GO, GO,
◁ SAID THE ▷
BIRD

A NOVEL BY

ANNE NALL STALLWORTH

◁ ▷

GO, GO, SAID THE BIRD

◁ ▷

THE VANGUARD PRESS
NEW YORK

Copyright © 1984 by Anne Nall Stallworth
Published by Vanguard Press, Inc., 424 Madison Avenue,
New York, N. Y. 10017.
Published simultaneously in Canada by Book Center, Inc., Montreal, Quebec.

Library of Congress Cataloging in Publication Data
Stallworth, Anne Nall.

Go, go, said the bird.
I. Title.
PS3569.T3217G6   1984   813'.54   83-25933
ISBN 0-8149-0883-7
Designer: Kay Lee
Manufactured in the United States of America.

1 2 3 4 5 6 7 8 9 0

The quotation on the epigraph page is from "Burnt Norton"
in FOUR QUARTETS by T. S. Eliot, copyright 1943 by T. S. Eliot;
renewed 1971 by Esme Valerie Eliot. Reprinted by permission of
Harcourt Brace Jovanovich, Inc. and by Faber and Faber Ltd.

FOR CAROLE AND CLARKE

Acknowledgment is also made to Harper & Row, Publishers, Inc. for permission to reprint six lines from "Heritage" from ON THESE I STAND by Countee Cullen, copyright 1925 by Harper & Row, Publishers, Inc. renewed 1953 by Ida M. Cullen; to Alfred A. Knopf, Inc. to reprint five lines from "Warning" from THE PANTHER AND THE LASH by Langston Hughes, copyright 1967 by Arna Bontemps and George Houston Bass and one line from "Blues in Stereo" from ASK YOUR MAMA by Langston Hughes, copyright 1959, 1961 by Langston Hughes; and to Twayne Publishers (G. K. Hall), Boston, and Carl Cowl to reprint six lines from "America" from SELECTED POEMS OF CLAUDE MCKAY, copyright 1953 by Mrs. Hope McKay Virtue.

Go, go, go, said the bird: human kind
cannot bear very much reality.
Time past and time future
What might have been and what has been
Point to one end, which is always present.

T.S. ELIOT
Four Quartets

GO, GO,
◁ SAID THE ▷
BIRD

CHAPTER

1

Bird Lasseter stood in the middle of a sandy dirt road, hands on hips, legs braced far apart, barring a smaller boy's way toward the town. A fiery July sun bore straight down on them, their shadows squat at their feet.

"You're not going into town, Arvin—"

"Git out of my way—"

"Something's happened to your daddy."

"Ain't nothin' happened to my paw you got any right to know about."

"Go tell your mama the sheriff sent me for her, tell her he wants her to come to Mr. West's hardware store."

The boy tried to dart past and Bird grabbed him, swinging him back into the road. Viciously, the boy knocked his hand away. "Don't touch me, keep yore hands to yoreself."

They stared at each other, eyes locked. Bird shifted more solidly in front of the skinny boy, who was barefoot and wore no shirt; his rib cage was hollow and protruding, his stomach sunken. Old sores pocked his legs, gray scalp showed through bristled, pale hair.

"You don't want to go there," Bird said. "Go tell your mama to come to Mr. West's store." But the boy only stared at the road behind Bird.

A gray board house squatted in a grove of cedars in the direction the boy had come, and in the yard a few thin chickens scratched at the hard clay earth washed clean by fierce spring rains. The flowing of the Alabama hummed through the piny woods to Bird's left, and to his right, in an unplowed field, bright yellow black-eyed Susans bloomed. Beneath the flowers and the weeds, old furrows, where once cotton had grown, stretched in wavy rows to converge on another piny woods. A cloud drifted over the sun, a July fly buzzed in the ditch, sounds of river and insect drowsily blending, the sound rising, falling, in the moist air.

"Let's go," Bird said, taking the boy's shoulder, turning him toward the house.

He jerked away. "Take yore nigger hands off me! I don't keer how white yore skin is, you got no right to touch me, yore a nigger bastard, my paw says so!"

The boy's pale blue eyes were flat with hatred. "All right then," Bird said, "go on, I won't stop you." He moved aside to let the boy pass. "Your daddy's dead. Coy Watson shot him in the head awhile ago for calling him a thieving bastard for taking that old wagon wheel out of your daddy's field."

"Yore a goddam liar, my paw ain't neither dead," and tears spurted from his eyes; he spat at Bird, the droplets spraying the air. He ran for the house, his feet kicking up puffs of dust.

Bird watched until the boy disappeared behind the dark rectangle of door, and then headed back to town. When he had walked along the highway for about a mile, he turned suddenly and jumped the ditch and went to sit just inside the woods, concealed behind tall blades of Johnson grass. He was hot and unlaced his sneakers and kicked them off, pushed his feet into the cool dirt, rolled up the sleeves of his soft white linen shirt. He trailed his finger along his arm and down his leg from the hem of his cut-off jeans to his ankle, observed that his skin was marred by no trace of darkness. It gave no evidence that his blood was tainted with black genes; and yet in Asheton, Alabama, in 1964, Southern law branded him Negro. But he did not accept this fiction of law anymore now than he had five years ago when his father had come to him in the night to tell him he was sending him away. He was asleep on his cot on the back porch, and his father had awakened him to tell him his heritage; he had lain listening to the horror of the whispered words while hundreds of fireflies swarmed in the branches of the pines.

I can't pretend any longer that you're my son. We can't live together anymore, in the morning you have to leave. I know I've done you a great wrong and I'm sorry.

He had gone back into the house, the screen door slapping softly shut behind him; and Bird had lain awake the rest of the night watching the fireflies go out gradually, like a dying fire, the arrhythmical flashes of light dimming until gray dawn extinguished them altogether. Then he got up and went inside and saw his suitcase sitting beside the kitchen door, only then believing that what had happened in the night was real.

Hatred rose now for the white-trash boy who had called him "nigger." Arvin Helms couldn't even try on shoes in the mercantile store; Mr. Miller made the flatwoods trash, just as he did the Negroes, bring in a sheet of paper with their footprint drawn on it to measure the shoes against. And yet the ferret-faced boy considered himself better than he. But what did it matter what Arvin thought? and he pushed down the hatred. His time in this town was almost over, he would be seventeen next month, and in September he was going to Birmingham to college and then to medical school. And his medical degree would be his ticket to freedom. When he became a doctor, he was heading north, maybe even all the way to Canada. He might go to Toronto, he'd read about that in World Book, had learned that its summers were warm and green, but its winters much colder than Alabama. Still, he didn't think he'd mind that—the moist river heat of Asheton made his sensitive skin itch and sting. And when he got North, he was going to pass for white, which, of course, he was. After he left Asheton he would never be called "nigger" again.

But with the gladness for leaving came the sadness. He'd have to leave his father. And Johnnie. And at the thought of Johnnie his groin tightened, but he willed the feelings away: not until he had finished school and gone North and gotten married would he make love. Mindless sex and bastard children were Negro—never would his child be called bastard. Many times when he walked along the streets of Asheton he'd look into white men's faces wondering if they were his father; some-

times he woke in the night naming these men over, looking for
resemblances of features. Sometimes he thought maybe the doctor was his real father, there were many similarities: his hair
was dark brown and silky like the doctor's, waving softly over
his ears; he was tall like him, he had reached nearly six feet this
summer. His father's eyes were deep blue where his own were
hazel, but then, he thought maybe he took the color of his eyes
after his mother. But he did not really believe the doctor was
his father—he would never have sent him away if he were his
son.

He lay back on the ground, pillowed his head on his arms,
closed his eyes. And at once the laughing image of Johnnie came
up, always she was at the edge of his mind, she danced like a
whirl of light on the velvet backdrop of his lids, and the feelings
of love for her came, the hard, rising swell of his penis. But he
would not masturbate, it would be abhorrent to have this
tender, protecting love for her played in solitude, that she
could not know of its happening. It would be taking his gift
for her for himself. Afterwards, his loneliness could
only be deeper.

But sometimes in the unguarded depths of sleep the feelings
came. He dreamed of holding her, her hair a golden cloak enclosing them, and he awoke in orgasm, floating upon the ecstasy, helpless, uncontrolled. As the feelings drained away and
reality returned, he would open his eyes to the dark and see the
pale outline of his windows, despairing that he could not carry
his resolve into his subconscious.

He gazed upward into the boughs that were deep green
with midsummer, and above them to the telephone wires where
thin wisps of cotton clung, blown there from endless wagons
hauling cotton to the gin. But that was a long time ago—wagons
didn't go to the gin anymore, pickups went, and then over to
the cotton mill at Carden.

He lay in the hot stillness of the July afternoon and thought
of how that old wagon wheel had probably lain rusting in Otis
Helms's field for years, probably he hadn't even known it was there
until Coy took it and painted it red and propped it beside

the door of his restaurant. Bragged about where he got it. What a pitiful thing to die for, a rusted wheel. But then, people had died for less in Asheton—loaded guns and hair-trigger tempers were the dark threads woven through the fabric of the town. He wondered that Arvin could love that fat, red-faced father who let his fields go to seed, his children starve, and who got drunk in Whiskey Alley every Saturday night and came home and beat his wife. He thought he ought to get up and go on the second errand he only now remembered: Mason Posey was drunk and stalking his father with an unloaded gun. This happened about once every couple of months and had begun about five years ago. His father said he didn't know why Mason came after him that way, but it had become Bird's job to take Mason home to Maybelle. After awhile, that was what he would do, but right now he needed to be alone, and he closed his eyes and slept.

Stinging, sharp-edged pebbles sprayed onto his arm and cheek, and, alarmed, he sat up, not remembering the time of day or where he was. He was in the woods, but which woods? He peered through the verticle slats of grass, saw the bleached streaks of sky, the sandy earth beside the pavement. The wheels of a pickup truck rolled slowly by, so close he could see the crazy, patchwork pattern of the tread. A huge lump lay beneath a brown wool blanket in the back, two muddy boots jutted out, jiggling in rhythm to the swaying truck. Sitting next to the lump was a woman, stolid, stoic, hands folded in her lap, a shapeless faded blue garment hanging over her shapelessness.

Mrs. Helms turned her face to him; he saw the hard, deep wrinkles about her mouth, the broad fleshy nose. He remembered then where he was, and watched the truck until it turned left and out of sight onto the Selma road heading for the Dillard Funeral Home. All the flatwoods white trash used Dillard.

He walked along the road toward the town, unreality clinging to him as when he had first awakened. Sharp points of tree shadows thrust across his path from a westering sun. On the blurred edge of fading afternoon he was homesick, this was the time of day when they were little that he and Johnnie would have been playing in the yard and begging for just a few more minutes when Mary Betty called them in to bathe before supper.

He began to run, eager to see Johnnie, for after he took Mason home he was going to the woods to meet her. He passed the "Asheton Police Jurisdiction" sign and just after that the one-room Negro grammar school that sat far back off the road at the end of a dirt lane. A sweet gum grew beside the door, a horse grazed in the meadow near the hedgerow of cedars and wild plum trees and blackberry bushes. He had never gone to that school. When he was little, sometimes he hid in the field across the highway and watched the children who did go there, some black like Mary Betty, some with skin like creamed coffee, some bright, as Mary Betty called the palest skin. But none was as white as he.

When he was six, his father tried to enroll him in the white grammar school. The sharp-nosed women behind the high counter in the office had stared, disbelieving, at his father. *Have mercy do, Jesus. Doctor, I believe you truly have forgotten who he really is.* And his father saying, *You have no right to deny him, my tax money supports this school,* the words forced through stiff lips gone deadly white.

The children had gathered around, whispering *nigger, he's a nigger,* and he had shrunk against his father, who led him from the building into the golden September morning, squeezing his hand so hard the knuckles ground against each other; but he did not pull away.

When they got home he had stood in the corner of the kitchen watching Mary Betty cook noon dinner. It was only they in the house; the daughters had gone to school, except Johnnie was gone with the Woman to oversee the harvesters in the wheat field; his father had gone to his office. He watched Mary Betty as she walked between stove and table and sink, stopping now and then to shake her head at him, muttering "po' chile, po' li'l chile, ain't done nothin' to *no*body 'cept git bahn."

He was not like her; his skin was not black and shiny, it

was she who was called "nigger," not he. He waited for his father to explain, but he never did and he wouldn't ask. And so he took the silence to mean that what the children had said was not true. How could it be? It made no sense.

His father hired a tutor, a retired schoolteacher who came three times a week from Selma to teach him to read and write and do arithmetic. She even taught him Latin because his father said Bird was to be a doctor. He remembered that she was kind and that through frizzed, wispy hair could be seen the domed curve of her head. She had a sweet, powdery smell when she leaned over him guiding his hand as he shaped the letters of the alphabet. He liked her, he even loved her, but intellectually; she was the instrument of his learning to read and he would have loved anybody for that.

He could not get enough of reading; in summers he read beneath the scuppernong arbor, in winter behind the stove in the kitchen. In two years he had finished all the Readers from first through eighth grades, and he had read the *Black Stallion* books and the *Hardy Boys* and *Robinson Crusoe*. His father checked out books for him from the library in Selma and let him join the Book-of-the-Month Club.

When he was twelve, the tutor told his father he was exceptionally bright and he ought to be sent away to school, to someplace where his background wouldn't matter. And his father had said, "And what background is that?" His voice was ominously mild and inquiring. And she had said, "Why, Doctor, you surely can't think I'm unaware of his background?"

Bird had heard this conversation standing in the hallway outside his father's study; the door was open and so he knew it was all right to listen. Again he waited for an explanation of this allusion to his background, but his father said nothing. The woman never came back after that, and he missed her, for he had no one to talk with about books. His father read only newspapers and medical journals, and Johnnie read only what was required in school. He had a note from the tutor saying how much she had enjoyed teaching him, and that she hoped he would always love books; so desperately did he want to share a poem or a chapter of a book he was reading, he would promise to play some game with Johnnie if only first she'd listen to him read. They'd sit beneath the arbor at the side of the house, the light through the vined roof speckling the book and her face and arms, he caught in the dream of words, in the bliss of saying them to her whom he loved. When, after only a few minutes, she began to twist her hair or fold a pleat into her skirt, he'd stop reading; and she'd jump up and grab his hand, pulling him up, not noticing his disappointment. Not noticing he had stopped in the middle of a sentence.

He came into the town in late afternoon, walked down the sidewalk of the one-block business district, his shadow long in the random sunlight cast between the board buildings. Nothing moved except that a small brown dog trotted down the deserted street.

He walked to the corner and looked down the hill toward the abandoned railroad station, looked up the hill to the white-frame Bide-a-Wee Hotel. But the only movement was heat waves shimmering off the fender of a parked car. He turned and walked back again, scanning the buildings across the street—his father's office, the bank, the hardware store, the general store—but he saw no one. He passed the vacant Standard Oil Station, looked into the windows of Mrs. Henderson's café, Mason Posey's office, the drugstore, and the pool hall. But everybody was home napping or sitting on the shady side of their houses drinking iced tea and fanning. He felt suddenly bereft, as if he had landed here on a saucer from Mars, and he headed in the direction he had come, to cut through the woods to meet Johnnie.

But then he saw the merest fleeting wisp of something—it could have been the shadow of a bird or the flap of a coat-tail, and he turned back and ran across the street and down the alley to the back of the hardware store where Otis Helms had gone that morning to buy cartridges for his shotgun and gotten himself killed instead. Mason shambled along the cracked cement, his graying brown hair straggling over the collar of his seersucker suit, his shoulder bumping the building. His arms hung loosely at his sides and in his right hand he clasped a gun.

Bird ran after him, jumping over croker sacks of alfalfa and guano, angry that he had found Mason and feeling guilty for his anger. Now he would have to take him home and probably be late meeting Johnnie. But the worst of it was that he would have to see Maybelle. But then pity flooded, for Mason looked so vulnerable, so needing caring for. Mason was his friend.

"Mr. Posey," he called. "Wait for me and I'll walk home with you."

Mason turned, smiling; he made no protest when Bird took the gun and stuffed it into his jeans' pocket. He took Mason's arm lightly, and thinking with any luck at all Maybelle would be gone selling insurance and he wouldn't have to see her. He was due for some luck that way.

"There was something I was supposed to do," Mason said, and he pulled against Bird's clasp, turned sad brown eyes on him. "What was I supposed to do, Bird?"

"It can wait, Mr. Posey. Let me walk home with you, keep you company. We can talk."

"But it was important, there was a case or something." His light-blue suit and white shirt were court clothes, except that he wore no tie and his coat was soiled, his shoes dusty. But for that, Bird thought he could have been swinging down the street, briefcase under his arm and on his way to see a client.

"There was something. . ."

"It's all right, Mr Posey, it can wait until another time," and Bird guided him toward the sidewalk.

He moved reluctantly, his feet scraping across the pavement. "I don't know if it can, Bird." and he rubbed his cheek, and Bird saw that old, dark blood had coagulated on his knuckles.

"Have you been by the barbershop today, Mr. Posey?"

"I don't remember. Have I had a haircut?" He touched his hair.

"No, I don't think so; it doesn't matter, I was just wondering."

They crossed the street, the smell of warm asphalt rising into their faces. He should have come to find him sooner, he should not have stayed so long in the woods. Undoubtedly Mason had run into the barbershop goons, the brothers Bro' and Walter Abel. When Mason passed by, if Bro' and Walter were lounging outside, they'd call to him, "Hey, Counselor, what you gon' do with that gun? Hit Doc over the head with it? Won't Maybelle give you a bullet?" And then Mason would hit at them and they'd laugh and dodge and Mason's fist would hit the wall. If that's where he was when Bird found him, the brothers would watch him lead Mason away, their eyes mean and speculative, beer bellies hanging over their big metal belt buckles. "Niggers take nigger-lovers home," Bro' would say. He was always the leader, Walter mostly just snickering and shuffling.

"When you're out walking, Mr. Posey," Bird said, "I wouldn't go by the barbershop if I were you."

Solemnly, Mason nodded. "There's bad people down there, Bird. I don't mean to go, just sometimes it seems I'm there. Don't let them cut your hair."

"Mary Betty cuts my hair," he said. He couldn't go in the white barbershop, and even if he could, he wouldn't let them touch his hair.

When he was ten, a teen-age boy had cut his hair. He worked on the farm, helper to the Woman, and he had grabbed Bird one afternoon when he came out of the woods after swimming in the river. The boy knocked him to the ground and sat on him, took his pocket knife and cut out chunks of hair, Bird understanding he did it because it was Caucasian—good hair, the blacks called it. *You think you so cute struttin' 'round jes lak you white, but you ain't nothin' but a nigger lak me.* The boy warned him if he told the doctor who cut his hair there were other parts of him he'd also take off.

They walked through the neighborhood in the glare of afternoon, the sidewalk like a stage stretching past the sprawling, elm-shaded houses where people sat on the porches in swings and rockers, lowering their afternoon papers to watch them as they passed. But no one spoke: they hated Mason as they hated him. Mason had defended a Negro man against a white woman who said the man had raped her, and though he had proved the young Negro could not have been in Asheton that night, still the jury sentenced him to twenty years in prison that he had not served. A posse kidnaped him from the tiny jail in Carden and took him into the woods and cut off his testicles and he had bled to death.

Mason lost all his practice except for a few renegade whites who thought Negroes had rights, and Maybelle had to get a job to help buy the groceries and pay the taxes on the old Nathan Ashe mansion Mason had bought for her when they married. She bought a faded red Volkswagen and went all over the state with policies and actuary tables in the back seat telling at what age you could expect what disaster. Mason had been drinking for years, but recently he started drinking more heavily, and the town said it served Maybelle right to be brought down. After all, she shouldn't be living so high; they said Mason had no business marrying her, for he was old-line aristocracy even if he was poor. At one time his daddy had owned half the town but had lost his money, for he too was bad to drink. Like father like son, they said.

After Maybelle married Mason, she sold the board house and the little dab of land her daddy had managed to leave her, and they moved into the mansion. She gave lawn parties just like she was quality, with tables under the trees covered with white cloths and centered with hurricane lamps flickering like fireflies. Colored strips of crepe paper streamed from the fans, couples danced on the veranda and in the grass to the mellow notes of Bing Crosby singing "Stardust" and "Deep Purple"; Maybelle, slender as a stalk, twirled across the lawn, the girls in white dresses fluttering like moths in the twilight. white-coated Negro waiters, who during the week were yard men and janitors, passed among the guests serving Ritz crackers spread with pink cream cheese with ripe olives stuck in the middle like round, dark eyes, and Methodist champagne made of sparkling water and ginger ale.

After the trial, people came in the night and threw rocks and broke out windows, and Mason wouldn't have the glass put back in upstairs—he said they'd just come and do it again and he boarded them up and had wire mesh put across the ones downstairs, giving the place the look of an ante-bellum prison. When they couldn't get to the glass anymore, some men came and burned a cross in the yard. The emerald lawns and the rose gardens went to weeds; over the years the house got the look of genteel decay, the paint peeled, the veranda sagged.

Sometimes Bird visited with Mason in his office. They had become friends, and Mason asked him to come. They'd talk about slave days and how Mason's great-grandfather was the first settler after Nathan Ashe. "I'm the last of the Poseys," he'd say, "my little brother died with diphtheria and all those aunts and cousins that lived here gone." But most of the time they didn't talk at all; Mason sat at his roll-top desk thumbing through a dilapidated *Alabama Code* passed down from this grandfather, and Bird sat drowsing in a chair across from his desk, an old copy of *Newsweek* on his lap. The door was open to the hot, dusty afternoon, heat reflecting off the sidewalk into the room. Sometimes a wasp flew in, batted against the walls, flew out again; and sometimes a Negro came up, stooping low, servile, to knock on the bottom of the door, saying, *This old nigger sho' am in a mess, Mista Mason, this old nigger sho' do need he'p*. These were the last of Mason's clients, the renegade whites and the poor Negroes who could not pay.

He waited for her in the hallway, angry that she held him here. She said she had a message for his father and he didn't believe her, or if she did, it would be something made up, of no consequence. Last time she had asked him to wait when he took Mason home, she had taken him into the gallery above the ballroom where in the gloom the phantoms seemed to lurk, and she showed him paintings of Mason's dead relatives: big-eyed women in deep-cut dresses, balding men in wing collars and beards. She had leaned close to him, breasts lightly brushing his arm.

Always she had something to detain him, and several times he had handed Mason over to her at the back door and refused to come in, and she complained to his father that he was rude and wouldn't help her get Mason into the house. His father had told him he must always be polite and help her, but Bird was afraid of her. Once when she had taken him to see the pictures, she had leaned against him whispering "I'll bet you've got a big one, a tall boy like you must have a great big one." He wanted to tell his father, but was ashamed, thinking it must be something he'd done to make her talk that way. So he continued bringing Mason home; they climbed the hill walking beneath the dense, dark-green foliage of the cherry trees, the columned house guant and stark against the sky.

He leaned now against the wall, staring through the filmy white curtains of the window at the end of the hall toward the meadow growing serene green grass, but that once had been covered with cotton, the glistening white black-dotted with slaves chanting back and forth. Yankee soldiers had also been in that meadow. During the war they took over house and land, shot Nathan Ashe as he stood beneath the crimson crape myrtles that overhung the veranda.

He heard them now, the clump of soldiers' boots echoing through the high-ceilinged rooms, heard their shouts as they made camp beneath the oaks, horses whinnying, pulling the big cannons and artillery guns. An entire regiment had ridden up one rainy summer afternoon the third year of the war, and before the sun had set, the horses' hoofs and the caisson wheels had ground the cotton fields and the vegetable and flower gardens into mud. In the space of only a few hours, weeks of labor had been canceled out. They said even the slaves had cried and begged the soldiers to stop when a rosewood table and a dozen hand-carved mahogany chairs were splintered into kindling for the campfires. They had stayed all summer before they finally headed out toward Georgia to join General Sherman.

▼

She came down the hall, feet moving quickly, whisper-
ingly, across the pale oak floor. Tall and broad-shouldered, she
moved toward him, the huge breasts preceding her, thrusting
pugnaciously beneath a white knit shirt—Bird thought she could
do battle with those breasts, could wield them like jousting
sticks. She was narrow at the hips like a man, the shirt pushed into
into black slacks. Bleached hair, once shining black, hung lankly
to her shoulders, and as she came up to him she sighed heavily
and pushed the hair off her forehead, running her fingers
through the limp strands.

"Well, he's asleep, finally," she said. "I'm so glad when he
sleeps, I don't have to worry about him, I can have some peace.
It's like getting a baby to bed, though I wouldn't really know
about that. I always wanted a baby—"

"You said you have a nessage for my father?"

"I think it's so sweet the way the doctor lets you call him
that. So enlightened."

"I have to go." His voice was hard and firm. He would not
allow her to toy with him; he saw the sharp gleam of pleasure
in her eyes as she lightly stroked her breasts, which was her
habit when she talked to him. "You said you have a message."

"Yes, yes, I do. I want you to tell the doctor I think I must
put Mr. Posey in Bryce. I want him to make the arrangements,
I simply can't cope—"

"But you can't do that, Mr. Posey's not crazy."

"You can say that when he hunts the doctor with a gun
and can't even find the way home? Come now." She laughed
lightly, tossed her hair, fingers idly, fleetingly, tickling the
breasts. "Just what would you call crazy?"

"The gun's never loaded," he said.

"That's so typical of Mason, not loading the gun. He's impotent." The words were malevolent, condemning. "He's so in-
effectual, he's not a man."

He backed away from her, shaking his head. He did not
want her confidences, did not want to know of his friend's hu-
miliations; he had to protect Mason against her intimacies. "I
have to go," he said, "I have to meet someone."

He was in the kitchen, and as he turned to the door a small dog ran at him, appearing suddenly as if he had been conjured from the gloom, and Maybelle scooped him up, nestling him onto the couch of her breasts.

"Naughty boy, Georgie, bad doggie to bark at the nice boy who brought our daddy home." She snuggled him close, he wriggled beneath her chin, licking her neck. "He's a Yorkshire, you know, I bought him at Lovable's in Selma. He cost one hundred dollars, yes, he did, he certainly did, didn't you darling?" She held him aloft, her face just out of reach of his flicking tongue. "He's a bad doggie," and she gently shook him. "Yes, he is, but he's mama's baby." She set him again on her breasts.

"He's spoiled to me, you understand. He doesn't mean to be unfriendly, it's just that we have only each other."

"Yes, ma'm, I understand, I have to go now—"

"Bad boy, Bird, to call me 'ma'm.' It's not polite to make me feel old."

"I'm sorry, I didn't mean to do that." He backed toward the door, and she swirled the dog's brown silken hair.

"I've had lots of dogs, but Georgie's the best, he loves only me, he won't have anything at all to do with Mason." Her voice was triumphant, pleased.

And Bird thought of her other dogs, all small, all male, two poodles and a dachshund. They were buried in the back yard beneath the crape myrtles, the tiny graves neatly in a row and with their names chiseled in marble markers: Jacques, Pierre, Rolf. Maybelle's family plot.

"I have to go now," he said. "I have to meet someone." It seemed he had stood forever in the long dream of afternoon, the dark shapes of birds hurtling past the windows. He went into the kitchen and she followed behind, standing in the doorway.

"Wait," she said. "Stay and talk; I can fix supper, I have some wine."

I have to go."

"Stay," she whispered, came close, almost touching. "I'll

turn on the phonograph and we'll dance." She took a couple of little waltzing steps, humming. "We can turn the lights off and dance in the parlor; you'd like that, wouldn't you, dance in a white person's house? I'm not prejudiced, I think you're just as good as we are, we can dance and you can rub your thing against me like the boys used to do out at the Blue Moon."

He stared at her clown face, bright red lipstick bleeding into the cracks of her lips, cheeks rouge-fevered, eyes puffy, crow-footed. But the breasts were young and high, they pointed at him like guns, and he was paralyzed, unable to move. She took his hand and placed it on her breast, and still he could not move, horror froze him there—he was shocked at her softness, he had thought they would be hard as iron.

"Stay," she said. "You know you want to stay, you like to touch me."

He fell back against the door, the sound reverberating through the high-ceilinged rooms, and he groped for the doorknob behind him, twisted it, whirled down the steps into the dusk, the clover of the deep grass warm around his ankles.

"Come back," she called, "you touched me, you want to be with me—"

She was a bulky form behind the screen door. "I did not touch you, you put my hand on you." He did not know if he had spoken or if he imagined that he spoke.

"I'm going to tell Mr. Posey what you did, you nasty little nigger, you come back here, you better listen when a white woman speaks to you!"

He ran around the side of the house and beneath the rose arbor, the thorns tearing at him, snagging his shoulders and his arms, the scent of the blood-red roses sweet and heavy. She screamed after him, her voice shrill, agonized, growing fainter as he ran into the deep shadows of the cherry trees.

She lay on her bed on the yellowed crocheted spread. Pendulous, white-blossomed crape myrtle hovered outside the window; dark-gleaming mahogany bedposts carved with cherubs surrounded her; the massive weight of the headboard loomed behind her. She saw the reflection of the bed—of herself—in the round dresser mirror across the room. She arched her back, unhooking the boned brassiere, pulled up her shirt, and the little dog crept onto her chest, her breath quickening as his warm, smooth tongue began slowly to wash her breasts.

After awhile she got up and walked out into the night and down the road toward the woods.

2

They lay in the dusk beside the river in Bird's magic place. He had called it that since he found it by accident the morning his father sent him away and he fled the house of Jake Bonner and his grandmother. He had watched his father's car drive away down the road, the billowing gray dust obscuring the car, obscuring his past. When the dust thinned, the road was empty, and he ran, not noticing, not caring where he ran, and when he came to the end of the road he continued into the woods, crashing through vines and tickets until he stumbled into this small clearing.

A screen of bushes and scrub pines had hidden the slew that jutted from the river, and he had stood in a mote-swirled glow thinking he had fallen suddenly into a dream—an enchantment. Mist curled off the river, hanging like moss from the trees. The water lapped gently onto shore, tossing up sparkles of light like golden coins. He stood for a long time, his heart gradually slowing, and the sounds coming to him, the wind in the trees, a bird calling—the roar of the river.

He had gone to sit on the bank of the pool where the silver minnows darted above waved sand beneath the water; the wind trailed branches of the willows across its flat surface, the outflowing ripples striking the rocks and making hollow music. He lay down on the moss and slept, and when he woke the terror was back again as strong as it had been when he saw the suitcase beside the kitchen door. He cried then, but not with sorrow, but with a terrible hatred for his father for sending him from his home to live with Negroes, and despair and disbelief washed over him again and again that his old life was over.

His father had said that night on the porch that Bird must accept his heritage, meaning that he, his father, agreed with the town and with the law that he was Negro. He cried until all the tears were gone, until his eyes were dry and burning. *She* (meaning the Woman) *will divorce me and take my girls away*, his father had said. *I have to think of them as well as you, they are my blood. I'll always take care of you, you'll never want for anything. When you're a doctor we'll practice together*, and him thinking, *Say you love me, I can bear anything if you love me*; but the kitchen door closed, the words unsaid.

As he had lain watching the fireflies, he heard them talking in the kitchen, their voices loud and angry: *I hope you're happy, Jenny, I'm taking him to the Bonners in the morning*; her answering, *I will not have him here with my girls as their equal, that bastard Negro child; I'll never understand why I let him stay so long, I suppose it was pity for you and him and my own guilt. He was my punishment....*

That morning, when he had lain on the bank and after the tears had stopped, a hard determination had gripped him; like a locust he had crawled through the ripped skin of his old life to lie drying, reborn, in his new. He accepted that though he must live with Negroes, that did not make him one—he was still himself wherever he lived. He was white. He did not hate his father, it was the Woman he hated, for it was she who had sent him away. His father had no choice.

He was twelve when he was banished, and three summers later, when he was fifteen, Johnnie came to him in the woods, materializing in his peripheral vision. He sprang to his feet to face her, and when she laughed he knew she was real, his old playmate come back. Plowed fields and black dirt sinking beneath their feet, broad-leafed cotton whipping their legs, flooded back upon him—she was the finder of all his hiding places when he tried to slip away to read, and that morning she had rescued him from his solitude. When he thought back on the years before she came, he did not see how he had stood it.

▼

He cradled her head on his shoulder, stroked the soft silk of her hair. She sighed, turned and kissed him, and he knew he could have her, he could do anything at all with her, for she loved him. He pulled her to him, her hair falling about his face, and he lay peacefully enclosed in the silken world.

The sweetness of her breath was warm against his cheek, her hands pushed beneath his unbuttoned shirt pulling him to her; his loneliness faded as it always did when he was with her; he melted into her, thinking he would die of love for her. Nothing mattered except that they should become one flesh. *Little yella boy ain't nothin' but a nigger jes lak me.*

Roughly he pushed her away, she rolled onto the ground, then sat up, turned her back to him, her head sunk against her chest, knees drawn up. She looked so frail, so like a sad little girl, that he sat up and put his arms around her. Angrily she shrugged him off.

"You're mean and hateful, you don't love me."

He put his arm about her again, held her tight, kissed the flushed cheek. "We can't do anything, I've told you that. I have to take care of you. I don't believe you even know how babies get born."

She struggled from his grasp, turned on him. "I do so know, I know as much as you do—"

"Well, then, *act* like you know. You know what kind of trouble we could get into. Nobody even knows we come here, that we see each other. We have to be responsible."

"Oh, Bird, I don't care about anything but us. *I* know how to keep from having babies so we can make love. Tommy Wooten carries one of those rubber things in his billfold; he says if he ever hits it lucky he'll be ready. It's wrapped in silver foil and has a picture of a sheik on it; Tommy showed it to us on the ball field at lunch one day. You know, it's just like those we found in Daddy's drawer at the office that time and we blew them up like balloons, remember?"

His jaw dropped. He did not believe what he had heard, this girl who looked like an angel was talking about condoms and calling them rubbers. He had imagined it, his ears had deceived him; but she sat coolly observing him, grinning at his shock that she knew something he hadn't told her.

"Everything's not in books, Bird," she said smugly.

"Who is Tommy Wooten?"

"Just a little short boy who's always trying to date pretty girls, but even the homely ones won't look at him. But the boys sure are impressed that he's got a rubber—"

"Shut up!"

She drew back, the joy fading from her face, and at once he was sorry to have hurt her and wanted to tell her so. But he did not, for he was jealous of this life she had that he could never share or know anything at all about except what she told him. Though he was sorry to be mean, he was also angry. "Don't you know how crude it is to talk like that? You ought to be ashamed."

Tears came in her eyes, and he looked across the rose-streaked water to the dying sun setting beyond the dark forest, and beyond were the fields and towns and highways that led into a world where he could never take her. Whenever he thought of marrying, imagining a wife, it was Johnnie. If he asked her to, she would go with him, but it would be a game, and when she grew up, if she tired of the game, what then? She would hate him.

He put his arm around her and she sat rigidly unmoving, would not look at him. "I love you," he said, "I'm sorry if I hurt you."

At once, as it had ever been, she forgave him, and she turned to him smiling, eager. "Next time you go to the drugstore in Birmingham for Daddy you can get us one of those things and we can make love; some of the girls already have, they've *told* me—"

"You won't stop, will you?" but he smiled, she looked so earnest. It was another game she wanted to try. "Making love is for marriage, Johnnie, I don't care what the other girls say."

"You're old-fashioned," but she looked at him, waiting for the next words he could not say: we have to wait until *we're* married. And he grabbed her and began to tickle her, and she shrieked and rolled on the ground, begging him to stop; and then he knew she'd forgotten the talk about marriage and he lay beside her, his arm pillowing her head. They stared into the sky, wished on the first pale star, refused to tell each other their wish.

"What are you thinking?" she asked.

"I was thinking of the river and wondering how many people have lain here beside it like us. I was thinking how it's probably been here as long as the earth, and that it will be here long after this town has turned to dust."

"Oh, don't say that. Asheton turned to dust? Asheton will always be here, it's been here since the slaves."

"*Since* the slaves? It's still slave days, just as much as when Nathan Ashe came down the river from Virginia and brought them here. Not one Negro in this town votes, not one owns a square inch of land. But there's something going on out there. It hasn't touched us yet, but it will. There's sit-ins in Birmingham and Selma, and freedom rides on the Greyhound buses. And that's just the beginning. Martin Luther King integrated the city buses in Montgomery after they arrested a Negro woman named Rosa Parks. And you know why? Because she wouldn't get up and give her seat to a white man; the driver said she was sitting past the colored section that was filled up."

"Mrs. Farrington in government class says they don't really want to associate with white people; she says it's Yankee agitators coming down stirring them up; she says Negroes are like children, they just want to laugh and fish and let white people take care of them. She says—"

"*Please*," Bird said, rolling his eyes heavenward. "Spare me any more of what Mrs. Farrington says, I'm glad I can't go to your school."

"Don't get mad again, let's just don't talk about it. When we're here let's let it be you and me. there's not any other world out there. I wish I couldn't go to my school either since you can't."

"There is another world out there; sometimes I think I dream this place and that you come here."

"I hate it when you talk like that. This place *is* real and we are together, I don't care what you think. When I'm out there it's as if I'm always waiting for when we can come here, because that's when time starts for me."

He took her hand, kissed her fingers. "I didn't mean it, I feel that way too. If I didn't have you and our magic place I don't know what I'd do. But lately when I go to Birmingham to get supplies I see things. People in this town talk about what they hear on television or read in the newspaper like it's news from Timbuktu, like it really doesn't have anything to do with them. The world just flows around us, as if time forgot all about us. But I get the feeling that pretty soon the world's going to glance this way and we're never going to be the same again. A line from a poem keeps going through my head, 'Wind in the cotton fields, gentle breeze: beware the hour it uproots trees!' "

She pushed closer to him. "That's scary, Bird, nothing bad's going to happen to us, the Negroes here aren't like in the big cities."

"Oh, but you're wrong; remember, I live with Negroes, I hear Jake and his friends talk. I saw it in Birmingham a long time ago when I first started going for supplies. It was when I—" He stopped. He had been going to tell her about the afternoon he suddenly took the notion to ride a city bus and pass for white; just suddenly he had decided to merge with the crowd climbing on board. He was going to tell her what had happened with the Negro woman and the white bus driver, but then did not. She might tell his father; she wouldn't mean to, but sometimes she let things slip like she had about poor old Tommy's condom. Surely he had told that in confidence?

"Go on," she said, "once in Birmingham, what?"

He looked at her, considering. Bright blue eyes so like their father's gazed at him eagerly. He wanted to tell her the story of the bus driver's cruelty to the Negro woman, but he couldn't risk anyone knowing he had passed for white.

"Once I saw a sit-in at Woolworth's counter." It was true, he had. "I was walking down the sidewalk toward the drugstore to get supplies for the office, and all at once sirens came shrieking down the street and police jumped out of squad cars blowing their whistles and they ran into Woolworth's and dragged out two Negro men who just went limp—you know, the way Martin Luther King tells them to. They were handcuffed and shoved into a black Maria. I saw every bit of it, it was really scary, lots of blacks gathered around and it could have turned into a riot, but then it didn't. A taxi was parked at the curb where I was standing and the driver leaned over the window and said they ought to all be shipped back to Africa and the Yankees with them."

"Oh," said Johnnie.

He raised on one elbow to look down at her. "Oh? What do you mean, 'oh?' "

"Just 'oh.' I thought it was going to be something, well, you know, *special*."

"Well, it was *exciting*, whistles and sirens and people running all around and crowds gathered on the sidewalks, and let me tell you it was scary to see those men dragged around like that. What did you want, a circus parade?"

"No, I've seen that over in Selma." She gazed blandly up at him.

He fell onto his back again, sighed, and looked up through the branches to the dusky sky. What he had told her was boring because in her mind it had absolutely nothing to do with her. "Well, I suppose you would have had to have been there."

"Bird?"

"What?"

"Wouldn't it be wonderful if we *did* have a baby? We wouldn't tell anybody, we'd hide it in one of those old slave houses back of the Ashe mansion and we'd take turns taking care of it."

He raised his head to stare at her, and she was looking off over the river, her eyes glazed, dreaming. He had thought she was acting silly, making a joke, but he saw she was serious, and he fell back into the pine straw, laughing, rolling on the ground, arms clasped across his stomach. "*Hide* the *baby*? Are you crazy?" and new waves of laughter rose. "What would you tell people when your stomach got big, that you're gaining weight and have to go on a diet? What would you tell them when it got suddenly small again? I can't stand it, I can't stand it," and laughter would bend him double again.

Gradually, as his laughter subsided, he felt the ominous silence, felt her eyes on him; she watched him as he'd seen dogs watch a snake in the cornfield. He sat up and could not meet her eyes; he looked off across the river that was dark now, the evening star risen just over the tops of the trees. She should already have gone home, their father would be worried about her; he did not like her out after dark. Johnnie had told him this, and he would have been jealous of this love his father had for her if he had not loved her so much himself.

He cleared his throat, glanced at her, and her face was tight with anger. "I'm sorry," he said.

She raised her hand, palm pushing against the air. "Stop. Don't talk to me. I hate you. I wonder how I could ever have loved someone so arrogant, so superior. Nobody's smart but you, as far as you're concerned I'm just stupid, but somehow nothing has ever seemed impossible when I'm with you. I never think of the details of our games because I thought you could figure anything out, I thought that together we could do anything." She dropped her head to her knees and cried.

He put his arm around her shoulders, and she did not push him away. "I'm sorry. I was laughing, but it felt more like crying. What it was is that I love you and I want to marry you and live the rest of my life with you. But on a street where everybody knows us and we know them and we visit each other's houses. I don't want us to have to hide our baby in a slave cabin; I'd be so proud if we had a baby."

He looked away, wanting to cry with her, but would not— he had not cried since that morning five years ago when his father had brought him to the Bonners. And despair rose for the black part of himself that would forever deny her to him.

Her hand was soft on his cheek, caressing it; she kissed his lips lightly. "Don't look so sad, I can't bear for you to look that way."

He took her hand, but still not looking at her. "Forget everything I said, pretend we didn't come here today. This has been the most horrible day."

"I won't forget what you said, at least the part about how you love me and want us to get married."

"I said forget it, we can't ever get married. Have you forgotten who I am? Have you forgotten why your father sent me away?"

"He never told us anything. But I hear them talking, and I don't care what your heritage is supposed to be. We can run away, we could leave this summer and find us a house and get jobs. We wouldn't ever have to come back here."

"You love Asheton, I would never do that to you."

"What do I care about this old town without you? I only want to be with you forever, don't you know that? I wish you'd stop trying to think up reasons why we can't be together. You just spoil everything." She lay back on the ground, pale blue eyes opaque with tears.

He leaned over her, gently kissed her lips, and when she smiled, he lightly touched where the dimples had shown. "God must have loved you very much, Johnnie."

"Loved me? Why?"

"Because of your dimples. He put dimples only in people He loved especially. You see, He had us all on an assembly line on a kind of conveyor belt, and as we went past for inspection, those He didn't like He'd push a dimple into their chin and say 'I don't like you!' But the people that were good and kind and beautiful, He'd put dimples in their cheeks and say 'I love you!' And that's how dimples came to be."

"I don't like that story. I wish you hadn't told me."

"Why not? I thought to make you happy."

"You don't have dimples, and I don't want God to love me if He doesn't love you."

"I don't have a dimple in my chin either, so I suppose He's waiting to pass judgment, and that's all right with me. Besides, it's just a story, I don't believe in God anyway, it's just a way somebody thought up to keep people in line."

"Oh, you mustn't *say* things like that, Bird, God might punish you. Quick, take it back, say a little prayer."

He laughed, smoothed the frown between her eyes. "You are just a bundle of contradictions. One minute you talk about having bastard babies and the next you want me to pray for saying I don't believe in God."

"God will forgive all sins except not believing in Him. That's what the Bible says, 'he soever who believeth not on Me is in danger of hellfire!' Or something like that. Wanting to make love is not a sin—"

"Wanting to make love *not married* is a sin according to Christians. And according to me too, only for different reasons. And God in Asheton, Alabama, is for keeping black people in line, to make them not worry about their terrible lives here on earth, because when they die they're going to heaven to fish off golden banks with heavenly fishing poles in their hands."

"If you hate it so much why do you go to church? You take Emma nearly every Sunday."

"That's right, I do, it's the least I can do, she's been good to me and she's an old woman. And the least you could do is call her 'Mrs. Bonner.' "

"Everybody calls her 'Emma.' "

"I don't, your father doesn't, everybody at church calls her 'Mrs. Bonner,' they treat her polite and dignified."

She sat up. "Why are you being so mean to me today, *nothing* I say is right."

She was right, he was being mean to her, and he hated himself for it. He was taking his feelings out on her because the flatwoods boy had called him 'nigger'; because Maybelle Posey had put his hand on her breast; he couldn't fight back with them, but Johnnie was easy, she wouldn't hurt him.

He put his arm around her. "I'm sorry. I've said that a lot today, haven't I? But I really am, I wouldn't blame you if you didn't even come here," and the words terrified him. The thought of going back to the way things were before she came—to the loneliness—was not even to be considered, it was a happening he refused to contemplate.

She laughed and flung her arms around him, and they top-
pled over, she wrestled him onto his back, tickling him, him
writhing, laughing, and she jumped up and ran away into the
woods, her footsteps crashing among the trees.

He ran after her, calling to her, but she had disappeared,
and he thought he would never see her again; he'd read of things
like that, of people just disappearing and never seen again. He
ran along the bank of the slew, panic rising, and then he heard
her laugh, the sound skipping across the water like a stone, he
saw her standing in the marsh grass, and she slapped her hand
against the flat surface of the pool, the sound hollowly echoing;
an egret flew up, wings whirring, beating the air, streaking like
a shooting star against the night sky.

Bird plunged into the water and swam to her, relief for
finding her causing him to tremble in the hot night; but then
she flipped forward and dove beneath the water, only the circle
of outflowing ripples to show he had not imagined her. He
plunged after her, groping for her, grasping clumps of grass and
thinking it was hair, ripping it to the surface, flinging it away.

She was standing naked on the shore, her hair streaming
about her shoulders, and she looked not much different now
than when she was little and they had bathed together: her hips
were narrow like a child's, her small breasts and pubic hair
seeming merely nature's reluctant acknowledgment that she was
female. He went to her, and she swayed against him like a large
white flower too heavy for its stalk, her arms twined around his
waist, and they sank to the mossy ground.

Her eyes turned dark as the water, her lips parted slightly,
and he kissed her, their breaths blending, her hair trailing across
his face, cool and musty with the river. From the earth rose the
scent of ancient summers, in the diminished light the purple
swamp lilies turned black, there came the music of the rippling
water striking against the stones, and the clatter of birds going
to roost.

She unfastened the buttons of his shirt, and he stood and
pulled off his clothes, then lay flat upon her. "You're so beautiful," the words whispered, strangled. "I love you, I have always loved you."

It seemed he stood apart and watching them clasped together in the dappled moonlight, and he heard the preacher in the Sunday pulpit: *and de woman took of de fruit and did eat and she give it to her husband and he did eat.* Triumphant, from the tall grass the serpent hissed *nigger.*

He thrust her away and stood up, trembling, and he went to the bank and brought back her clothes and dropped them on the ground beside her. "Get dressed," he said.

She stood in the shadows, her arm across her breasts, her hand covering the mound of pale pubic hair.

...and they knew that they were naked; and they sewed fig leaves together and made themselves aprons.

At seven o'clock on Saturday morning, Dr. John Lasseter—tall and straight—stopped in the middle of the street in front of his office and looked skyward, checking the weather. He did this each morning, and his eyes squinted against the sun rising between the buildings; the flagpole in front of the general store cast a long, angled shadow against his office.

A rattletrap pickup rolled by and a man leaned out and yelled "Gon' be another hot one, Doc, it's already eighty-five in the shade," and the truck drifted around the corner, the strangled sound of the engine dying away.

Dr. Lasseter continued across the street, thinking there were no clouds, cirrus or cumulus, to read against the bleached sky. No rain would come today to cleanse the air, to wash the dust off the streets. Killer weather for old people and asthmatics.

Already a group of people outside his door—were divided by the door—blacks on one side, whites on the other. All that identified the races was their skin; their clothes were the same— bibbed overalls, faded workshirts. Flatwooders and Negroes. He'd lost part of his town white practice when he took Bird, and the rest of it when he started living mainly with Zella five years ago. That is, he'd lost all of his town practice except Katie Hunt, the high-school Latin teacher. The school board would have fired her if they could for continuing to come to him, but she had tenure, so they had settled for hating her, and she'd also lost her private students and those from her classes who needed tutoring. She needed the extra money, she'd never married, and he'd tried to make it up to her by charging less. He wouldn't have charged her at all except that she would have been offended. Once he tried to tell her he appreciated what she'd done, that he knew what she'd given up, but the words just weren't there, and she'd waved away his muteness. "We go back a long way, John, words don't mean anything between us. Friends don't have to explain. You're John Lasseter and that's all that matters to me." How did a man repay kindness of such magnitude, how make it up to her? Later, he thought it might be that he had.

When she died, his last link with the town was gone, at least as far as doctoring went. The whites went to the young doctor over in Carden, and that was all right, the blacks came to him from all over the county, some from as far away as Marion and Selma. He was on the staff of St. Francis Hospital in Selma, he did some surgery, took out tonsils, appendixes. He could work twenty-four hours a day, seven days a week, if he wanted to and could hold out. Last year he'd started taking Wednesdays off. He needed to be with Zella more. But he'd gotten rich off five-dollar office visits and fifteen-dollar house calls, and to hell with the hypocrites who hated him for loving Zella.

Oh, they accepted—condoned, even—that most men had to have their little roll in the hay now and then with a black woman; they even accepted that some went to Whiskey Alley to the Negro prostitutes. After all, unless a man was a boor and insensitive to his wife's delicate feelings, he hardly ever forced himself on her after the children were born. They understood that Southern women were different, more fragile than Northern women—that for them the sex act was a sacrifice to enable men to carry on the family name.

When he was a young man and sometimes went to parties on twilit lawns, the girls languishing in swings in their summer dresses, the boys in white suits would drink a toast to them: "to Woman, lovely Woman of the Southland, as pure and as chaste as this sparkling water, as cold as this gleaming ice, we lift this cup, and we pledge our hearts and our lives to the protection of her virtue and chastity."

But that had not been Jenny. When they were first married, many times she had wakened him, her arms clasping him, puling him to her; and he was glad that nature had not been so stupid as to make the act of love abhorrent to women. Men were, for making such stupid tributes. The making of life was an ecstacy he and Jenny had shared. At least in the beginning.

He pulled his thoughts from her. He would not think about her; all that was over, the sighs and pledges of love in summer nights, the breeze blowing the curtains, the smell of turned earth and honeysuckle in the air, the moon shining in upon their naked bodies. And on winter nights, covers pulled over their heads, laughter and breath warm and blending as they strained in love that was not only for making babies but just because they loved each other; they had truly become one flesh. But all that was gone, relegated to the world that was called the Past.

But he had Zella now; he had broken the code and fallen in love with a Negro woman, had brought this love into the open by giving her a house and living with her. And he was not sorry, all the town's condemnation and punishment could never make him sorry.

He walked along the sidewalk to his office and wished he could spend more time with her, that it was nearer the time Bird could practice with him, but that was still years away. He'd hoped for awhile some young doctor would come here and give him a hand, just for a few years until Bird finished school; but no young doctor was coming here, they'd have to work too hard. They had it easy in the city, they didn't make house calls— at least that's what he'd heard—and they loaded their patients into hospitals that were run like garages, people just parts, a gall bladder or a kidney or a liver. They didn't seem to appreciate that the body was a miracle of craftsmanship to be treated reverently, tenderly. Big-city doctors had become nine-to-fivers with weekends off to play golf at the country club. Damned silliest game he'd ever heard of, golf—grown men riding around in toy carts trying to knock a ball into a hole. That's what they did for fun; he'd met them at conventions, listened to them talk. And as soon as they found out he was from a country town they'd edge away, their eyes glazing over as if they didn't see him anymore, and pretty soon he'd be by himself. Hell, he didn't care, he hadn't gone to talk about golf but to see if they'd come up with any more miracles like penicillin.

Doctoring was his work and his fun; since he was nine years old he had known he was going to be a doctor; it just came to him one day when he was sitting high in a tree in his back yard that that was what he was going to do. Nothing had happened to make him decide this, no inspiration from a doctor, and nobody in his family had ever been a doctor that he knew of. But he was as certain that that was what he would be as he was that tomorrow the sun would rise. And it had never disappointed him, it had filled his life completely. Until Zella. She possessed him now as his work never had. As Jenny never had.

"Here now," Dr. Lasseter said, stepping up to his office door. "Leave LeRoy alone, you ought to be ashamed of yourselves, grown men picking on a child that way."

He took his keys out of his pocket, pulled the small black boy up to him, noting that the bare arm was hot, yet prickly with goose flesh, that he was shivering with fever. He unlocked his door, pushed the loose thumbtack tighter into the white card on the door on which he had typed DR. JOHN LASSETER, M.D.; OFFICE HOURS SUN. 8 A.M. - 4 P.M.; MON. - TUES. 7 A.M. - 4 P.M.; THURS. - SAT. 7 A.M. - 4 P.M.; AVAILABLE ONLY FOR EMERGENCIES WEDNESDAYS.

The flatwoods white men crowded to the door, pushing the boy aside, and again Dr. Lasseter said, "Here now, quit pushing at LeRoy, can't you see how sick he is? Haven't you any feelings at all?"

They grinned and shrugged. "Well, hell, Doc, we're sick too, and we warn't hurtin' him none, we was just teasin' him about his name. He thinks he's a king."

"My name," the boy said, "is Le *Roi*. Capital l, small e, capital R, small o i. It means 'de king,' Bird told me so." His thin shoulders beneath the ragged shirt were stiff with pride, and his chin trembled though he did not cry when the men guffawed. Even the blacks were laughing.

"Well, you shore don't look much like no king. Whut you king of, the shithouse?" and they laughed harder, slapping their knees. "You look more like you ought to have a ring in yore nose and bone in yore hair than a crown on that burr head."

"You quit laughin' at me, Bird say that's whut my name means—"

"Well, he shore ought to know, seein' he's one of yore kind."

"Get out of here," Dr. Lasseter said. "Go find yourselves another doctor; what's wrong with you men I can't fix. I wouldn't dirty my hands on you."

"Here now, we got as much right to git doctored as these here niggers, I been awake all night, cain't hold a thing on my stummick—"

"I said 'get out of here.' "

When they did not move, but only grinned, the doctor said, "I can help you on your way. I can get my thirty-eight from the office."

They walked away, slowly, looking back over their shoulders and muttering, and just as they turned the corner flung up their arms, middle fingers pointed skyward.

"Well, good riddance," the doctor said, "now come on in here, LeRoy, and all the rest of you."

He took Leroy's hand, leading him in first, and saw that his stubbed toe was twice its size, the skin tight with green pus that oozed from around the edge of the nail. He could not see the stripes because his skin was too dark, but they were there, he'd bet his life the boy already had blood poisoning. The fever indicated the infection was generalized.

In the old days, even as recently as the forties, the boy might have died. He'd lost a young man to blood poisoning when he'd first started practicing; it had been a terrible blow, he'd come out of medical school thinking he would save everybody by sheer force of will, if nothing else. Foam had bubbled from the man's mouth, and not a thing he could do but sit by and watch, hold the fading, fluttering pulse until he was gone. Close the eyelids. Cross the hands. Pull up the sheet. Keep telling the weeping mother how sorry he was, feeling so like a failure, wanting to chuck it all and just go on off down the road, walking and walking, he didn't care where. But it was different now; he'd give LeRoy a shot of penicillin and by this time tomorrow he'd be practically well, his mama would have to hold him in the bed. And fresh pity rose for the young man he couldn't save, the beautiful young man with the pale cheeks and long eyelashes.

Now and again he'd find somebody who was allergic to penicillin, and he'd have to treat them in the old way, hot salt water and poultices, sometimes herbs he'd learned about from the old women in the flatwoods. He'd thought he knew it all when he came out of medical school, he was fuzzy-cheeked and brash, but he'd finally learned to listen. Those old women had knowledge passed down through the generations, some sixth sense he'd seen work more than once when he'd used up all the tricks out of his black bag. And then he'd just stand by and watch: they'd brew teas and grind leaves, and he'd even seen prayer work—he'd learned not to scoff, to discount, anything. No explaining the mind and the effect it had on the body.

Frank and Maxine Wesson sat on one side of the waiting room, the blacks on the other. The patients had worked out this system a long time ago, the doctor hadn't planned it that way, and they talked back and forth swapping symptoms, talking about crops. Frank and Maxine owned a piece of land between town and the flatwoods, so they were not white trash nor were they townspeople. There were only three or four farms like this, and those people were a breed unto themselves, they kept mainly to themselves.

Ordinarily, he took whites first; he didn't like that system, it galled him, but the blacks wanted it that way. The flatwooders had ways of getting even with uppity Negroes that got taken first in the doctor's office. But this morning he didn't care who wanted what or who hated who, he was taking care of that child first even if the waiting room had been full of flatwooders. He was going to lance that toe and get some penicillin and tetanus antitoxin into LeRoy.

He went into his office and hung his coat on the hatrack, then into the examining room and helped LeRoy onto the table. He washed his hands, noting with pleasure the sunlight streaming through the window. Best thing in the world to kill germs, sunlight. After he dried his hands he flicked the switch on the fan on the wall, adjusting the angle so that it moved the air without blowing on the patient. He didn't have air conditioning, it was unnatural; but the body adjusted to heat, sweat was cleansing and got rid of toxins. People weren't made to live in refrigerators.

This room suited him exactly: nothing unnecessary was here, no pictures on the walls, no curtains at the windows, only a Venetian blind that was raised most of the time except during the hottest part of the day. The floor was spotless red tile, the benches in his waiting room from the basement of the First Baptist Church that he'd paid fifty cents apiece for twenty-five years ago. A bootlegger told him once he felt like he was in the amen corner of the church, and he'd asked the man what he could possibly know about churches, that it seemed like he ought to feel more at home in jail. He joked with the flatwooders and they liked that; they were poor, but they were human beings, after all. Of course, some of them were mean as snakes, like those two out front this morning. But mainly they were just poor, and people despised them for that.

He'd lost some of the flatwooders after Zella, but mostly they kept coming; he'd been their friend during hard times and let them pay in corn and potatoes and pigs and chickens, many times not taking any pay at all. And they understood that white men slept with Negro women, for them it was as natural as sunrise. But they were like your horse or dog: you might like them—you might even love them—but you didn't bring them in your house and put them in your bed. They were utilitarian, objects of use for satisfaction. Sometimes he caught their puzzled, measuring looks: they did not understand him but they accepted him.

When he had finished with LeRoy, he sent him home with a note to his mother telling her to keep him in bed, not to let him out anymore, he would come to the house the next morning to change the bandage. LeRoy's mother had two younger children, one a baby on her lap. And she had two older. "Folks tells me, Docta, that I always got one in my stummick and one on my lap." And she looked so tired, so defeated. He wanted, first chance he got, to go by there and talk to her husband again about birth control. He didn't know how many times this would make, she simply wouldn't go to Selma to get her tubes tied, and George wasn't a bit interested in the condoms he left for him. He'd just have to keep trying.

He went to the sink and washed his hands again, scrubbing them with a stiff brush and Lifebuoy, wished that he had time to drive LeRoy home, that he didn't have to walk home in the hot sun. But the waiting room was filling up, mostly with share-croppers who'd saved their illnesses until the weekend if they could. Overseers didn't want them taking time off if the croppers could still stand, they thought most times they were just lazy; they'd told him the blacks came back from his office saying what "Mista Doc," said like it was the gospel. "Quit telling them to go to bed," the landowners said. "They're like children, give them an inch and they take a yard. You ought to know they'll get away with whatever they can, especially if they're encouraged." And he'd told them that he'd practice medicine the best way he saw fit, he wasn't telling anybody who was sick to go slave in a hot field.

He dried his hands and went to the door to see who was next, decided to take Maxine Wesson and get it over with. He was absolutely out of patience with her, it was the third time this week she'd been in. She was a hypochondriac, she still had morning sickness even though she was in her ninth month. Frank said she had told him she hated him and wouldn't let him come near her, wouldn't even sleep in the same bed. Frank said that when she knew she was pregnant she jumped off the end of the bed trying to jar the baby loose. He said she screamed and cried and tried to beat him up.

He'd tried to explain to Frank about condoms but Frank just kept shaking his head and saying it sounded to him a lot like washing your feet with your socks on. Still, he had to keep trying; after the baby was born he'd talk to Frank about it again, he needed a rest before he took on another one of Maxine's pregnancies. He started to call her in, then waited to hear the end of a conversation between Frank and Dave Crenshaw.

"You know anything about that mule out to Ellard Willoughby's place?" Frank asked. "You work down there sometimes, don't you?"

"Yassuh," Dave said, "dat's right. I he'ps out Mista Ellud sometime, shuck de cawn, bale de hay."

"Well, either I'm crazy or I seen a mule stickin' its head out his window last winter. Ain't that so, Maxine, didn't we see a mule along about last February?"

She nodded that they had, her hands folded upon the huge mound of her stomach.

"It was blowin' great big puffs of steam out its mouth," Frank said. "And then it snorted and it was gone and I thought I maybe was imaginin' things."

"Nawsuh, you din't 'magine it, he got a mule all right."

"But in the *house*? Is that fuckin' mule livin' in the house, Dave?"

"Well, suh, Mista Frank, I don't rightly know nothin' 'bout is the mule zackly *livin'* in de house wid Mista Ellud, but I *do* know it got de run of de place."

A burst of laughter, blacks and whites together, and the doctor smiled. Ellard Willoughby was lonely, last winter he'd kept a goat in the kitchen. And he wondered at the complexity of human nature that whites could sit in his waiting room laughing with blacks one day and cut off their balls the next.

He went back into his office and sat down at his desk, deciding to wait until Gertrude came in before he called Maxine. No one seemed very sick, and all of a sudden he felt tired, it just came over him, a great lassitude. He supposed it was because he wasn't sleeping much lately. And Maxine did better when Gertrude was there, Gertrude could handle her better than he, she'd pat Maxine and stroke her hair. It was just about time for the baby, probably not more than another week, and he'd be glad to have it done with. Glad for Maxine.

He'd lain awake most of last night worrying about Zella because she had said she was leaving him, that she wanted more, a home and children. And he had thought that he'd already had that, that he couldn't go through all that again. And he knew that was selfish, and that if Zella was going to have children it would have to be soon. She was thirty-five. But he would be fifty-three in July and he couldn't do it all again, and certainly not in this town. Neither of their lives would be worth a plugged nickel, a white man and a black wife.

He leaned forward and took his testosterone tablets out of his desk drawer and slipped one under his tongue, leaned back again, closed his eyes. The hormone made it possible to sleep with Zella two or three times a week, whereas without it he doubted he'd be able to make love once a week. Too tired, too many late-night house calls. Too damned old, and too many years of regret weighing on his shoulders. And Zella's lust was a burden. He thought that a black trait, not inherited, but from lack of inhibition. He doubted Negro women ever had toasts drunk to their purity. "You haven't lived until you've fucked a nigger woman." How many times had he heard that? Hundreds, probably. Men talking in barns on rainy afternoons shelling corn, high-school boys smoking rabbit tobacco behind the barn bragging about seducing the maid, thinking they were big men now they'd had a Negro girl who couldn't refuse.

Zella had wanted him to divorce Jenny and go North with her, for them to get married, and he'd considered it. The girls were grown, except for Johnnie. Even if she were grown, he couldn't leave this child who loved him, who had never judged him. Sarah hated him and took Jenny's side, the twins were oblivious to the turmoil, they had each other, it seemed they loved only the mirror image of themselves. But they were always polite to him, and kind. None of the girls knew the whole story, and better all of them hate him than know the terrible thing about their mother. But whatever he had done, Johnnie loved him; from the beginning of her life there had sprung a bond between them, a sympathy.

He loved her as he had loved Jenny in the beginning, wanting to protect her, to make life easy for her. When he had found Jenny, he was gloriously happy that he could put this searching part of his life behind—as he had never wavered in his determination to become a doctor, so he had intended he would love only Jenny and forever. It just went to show how wrong you could be, how much of life was a matter of luck. He never would have believed how wrong he had been about Jenny. Too bad, too bad, to err on such a crucial matter as choosing life's partner. His deepest desire had been to cherish her for all of his life....

He sighed and leaned back, slumping in his chair. He would not think about Jenny, he was through agonizing over her. They lived now as courteous acquaintances, and that was a miracle, for once he had nated her so much he had wanted to kill her.

He considered a trip for Zella. That might be an excitement that would pacify her for awhile, make her less restless. He could take her to Canada, they could take the same trip he'd had as a boy. When he was sixteen, his mother had decided he needed to see someplace besides Asheton, he'd never even been out of the state. He'd gone all the way to Banff, and when he got back home they had sat at the kitchen table looking at the pictures he'd taken. And he saw the longing in her eyes as she fingered the pictures—he understood, finally, through his thick-skinned, egoistic youth, that he had taken her trip, that in her love for him she'd given him her dream. It had been her longing for the greenness of mountains, the coolness of lakes, her longing to escape the flat, hot land. Too late he had remembered her sitting in the lamplight reading his geography books, too late to make her who had never been farther north than Tennessee take the trip.

He reached for her picture that sat on his desk, and a smiling woman with large, dark eyes looked back at him; but she didn't seem real with the wavy black hair and smooth, placid hands folded in her lap. Memory told him she was tiny, with gray-streaked, faded hair, with hands never still: washing, hoeing, ironing, canning, loading the wagon to take to town to sell that which she'd grown and preserved. The little house where they had lived together on the edge of the town was gone, just a vacant field now mostly trees and brush. But she was there; sometimes he parked his car on the side of the road and looked at the place, and it would all come back, the mulberry tree where he climbed to hide to get out of chores, her standing looking up at him with the buggy whip and not having to say a word. He didn't remember his father, who was bucked off his horse and his neck broken. His mother had been his security, his evidence of an unchanging world. And then she died, she whom he had thought would never leave him, had left him. He had not been able to believe so much motion could be stilled. She became the yardstick by which he measured all other women, and Johnnie looked like her, except that Johnnie was blonde, like Jenny.

He set the picture back and thought again of Zella. They couldn't travel together, no motel in the South would take a mixed couple, and even in the North he'd heard it was bad. He couldn't subject her to that. And besides, he didn't want to go on a trip, too many people were counting on him here, what would they do if he were gone? He had to think of something else, some other way to make her happy. He could send her by herself, buy her lots of clothes, give her lots of money to spend. But he was afraid she would never come back.

He went to the window and looked out into the street and thought that he would have to marry her and go North, take Johnnie with them. And have her persecuted for his and Zella's sins? Never. He would die first before he would do such a thing to that dear child. But besides, his life was here, and his heart. He could not live among strangers.

He looked out into the dusty early-morning street, and knew that if he shut his eyes he could name each building and the year it was built; he knew each house of the neighborhood, who lived in it and who lived in it before them and who before that. Up the street and to the left was the First Baptist Church and in the graveyard next to it were the bones of his mother and father and his son. Quickly he pushed away the thought. He would not think of his son. Even after all these years the hurt was as fresh as if it happened yesterday. Bird, finally, had made the grief bearable. He could not see how Jenny could have been so heartless as to make him send him away.

He had found Bird in Berry's Woods. Early one August morning he'd been walking at dawn because he couldn't sleep; he'd lain awake most of the night worrying about Jenny, just as last night he'd worried about Zella. Jenny had asked him not to move back into their bedroom, she said his being called out at night disturbed her sleep. She had the storage room painted and new carpeting put down, and he moved his wardrobe and his magazine stand filled with medical journals and pamphlets from drug companies to join the iron bed that had already been set up there. He hadn't cared about the paint and the carpet, it was going to take a lot more than that to fix what was wrong between him and Jenny.

Six months after the twins were born, he and Jenny had made love twice, and it wasn't the number of times that broke his heart, but that she had withdrawn from him. The joy and hope of their lovemaking was gone. He went to her room and they sat together on the side of her bed, and he held her and told her he loved her just as he had in the beginning, only more. But she had only stared into her lap, worrying a piece of string in the seam of her gown. Finally he had left, heard the lock click after she closed the door. He stood in the dim hall, knowing she was waiting on the other side for him to leave.

He had lain in his clothes on top of the covers, and at dawn went to the woods. He walked in the roseate light, thin mist off the river kicking up like dust, and he accepted his situation: Jenny hated him for their dead son, she was never going to make love to him again, and the knowledge stabbed his heart like a knife. He did not know how to make her love him again; her face as she closed the door was set hard as plaster of Paris.

He turned back to the house that morning, and when he heard a racket of birds fussing and twittering just above the ground in a pine thicket he went back to see what it was. He waved his arms at them, and found a market basket sitting beneath the trees holding a baby wrapped in a white blanket.

He knelt beside it, the baby staring up at him with dark eyes and sucking its fist. He peeled back the blanket as if unfolding the petals of a budding flower, and a naked boy baby lay revealed, a thin gold chain with a small cross fastened about his neck. He touched the velvet-skinned hand, and the tiny fingers popped around his finger; he smiled at the baby's strength, and gently felt the frame that was solid and straight, palpated the stomach. He lay his ear against the rib cage and heard the wonder of the strongly beating heart. Loosely, he folded the blanket over the child again, only then aware of the birds fluttering and scolding from the low branches of the trees.

He sat for a long time beneath the tree, his hand resting lightly on the basket, and for a moment he was beside Jenny's bed; their son lived; he rose and, immersed in flooding, baptismal sun bore the baby home, calling to Jenny as he entered the house. She was standing at the top of the stairs in a long white gown, her golden hair flowing about her shoulders: *a woman clothed in sun, the moon under her feet.*

He climbed upward to her, proffering the baby; she could take her son to her breast—she could forgive him and love him again. *This is our son, Jenny, I found him in a basket in Berry's Woods. He has been sent to us.*

For the first time in months she looked straight into his eyes, as if she really saw him—as if he were crazy. *It's that nigger whore Phoebe Callins's baby, haven't you heard? she's had a white man's child. Undoubtedly she's thrown it away.*

He took the baby and gave him to Mary Betty to care for, setting up a crib in her room off the kitchen. She cradled the baby to her large breasts, crooning to him while he wrote out a formula of canned milk and Karo syrup, directing her how to mix it and how often to feed him; and he had told her how he came to find the baby, how the mockingbirds swooped at his head trying to protect the child.

"His name is Matthew because he is a gift of God," he said. "And his second name is Memory in remembrance of my mother." But Mary Betty called him "Bird."

"Listen how he coos like a dove, Docta, the birds done put their mark on him." And the nickname stuck.

In the afternoon, Phoebe's father had come, crying and saying Phoebe had left the baby in the woods and then drowned herself in the river. He asked for the child, he'd got word through Jenny's sharecroppers that the doctor had the baby. *He's mine, Mista Doc, he's all I got left of her. I wants to take 'im ovah to my sister's in Carden, God as my secret judge knows I thanks you fo' whut you've done.*

He unlocked the medicine chest over his desk and took out a small glass vial of clear liquid, held it up to the window. Morphine. Derived from the poppy, the genus *Papaver somniferum*, nodding its scalloped, scarlet head in the breeze in almost every garden in town. So lovely. So deadly. Saint and devil. He rotated the bottle in the sunlight, the translucent liquid refracting the rays into rainbows. *O Lucifer, son of the morning.*

Morphine, the genie locked in this tiny bottle; if he loosed him his power became his, according to how he chose to use it—to ease pain, to comfort. Or to enslave. How terrible to have such power, and quickly he replaced the bottle in the cabinet, locked the door, dropped the key into his pocket.

He was trembling, as if he had escaped some danger, some awful knowledge. He went to the sink and washed his hands, splashed cold water on his face, then sat again at his desk. He could not believe it had been five years ago that Zella had come up on the porch knocking at his door.

She came just after midnight; at first he thought he dreamed, her voice called so softly, moaning at the door like wind sifting through the cracks, *Docta, Docta*. It nibbled at the edge of sleep until at last he understood someone called, and he went to the porch and found her fainting on the steps, holding onto the banister. In the light that shone from his room he saw dark blood on the floor and on her dress, and he picked her up and carried her into the kitchen, lay her on the table, knowing he had no time to get her to the office.

He yelled for Mary Betty, and they ripped off the bloody clothes, got a pillow under her hips, and with the curette scraped away the embryo and packed her with gauze to stop the bleeding. He gave her a shot of penicillin and put her to bed in Mary Betty's room, brought in a practical nurse to take care of her. When she was well enough, he moved her to the house on the river that he had built for himself to have a place to be alone, to sit and think. Jenny didn't want Zella at the farm, though there was certainly nothing between them at the time. It was, she had said, that she didn't want the house turned into a hospital. The Negro practical went to the river house with Zella and stayed until she was able to be up again, and he got to looking forward to going out to see about her, liked thinking someone was using the small snug house. It had only a living room and bedroom, a kitchen and a bath, and a screened porch where he could sit and watch the sun rise.

Zella had come to Asheton from Carden; she said if she got tired of one place she went somewhere else. Henry Jerald, a big dark Negro, came looking for her at the office, and Gertrude said the word was that Zella had prostituted for him. Later, after they had begun to love each other, Zella told the doctor this was so, and he believed the baby was Henry's. Henry left Asheton and went to Chicago and Zella hadn't heard from him since.

Late one afternoon when he came to see about her, when he was thinking it was nearly time to send her home, he found her swimming naked in the river, though it was late autumn and the weather turning cold. The first time he saw her, she was walking along the edge of the water, her dusky form blending with the twilight. She stood in the shallow pool, bubbles rising about her from a spring that fed into the river. She was tall, with long, strong legs, and coarse dark hair halfway down her back; he was happy that nothing about Zella reminded him of Jenny.

"I don't care if you look at me," she said. He was surprised that she knew he was there, so quietly had he walked down the slope.

He was embarrassed, like a pubescent boy caught peeping at his sister while she dressed.

"I'm sorry to intrude on your privacy. I apologize." He had said this, stiffly formal. "I should have let you know I was here."

"I don't mind for you to see me. I like for you to look at me."

He made love to her that night, and after that spent every spare minute with her.

The screen door at the back of the office creaked open, and Gertrude appeared in the doorway in white stockings and white oxfords, her uniform so stiffly starched it looked as if it could stand alone. Her kinky gray hair was pulled into a tight bun on her neck and fastened on the sides with genuine tortoiseshell combs the doctor had given her last Christmas. She told him they were her proudest possessions. Her black skin was scrubbed to antiseptic cleanliness, and he sniffed with deep approval: he had taught her that, in order to be his nurse, she must meet the highest standards of personal grooming and she had surpassed even what he demanded.

"Docta," Gertrude called, going at once to the sink in the examining room to wash her hands, "when I pass by de barber shop de mens down there say they seen Mista Mason out dis mawnin', lookin' fo you, they say he got de gun. They say he jes wanderin' roun' lak he don' know where he at."

He shook his head, considering the information. "Well, I'm sorry," he said. "I wish I knew what to do for the man. I've tried to talk to him when he's sober, but he doesn't remember anything he does when he's drunk. I've read of cases like this, people have even committed murder and not remembered. I guess I'm going to have to consult with somebody, if I can ever just get the time to get away; I don't want to do it on the telephone."

"Yassuh." She stood now in the doorway, drying her hands on a rough brown-paper towel.

"There's nothing for it but to send Bird to look for Mr. Posey. He's picked a bad day, the waiting room's full and I wanted Bird here to observe and to run errands. That'll be just the excuse he needs to stay gone all day. To tell the truth, Gertrude, I don't think my son likes doctoring all that much."

"Well, Docta, he young, you got to give 'im a chance, give 'im a little growin' time. He jes a baby."

"He's nearly seventeen years old; when I was seventeen I was practically running my mother's farm, and by the time I was eighteen I was off to medical school and I don't mean *pre-medical* school. Gertrude, I'm afraid he's lazy."

"Yassuh."

Dammit, the woman was patronizing him, she didn't agree with a word he'd said about Bird; she was crazy about the boy, as was most everybody who knew him. But the boy needed discipline, he needed to show some signs of maturity. Last summer he'd made him work in Wesley Turner's field; he thought Bird too cerebral, that he needed to know physical labor and to learn the value of a dollar. His own childhood had toughened him, he'd never had things handed to him on a silver platter. He didn't want Bird spoiled, and so he'd sent him to work for Wesley, had outfitted him in sun hat and overalls, and from a distance you couldn't tell him from the cropper who chopped alongside him. His face had blistered, his hands had rubbed raw beneath the gloves, and he begged to quit; but he wouldn't let him, he made him finish out the month he'd promised Wesley. At night Emma Bonner said he fell into bed without supper, he was so tired, and several times he parked his car on the side of the road and watched Bird moving slowly down the rows, and he nearly went to tell him it was all right, he could quit. But he didn't. During the month Bird grew leaner and his slender arms filled out, became more muscular. But when the month was up he'd gone straight back to his old habit of spending hours reading under the scuppernong arbor. Sometimes when he left for the office he leaned under the twisted, leafy vines to tell Bird good-by, saying, "Better move every now and then, son, the buzzards might get you, you're so lazy."

"Docta?"

"Yes, what is it, Gertrude?"

"You ready fo' me to start callin' in de patients?"

He nodded that he was. He should have already started; he was making himself run late to make calls in the afternoon. He went into the examining room and stood next to the table, waiting. Gertrude came back, alone.

"I expects, Docta," she said, "dat you ought to see Hattie Crosby first, she jes' come in, she say Bill got drunk las' night and beat her up 'cause she fussed at 'im. She got a ice pick stuck in de bone in de side of her haid; you think the white folks gon' mind if you take her first?"

"My God, woman, get her in here, why didn't you just bring her on in?"

Before she could turn to leave, there came a sound like a car backfiring, or a gun shooting, and his first thought was that it was Mason, that he had gotten a bullet for his gun. But then people were running down the street hollering, someone opened the waiting-room door shouting for him to come to the hardware store, and he grabbed his stethoscope and his bag and ran down the sidewalk; Harley Miller had left the flag half-raised outside the mercantile store, a Rich 'n' Creamy Dairy truck was stopped in the middle of the street, the driver gone.

He pushed through the crowd gathered at the curb in front of the hardware store and saw Otis Helms lying on his back in the street, arms outflung. He stopped in his tracks, cursing, closed his eyes, sickened. Almost half the man's head and part of his face had been blown away; Coy Watson stood on the sidewalk, nickel-plated gun clasped in his hand. The smell of gunpowder and pale-blue smoke hung in the air.

He knelt beside the man whose eyes were filmed, opaque, his mouth a half grin of gapped, brown-stained teeth. He made the confirming gestures of feeling wrist and neck, shook his head, and stood up. When he turned, Bird was standing behind him, staring at Otis Helms, his face deadly pale.

Quickly he told Bird to hand him his bag he had set on the pavement, and when he had picked it up the color was coming back in his face, his lips were not so white. Then the sheriff was there pushing through the crowd telling everyone to step aside; he took Coy Watson by the arm, told Bird to go and get Mrs. Helms when the doctor said Mr. Helms was indeed dead.

He followed Bird onto the sidewalk, walked as far as his office with him. "After you've told Mrs. Helms, Bird, I want you to find Mason Posey and take him home. He's drunk again and coming after me with that empty gun."

And he went on into his office to see about the ice pick stuck in Hattie Crosby's head.

4

On Saturday morning Faye Watson sat on a tall stool behind the cash register in Koy's Kountry Kitchen truck stop, two miles outside the city limits of Asheton on state highway 12. Most people referred to the restaurant as the KKK, not only for the initials, but because of Coy's political activities.

The sun had just begun its climb up the sheer face of eastern sky, and the red glow shone in through the plate-glass window, turning Faye's auburn hair redder, and washing to anemic whiteness her pale, freckled skin. The cigarettes and candy bars in the glass case, the cheap plastic toys in plastic wrappers hanging from spindles on display racks, the red juke box, silent since 3:00 A.M., all blended together, bound by the rosy light.

A Mack truck pulled into the parking lot, and she craned to see the license plate, then took a small notebook from her pocket, flipped it open, pulled a ballpoint pen from its spiral binding, and entered *Idaho* beneath the list of states recorded there. A truck with Idaho plates had never stopped at the Kountry Kitchen before, and later she would look it up in the World Book. The next time a driver came in from Idaho she'd know all about it, and he'd be surprised and admiring of her knowledge. She liked for men to look at her that way, to think she was smart. But she couldn't talk to them if Coy was there, he got jealous and accused her of flirting, "twitching her ass around," as he called it. She wished the truck that had just pulled in was a Red Ryder from California, because that would have been Hayes, and she really liked him, they talked about everything, about God and civil rights and President Johnson; about hippies (Coy said Hayes was one because of his jeans and beard) and flower children and all the places he'd been and she hadn't. Hayes liked her too, she could tell; he brought her a necklace with a sand dollar painted with palm trees and blue ocean from Florida, but she'd hidden it under the tablecloths in the buffet so Coy wouldn't know. She wished she could wear it because it was so pretty.

She stretched and went to the coffee maker behind the counter and poured a cup for the driver, who had come in and sat down in a booth; she returned to the stool and thought how tired she was after being up all night. Ordinarily Coy took the night shift, but three times during the night she'd had to take him Maalox for his ulcer.

Idly she unfolded the Friday-night *Selma Times* lying beside the cash register, flattened it against the counter. FOUR BLACKS ATTACKED BY WHITES, the headlines said. And in small letters beneath, Try to Enter White Theater in Downtown Selma. Briefly she scanned the article, saw that three other blacks had been arrested for trespassing when they sat in a white restaurant. It said the Negroes had tried to integrate the theater and the restaurant to test the new federal civil rights act.

A smaller article near the bottom of the page said that President Johnson had ordered the bombing of some unpronounceable city in Viet Nam and that four American planes had been shot down. How strange to die in a place almost impossible to find on the map, but some of the customers had violent opinions about it. They said the United States had to contain Communism. Well, in Asheton it was the flatwooders and the Negroes containing it, she'd never seen any of the well-off white boys in uniform. It seemed to her like the war in Viet Nam had a whole lot less to do with them than the civil rights movement, which had affected them not at all.

Faye thought she ought to burn the paper, she dreaded how mad it was going to make Coy when he saw that article about the sit-ins so close to home. But he would be even madder if he couldn't find his paper; he went in every afternoon to buy it because the young boy who delivered it wouldn't come so far. The loss of the paper could turn into a major crisis. But it really didn't matter all that much whether she saved it or burned it, if he didn't get mad about that he'd get mad about something else—it was time for the explosion, she'd been watching the tension build for several weeks. Sometimes she couldn't stand the waiting, and she'd do something to push him over the line. And when he was dead ripe it took hardly anything at all to make it happen—a smile or a wink at a driver, a twitch of her skirt, and his fury would come roaring down on her and she'd be glad to get the beating over with. And she knew that in a perverse sort of way she enjoyed this power over him, this ability to control when he would beat her. It was never a question of if, but when, and she might as well at least decide that. She folded the paper and pushed it away, smelling the beating like ozone before the rain.

She did not understand Coy's violent hatred of Negroes, just as she did not understand the rage that always lay so shallowly beneath the surface. No blacks worked in the Kountry Kitchen except for the cook, Nellie. He believed that truck drivers liked Negro cooking because of its high seasoning, and he'd laugh and say he never let principle stand in the way of making money. He only let Bird Lasseter come to clean the yard and trim the shrubs on Sunday afternoons because Dr. Lasseter had asked him to, saying Coy didn't have to pay the boy, it was for building character and exercise.

Coy didn't want to do it; he called Bird "the white nigger," but he'd let Bird come because when Coy had had pneumonia and been sick nearly a month, Dr. Lasseter let them pay the bill as they could and then hadn't charged nearly what he should. They'd just opened the restaurant and didn't have much money, so Coy felt like he owed the doctor a favor. After the bill was paid, he kept saying he wasn't going to let Bird work there anymore, but then he said maybe the doctor would go easy on the charges when the baby was born.

Fear streaked her stomach when she thought of the baby. And then because it seemed to know she thought of it, it fluttered like the brush of a butterfly's wing inside her, and she held her breath, waiting, praying for the movement to stop— she was ashamed of her fear of the gentle touching. She looked at babies when the mothers brought them into the restaurant, the little red-faced, newborn babies, and she was terrified that such as these grew inside her, gradually swelling her stomach so that someday she would burst. And thinking of it she felt faint and giddy, and quickly bent her head between her knees as Dr. Lasseter had instructed her to do. When she straightened, she saw the driver looking at her curiously, and, embarrassed, she looked across the highway to the still dark woods.

She had kept from getting pregnant for over a year simply by having a diaphragm Coy hadn't known about. She told him before they were married she didn't want any children, and he didn't say anything then, but when she told him again after they were married, asked him oughtn't he to be using something, he told her he was the man, he'd decide whether or not she had children. And she'd gone to Dr. Lasseter, asked him wasn't there something she could do, she'd heard married women talk. And he didn't understand why she was so scared; he told her having babies was the most natural thing in the world, that she ought to want to have a big family. But she just sat stubbornly staring at him, ashamed to tell him that she knew that if she had a baby she would die, and he'd shaken his head and fitted her with a diaphragm, shown her how to use it. She'd had it for a year before Coy found it in her dresser drawer hidden under her nightgowns, and he wanted to know what it was.

He dangled the round, shallow cup of thin pink rubber in front of her face, holding it between thumb and forefinger as if it were dirty, and she had tried to grab it from him, furious that he touched this most personal possession. She bitterly hated him, and struck at him, and his face became shocked at her anger; always she had been conciliatory, pacifying. But then he laughed and gripped her shoulder, holding her just out of reach of the diaphragm. *You have no right, it's mine, give it back, you have no right.* And he said, *Nothing's yours, I own everything, the clothes on your back, the food you eat. I own you, because you are my wife and God made you for me. I own this thing, whatever it is. Now, what in the hell is it?*

She screamed that it was to keep from having babies, and

he ripped it into tiny pieces that fluttered to the floor, held her by the back of her neck, his hand a vise holding her head; he cursed her, his face white, drained, his lips bloodless, and he told her if he wanted her pregnant, then, by God, she'd be pregnant. He knocked her down and tore off her slacks, raping her among scattered strips of pink rubber that looked like confetti, as if there had been a celebration.

She lay on the floor a long time after he went to pick up the night shift, and then she went to the bathroom and climbed into the tub and bathed, scrubbing away his smell, his sweat, and semen that ran down her legs. Afterwards she sat on the couch in the dark watching the streaks of headlights of cars on the highway and praying that he would be killed, that he would be crushed and bleeding among broken glass and smashed metal of the black Continental.

He was late coming back, and she grew happier as time passed; she thought *maybe he is dead, maybe the phone will ring and some deputy's somber voice will tell me the good news.* She must try to keep from laughing, she must not let him know she was happy. But then headlights swept across the windows and she put on her nightgown and went to bed.

The trucker from Idaho paid her for the coffee and automatically she reached beneath the counter and took out the canning jar of bennies, dropped six onto the counter when he said that was the number he wanted. When the door opened and two men came in, he looked quickly over his shoulder.

"Don't worry," she said, "the sheriff buys bennies from us too," and he paid her the three dollars and left.

She poured the two men their coffee, found they didn't want breakfast and was glad; Nellie wasn't here yet and she didn't want to have to cook—the smell of food sickened her. Dr. Lasseter was worried because she was losing weight instead of gaining, she had lost down from a size ten to a size eight; but she hated to eat, to feed the baby, because it would gain also, and get bigger and bigger. . . .

She took out her notebook and walked to the window to

check the license plates of the truckers who had just come in, found they were the ordinary variety of Mississippi and Tennessee, dropped the notebook back into her pocket. She turned off the floodlights, the sun was up and streaming through the windows. It was going to be hot again, no rain, the fields turning harder and grayer. The weather was bad for corn but good for her daddy's cotton, and she wished she still lived with him, that she had never left him; she wished Coy had never come up out of nowhere that moonshiny night and turned up their walk to the porch where she and her daddy sat talking.

"Hidee," he said, his Bible tucked under his arm. He put one foot on the step, his hand on the banister, waiting. But her daddy didn't invite him up. "I'm a lay preacher," he said. "I preached at prayer meeting at the Holiness Church tonight. But that don't pay anything but supper. You all know the church?"

"I've heard of it," her daddy said, "But me, I don't go to church. My church is right here, beneath this sky."

"That the way you feel too?" he asked Faye.

Before she could answer, her daddy had said, "I don't see as it's any of your business whether we do or we don't go to church. Who are you?"

He came up onto the porch then, without invitation, and he held out his hand, which her daddy ignored. "Name's Coy Watson, I don't have a regular church right now, I just fill in wherever I'm needed, trying to do the Lord's work." When he kept his hand extended, as if he would stand there forever with his hand stuck out if he had to, her daddy had finally shook it.

"Name's Wesley Turner and this is my daughter, Faye."

"Pleased to meet you,' he said, shaking her hand also. "I'm looking for a job, I don't mind hard work."

"Where you from?"

"Oh, all around; I call the world my home, heaven's my destination, but I was born in the flatwoods."

"I haven't heard the name," Wesley said.

"Well, the flatwoods is a pretty big place. My daddy scrabbles out a living, raises corn, potatoes. It wasn't the life for me."

"What kind of work you looking for?"

"Any kind; like I said, I've kind of fallen on hard times."

Wesley hired him for the field, but before the cotton was half chopped Coy had talked Faye into marrying him. She wondered now what she had thought she saw in him, wondered why in the world she'd ever thought he was good-looking. Her girl friends thought he was, and that pleased her; they thought he was a natty dresser in his wing-tip shoes and pin-striped suit. His hair was coal-black, with a swirl he put in it when he combed it, but his eyes were a peculiar kind of gray that seemed no color at all. She supposed she fell in love with him because he was sweet to her; before they married she never saw a sign of violence. He bought her presents with what her daddy paid him, a cheap watch, a zircon bracelet. She'd been so fooled she even gave him her mother's money.

She never should have told him about the money, but she thought she loved him then, and she trusted him. He asked her a hundred questions about her daddy's farm, whether he owned it and how many acres he had, and before she knew it she'd told him about the twenty-five thousand dollars her daddy had in a savings account for her that had come from the sale of her mother's house and five hundred acres of timberland. It was right after she told him this that he proposed and got her to talk her daddy into signing the money over to her to buy the restaurant.

And she'd really done that, she'd badgered her daddy until he'd given her the money she knew now was rightfully his— they'd never gotten a divorce and her mother had died without a will. Her daddy wanted her to use that money for college, he said it was a chance to make something out of herself. "What in the world do we know about Coy Watson except what he's told us and that he can't look you in the eye?" he said.

But Coy said the words that no one had ever said to her before, not her mother, who did not love her, or her father, who did. The words weren't necessary from him, all his deeds revealed his love for her. In her heart she knew that showing was better, truer, than mere words, but still she wanted to hear them. *I love you, Faye darlin'*, Coy said again and again. Oh, he understood her, sensed this need in her.

So she pestered her daddy until he gave in and signed over the money, but he wouldn't give an inch on one point: he wouldn't sign anything until her name was also on the deed to the restaurant. And he made her sign a paper that said her share of the restaurant went to him if anything ever happened to her, and that she could never sign her share over to Coy. Coy argued hard about that, he gave all the reasons it ought to be just in his name, that women ought not to have to worry about business, their brains just naturally weren't suited to complex matters; he said that as head of the house he ought not to have to get Faye's permission to do what was necessary in the restaurant. But her daddy looked him level in the eye and pretty soon Coy shut up. And many's the time she'd been glad her daddy had seen to her interests, it gave her a feeling of security and respect. Once when Coy kept ordering her around in the restaurant she finally got tired of it and told him she had as much say as he did, and he'd slapped her face, but it had been a great satisfaction to have said it. She owed her daddy for that privilege, of being able to say that to Coy. But she felt guilty about the money; it ought to have been her daddy's, he could have bought more land, built a bigger house; but he said what did he need with more land and a bigger house? he had all a man could want. Nevertheless, she felt guilty.

Guilt was her earliest recollection at her mother's knee. She had cried as her mother told her the story of her, Faye's, birth, of how her feet had been born first and that she had begged the Lord to let her die; she said having a baby was the worst pain a mortal could bear and that men were beasts who caused women to suffer this way.

The day she was born her mother had ordered her daddy away, she told him never to come back, and he left her mother's house in town to go back to the farm where he was born, and his father too. He let the black man who'd always lived on the place move in with him, and when he died, because he didn't have any family, he'd buried him in the family cemetery back of the house.

Her daddy's interval with her mother, that one year that had caused her birth, deflected the flow of his life hardly at all.

But he did not forget Faye; when she was three he visited her, and her mother, looking out the window, would call, "Here comes the beast, Faye, it's your daddy coming." Faye would run and hide, trembling in her mother's closet, the musty clothes pulled about her head. She would never come out when her father came to see her, and after awhile he stopped coming. Faye had to pass his field on the way to school, and when she saw him plowing in the distance she would run, her heart pounding, lunch bucket bumping her leg.

In the summer of her tenth year, her mother died of typhoid. At the funeral, pressed among the crowd, remorse washed over her, wave after wave; it was her fault her mother had died so young, barely thirty years old. Everyone said her mother was never strong after Faye was born; she remembered her mother lying on her bed as twilight filled the room, the Negro maid laying cool camphor cloths on her head, the smell sweet and heavy, her Bible, the pages damp and wilting, pressed to her bosom.

So young, so young, the people whispered, and stony-faced, Faye stared at the silvery coffin, her eyes dry. And then a warm, callused hand enfolded hers, she looked up and her own bright blue eyes looked down at her, a weather-beaten face smiled at her. The man's hair was red, his neck checkered with deep lines above a stiff white shlrt, and she knew this was the beast. Her vision faded, the preacher's voice echoed as through a tunnel; and yet, at the same time, she saw clearly each grain of black dirt piled high beside her mother's coffin, each petal of flower heaped around. When she slumped, her father's strong arm came around her waist and held her up, and she wasn't afraid anymore.

By midmorning, the sun shone poker-hot on the asphalt of the parking lot; across the highway the leaves of spindly pines that the paper mill had planted hung limp, the taproot not yet long enough to draw the deep moisture. Nellie was in the kitchen and was handling the breakfast rush, Coy would probably sleep another two hours, the baby did not move, and so for awhile she could be happy. She decided to have a cigarette, but first looked warily toward the door of the apartment. It was too early for him, she knew that, and yet she was afraid.

She took a cigarette from a pack of Kool's from the carton beneath the counter and lit it with a match from the display bowl beside the cash register. After a long, deep drag, she waved the smoke away with her hand, and the menthol soothed the nausea. She'd smoked before they were married, it was her daddy taught her, and they'd sit on the porch in the dark talking and smoking. It was companionable, and Coy hadn't said a word, but on their wedding night when she lit a cigarette in the apartment (that was where they spent their honeymoon), he'd snatched it from her mouth and told her never to smoke again. "You're my wife," he said, "and I'm a preacher, you got to have respect." But when she went up to her daddy's she still smoked with him, she'd chew some coffee grounds before she came back to the restaurant. Her daddy fussed at her, he said he'd bet his last dime that Coy Watson had committed more sins than the whole town put together. But she still loved Coy then and tried to please him.

She didn't smoke at the restaurant for several months, but then one night when she was working the night shift, sometime between midnight and dawn, she got to craving a cigarette really bad, and when a trucker came in and offered her one while she stood talking to him at the counter, she took it. She just reached right out and took it and didn't think too much about it, the thought barely crossed her mind about Coy telling her not to smoke. She just assumed he was asleep. But he'd gotten up and come to the door checking on her, and when he called to her, she quickly dropped the cigarette on the floor and stepped on it.

He was in his shorts and tee shirt and standing in the shadows just outside the door, and he motioned to her, and she followed him into the bedroom. "I got a stomachache," he had said. "I got a fucking-a, first-class, son-of-a-bitch stomachache from a fucking ulcer, and I got a no-good wife that don't give a damn because she's too busy smoking and flirting with some asshole trucker."

He slapped her hard across the mouth, splitting her lips,

and when she screamed, he hissed, "Shut up, bitch, you want your boy friend to hear?" and he squeezed her jaws hard against her teeth, shoved her against the wall. She was quiet, and did not take her eyes off him. "Fucking-a," he said, "you better be scared. You better remember who you're dealing with. I told you not to smoke, didn't I? Didn't I tell you I won't have you disgracing me? Think you can remember that? Huh?"

He pushed his face so close to hers that she could see the pores of his skin, the golden flecks in the gray eyes; and suddenly he was the terrifying something that came in nightmares that she could never remember what it was when she woke up. She struggled against the hairy, rock-hard arm that held her so effortlessly; and then he hit her with the flat of his hand across her head, and the pain blossomed in a huge burst of light, and she screamed again, and he grabbed her shoulders and shook her, slamming her against the wall.

"You're gon' learn to do what I say," he said, the words gasped. "You're gon' understand who you're fooling with," and his fist smashed into her stomach, knocking the breath out. She sagged onto the floor, her cheek resting on the cool tile. She drew her legs up against her chest, waiting to die, for she had never known such pain. He leaned over her, dead-white face peering into hers. "You got to learn respect, you got to learn who's boss."

The pain possessed her completely, she was reduced to flesh only, she was without soul or dignity, quivering at the muddy edge of the beginning of time. No one had ever hit her—not mother or father or the Negroes who had cared for her before she went to live with her father. She watched the light behind the curtains turn from black to rose to crystal, the pain slowly diminishing. She studied her freckled arm and the short, stubby, nail-bitten fingers of her hand lying on the green-flecked tile, and she despised herself. Her old feeling of worthlessness washed over her—there was something wrong with her to inspire such contempt, such violence.

After a long time she pushed slowly to her feet, braced herself against the wall, and crept onto the soft, faded green chenille spread of her bed, and he was gone, though she had not known when he left. The smell of spicey after-shave lingered in the air. She slept all morning and into the afternoon, and when she woke, the gray wolf that had lain beneath her bedroom chair when she was a child with her mother had come back. It had disappeared while she lived with her father, but he lay now in the corner, his yellow eyes gleaming with hollow light.

Coy knew it was going to be a bad day when he woke up. It was only five o'clock, and already the small bedroom was a hotbox, the tiny Zero fan on the dresser barely moving the air. A dusty shaft of light stabbed through the thin curtains and into his eyes, and he flung onto his side to face the wall. He'd drunk too much beer and smoked too many cigarettes yesterday, and that was what had given him the stomachache; his mouth tasted like unwashed pussy.

He flopped onto his back again, and the scrape of the rough sheet across his balls caused an instant erection, and he was proud of that—it eased for a moment his bad humor. God, it was great being a man. For the life of him he couldn't see that women had anything to enjoy sex *with*. His organ seemed a thing apart, he thought of it sometimes as his "joy stick" and sometimes as "him" or "John Henry." He'd been horny since he was ten years old, kept getting hornier, and if this was "sickness," he hoped never to recover. He believed fucking was as close to heaven as he was ever going to get.

He raised his head and stared down his hairy chest at the tented sheet. *Bring the baggy pants, Jeeves, we'll smuggle this one into town.* His chuckle slid into a scowl because he had no place to put such a magnificent hard. As he stared at the gradually settling sheet, his black mood turned blacker. Only moments before, his shrinking penis had throbbed with blood, and briefly he considered jacking off rather than wasting it. But damned if he'd sleep with five-fingered Mary when he had a wife who was supposed—by God, whose *duty* it was to get fucked. There wasn't a goddam reason in the world Faye shouldn't sleep with him, that Dr. John goddam Lasseter was in on it with her. His father had had his mother any time he wanted, and she'd had five children; hell, she'd thrived on it, lived to be nearly eighty years old. She wouldn't have dared refuse her husband, she was scared of him, he'd slapped her around a lot—sometimes more than slapped. But hell, he'd slapped the kids around too, him and his two brothers. Once his daddy had kicked him for staying out late playing ball; he still got mad when he thought about that, the hard toe of his daddy's boot in his groin.

Hell, he didn't want to think about it. That was all water over the dam, and he kicked back the sheet, willing a breath of air. But the curtains hung limp, the only thing coming in the window was the smell of diesel fuel. But shit, that was all right, the more gas pumped, the more money in his pocket, and that cheered him some—that was *his* gas, and this was *his* restaurant, he didn't give a good goddam how many times Faye's name was signed to that deed. Her old daddy was gon' spend it on college, and what the hell did Faye need with college? Too much learning gave women funny ideas, made them uppity, got them started talking about things like women's lib and thinking they weren't subject to their husbands. That's what the Bible said, *a helpmeet unto thine husband.*

He was really down on his luck that day he walked up on Wesley Turner's porch. He was so down, in fact he was desperate enough to even consider going home to that half-ass dirt farm of his daddy's. He didn't have a red cent in his pocket and no place to stay. The most he'd hoped for at Wesley's was a couple of squares and a bed in the barn. He was hitchhiking across the state hoping for something to turn up, some church that just *might* need a preacher for awhile. He'd found a Bible stuck under your arm got you a passport to almost anywhere, people trusted you; just stick that old Bible under your arm and bend your head just a little, real pious.

Except that son-of-a-bitch Wesley Turner. Wesley just sat there staring at him like he could read his mind, it gave him the willies the way he did that. He'd look you square in the eye and finally you'd have to look away. But for normal people if you said a few "thou arts" they'd invite you right in and feed you and give you the best bed in the house. Spread their legs. And that was the best part, the heavenly nooky. He smiled at his humor, but stretching the muscles made his head hurt, and he scowled.

Tomorrow he was going to preach at Mount A'rat Baptist Church in the flatwoods. Shit, he wished now he didn't have to go, that that new little black-haired waitress Bonnie Sue had not said she'd meet him at the vacant sharecropper's shack back of her house on Sunday morning. Hell, he couldn't preach and meet her too, and that looked like a mighty sweet little piece to turn down. For a moment he considered not preaching, but then Mount A'rat might not ask him again if he didn't show, and he liked preaching. He liked it a whole lot, having people look up to him, listening so seriously to what he said.

It was purely an accident how he'd got started preaching. He'd gone into a Holiness church revival tent meeting at the fairgrounds in some jerkwater town he couldn't even remember the name of, only that it was just over the line into Mississippi. The preacher was late and the kids were running around and babies squawling. The noise was driving him nuts, he'd only gone in because it was raining and he'd didn't know where he was going next, he didn't have anywhere to sleep, and he was hungry. He'd thought he might luck up and get communion, a cracker and some grape juice, participate in the ritual of eating Jesus.

All of a sudden he just decided to go down front and tell them to shut up, but when he stepped onto the platform they got quiet and looked real respectful at him. He had on his dark-blue pin-stripe suit and red tie, and it sure paid off, his always looking his best. They thought he was the preacher; he just started saying what he'd been hearing revival preachers say all his life, hell, he'd heard it enough. His daddy had them in church twice on Sunday and every Wednesday night for prayer meeting and two weeks every summer for vacation Bible school and revival.

There was a Bible lying on the piano, and he picked it up and flipped it open and started reading; it was some kind of hell-fire verse about vengeance is mine saith the Lord. He told them they were hell-bound sinners, that they were nothing but worms in the eyes of God; he stomped his foot and pointed his finger at them, shook his hair all around—hell, he really got into the spirit of the thing, and they loved it, they shouted *hallelujah!* and *amen!*, some even started blubbering and talking in tongues, and when he was through they gave him twenty-five dollars and he hotfooted it out of there. He'd saved a few sinners that night, laid his hand on their heads and said go and sin no more. He liked that, *go and sin no more.* He often wondered what had happened to the real preacher, why he hadn't shown up. It was storming, the rain beating on the tent in sheets. Probably he'd gotten stuck somewhere in traffic—whatever traffic there was. He'd taken the Bible with him, it was the one he still used. His good-luck charm. And he was now a genuine, bona fidee lay preacher—no telling how many gals he'd laid as he made his way across the South.

Before he'd lucked up on Faye, he'd been going from one job to another ever since he got out of the army in '51. Seemed like he just couldn't find anything to stick to, and he sure as hell wasn't going to farm with his daddy like his two brothers. Anything he hated was getting sweaty and dirty. Always he'd tried to figure a way to get rich quick; he'd sold insurance for awhile, but then a husband came home early one night and caught him feeling up his wife. He was just beginning to make a little progress when that son-of-a-bitch came in and ordered him out of his house. It wasn't his fault the woman had "round heels"; hell, if a man had balls he could control his wife, simple as that.

After the insurance, he tried selling a kind of spray-on liquid that made things look like suede—purses, billfolds, shoes, vases. You name it. He'd have put suede on his balls if that would have helped sell it, but shit, the stuff just wouldn't go. Cost too much and people didn't seem all that crazy about suede. It was right after that that he came on Faye and her daddy on the porch of that little bitty white house like a couple of sitting ducks. He almost walked on by, but he was hungry and it was dark and he'd thought, what the hell, but not expecting a damn thing. Hell, bells should have rung and whistles blown. Whoever would have thought that little half-ass farm was a gold mine? Just went to show, you never knew where fortune might turn up.

He turned on his side, closed his eyes, wishing he could go back to sleep, wondered what might turn up in church tomorrow. Might hit pay dirt there too. When he preached, he scanned the congregation to see what sweet tender young thing was there that he might talk to after the service about her salvation. When he got going good he'd begin to touch them, just a friendly clasp of the arm at first, a touching of the hand. And if they took that all right, he'd get a little bolder, maybe brush his hand across a tit and then act all flustered like it was an accident. Those little flatwoods gals were so dumb they didn't even know when they were getting felt up. Once, a long time ago in Tupelo, he got a girl in the choir loft and had her pants off before she finished saying, "Here now, preacher, whut you thank yore doin'?" That was a bad one, though, turned out she was a virgin, and God, what a mess, blood all over his legs and on his shirttail. It was disgusting; he'd cursed her, and she'd started crying and said she was going to tell her mama. He hid out in the woods the rest of the day and left town that night. Didn't even get the noon meal he'd been invited for.

He couldn't sleep, and he got up and stripped away the sweaty shorts, wadded them into a ball and threw them into a corner. Maybe the next summer he could afford an air conditioner for the bedroom, but he'd wanted to get the Continental first, he could show that off. Hell, he felt like king-of-the-mountain when he rode down the highway in that car. Longest day he lived, he never thought he'd own a car like that.

He went through the kitchen onto the screened back porch and got into the shower, ran cold water over his head and back, over his shriveled penis. He blamed that loss on Faye, it was her fault. Everything was her fault. He considered again skipping church, hell, he needed *some*. But he couldn't risk losing that church, they called him a lot to come there, and being a lay preacher gave him status. And he'd found status was a lot harder come by than pussy.

He lathered deodorant soap over his stomach and chest, pleased that at thirty-four his muscles were still hard and tight. He went to the Y over in Selma twice a week and pumped iron. It was a man's world, and for awhile he could forget about always being on the make. He shut off the shower and pulled a towel from the back-porch line and dried off, went into the bathroom and shaved, splashed on pale-green Aqua-Fresh, sprayed deodorant under his arms.

In the bedroom he put on clean underwear, then pushed aside Faye's clothes in the closet. Shit, he needed his own closet, the perfumy smell of her stuff got in his shirts, people would think he was some kind of goddam fairy. One of these days he was going to build himself a house with his own closet and big enough to fill with suits and shoes and shirts, different ones for every day of the month. He put on sharp-creased khaki pants and a white sport shirt, then sat on the side of the bed and pulled on white rayon socks and loafers he kept polished to a brilliant shine. He used to sit in school envying those rich boys their shiny Weejuns while he'd had to wear high-top sneakers. And he'd hated their smug faces, their eyes that slid over him when they passed in the halls like he wasn't there. And those rich gals in Sloppy-Joe sweaters and pleated skirts, charm bracelets dangling on their arms, holding hands with the boys.

He went to the dresser and took the bottle of hair oil, shaking exactly two drops into the palm of his hand, rubbed it into his hair that he swirled into a pompadour. He leaned back to appraise, gently pushed it a tad higher, and thought how sharp he looked, and his mood improved considerably. He began to hum as he started for the restaurant, *look* sharp, tum-te-tum-te-tum, *be* sharp, tum-te-tum-te-tum. And as he opened the door, thought that Faye better be behind that cash register where he left her last night, she better not be swishing that shiny, jersey-covered ass between the tables.

She was not there, the stool was empty. He stood just outside the door and saw her standing at a table talking to a driver with a short black beard; they were laughing, Faye tossing her hair, throwing back her head. Hard, cold anger shot through him like electric shocks, and the foul mood came down again, blacker than when he first awakened. He was going to have to straighten her out again, he'd seen her scuttling away from this goddam hippie driver before, but he'd never actually caught her at anything concrete, nothing he could for sure call flirting. But he for sure the hell had this time; it was plain she didn't expect him out so early, and he didn't know why it made him so mad to see her looking so happy. He just didn't like it, that was all, and he had a right to expect that his wife not play hostess to the goddam Commie hippie community.

And then he saw the cigarette hanging loosely between her fingers, and the blood rushed to his head so that his brain felt hot—sound faded, the country whine of the juke box, the clatter of pans in the kitchen, the clink of silver against china; and sight blurred except for her, she stood in profile, tauntingly raising the cigarette to her lips that closed around it, sucking, pursing, lazily blowing out the smoke.

He walked toward her and he was almost happy, he almost loved her, because his fury had someplace to go, and he went to stand behind her, had circled back through the tables, stalking her. And neither of them saw him coming, she blocked the hippie's view.

Close to her ear he whispered, "Cunt, bitch," and when she whirled, he jerked the cigarette from her mouth, ground it into the floor. Slapped her across the mouth.

But then a fist smashed into his face and he flung out his arms, grabbing at chairs and at a table that crashed down with him, and he slammed onto his back. He looked up into dark, enraged eyes and a bearded face; burning pain and blood spewed in his mouth, strangling him when he breathed, and he coughed and bright red drops sprayed onto his white shirt.

He bellowed as he braced to rise and a boot stomped his hand, grinding, and then silence and blackness came down as the fist ground into his face again.

When he opened his eyes Nellie leaned over him, and her

Negro smell was in his nostrils, and the soapy, dishwater smell of the dishrag she lay on his forehead. He snarled, pushing her away, and he sat up and rubbed his arm across his face, the dark hairs soaked with blood. He clutched a table leg and pushed to his feet, swaying and cursing, fists doubled, looking for the hippie, who was gone. Two drivers stood by the door watching, and he yelled at them, "Get the fuck out, go on, get out of here, the show's over. And you tell that hippie Commie son-of-a-bitch friend of yours if I ever see him again he gets a bullet between the eyes."

They walked into the bright glare of morning, and he turned to Nellie. "Where is she?"

"Miss Faye?"

"Who the shit you think?"

"She gone to the 'pahtment—"

He nodded. That was good, that was where he wanted her; he was afraid she might have run off to her daddy and then it'd be a bitch to get her back down here, she'd know what was coming. But he needed something else first, he wanted more than just her, and his gaze lit on the dishwater-blonde waitress standing big-eyed by the counter.

"*Boo!*" he said, and she scuttled off into the kitchen and he chuckled. Not enough, he needed more, and he looked around for Nellie, but she was gone, and then he saw an old farmer and his skinny wife sitting at a table by the window. Might be something there, and he walked slowly over to them, the red-hot anger forged like a lump of iron in his chest.

"Well," he said, "get your eyes full?"

Their forks stopped midway to their mouths, and they stared up at him, the old man cleared his throat, looked down at his plate, dabbed at coagulating egg yolk with a piece of biscuit.

"What's the matter, cat got your tongues?"

"It's a shame," the man said, "what happened to you, there ought to be a law—"

"There ought to be a law against old farts like you two," Coy said. But they said nothing, stared down into their plates.

The old woman reached a blue-veined, brown-spotted hand to clasp her husband's, and then she looked up at Coy, her jaw slack as she grunted at him. Partially chewed food, stringy with saliva, hung between her yellow dentures. His stomach curled, and when she put her hand on his arm it was cold like she was dead, and he jerked away.

"Get out of here, both of you, you're disgusting, you're repulsive—"

"See here now," the old man said, "you show a little respect for us, we ain't dogs, my wife's had a stroke and cain't talk—"

"Old man, you take that ticket and walk right over there to that cash register and pay and then get out of here. Just lay your money on the counter." The words were lazy, but his eyes were flat, deadly.

"We ain't finished our breakfast, how come we got to pay if we ain't finished?"

"Because I said."

When they were gone, Coy went behind the counter and opened up the metal box where he kept his snub-nose Chief's Special. He kept the nickel plate so gleaming he could see his reflection, and ordinarily he was careful not to mar the shine with his fingerprints; but this morning he didn't care about shine, he cared about performance, and he decided to take the gun down to Byron West's hardware store and have Byron cut the spur off the hammer to make sure it didn't snag on his pants pocket when he whipped it out. He wanted everything perfect, he would be ready any time, anywhere, when he came up on the hippie Commie son-of-a-bitch. He'd of had it in his pocket this morning if he hadn't been thrown off by that filthy cigarette hanging out of Faye's mouth. And he chuckled over the plans he was forming for her.

He flipped open the chamber and emptied the thirty-eight shells into the metal box. While he was at the hardware store he was also going to load the gun with hollow-nose dumdums. Bullets like that could blow off a horse's head—he'd target-practiced on a skull in the pasture once.

▼

He paused in the door of the hardware store, ran his hand down his pants leg, loving the shape, the feel, of the gun pressed against his thigh. He'd drawn it several times after Byron cut off the spur, whipping it out of his pocket smooth as silk. He was ready—wherever, whenever, he was ready for the hippie.

A bulky shape moved across his vision, and he squinted his eyes against the sun risen over the giant water oaks across the street. Otis Helms faced him from the sidewalk; he had just climbed from his pickup parked at the curb, and his shotgun was slung across his arm, barrel broken.

"Well, if it ain't that thievin' bastard stole my wagon wheel," Otis said. Both stood unmoving, tensely waiting.

"You are a goddam white-trash mother-fucking liar," Coy said. His hand hovered over his pocket, and Otis flung up the shotgun, locking the barrel with the same motion. But the dum-dums smashed into his head before his finger touched the trigger, and he fell back, blood gushing.

Coy ran down the steps, gun still upraised, and looked down into the filmed eyes of his enemy, a violent thrill of joy tightening his groin.

People ran into the street shouting, shrill screams splitting the morning air and rising in intensity until the sound passed almost beyond hearing. The doctor came, and they parted to let him pass, the air becoming deathly quiet; and when he had knelt and closed the sightless eyes, the women took the children's hands and led them away, scolding them for looking at that which they could never forget.

5

The black mood that descended on Coy after the incidents of the hippie and of Otis Helms was the worst he had ever had. The sheriff had arrested him and taken him over to the jail in Carden and kept him overnight in a cell with two sour-smelling drunk millworkers. He'd been fingerprinted and mug-shot, even though there were plenty of witnesses who said Otis threw up his gun first. But shit, that hadn't cut any ice with the tin-horn sheriff, he'd arrested him anyway. And since he didn't know any lawyer except that nigger-lover Mason Posey, they'd sent over some snot-nose kid in an ivy-league suit to defend him. After the kid talked to the D.A., the D.A. said it was obviously a case of self-defense, so why waste the taxpayers' money by taking it to the Grand Jury? The scrawny little sheriff's mouth had puckered like a duck's ass when he had to give Coy back his belongings and let him go.

It was nearly seven o'clock when he picked up the Sunday-morning shift on his way back from Carden, and he was afraid he'd miss the breakfast rush, and that the drivers would go on down the highway to the Donut Hole to eat. So he drove along the straight stretch of road a hundred miles an hour, and the dishwater-blonde waitress fainted when she got out of the car at the restaurant, so he had to take her back home again. And that just fanned the flame, made him even madder, because now he was short-handed and he'd have to let Faye come out and work the cash register until he got back from preaching.

After that, he sure had plans for her. No more excuses, no more Dr. Lasseter said this or Dr. Lasseter said that. Fuck Dr. Lasseter. She was his wife and he was going to screw her every way imaginable: frontward, backward, sideways, upside down, oral, anal, you name it. He was going to have a ball, make up for all those weeks she'd twitched her butt around and wouldn't let him have any—all those weeks when she looked like she couldn't stand for him to touch her. It just might be she'd turn into a good little wife once she got the hang of how to do things—after all, she'd been crazy about him when they first got married. Actually, he was sorry he got her pregnant, he ought to have let her use that little pink thing he found in her drawer, but he didn't want her getting wrong ideas about who was boss. The good doctor had no business giving it to her without consulting him.

After he got things organized in the restaurant, he hauled Faye out of bed and sent her ass to the cash register, and he saw how disappointed she was when she saw him. Probably wished he hadn't come back at all. She knew she was going to get it, the way she kept looking funny at him, like she was wondering what was coming next. Well, let her wonder, no need to spoil the surprise of what was coming this afternoon. And he didn't have to worry whether he got any or whether he didn't, before church or after church, he had all he needed right here in his own house. And he was married to it.

He showered until all the hot water ran out, and then he showered some more in cold water, and then he put on his preaching clothes, and when he passed by the register he leaned in close to Faye and told her he had someone keeping an eye on her and if she moved her ass one inch off that stool he'd know about it. And he waggled his eyebrows at her, but the movement sent pain shooting through his scalp where the hippie's fist had hit. And his mouth was sore where his teeth had cut his jaws, and all his anger came back, and he hesitated, thinking to skip church and take care of her now, pay her back for what she had caused. He saw the flicker of knowledge in her eyes of what he was thinking, and she turned pale. Damn right, she better be scared. And he decided to go on, he could have both, preaching and revenge.

He put on his mirror-lensed sunglasses and walked out into

the humid, late-morning sunshine, climbed into the Continental and screeched off, burning rubber as he turned left, and after about a mile he turned right onto a dirt road that descended gradually into the flatwoods. He passed shacks and shotgun houses, and except for the patches of corn and potatoes and pole beans, weeds grew mostly in the fields, and chinaberry trees and sycamores and red oaks shaded the swept yards; beneath the trees were rusting tricycles and pieces of plows and harness and rickety chairs where old men sat watching the black car pass. And people came onto the front porches, long, sad, stubborn faces also watching him drive by, wheels spinning up the dust, his elbow resting on the window sill of the big car, fingers lightly hooked on the steering wheel.

Those walking along the road stepped aside to let him pass, handkerchiefs pressed to their noses against the dust; they moved with plodding deliberation toward the church, women in starched cotton dresses, men in cheap brown or black suits bought secondhand, children also in starched dresses but barefoot.

The road rose gradually upward and ended in the churchyard, the gray-board church dwarfed beneath giant oaks, and a small tin steeple protruded from the peaked roof, cut so short it seemed merely a symbol, a reminder, of what their status would be in heaven. Everywhere was bare earth; even in the cemetery only the yellow-blossomed bitterweed grew along the fences, and the graves were bare and marked with cedar crosses and concrete slabs. It was as if the grass hated to grow even for the dead, that mud and dust were punishment for being poor, that they were doomed always to wipe and scrape and sweep, the dirt seeping into their houses, the pores of their skin, beneath their fingernails.

Coy parked beneath the trees in front of the church, and the children swarmed over the car smearing the gritty dust over its once-gleaming polish. They hung in the windows and he scowled and told them to get their goddam sticky hands off the upholstery; they ran for the church, hollering and laughing and shooting birds back at him. He watched the little bastards, despising them, and wondered how in hell he was going to stand having a kid around him all the time. He took a Wash 'n' Wipe out of the glove compartment and viciously tore away the foil wrapper, scrubbing at the smudges on the maroon vinyl. Goddam kids with their skinny faces and wise eyes. They loved tormenting him, they'd done it before, and as he was scrubbing, one of the older boys, about thirteen, stuck his head in the window, grinned at him. He hadn't even heard him come up, and the boy said, "You really love that car, don't you, preacher? You ought to fur-line the tail pipe and fuck it." He laughed and ran for the church, his bare feet making wide prints in the dust, his shirttail flapping, and Coy yelled after him, "You little bastard, you ever push your face in this car again you're gon' be missing some teeth."

He got out of the car and locked it, dropped the keys in his pocket, and a cur dog ran up and began to hump his leg, and he kicked it away, thinking, by God, there was a conspiracy against him. Everybody was inside, they were waiting for him, but he thought he just might skip it, go back to the restaurant. Why should he cast his pearls before swine? He could be having fun and games with Faye right now. Bunch of ignorant flatwooders with their bristle-headed kids. But as he reached for his keys he stopped and turned toward the church. He still had this hope of a little something after the sermon. One good piece of strange ass would go a long way to easing his humiliation by the hippie and loosening his screaming nerves that were wound like a too-tight spring.

He walked into the cool dimness of the church, and he felt their eyes on him, noting his progress as he strode toward the pulpit, his Bible under his arm. He bowed his head, a pondering frown between his eyes, and it was so good, so good, them watching him, no matter the children or the dog, the smart-mouthed boy: he was somebody for awhile, they waited for *him*, for *his* instruction. They admired him. But he deserved more. This church didn't even have a bell; hell, he'd seen men at the Y with bigger dicks than that steeple.

He climbed into the pulpit and sat in a straight chair beneath the picture of Jesus praying in the Garden of Gethsemane, and he folded his hands, let his eyelids droop. He looked as if he were meditating, but he was watching. The people sat slumped on the benches, their faces turned to him, flat flesh against flat bones. White trash. Born, live, die, right here in these woods scrabbling a little food out of the dirt, the men boozing it up weekends, the women with a gang of kids stuck to their skirts like cockleburs. Women old in their thirties and wrinkled and ugly, hair balled up on their heads. Jesus, he was glad he wasn't born a woman. That's one thing to be thankful for, he didn't have to have babies and hate sex. Most women didn't like it. Except niggers. He didn't blame the doctor, black ass was the best. He hadn't had any lately and it might be he ought to pay a visit out to that river cabin sometime; hell, the gal was a whore before the doctor took her out to the woods and locked her up.

A baby cried, and a woman in the front row hauled out a swollen, bluc-veined breast, and the baby's greedy mouth caught hold. And Coy thought that soon that would be Faye with a yelling, wriggling being attached to the breast that he had fondled—that he had sucked. And his stomach curled. As far as he was concerned, the baby could have it, unless, of course, he made her put it on a bottle. Forget about what Dr. Lasseter said about nursing it, that was a lot of old-fashioned bullshit, it was disgusting too that the baby came out of the same place he fucked, and he wished again he hadn't knocked her up.

The congregation rose to sing, and he rose also, but he didn't have to open his hymnal, he knew the words by heart, hell, he ought to, he'd sung them enough, *On a hill far away stood an old rugged cross the emblem of suffering and shame.* Well, he knew all about that. He'd sure as hell suffered in his life and most especially this weekend. Shit, Jesus Christ didn't have any corner on the suffering market. He thought the people watched him as they sang, and that their eyes were accusing that he had killed one of their own. He looked over their heads out the window toward the road, and in the hard noon sun he thought the landscape looked threatening and somehow ominous; and he wondered if they had something planned for him, maybe they were going to ambush him and kill him. And he was afraid. He considered making a break for it, running down the aisle and jumping into his car, get the hell out of there.

To that old rugged cross I will ever by true, its shame and remorse gladly bear, their voices toneless, off-key, with no instrument to guide them; their eyes were unwavering, faces bland, without expression. And he began to sweat, the rough leather of the Bible slick in his hands, his sore lips stiff as he forced the words of the song. Goddamned mother-fucking draft-dodging hippie who had hit him, he'd get even.

The yellow dog that had humped his leg trotted down the road through the heat waves shimmering in the ruts like pools of water; he looked back to the people, at their plain, tired faces, and he knew they didn't care anything about Otis Helms, they weren't going to bother him. All they cared about was making it from one day to the next. They were fair, they knew Otis had thrown up his gun first. On the floor in front of the pulpit, where now stood a fruit jar of wild roses, on Wednesday would lie Otis's coffin, and the people would gather to mourn him and then go to visit with Mrs. Helms and to eat the food each of them had brought. He wondered if he ought to announce the funeral and try to look sorry, but the fact was, he didn't feel anything any more than if he'd shot a rabbit. He decided it would be better not to say anything.

After the singing the collection plate was passed from hand to hand, with only an occasional clink of a coin and no folding money. They set the offering on the pulpit beside the lectern and he rose to face them; they shifted and settled, looking up at him, holding him in their placid stare. The baby drowsed over the diminished breast.

"Paradise lost!" he shouted, and stomped his foot, the blood rushing into his face as he leaned toward them, hands on hips. The baby cried out, clamped its mouth again onto the breast.

The people stirred and shifted, settled down again, and he thought, by God, that made them move, showed they were alive. An invisible car passed on the highway, the sound fading away, a mockingbird sang in the tree outside the window.

He opened his Bible to the place he had marked with a faded strip of purple ribbon. *And when the woman saw that the tree was good for food, and that it was pleasant to the eyes, and a tree to be desired to make one wise, she took of the fruit thereof, and did eat, and gave also unto her husband with her; and he did eat.*

Sadly he watched them. "Because of this woman Eve, who could not resist the temptation of the serpent, all of us are damned to live forever in outer darkness! 'Eat! Eat!' she told her innocent husband. 'Here, darlin',' she said, 'take a bite,' and she took a bite first, and smacked and slurped, saying 'uhm-*uhm*, that's good,' and the snake ate too, smacking and drooling until, naturally, old Adam just gave in and joined the party, and they gorged until they were so stuffed they fell on the ground!"

The men nodded and called out *amen!* but the women only sat passively, and Coy thought as he watched them, damn right, they're guilty as sin and they know it, and he strode back and forth across the pulpit, the dark mood lifting. He was glad he had come, he was right to come, these people paid attention to him, listened to him; he was important, somebody.

He told them the rest of the story of Adam and Eve, closed his Bible and quoted the scripture to them, and he thought that would impress them, how he knew it by heart—shit, he ought to, it was his standand sermon, he got a kick out of preaching about the wickedness of women. He'd heard it since he was a baby and sucking at his mother's tit like the kid in the front row. And when he was older it was a delicious kind of horror to hear the part about how God kicked Adam ad Eve out of the Garden and put up the flaming sword that turned in every direction to keep them out.

"And so, brothers and sisters," he concluded, "because of the sin of one woman, we have all lost our right to Paradise. And now we have to earn it, we have to accept Christ as our Lord and Saviour to regain our right to enter that Paradise which is called heaven. We will now sing page two hundred and seventy-two, 'Just as I am without one plea, but that Thy blood was shed for me.' "

He walked down from the pulpit to stand in front of the jar of red roses. "Won't you come?" he begged. "Won't you come and settle accounts with that old serpent the Devil?" He raised his arms as they stood and began to sing, and he saw that the baby had been shifted to the other breast, and he thought it was the first time in his life he ever preached a two-tit sermon.

They sang "Oh, Lamb of God, I come, I come," but no one did, no one moved one inch toward the front of the church to receive salvation, for him to perform the laying on of hands, the drying of tears, and that was just in keeping with the whole mother-fucking weekend, not one sinner brought into the fold. Hell with it. Hell with all of them. One more verse and he was going back to the restaurant so Faye could get all powdered and perfumed and lie waiting for him back in the apartment.

He stood at the door shaking the people's hands as they filed out, and a small, rounded, dark-haired girl with big brown eyes stopped and smiled at him. She didn't have those flat face bones like your average flatwooder, and she was dressed real cute in high-heel pumps and a pale blue suit with ruffles at the throat. He wondered how he'd missed her when he scanned the congregation, and his spirits lifted; maybe he'd hit pay dirt the way she was looking at him, kind of smiling and her head tilted to one side like she was sizing him up. She was a little older than he liked, maybe thirty, thirty-five, but what the hell, she had a sweet little figure and big boobs. He wouldn't have to worry about whether she was a virgin or whether she was going to start crying and run off to her mama; she was old enough to know what she wanted, and from the looks of things, she wanted him.

He smiled, and she gave a big, broad smile back, and he bent to her as she crooked her finger at him; shivers went down his spine, she wanted to tell him where to meet her, and the soft, warm breath of her words whispered against his ear.

"You're full of bullshit, you know that, preacher?" She turned and walked away down the crumbling concrete steps.

He was in a rage when he got back to the restaurant. Faye sat behind the register, and she did not look at him; he saw that her lips were swollen and already turning blue where he had slapped her. Good. Only it wasn't nearly enough for what she'd done to him, and he planned to settle that score this afternoon. One of these days he'd get even too with the smart-ass girl who had called his sermon bullshit—he'd like to have a few hours with her in a lonely place.

"Go on back to the apartment, Faye", he said, walking beind the counter to stand beside her. Her face went completely blank as she looked at him, she was like a walking dead person, and it gave him the creeps the way she could do that, like she'd moved out of her body and nobody lived there.

Hell, he didn't want to fuck a zombie, he wanted some action, some response. He might slip a bennie in a Coke and make her drink it, maybe that would get a wiggle out of her behind. Last time she moved when they had sex was about a year ago on a foggy night. He chuckled, but without amusement.

Faye went into the apartment and he worked the cash register, loving the feel of the bills, the smooth hardness of the coins. The ding of the bell as he rang up the money was the sweetest music to his ears. If business was still going this good by the end of the year, he ought to have enough money to buy a house in town, maybe even build on the hill near Griffith Hodge's big brick house. Now, wouldn't that be something, a flatwoods boy living next door to the banker. Hell, on Sunday the restaurant was filled not only with truckers but he got a lot of the after-church crowd—his was the only place for miles on this stretch of road that served home-cooked vegetables and homemade pies; the other places were all short order.

Handling the money made him feel a little better after the blow of the smart-ass gal, and he stayed until three o'clock ringing up money and keeping a check on Nellie, making sure she never sat down. He kept the waitresses hopping, he didn't want any dissatisfied customers complaining about the service and maybe not coming back. When the rush was over he decided to go on back to Faye. He'd make her put on that shiny black negligee he'd given her a couple of Christmases ago that she'd never worn. Well, she would wear it today, and she would wear it a hell of a lot more from here on, now that he'd decided to be boss again and quit letting Dr. John goddam Lasseter run his private affairs.

As he turned to leave, three Negroes walked in the front door, and for a minute he thought they didn't know where they were, that they'd gotten mixed up and thought this was a nigger joint; but hell no, they came right on in like they owned the place and sat down at a table. He shook his head, not believing they were still there, but they were, two of them black as the ace of spades, but one of them was slim and one was fat; the third was a high yellow and nearly bald. They had on suits and white shirts and ties.

The sign on the front door said in big letters WHITES ONLY and underneath, MANAGEMENT RESERVES THE RIGHT TO REFUSE SERVICE TO ANYONE. Maybe they couldn't read, maybe he'd have to go over there and give them a quick lesson in the alphabet, sound out the letters to them. The two drivers still in the restaurant had stopped eating and turned to stare, watching him as he lazily made his way toward the Negroes.

"Afternoon," he said, propping his foot on the rung of the dark, fat man's chair. The waitress who served this table stood close by, pad and pencil in hand. The men looked up at Coy, returned his smile.

"Afternoon," the yellow Negro said, and with only the barest trace of black accent. "Sure is a hot day, looks like you could stand some rain around here."

"Sure could," Coy said. "You folks from around here?"

"No, as a matter of fact, we're not. I'm from Atlanta, my two friends are from Chicago."

"Thought not. You don't know our ways and probably you can't read—"

"Yes, of course we can read."

"Then you missed that sign on the front door that said we don't serve niggers?"

The three men exchanged long glances, but the yellow man continued to speak for them. "That's all right with us," he said.

"We don't know any—'niggers,' did you say? If we happen to meet any we'll pass your message along."

"It might be," Coy said, "that you don't understand exactly where you are or who you're dealing with." His voice was conversational. "Now, you three jigaboos fit my definition of nigger exactly—you got nigger hair, nigger eyes, nigger skin. In my book that makes you niggers. But we're nice folks around here, we don't let anybody go hungry, so if you'll go around to the back door and tell my cook Nellie what you want, she'll fix it the way you people like it. Then you can be on your way and I hope a little smarter than you were before you uppity-assed through that front door."

One of the drivers sitting at the counter called, "The Kountry Kitchen's gettin' to be a reg'lar meetin' place for coons and hippies, I swear, Coy. I might have to start eatin' down to the Donut Hole, they got a higher-class clientelle." He laughed, nudged the driver on the stool next to him.

Coy shot him a black look; there was enough truth in the remark to scare hell out of him. Word got around, people would stop coming there. They hated hippies, but they hated coons worse.

"Go on, get out of here," he said to the Negro men. "If you're hungry, go to the back door, I wouldn't turn away a dog that was hungry. But if you came in here to make a point, get in your car and *take off*! You agitators come down here stirring things up gon' get your heads blown off! Now get!"

"We have the right to be served," the slim black man said. It was the first time he had spoken and his voice held only a faint tinge of the South. "It is the law of the United States of America that we be treated equally in public places—we have the same rights under the law as you."

"You got no rights at all in *my* restaurant except what I say you got.It's called free enterprise, but I expect that idea is a little too complex for you people's brains. All you're gon' get served is some lead right between the eyes unless you move on out of here. I shot a man yesterday, name of Otis Helms, you might of read about it in the newspapers?"

"We've been traveling, we haven't seen any papers—"

"I blew a man's head half off yesterday." He spoke the words quietly, but with a certain note of pride, and his hand slid into his pocket, closed about the gun. Oh, it was sweet to be ready, he wouldn't be caught off guard again like he was with the hippie yesterday.

The big man swallowed, his eyes following the movement, and Coy saw the flicker of fear in his eyes, knew he saw the shape of the gun. He smiled, an aching sort of pleasure spreading through his stomach. Hell, he was glad they came in, he felt his esteem had been raised after the hippie of yesterday. By tonight the drivers sitting at the counter would have spread the word up and down the highway how old Coy had dealt with the niggers. That and shooting Otis Helms ought to make things equal again. Hell, more than equal, the goddam hippie took him off guard, he could have ground the little bastard into mush if he hadn't been caught off guard. And the rest of the afternoon was still ahead, a sweet little piece of ass waited for him on the other side of the door. Hell, he wasn't even going to have to wheedle for it or ask permission. No more of that shit, it belonged to him. Legally.

The men left, walked out into the fiery daze of the afternoon, and Coy strode back to the counter, the drivers smiling at him, nodding and approving, touching him as he passed. His good humor swelled, blossomed in his chest, he was on a high, and hell, he hadn't even had a bennie. He opened the cash register and counted the money, made a great show of writing down on a pad the exact amount, saw the broad-assed, black-haired waitress watching. Had to let them know every minute that you were on to them, that you knew they'd steal you blind you give them half a chance. He saw the contempt slide across her face as she watched and turned his gaze flat as he stared at her. She looked quickly away, and he thought he was going to have to fire that girl, she was out of the mountains and mean. All those mountain people were mean, women included. Besides, he wanted to get somebody better-looking; when Faye had the baby she'd be out of commission. Made him sick to think of the condition her ass was going to be in. He didn't relish fucking her all that much with that baby inside her. But he blocked that out of his mind, she was a pretty good lay those first months, and he could get her back on the track. Hell, it was available, at least until her stomach got too big and repulsive. But he wouldn't think about that now, this afternoon was this afternoon; when he became lost in the glory of fucking there was no past and no future.

He had started toward the apartment when Nellie called to him. "Mista Coy," she said, sticking her head out of the kitchen door. "Them colored mens ordered some cheeseburgers, but when I took 'em out to 'em, they's gone; I run out and try to catch 'em an I seen a blue car way off down de highway headin' toward de Selma road."

"Goddammit, did they pay?"

"Nawsuh, I don' never take no money, you tell me not to an' I don' never take no money, you say I ain't sposed to—"

"Shut up!"

The black head popped back inside the door, and the two drivers at the counter laughed and looked at each other, shaking their heads. "You got to eat three cheeseburgers, Coy; I hope you're hungry, they sure put one over on you."

He ran into the kitchen and grabbed the brown paper sack out of Nellie's hand, and then he was driving down the highway, not remembering leaving the restaurant or getting into the car, his mind fixed on only one thing, a pale blue dot far in the distance, disappearing over a low rise of hill. He slammed the accelerator against the floor until the shimmering dot appeared again, and it seemed as if he were standing still and the blurred green of landscape shooting past, the hard bright streak of highway a silver cord reeling in the blue dot, him playing it closer and closer, like a fish.

Gradually he came up behind it, the orange numbers leaped out at him, AC 92547, Michigan, Land of Lakes, and then he was beside the car, black faces staring out the window at him; vaguely he heard a horn blowing, and then they whipped right onto the Selma road, and him still beside them, gently, gently, nudging the car onto the grassy strip, careful not to touch it, not to scratch the shiny paint of the Continental. He grinned at the Negro faces with the bulging, terrified eyes, mouths open wide and screaming at him, but the sound whipped away in the rushing air. They bumped to a stop on the edge of a ditch, and he came up behind them, lazily climbed out of his car and walked to the driver's window.

"Hey," he said affably, "you didn't have to be in such a hurry you forgot your cheeseburgers. I told you to leave, but shit, it didn't have to be *that* fast." He tossed the sack in the window and it fell into the lap of the yellow-skinned driver who, entranced, watched the grease seeping through the brown paper onto the pale blue of his cotton cord suit.

"That'll be fifty dollars," Coy said.

"Fifty dollars?"

"Yeah, I got to charge you for the extra service; usually I don't deliver to runaway niggers in my Continental—there's the gas and the aggravation as well as the food. You understand." The words were soft but deadly, like the soft shake of rattles from tall grass.

The fat man leaned over the driver, his face stiff with rage. "We don't owe you a cent, you bigoted son-of-a-bitch," he said.

And the gun was in the window; suddenly it was just there, as if it had materialized, Coy backing away, the gun sight aimed square in the middle of the fat man's forehead. "My mother was," he said, "the flower of Southern womanhood. Maybe you Northern niggers don't know that down here it's a killing offense to call mothers dirty names? I was born within the bonds of holy matrimony."

The yellow-skinned driver said, "My God, all this over a couple of cheeseburgers?"

"I shot a man yesterday over a piece of scrap iron."

The man swallowed, Adam's apple rising convulsively above the knot of his tie. He gestured, shook his head. "I don't understand, I just don't understand."

"Well, you will understand that there is a right way and a wrong way niggers act in the South."

"By God, if you're going to shoot us, *go ahead and shoot*, you white ape." The fat man screamed, beat his fists against the dashboard. "By God, we are human beings!"

The slim black man in the back seat leaned to grasp his shoulders, saying, "It's all right, George, it's all right," and he held him until he slumped back and was quiet. "If you are going to use that gun, go ahead. All of us understand in this fight we've joined that we might die."

"Well, well, mighty brave, aren't you?" Coy said. "But hell, I'm gon' let you shoot yourselves. Considering how I killed a man only yesterday, it might not look good for me to shoot anybody else for awhile even if they are niggers. It might give us a bad name, and shit, this is my home and you are just passing through. You thought you could sashay through here and shit on our town and then walk away laughing at what fools you made of us, didn't you? You've messed up my day pretty bad; I had plans and it's plain put me in a foul humor."

"You want us to die over cheeseburgers?" asked the yellow man.

"It ain't cheeseburgers, chrissakes, it's the principle."

The slim man in the back seat took out his billfold and offered two twenties and a ten to Coy. "Here, take your money, we're sorry we came into your place and we'll never come in again."

"Put the money back," Coy said. "I'm not dumb enough to come close to the car and let you grab my gun. Just settle back there, take your hands away from the door handle, you're not gon' rush me."

The man put the money back in his billfold, leaned back, the white-hot afternoon becoming laced with slow shadows edging from the woods. The men were dark shapes in the gloom of the car, and they gazed out at him, almost dreamily, in the silence. A bird whistled deep in the woods. Finally Coy told them to get out of the car, but they did not move, just sat staring, faces turned up to him, the light glinting softly on the gun.

"Get out," he repeated.

"You're crazy—"

"I didn't ask your opinion of my mental condition. I might resent that if I wasn't having so much fun. Now, get out, I'm tired of having to argue with you people; all I've done since you set foot in my place is argue with you." He waved the gun at them, motioning them out.

They climbed heavily out and stood facing him, and he stepped back, gun held close, his back to the road where no cars passed. He kept a wary eye on the big Negro; he looked like he might have played football, he was fat but he looked dangerous. That one, more than the skinny ones, might try to jump him, he was unpredictable, not in control of himself like the other two were. He half hoped he *would* try to jump him, the gun felt so smooth, fitted so neatly into his hand, the hammer cocked, the dumdums all in the chambers. It had whipped out of his pocket without a whisper; their eyes had nearly popped out of their heads. They were afraid of him, and that fear on their faces was nearly about as good as the pussy they were causing him to miss this afternoon.

He made them line up and lean on their car facing it, legs spread, arms braced, and he backed away from them, switched his gun to his left hand and leaned in the window of the Continental and took the keys out of the ignition, and still walking backward, went to the trunk of his car; he glanced down only for a second to fit the key into the keyhole, and when he glanced up again, the big Negro was roaring down upon him, snarling, face bunched with rage, and in the explosion of the gun that reverberated through the woods, the man spun backward, slamming onto the dry, spiked grass.

The other men did not move; they stared, faces tight, sweat running down the sides of their faces and staining their suits in wide circles beneath their arms.

Coy still held the gun in his left hand; hell, he could shoot with either hand, the man probably didn't realize that. All those hours of target practice had paid off, and he watched the man stagger to his feet clutching his upper right arm, the coat split, bright red blood seeping around the tear.

"I don't think you're hurt bad," Coy said. "If I'd wanted you dead you'd be dead. I'm what you call—ambidextrous? Y'all know the word? It means I'm as good with either hand; shit, I can eat or play baseball—or shoot—just as good with my left as I can my right. You can go on back and stand with your friends now," and he gestured with the gun.

The man walked slowly to the car, slumped against it. "Spread your legs," Coy said, and the man spread his legs, stared down at the ground.

Coy opened the trunk, took out his rifle, watching the men all the time, his eyes never off them, and he took the rifle off safety and pushed it under his right arm.

"Okay," he said, "let's go, y'all march on down there into the woods."

"My God, man," the yellow Negro said. "What do you think you're doing, you've made your point, we won't ever bother you again."

"Damn right you won't, I'm gon' see to it. Teach some of these other niggers got funny ideas a good lesson. Save 'em the trouble of trying to act like white folks."

Slowly, one behind the other, they walked across the grassy strip and into the smothering heat of dense foliage of the woods. He told them to sit on a rotted log, and he told the big black Negro to take the white handkerchief triangled in his suit pocket and tie it around the top of his arm. He did not, he said, want the man to bleed to death before he got a chance to play the game he had planned for them.

"I don't believe any of this," the yellow Negro said. "I'm dreaming, in a minute I'll wake up and tell about my nightmare."

"In a minute you'll be waking up telling it to St. Peter. Or to Ole Scratch, according to whether you been a good nigger. Judging from today, I believe it's gon' be Ole Scratch." He laughed. "Y'all don't think that's funny? Well, I don't blame you, this here's serious business we're having. I apologize for making jokes at a time like this."

In the silence was the far rushing of the river, the twittering of sparrows in the trees. Coy broke open the gun, shook the shells into his hand and dropped them into his pocket, twirled the chamber and tossed it onto the ground at the feet of the yellow man.

"Don't touch it," he said. "Not yet, I'll tell you when. There's one bullet in there. If you try to turn the gun on me it's the last move you ever make. Next time I shoot, I shoot to kill. Understand? Nice and easy now," he nodded to the yellow man. "Pick it up."

The man stared at the gun but did not move. His shoulders were slumped, his arms resting heavily on his legs. "No. I won't." He did not look at Coy.

Coy raised the rifle, braced it on his shoulder.

"Your head is dead in my sight, I pull this trigger you won't ever know what hit you, it'll be just like switching off a light."

The man closed his eyes, licked his lips. The other two men stared at him, mesmerized. Slowly he stretched his hand to the gun, but just before he grasped it, Coy said, "Don't even think it. Even if the bullet is in the chamber you wouldn't stand a chance. I got a hair trigger on this rifle just like on my gun."

The man showed no sign that he heard except for the barest flicker of nerve twitching in his cheek, and his hand tightened about the gun, swiftly he raised it to his head, the click of the hammer striking, the turning barrel shattering the silence. The man dropped the gun onto the ground next to the big man's feet. "Lord, Lord," he moaned, shaking his head.

"Go on," Coy said. "Pick it up."

The big man was holding his hurt arm, and he looked up at Coy, his eyes pleading; soft dark flesh glistened, sweat ran down his neck into the starched stiffness of his collar. "God as my witness, I'm sorry." he said. "Let us go, we won't ever come here again."

"That's funny, I thought y'all said a little while ago you were ready to die. What happened to all that courage?" He looked at the yellow man. "You should have seen your friends' faces when you pulled the trigger. You should have seen the disappointment. I never saw two men wanted somebody to die as bad as they did you." He laughed, told the big man again to pick up the gun, leveled the rifle at his temple.

"I'd like to let y'all go, I really would, but I can't let the word get around that I let a bunch of niggers come in my place and beat me out of my money. Now *pick up the gun!*"

Stoically, woodenly, the big man picked up the gun, put the barrel to his temple, but as he squeezed the trigger, jerked the gun away, pointing the gun at the ground.

"I'd of blown your head off if there'd been a bullet in the chamber. If your number had come up you'd of got it one way or the other. Pass it on to your skinny friend."

The slim man took the gun, held it to his temple and fired, the third click echoing in the stillness.

"My, my, you're a cool one. Not scared like your friends, are you?"

The man dropped his arm to his lap. "I'm sorry for you. Yes, I'm afraid, everybody has to die, this isn't the first time I thought I was going to. I don't want to kill myself and I'm not going to do that again. If I have to die you'll have to shoot me."

"I just might do that," Coy said.

The man shrugged. "Whatever."

"Pass the gun to the high yellow."

The man looked at him, surprised.

"You think I'm stupid, don't you? You wanted me to reach for that gun, you were going to come for me. Well, it didn't work, so pass the gun to your friend."

"No. I won't. I told you I'm not going to play your game. You're right, I *was* hoping one of them would get the bullet, and I'm ashamed. I was terrified, but God, I didn't want to die for a cheeseburger. I was on the freedom rides, hell, I've played in the big leagues, you little backwater, redneck son-of-a-bitch."

For a moment Coy waited, head slightly cocked, eyes narrowed. Then he sighed and shook his head sadly. "You're right, I'm just a hick, a redneck flatwooder. I guess I just didn't understand that before you came here and explained it to me. I can't stand it, the knowledge is too terrible to live with. Throw me the gun."

No one spoke. The man continued to hold the gun. "Come on, throw it to me,' Coy said. "Pitch it over here." His voice was sarcastically wheedling.

Resigned, weary, the man tossed the gun and it fell at Coy's feet, who picked it up, held it to his head. "I'm so ashamed for being a redneck hick that I'm gon' kill myself, so you all watch how a *white* man dies." He pulled the trigger, yelling *blam! blam! blam!* over and over, the men staring, mouths agape. He laughed great whooping bursts of sound that crashed in the woods, and a covey of quail whirred up, stirring the still air.

"You niggers really think I was stupid enough to give you a loaded gun? Shit, I was disappointed not a *one* of you had the guts to try and shoot me. Bunch of goddam cowards think you're so brave come sitting down in *my* restaurant. You all really thought I put a bullet in there, didn't none of you notice the chambers were every one empty. Shit, you can see that when you got the gun if you had brains enough to look." His voice had patiently explained, as if to children. He dropped the gun in his pocket.

"I got to get on back. It's been real interesting meeting you all, but us hicks got to work, we don't have time for freedom rides and integrating truck stops. We got to work to keep you niggers on welfare. But feel free to sit right there long as you want to. I 'spect you got a lot to think about."

Just before he climbed in the car, he called back to them. "It might be you all might not want to try to integrate any more restaurants. 'Bye now."

He U-turned the Lincoln and headed back to the Kountry Kitchen and to Faye.

6

When Bird left his magic place on Sunday morning a cool breeze blew, but he knew that when the sun came up full it would be scorching hot again. He was only glad he didn't have to work Wesley Turner's cotton field this summer, then with a pang remembered he had to go to Coy Watson's after church. He had to rake and trim shrubs for the development of his character and also because it helped out Mrs. Watson; she was pregnant, and his father said that when he'd stopped in one afternoon to get a Coca-Cola after making rounds, she was raking and mowing, and she wasn't strong enough for that, she might lose the baby.

He didn't really mind the work all that much, yard work was child's play compared to the field, and Mrs. Watson was really nice to him, at least when Coy wasn't around. She was friendly and smiled at him and had Nellie bring him ice water and sometimes a Coca-Cola or a Seven-Up. But Coy despised him; sometimes he'd come onto the back porch and stare at him. Bird never challenged that look, never stared back, but kept his back turned until he heard the door close; and it was as if some terrible intensity had gone from the atmosphere, as if someone had flipped a switch and the air had become clear again.

He walked now through the neighborhood that was caught in the dream of Sunday morning, the sunlight pouring like pale molasses across rooftops, dripping through trees, speckling the dry, crisp grass. It shone on the Negro Sanctified Baptist Church, glinted off the tin steeple that reared against the cloudless sky, the hammer scars of its forging reflecting iridescent light like emeralds and rubies. The white citizens of Asheton hated that steeple, a committee had gone to the town council to protest it, saying it was disgraceful for Negroes to have a taller steeple than the white First Baptist Church. But Griffith Hodge, who was the president of the Asheton Merchants and Planters Bank and who had given them the piece of left-over tin after the new bank was built, said they better leave the nigras alone, they better let them have their metal gewgaw. "It keeps their eyes toward heaven, keeps them from looking too hard at their shacks and from thinking too much of how poor they are. You don't want their church to turn into a political meeting place like they have in Birmingham and Selma and Montgomery, do you? You've seen the foreign license plates on the cars coming through here, you've seen the strange nigras coming out of the pool hall. I am warning you, you had better leave their steeple. You had better leave well enough alone."

Bird walked through the streets thinking of how he would be going to that church this morning, and of how he didn't belong there. And yet he had to take Mrs. Bonner because Jake wouldn't. And he took her not because anyone made him do it but because she was getting old, and as he watched her sitting beside the fireplace one morning he had thought she wouldn't live much longer and was shocked at his sadness. He loved her and hadn't meant to, and not as white for black, but because she was Emma Bonner and she loved him: she had nursed him when he was sick, scolded him when he was bad, held him to her breast that first morning when he had come back from the woods though he had struggled to get loose from her. He remembered her smell of starch and powder, the dry-leaf color of her skin, her thin face, pitying dark eyes. He had, finally, sunk against her chest, given himself up to her murmuring. He thought that morning that she had become his second mother, the ache of losing Mary Betty eased. His real mother, as his father called the woman who had drowned herself, he could not imagine—she was less believable than people he read about in books.

He smiled as he walked along to think of those who had raised him, cared for him: white man, black mother, brown mother. Birds. And he thought of how wild things trusted him; raccoons and squirrels sometimes came so close to him as he lay reading on the riverbank that he could have reached out and touched them, but he never tried, he was afraid to frighten them. Sometimes birds lit on the low branches of the scrub pines, and he could look into the shining black dots of their eyes and believed he could have caught one; in his mind he knew the cool slickness of the gleaming feathers, the fluttering beat of their hearts.

He left the neighborhood and crossed into the business section, feeling sorry for those who slept, not caring that the firmament exploded over them, that the laboring sky gave birth to morning, red light hemorrhaging across the heavens. He stopped and stared toward the horizon where dark, pointed trees thrust against the bloody sky, and love surged in his heart for this land that had birthed him; he knew its ugliness and its beauty, its fields and woods, its river. Its people. But he knew that though he loved it, it was not his home. He had known that since the morning his father had tried to enroll him in the white school, when the children had whispered *he's a nigger*. He had not known he knew it that morning, but on looking back, that was when he had begun keeping himself apart. On Christmas mornings and on birthdays he had hung back, knowing he was not really part of the family; it was his father and Johnnie who would notice him standing alone and pull him into the circle. When company came for dinner, Mary Betty always managed to have him needed to go somewhere with her, saying she was scared to walk alone after dark or that he had to carry some heavy package for her.

He stared at the red sky that faded as he watched, and he knew he was only passing through, that all he so loved, black earth and sandy lanes and green-shadowed woods were fleeting, temporary. And, like this land, Johnnie would always be a part of him, but he could never have her, and he continued down the sidewalk, saw at the next corner Bubba Dodson and his smiling black-and-white dog sitting on the curb next to the Standard station.

"Morning, Bubba, morning, Spot," he said, and the small blond boy looked up from rolling his Sunday papers and smiled, the dog wagging his tail but not leaving Bubba's side.

Bird read the headlines as he passed, and saw that five Negroes had been arrested in Selma for trying to integrate a white theater and a white restaurant. And he thought they might as well give it up, whites were never going to accept blacks as people, they were never going to give up their power. Why should they? What gain for them? And that was why he had to be white: he could go to bed at night knowing no one would come and smash in his door and drag him to the woods and cut off his testicles even though the law had proved him innocent. But more than this, more than justice or liberty, he would gain passage into the world of human beings—he would be allowed to grow up. That would be enough, to be able to be a man.

He passed by the alley that ran between the drugstore and the pool hall, and he looked down its length thinking how evil it seemed even in the innocence of Sabbath morning. It was called Whiskey Alley because the black bootleggers who lived close to the woods behind the railroad station brought the white liquor there on Saturday nights to sell. The black men drank it out of Coca-Cola bottles, blowing hollow, airy tunes on the bottles when they were empty, and the alleybats leaning against the walls in tight, low-cut dresses bumped their hips in slow rhythm to the beat.

Sometimes Mrs. Bonner drank. And when Jake was gone off somewhere she'd send Bird to buy whiskey for her, and he was scared to go in that alley, but unable to refuse her when the sadness came. She'd stand in the kitchen door at dusk looking over the fields, her gray, kinked hair bright with fading light. And he'd know she was thinking of Jake's father (who was her son, Billy) who one morning, all of a sudden, walked off and never came back. He'd left a few months after Jake's mother had run away with a man when Jake was less than a year old.

"Baby," Mrs. Bonner would say, "you puts me in mind of

Billy, the way you reads and stays to yo'sef. He couldn't stand the field neither, and one night he kissed me good night and put his arms 'round me and say he loves me. An' de next mawning he gone, an' I know it ain't to find Jake's mama, he jes gone 'cause he cain't stand it here. He ain't never comin' back, an' I wouldn't try to find him, but, Law, Law, I miss him."

He'd go to the alley for her, the dollar bill crushed damply in his hand, and the deep-throated male laughter floated around him, and the musky woman-scent and smells of sweat and whiskey clogging his nostrils. The prostitutes brushed their hands across his crotch as he passed, and grabbed his hand, stroking the palm. "Do you have hair?" they said. "Virgin boys cain't grow hair in they palms, only grown mens come in this alley. Little white boy better stay away."

Two years ago there had been a murder in Whiskey Alley. Early one Sunday morning Dr. Strong went to his drugstore to get a headache powder for Mrs. Strong and had found Obediah Johnson with his throat cut, the blood congealed and black in the sandy dirt. Obediah was the distributor of the white lightning, and the rumor was that sometimes he sold it for more than he said he had, and kept the extra money. He had a glass eye, and Dr. Strong said that his eye stared fixed and straight out of his saffron face, but that somehow his good eye had closed, and it was as if Obediah was winking.

"It's bad enough to find someome murdered without having them wink at you about it," Dr. Strong said. "We have got to clean out that alley, stop the nigras from going there.'

Again Griffith Hodge talked to the town council. He told them that refusing them this pleasure was folly. "Weigh the consequences,' he said. "Weigh the consequences."

And again they did what he asked, but the sheriff didn't even try to find Obediah's murderer. "What's the difference?" he said. "It's just niggers killing niggers."

The sidewalk ended in the dimness of a wide, dirt road lined with oaks and silver-leaf maples. This was the neighborhood of the town blacks; the preacher, the deacons, the maids and nursemaids and cooks lived here, the houses bigger and sturdier, with swept yards and flowers planted around the porches. Most had two bedrooms, a living room, and a kitchen. All had outhouses and dug wells. Some of them, like Jake Bonner, had gotten permission from the town council to clear new ground, a half acre, sometimes an acre, into the woods, and they grew corn and pole beans and potatoes. Most of the houses were painted dark green, though some had peeling white paint. His father had bought the Bonners' house and land from the bank and had added on a bedroom and a bathroom for Bird. He also had a coat of white paint applied each spring.

Once a huge magnolia tree had grown in the front yard, but that first spring after his banishment, the power company had cut the limbs away from the lines and for weeks the sap had poured from the chopped wood, gradually slowing to a drip that lasted all winter. No new leaves appeared in the spring, the old leaves dropped off, and the men came again and cut down the mutilated tree altogether. And he was sad, and told the men they ought not to have cut the tree that way, and they said what did he care, it wasn't his neighborhood. But from its top branches he had been able to see the road that led to his old house, knew that beneath the far, green canopy of trees was where his real self had once lived. He had hidden in the leaves of the magnolia, casting out the silver thread of memory, yearning toward his lost life—losing that vista panicked him as if his life had always been, and would always be, limited to the dusty street of Negro houses.

He walked down the road, and smoke plumed from the chimneys where Sunday dinners, mostly cooked the day before, warmed on the backs of wood-burning stoves. Sunday was emancipation day, the day when washwomen turned into flower-hatted leaders of the Women's Missionary Society, and sharecroppers and janitors became dignified deacons in black suits. Maids and cooks became teachers, telling wide-eyed children that white Jesus died for their sins because He loved them too. They told them that inside their dark skins their souls dwelt white as snow.

On week nights, in the still, hot darkness, these same people sat on their porches talking, their voices softly bitter, sometimes Jake and his friends sat there, sometimes neighbors sat on the steps. *Sometimes I git so mad watchin' nobody but white folks on teevee I feels like smashin' my hand through the set sometimes I git so mad 'cause I got to leave my sick chile and go nurse little white baby I pinch him and laugh when he cry sometimes I git so mad I got to smash somebody beat up somebody sometimes I git so mad sometimes sometimes sometimes,* on and on, until finally one of the men would leave the porch and then somebody else and they'd go out to the Spotlight on the highway and get drunk and cut each other, kill each other, their anger turned on themselves because they couldn't turn it on the white man.

She sat at the kitchen hearth, a white crocheted shawl draped about her shoulders, her hands outstretched to the empty grate as if a fire burned there. She gave no sign that he entered, though he stood in the line of her vision. He went up to her, touched her lightly on the shoulder, and she looked up, awareness spreading across her face, dark eyes clouded behind milky cataracts. Her thin hand clutched his, and he thought how fragile she was, how cool her satin skin.

He bent to kiss her cheek. "We're going to church this morning, remember?" and she nodded. She was already dressed in her navy-blue voile dress, a cameo pinned at the neck of the round collar, and he thought how delicate were her features, in profile she was but a darker version of the profile carved in ivory, and he wondered where she had gotten the brooch and why she wore it.

She rose and brought his food to the table from the gas oven where she had kept it warm. She no longer had to burn wood to cook with, his father had bought her a stove and a refrigerator, had had the kitchen remodeled with walnut cabinets and a tile floor. But the table was covered with a yellowed cloth she had told him her grandmother embroidered. She had been one of Nathan Ashe's house slaves, and he had sold her lover to a family in Georgia. In white satin floss, this slave girl had worked the crude pattern of a man and woman facing each other, their hands outstretched but fingers not quite touching. The sadness of those fingers never touching always smote Bird, and he would take the material and fold it so that at last the hands could meet.

He sat at the table, set next to an open window, and he was not hungry but could not refuse the food she put before him, for it worried her for him not to eat. She watched him take the first few bites, peering at each mouthful, smiling approval as he gulped the scrambled eggs, washed them down with coffee. Then she sat again in the rocker, pulling it closer to still observe him, and his heart sank. Sometimes she would have further dressing to do and would leave him alone and then he would scrape his breakfast into the garbage sack, and she would be happy, thinking he was full.

She never sat at the table with him, nor would she allow Jake to sit with him. She considered him still the doctor's son, with her given only the privilege of being allowed to care for him. Sometimes he would stand in the doorway of his room where they could not see him, listening to the easy talk between Jake and Mrs. Bonner as they ate, the affection in their voices, their shared memories of people he had never known emphasizing his loneliness. He wished she were not always so courteous with him, but knew he did not really want her to treat him as she did Jake: her deference set him apart, it was further affirmation of his whiteness; she loved him, but as a black woman for her white charge.

"You out all night, baby?" she said.

"Yes. In the woods."

"They's bootleggers in dem woods."

"Not my woods."

"I worries 'bout you."

"You don't have to, I'm all right." He smiled as she peered into his face. "Don't worry about me. I worry about you."

She patted his arm, and he stared out the window toward where the sun crept through the cornfield, and he wished the

day could be his, wished he had nothing to do but lie beneath
the trees and read and think. He turned to her, thinking to tell
her he couldn't take her to church after all, but she was asleep,
her head resting on the high back of the oak chair. She looked
dead, with her hands folded across her chest, her flesh stretched
across the high cheekbones. And he knew he could not disap-
point her, this was something he had to do, it was little enough
to repay her for all she had done for him.

He left the table and went to his room off the kitchen, laid
out on his bed his tan linen suit, white shirt, brown and red
striped tie. On the days he could not go to the woods, this room
was his haven, he had all his possessions gathered about him,
he was fiercely protective of them: his Magnavox, his roll-top
desk, the journals he kept sporadically. He could not bear for
Jake to even look at his things and when he was gone locked
his door and his windows.

His father had bought him all the things he asked for when
he sent him away, and on summer nights when men sat on
porches playing their harmonicas, Beethoven's *Pastoral* drowned
the mournful notes of "Deep River" and "Yellow Gal Where
Did You Sleep Last Night?" On winter nights the electric heater
did not keep out the chill of raw, wet days and he pushed his
bed against the chimney, pressing his back against the rough
stones, glad his room had been built onto that outside wall. But
on clear cold nights he missed his back-porch cot, blankets
heaped upon him, his head wrapped in them and with only his
eyes and nose exposed. And the stars had glittered through black,
bare-limbed trees.

When he had dressed, he stood at the mirror examining his
reflection, tilted the mirror and stepped back to get a full view
of himself, and a dark shape behind him was also reflected like
a darker image of himself, like an omen—a threat. He whirled,
and Jake stood in the doorway watching him, shirtless and barefoot, sardonically smiling, eyes mocking. His body was massive
and heavy in the light that shone behind him, his muscles hard
and bulging.

"Little yella boy sho' do think he cute."

"Get out of my room—"

"Little yella boy goin' to church, mustn't get mad."

"Don't sneak on me, just go find something to do. Don't you have any business of your own?

"Oh, yeah, I got lots of business, but I just lak to watch you primpin' and preenin'."

"I've got to remember to close my door, I didn't think you were home. My father built this room so I could have privacy."

"Yo' father? Ha! Yo' father throwed you away—"

"You *shut up!* You don't know anything about anything, stay out of my room, stay away from me. I don't bother you, what's my fascination for you?"

They faced each other, there came the sound of Mrs. Bonner's feet scuffing across the kitchen floor, of water pouring, the rasp of dishes being scraped.

"You ain't nothin' but shit in white man's clothes, who you think you is? so high and mighty takin' Gran'mama to church so you can strut aroun' and stick up yo' nose lak you smell something bad."

"You're jealous, aren't you, you're jealous because she loves me."

"Shit, she feels sorry for you, you're plumb pitiful."

"She loves me. And I love her."

For a long minute they looked at each other, Jake lounging against the doorjamb, his dark skin shining in the electric light, and Bird looked past him out the living-room window to the blurred green of the summer morning. He saw in Jake's face the same hatred he had seen yesterday in Arvin Helms's face, and he wished the time had come for him to leave—not for church, but for good. He wished he could just walk away down some dusty road and never look back, forget this place as if it never had been.

He went to the dresser and uncapped his hair tonic, shook a drop into his hand, rubbed it across his hair, and brushed the deep waves flatter.

"Whut you puttin' on yo' hair, yella boy?"

"Hair tonic, what do you think?"

"Turn the bottle 'round."

"Why should I?"

Jake did not answer, but waved his fingers at the bottle, and Bird turned the label toward him.

"Vitalis," Jake said, and his voice was flat. "Little yella boy kin use Vitalis jes lak the white folks. I never thought 'bout dat you could use Vitalis."

They were silent, the bottle between them like a hope, an attainment—the trophy grasped after the struggle to the mountaintop or at the end of a race. Black skin diluted to white, kinked hair tamed and docile with white man's oil.

Jake left, the back screen creaking closed behind him.

They turned off the sandy road into the churchyard, walking across the dappled ground toward the gray-weathered church that was barely a block away, behind the houses on the street across from them; yet it had taken them almost a half-hour to get there. Mrs. Bonner had had to stop many times to rest, her breathing sighing heavily from her chest, and Bird had looked anxiously at her. "I'm all right, baby," she said, and finally they had arrived, the summer air filled with bells.

People trudged along with them, the women fanning with their white handkerchiefs, and beneath the trees the children still sat on the humped roots of giant oaks, for this was where Sunday school was held in summer. The boys' napped hair was shaved close to the skull, the girls' hair braided and tied with bright scraps of cloth.

The people spoke to Mrs. Bonner and she smiled and said she was feeling well, thank you, no matter what they said. They did not speak to Bird, and he no longer told their messages to Mrs. Bonner as he had when he first began bringing her to church. He had kept himself aloof, apart from them; he could not let them become familiar with him, for he had always to keep his image of himself sharply in focus. He could not allow himself to become attached to them, to care about them, for that would only make it harder to leave when the time came. He had cared too much already. And so the people turned away from him, not understanding, yet understanding in part—he did feel superior to them, and he was ashamed, and could not meet the hard accusing of their eyes, could not look at them directly. But to become white he had to reject them or he was lost. With his white skin he held the power to one day seize all he had lost the morning he was banished.

She held his arm as they walked, and Bird looked toward the cemetery where the sun edged over the trees, throwing the pointed shadow of the tin steeple across the gently mounded graves. And he thought the cemetery beautiful, the only adornment wildflowers, daisies and forget-me-nots, all blooming together as if some giant hand had flung the seed into the wind and scattered them there. It was like a field, giving no feeling of death or loss, and he watched the children playing tag, leaping back and forth across the graves—after church people would stroll there, reading the names on the cedar markers that had silvered and now seemed part of the ground. He thought how good it was that the dead should be included in their weekly affairs, that they were remembered. And a flame of pride shot through him that he had roots there, that it was his ancestors also who went back to Nathan Ashe, and beyond that to the Creeks who had farmed this land—he had found their arrowheads and bits of pottery in the muddy banks of the river.

Quickly he thrust those thoughts away. He could have no pride in such heritage: his survival depended upon its obliteration. So what if some chromosome, some infinitesimal part of himself lay in that cemetery? So what? Other ancestral chromosomes, and many more of them, lay in the white cemetery of marble tombstones and granite angels, of thick, mowed grass and rounded shrubbery. He turned his face from the gently blowing flowers and helped Mrs. Bonner up the wooden flight of steps and past the black-frocked preacher who lightly touched her as she passed.

He escorted her to her place on the first bench, and went to the back of the church to sit in the last row beside the door. No one would sit beside him or speak to him, they accepted his separateness; they drifted past him as if he did not exist, they gave no indication that he made a picture upon their retinas, and he had the eerie feeling that he really did not exist, at least not for them. He wondered if he walked across the road and were hit by a car if he would be killed or if he would pass through the metal? He and his tutor used to talk of such things, of spirits and reincarnation, when they read the great philosophers, and one of the things that had always mystified him was how it was that he was himself and not somebody else—what had made him *him?* When he thought too hard about it, he'd become dizzy and disconnected from the world, and he'd quickly think about something else. That was why he liked math, he felt safe in that world of exactness.

Behind the pulpit hung a gilt-framed picture of a kneeling Jesus, His robe parted, His exposed heart dripping great ruby drops of blood down his chest. His face was turned to the shining rays of a rising sun. To the left of the picture, written on a blackboard, were the page numbers of the hymns to be sung that morning, and also an announcement that it was baptismal day. He had watched this ritual many times from a pine thicket near his magic place. The preacher would push through the river, balancing against the river's flow with his arms stretched before him, white robe billowing upon the water. His flock gathered on the shore singing *when they ring those golden bells for you and me* as he immersed each repentant sinner; he told them he buried them in sin and raised them to life everlasting. Once, a little boy thought the preacher held him down too long, and he came up from the water thrashing and sputtering, drops of water sparkling like diamonds in a heavenly crown already set upon his napped head. "My God, Rev'rend, you lak to drownded me, I thought I was gonna die and me only in my sevens," and the laughter of those on the bank shattered the golden stillness of the afternoon.

In the vibrating air of the stilled bell, the people settled themselves for worship, men on one side of the church, women on the other. Teen-agers sat on mourners' benches that lined the walls on each side of the church, boys and girls together.

They were supposed to sit on these benches to grieve for their sins, but they giggled and elbowed one another, rolled their eyes, and Bird thought how glad he was not one of them. Sex was a trap that would force them to repeat the cycle of their parents and grandparents and great-grandparents; most of them would not even try to break the pattern of breeding and farming the white man's land.

The preacher strode down the aisle and into the pulpit, braced on the lectern as he stared into the congregation and waited for complete quiet. When nothing was heard but the shrill call of a bird, when nothing moved except the indolent cardboard fans imprinted with the message *Asheton Merchants and Planters Bank, Your Friend,* he said, "De Lawd is in His holy temple, let all de earth keep silence befo' Him."

A sigh rippled among the audience, and Bird thought the preacher kingly in his hugeness, his shoulders straining against the black cloth of his frock coat; his stern protruding eyes stared barely over their heads, and he did not speak for a long time; a tautness came into the air, it was as if he were tuning them, tightening the strings of his instruments.

"Let us pray," he whispered, and he reached heavenward. *Our Father, who art in heben, hallowed be Di name, Di kingdom come . . .*

The people's voices joined with his, but his voice rising above theirs, and a car chugged by on the road, faded, a faint breeze stirred in the trees outside the windows, the sun blaring on the dusty leaves. During the prayer the choir gathered behind the lectern, humming; the announcements were made and the collection taken up.

"Bredren," the preacher said, facing them again. "Sistern." His deep voice was soft but carried as if he had shouted. "Old Jesus wasn't nothin' but a sweet-talkin' liar!"

"No!" they shouted, "Ain't so, ain't so—"

"*Jesus* was a *liar* when he promised us salvation!"

"No, no," they moaned, shaking their heads, fans moving faster.

"You mean you believes Jesus *saves?*" He put his hands on his hips, leaned toward them.

"Amen, dat's right, dat's right!"

"Den how come you ain't livin' right? How come ever' day you break ole Jesus' heart?"

"Oh, Law, we sorry, we sorry!"

"Ever' day, *ever'* day, you kill Jesus all over agin, I hears de weepin' an' de lamentation of de angels, I hear de mother weepin' fo' her child Jesus dat she love jes lak you loves yo' own cheer'n. I see sweet Jesus climbin' Calvary's Mounting carryin' de cross on His back. I hear de cryin' and de moanin' 'cause you crucify sweet Jesus all over agin!"

A woman wailed from the choir, another female voice picking it up from the congregation and then another, the wails spreading like ripples from a stone cast into the water.

The preacher picked up his Bible from the lectern, pounding it with his fist as he tramped back and forth, his shoulders thrust back, face tilted up. "Thou shalt not *steal*," he shouted, facing them again. "You all been stealin', you been stealin' from de white folks, been slippin' in his chicken house in de middle of de night, sneak in de smokehouse, steal de meat. Now ain't that so? *Ain't that so?* Say *amen!*"

"*Amen*," they called. "*Amen, amen, amen* . . . "

"Been killin' too, ain't you? Been killin' each other, been out on de highway cuttin' each other, been killin', stealin', fornicatin' and *lyin'!*"

He stomped and he shouted, he shook his finger at them, he shook the Bible at them, then threw back his head, eyes closed, moaning. "Lawd, Lawd," he sighed. "Dey killin' You all over again, my sweet Jesus that died fo' us. Lawd, Lawd," he said again, shaking his head; his voice faded to a whisper, and he moved into the back of the pulpit to stand beside the picture of Jesus.

"Save us, Jesus, save us," the people cried, while the preacher shouted, "Lawd, Lawd, Lawd," over and over, the sound bouncing off the walls, the sound beating them, binding them.

Slowly he held up his arms for them to be quiet, and he walked back to the edge of the pulpit. "Wasn't that sweet Jesus you crucified?" he whispered, and their voices expelled in the unison of a common sigh, "Yes, Jesus," and they moaned as he swayed, repeating "Lawd, Lawd," the fans moving faster and faster as they rocked back and forth in their sorrow.

The faint breeze that had begun earlier had died, and the leaves of the trees hung limp and heavy, the air in the church was moist and steamy. He waited until they became quiet again, and he said, "Thou shalt not commit adultery!" But his voice was calm, conversational, and they stared at him seeming not to comprehend this *thou shalt not.* He leaned so far over the edge of the pulpit it seemed he would topple over, and he shouted, tendons of his neck bulging, eyes blaring. *Thou shalt not commit adultery!*

And they moaned and fell upon one another, crying, trembling, and a woman shrieked and stood up, flinging her arms about and wildly sobbing, then pitching backward. The women caught her and stretched her out on the bench, fan knocking against fan as they tried to tend her, and her red-flowered dress slid high over knees, her dark breasts half spilling from its low neck.

Bird looked out the window and thought that all they needed were loincloths and tom-toms, thought that the dense foliage, the smothering heat, might well be Africa. Each time he came here he swore it would be his last, or else that he would wait outside. But each time he could not resist the chance to wear his good clothes and to walk as a white man among Negroes. He wondered that they allowed themselves to become so excited, was disgusted with their religious orgasms. He thought he would get up and leave, go on to the Kountry Kitchen, let somebody else take Mrs. Bonner home. But he could not, it would scare her if she couldn't find him, he couldn't simply leave without seeing to her.

He looked back to the pulpit, and the preacher was mopping the back of his neck, his face, with a white handkerchief, and the woman who had fainted was sitting up again. Slowly the preacher walked back and forth, hands clasped upon his chest.

"I'se got a mother in heben," he said.

"Outshines de sun," the congregation answered.

"I'se got a father in heben!" He stood still now, facing them. His foot began a barely perceptible tapping.

"Outshines de sun!" they shouted. They began to sway.

"I'se got a sister in heben!"

They began to clap their hands, preacher and congregation, marking the rhythm of the words that had become a chant. The preacher began to dance slowly about the pulpit, face turned up, eyes closed, and the people shouted and clapped, their feet stamping out the beat that vibrated inside Bird's head and in his chest, that seemed like the throbbing of his heart.

"Outshines the sun!" Bird shouted with them, swept into the wild current of their emotion, his voice blending with theirs. And, as if from a great distance, he saw the blurred white of his hands clapping, and his brown shoe stamping was the flat, splayed foot of Africa. Sweat ran between his shoulder blades, and along the bony curvature of his spine; he shivered and felt nauseated in the intense, pulsing heat. People danced in the aisles, the bright colors smearing together; sweat formed on his forehead, burst and ran down the sides of his face; he saw the preacher profiled against the white wall of the church, his flared nostrils and heavy lips outlined sharply; his shadow jumped and writhed as if pulled by puppet strings.

He sat in rigid horror, his hands poised to clap as realization gripped him: for those few seconds he had become one of them, and his head rang as when he was sick. He thought he would sit in this position for all eternity, caught in the maelstrom of frenzied sound, that when eons had passed some paleontologist would find him in the ruins turned to stone.

"When we get to heben," the preacher shouted, "whut we gon' do?"

"Outshine de sun!"

In the long, jubilant expulsion of sound women sank to the floor, some talking in tongues; the men moaned and swayed, eyes closed; and the preacher danced upon the stage, hands clapping, dark and strange, yet somehow familiar, somehow profound.

Bird left the church and stood beneath the tree where the children had been, he leaned against the trunk and rubbed his head back and forth against the rough bark. With the pain, he felt connected again, the world seen as it really was. But he still felt sick at his stomach, and he thought how wily were black genes, how like a panther, cannily creeping upon him. And he knew he would never come here again.

Faye ran to the living-room window and watched Coy scratch off from the parking lot, the wheels spinning up gravel that bounced off the gleaming black paint of the car. She wondered what else had happened to make him roar off in such a fury, and she watched until he was out of sight, the car seeming distorted, misshapen, in the shimmering heat waves. Then she sank onto the couch, relieved that he was gone, if only for a few minutes.

She had been sitting at the kitchen table drinking a cup of coffee, jumping each time she heard a door open or close, dreading when he would come to lie heavy and sweating on top of her—to masturbate on her. She thought of slipping out the back door and going to her daddy's house, yet knew she would not. Her lips had swollen and he'd know Coy had been hitting her again, he'd curse and say he was going to kill Coy, only he wouldn't, he couldn't even shoot a dove or a squirrel, it was just talk. She had promised herself she wouldn't go there any-more with bruises on her.

She looked down the empty Sunday-afternoon road and knew that even though she dreaded what was coming, still it would be good to get it over with, she was glad for the weeks of peace that would lie ahead. And she'd act like she wasn't mad at him, she'd even say she forgave him, but all the time waiting, waiting, until she had the baby and could figure out a way to get the money back. Then she'd divorce him.

When she thought of divorce, she thought of Hayes. He'd told her many times she ought to get a divorce, he said he didn't buy her excuses about the money. "Your daddy doesn't need or want the money," he said. "Let Coy have it, it's a small price to pay to get rid of him."

But she couldn't, there was something in her that wouldn't let her just walk away, call it excuses or guilt or whatever—all she knew was that she couldn't give Coy the restaurant.

She left the couch and went to lie on the bed, the fan blowing hot air across her face, and she wished she had chucked everything and gone with Hayes as he had begged her to that morning. She'd had to convince him that it would be worse for her if he stayed as he had wanted to do, that Coy might kill them both.

She knew Hayes loved her though he'd never told her so; they'd never set foot outside the front door together, even touched, except a light meeting of the hands when Coy was gone or asleep. He wanted to marry her when she was divorced, but she would never marry again; Hayes would want sex too, as his wife that would be his right. But she was frigid, she'd found that out from the book at the library. Coy kept telling her there was something wrong with her (the only information she'd ever had was from talk among her girl friends in high school and from a Sunday-school teacher who told the Inter-mediate girls' class that sex was evil outside marriage and inside only to be endured), and she had gone to the library in Selma and sat in a corner and read a book about sexual joys, hiding it beneath a *National Geographic* magazine if someone walked close by. And Coy was right, the book said that women who couldn't respond, who never achieved orgasm, had psycholog-ical problems. She had gently closed the book and sat for a long time in the musty quiet, the hissing warmth from the radiators so peaceful she had dozed. She put the book back on the shelf when she sharply nodded and went back to the restaurant.

After that she stopped trying so eagerly to please Coy, and he didn't seem to notice any difference; she knew then there would never be any tender words or embraces, knew that in his frenzied humping he forgot who she was—didn't care who she was. *Slam, bam, thank you, ma'am.* That was a joke in high school, only she hadn't known what it meant then.

Once, when Coy had stripped in the darkness and, spraddled on all fours, had climbed on top of her, he had been outlined against the filmy window, his testicles swinging; and she had been struck with the most awful knowledge that it was as it had been in the beginning—clothes and civilization had not caged men's savage sexuality; it was always ready to spring like the tiger in the picture hanging on the wall in the living room.

She sighed and wished Coy would come on back, that she could get this horrible day ended. This time tomorrow it will be all over, she thought, the words comforting as they had been when she was little and living with her mother. Her mother's headaches, her bad humor, many times eased somehow with a night's sleep. She closed her eyes and the blood throbbed in her temples, and she thought that when he came back she would have to endure the sweaty heaviness of him pressing down on her, his tongue thrusting in her mouth, and she jumped up and ran into the bathroom and vomited. She splashed tepid water on her face and brushed her teeth, and as she went through the bedroom the wolf was plainly visible beneath the chair, its head up, its yellow eyes fixed on her. She sat on the couch again, leaned her head back on the warm, dark-green plastic.

Dully, as she scanned the room, she thought how much she hated this place: pale green, concrete-block walls, Coy's snarling tiger, full face, ears flattened. The picture had been here when they bought the restaurant, and when she was in the dime store she had bought a picture of a bowl of wildflowers to replace it. But Coy said he wouldn't have a fag picture hanging in his house, so she had put it in her dresser beneath her nightgowns, hurt that he didn't like it. That was in the early days when she still loved him and cared what he thought. Sometimes she took the picture out of the drawer and looked at it; the colors were garish and unsubtle, she knew that; and yet the artist had caught a certain light, a glow, the yellow daisies held the sun, and the radiance in the green leaves made her happy.

A console television set and a hotel-room chair, Danish modern, was the only other furniture in the room, and she closed her eyes and saw dark, gleaming floors, high ceilings, lace curtains and crocheted doilies; willow rockers on a wide front porch veiled by twisted wisteria vines and althea bushes. That was her mother's house. Her father's house was small, it could have been set inside her mother's three or four times, but it was built by her great-grandfather of heart pine, it was strong and durable, like the Turners. And he had built most of the furniture too, the oak swing on the front porch, a round, cherry dining table and chairs, the red-swirled wood rubbed smooth as satin. And a great longing came to be the child again who had lived in those rooms, attic ceilings sloping into walls that protected like arms, lying in the swing with her father holding her hand until she slept, while she slept. Oh, the wolf had not dared to follow her to that house.

She could bear it no longer; no matter what Coy did to her, she had to go outside before she went crazy, and as she rose she took a last look out the window, but the highway was as empty as before. She left the apartment and went through the restaurant, where only one driver sat hunched over a mug of coffee, and she wondered how much coffee had been filtered through how many kidneys in the three years they had been there. She did not know the driver, and when he looked up she nodded and passed on into the kitchen.

Nellie stood at the stove stirring a large pot of vegetable soup, steam swirling about her black face, her hair caught tightly into a net, the elastic cutting into her forehead. The flesh of her upper arms rippled with her stirring, her shoulders slumped beneath the white uniform; she had four children and no husband and when she went home at seven o'clock she still had her own supper to cook, her clothes to wash, her house to clean, her children to tend. The oldest was twelve and caring for the younger ones while she was gone, and tomorrow morning she'd get up and do everything all over again, on and on and on until she died and with no hope that things could ever be better. She didn't even have church on Sundays because Coy wouldn't let her off. She had Thursday afternoons and that was all.

"Lawd, God, Miss Faye," she said when she saw Faye

standing just inside the swinging doors. "I didn't hear you come in, you better git on back to the 'pahtment, I'se sposed to tell if you come out—"

"It's all right, Nellie, I know you have to do what he says, and if he comes in you go ahead and tell him, don't get yourself in trouble. But if I don't get outside for awhile I'll go crazy, I don't care what he does."

"You hush talkin' lak dat, it ain't jes you no mo', you got dat baby to think about. Mista Coy got great big ole hands and you jes' a little bitsy ole thing. You do whut he says, leastways 'til that baby gits borned."

Faye felt like she would cry for the worried kindness in Nellie's face, and a bond sprang between them for being women together and for their condition of being abused by the white man.

"Don't worry, Nellie, I'll be all right. Maybe he won't come back," and Nellie looked at her sharply, knowledge in her eyes at what she meant.

"Might be he won't," she said softly. "But I'll listen out fo' him, you go on outside and git some air, I'll come tell you when I heahs de car . . . ."

Faye went out the back door, and the heat wrapped around her, heavy, smothering, like a wool blanket, and she kicked off her moccasins and walked barefoot through the brittle grass to the willow tree that grew at the edge of the woods. She pushed aside the weeping branches and sat down in the gloom, looked back at the sun beating against the whitewashed walls of the restaurant and wished God would strike it with lightning and splinter it to bits or that it would burn down. It was a wicked place, she felt guilty selling bennies to the drivers, knew Coy was supplying sugar to the bootleggers. Maybe God *would* strike it down, like Sodom and Gomorrah.

She lay back on the bare earth and heard the rumble of the river through the ground, and she grew sleepy listening to its flowing and thought she'd take a nap; and then a door slammed and fear streaked her stomach—she listened for Nellie's voice calling to her that Coy was back. She pushed farther back, and footsteps brushed across the grass coming toward her; she hooked her arm about the low limb of the tree and squeezed her eyes shut, waiting for Coy's huge hand to tear away the branches and drag her from beneath the tree. Nellie had not heard him in time to warn her and she waited for a long time, and then there came a peculiar scraping sound; she listened intently but could not identify it, and opened her eyes and peered through the trailing limbs, seeing not size eleven loafers, but narrow bare feet and legs fuzzed with curly brown hair.

Bird Lasseter stood about fifteen feet away in cut-off jeans and a white tee shirt, idly raking the grass, now and then stooping to pile up small mounds of pine straw. She watched for awhile, joyous that it wasn't Coy, and impulsively she parted the branches and called to him.

He stopped raking, looking for the sound, and she called again, and he turned toward her, squinting his eyes as he walked slowly to the tree.

"Come in and sit down," Faye said, parting the branches like curtains, as if she invited him into a room.

He poked his head inside. "Nice place you have here," he said.

She smiled. "It's home. Come in for a minute and rest."

"I'm not tired, I just got started."

She saw the wariness in his face and that he had glanced toward the restaurant. "He's gone, he won't be back for a long time. If at all."

"If?"

"He'll be back, but not for awhile. We can talk."

He stepped inside, the leafed bars shutting behind him.

"I like to do this too," he said. "Get in places where nobody can see me but I can see them, see how they do when they don't know they're being watched. It makes you feel kind of superior."

"That isn't what I was doing, I wasn't really watching you, I thought you were Coy." She stopped. She never talked about her affairs, not to anybody, not to Dr. Lasseter, not even to her daddy—all they knew was what they learned from the bruises.

She'd gotten herself into this mess with Coy and she wouldn't burden anybody else with it. But she was glad Bird was with her beneath the tree, it was like inviting a friend home. Her mother would never let her do that. But she had not meant to offend him, for him to think she was spying. Coy was mean to him and rude, and she didn't want him to think she was like Coy.

"I wasn't spying on you," she said.

"Oh, I know that," Bird said quickly. "I never meant for you to think that was what I thought, I just meant I like to observe people—"

They laughed, and he sat down; she tucked her legs beneath her, pulling her skirt carefully over her knees. They looked at each other, laughed again, and Faye was embarrassed, she didn't know what to say, she was sorry she'd called him because she didn't know how to make conversation. She tugged at a piece of hairy willow root protruding from the ground, gazed beyond him to the woods.

"This must be a very good place to read," Bird said. "I used to read under the scuppernong arbor when I lived with the doctor. This reminds me of it, it hides you but yet you can see what's going on outside."

"I don't read much. Sometimes I read the romance serial in the *Selma Times*, but the stories are kind of stupid, nobody acts like those people. Seems like their biggest problems are what they're going to wear and whether they're going to catch some man they're after."

"That's trash," he said, then quickly apologized. "I'm sorry, I shouldn't have said that, it's just that I thought you'd probably like some other things better—William Faulkner, Flannery O'Connor."

"I don't know who they are, except maybe Faulkner; it seems like I remember we read a short story of his in high school, something about an old Negro woman who lived in a cropper cabin and the man she had lived with was going to kill her and the white people let her stay with them awhile but then made her go back."

Bird was nodding, his face excited. "That was 'That Evening Sun.' It's one of my favorites; if you liked that, you'd probably like some of his novels, I could lend you a book—"

She shook her head. "No, I couldn't borrow a book from you, Coy would get mad," and she blushed deeply, ashamed that the words had slipped out, that she had said such a thing to this beautiful boy whose eagerness had vanished with her words, whose jaw had hardened. "I'm sorry, I shouldn't have said that."

But then she saw pity in his eyes for her embarrassment and understanding sprang between them as it had between her and Nellie. "You're lonesome too," she said.

A mask of blandness slid over his face, and he shrugged. "Isn't everybody? Thomas Wolfe said, 'which of us is not forever a stranger and alone?' "

"Oh, no, I could never believe that, even as lonesome as I've been, I've had my daddy, there's always somebody—"

"I've had Johnnie, that's true." His voice was musing, he drew up his legs, rested his arms on his knees.

"You mean your sister?"

"She's not my sister. I wish she was, it would sure make my life a whole lot simpler."

The heat and the gloom bound them, time became distilled, compressed, so that it was easy to talk, as if they had known each other for a long time. They told things they might never have told except in these circumstances: they talked about Coy shooting Otis Helms and he told her how Johnnie met him in the woods, only nobody could know that, and she promised she would never tell. The world outside the leafed confessional was not real—all that existed was themselves and the hot breeze trickling through the branches.

When they finally became silent, Faye thought how light she felt, the sick burning in the pit of her stomach that had begun the day she found out for sure she was pregnant was gone. She was hungry, in fact, ravenous, and she jumped up and said she was going to the kitchen for some tea. "Iced tea with lots and lots of sugar and lemon, so much sugar that it swirls in the tea like snow, like in those toy paperweights with blizzards on Swiss mountains."

She ran for the restaurant, happy they were friends and trusted each other so that they could share. Her feet skimmed the ground, all that she saw—trees, ground, sky—were seen as through the mist of a pleasant dream. The slanted sun struck the kitchen window like the splintered light of a jewel, and she burst into the kitchen, startling Nellie, whose hand flew to her heart.

"Lawd God Almighty, Miss Faye, you lak to scared me to death. I been so busy gettin' ready fo' de supper rush I fo'got about you. You better git on back to de 'pahtment, Mista Coy bound to get back any minute. How come you smilin' lak dat, I ain't seen you smile lak dat since I knowed you."

"Why, Nellie," Faye said, her voice light and teasing, "I smiled a year ago last Tuesday, the night Coy left town for two weeks."

They laughed, Nellie's fat stomach shaking beneath her apron, and she turned back to the wooden table and began again chopping the lettuce for the salad.

Faye filled tall plastic glasses with ice and dark brown tea, poured in sugar from the sugar sack until the tea was nearly white, then floated wedges of lemon on top. She put two huge pieces of gingerbread dripping with lemon sauce onto paper plates, put it all on a tray, and went back to the tree. Saliva flowed beneath her tongue, her stomach cramped with pleasure. She reveled in her lightness, she felt like she might float right up through the trees to the great fluffy clouds that had built on the horizon with the setting sun. She took great bites of the cake and washed it down with tea, and Bird laughed and shook his head at her, and she thought what a good time they were having. A small white butterfly drifted into the cloistered dimness, dipping, rising, lighting on the cake crumbs on the paper plates.

"The Creeks called them 'those that fly crooked,' " Bird said.

"The butterflies?"

"Yes. I've never seen one fly straight, have you?"

"No, now that I think about it, I guess I haven't. I like it, though, so that's what I'll call them from now on. We're having a good time, aren't we?" Faye said.

"Yes," he said, smiling. "You're like Johnnie, you can have fun like a child."

"Is this what children do? I never had a friend when I was little, nobody liked me, except once a girl in third grade did, her name was Juanita, and I brought her home from school one afternoon. We came up on the porch and Mama came to the door and told her to run on home, that I couldn't play, and when she left she said that Juanita was common, she lived down at the old convict camp. Only I liked her, I didn't know what common was and I didn't care."

She lay back on the ground and the ginger still gently stung her tongue, the tea still felt cold in her throat, her stomach, and the day spread out around her, the washed sky arcing over them, dimming with the dying sun. She closed her eyes and felt a glorious emptiness, the absence of a presence, and realized that for the first time in months she had forgotten for a little while about dying. Then Bird stretched out beside her, and he told her that Beethoven's *Eroica* was his favorite symphony and Faulkner his favorite author. And she told him that her uncle who had been a preacher over in Carden hadn't wanted her mother to marry her father, that he didn't think he was good enough. She said she wished he was still living so she could tell him what a good man her daddy was, probably even better than a preacher. She told him about how she had quit being scared of the devil or the end of time after she went to live with him, and she nearly decided to tell him about the wolf, but then didn't. She was afraid he would think she was crazy, as she did herself sometimes. How else explain something that wasn't there?

They lay silently for awhile, and then Bird said he had to quick finish the raking, wasn't it time for Mr. Watson to be home, and she said maybe he wasn't coming back. He didn't answer and she heard the regularity of his breathing, and looked at him, saw he slept, and shut her own eyes. When she woke she thought she dreamed, for a head floated inside the branches, a hand appeared and hit her across the side of her face so that her ear rang and went numb.

She screamed for her father as she always did in nightmares, and then the twisted face screamed *slut, bitch,* and another hand appeared, the two hands gripping her shoulders, shaking her so hard she thought her neck would break. She shoved backward, pushing along the ground, but he was falling down upon her; now she was going to die, but then he fell sideways, Bird had kicked him away, and he was cursing and screaming *whore! bitch! slut!* All this she saw through a haze of terror, the male forms blurred and moving as if in slow motion, and she crawled away and it seemed a long time before she reached the curtain of branches, the thin limbs catching in her hair as if trying to hold her.

She was running down the road between two weeded fields where once had been a cropper's cabin, and she did not remember getting there, and faintly she heard screams of *white nigger* over and over; she looked back and saw Nellie running across the yard toward the tree, white apron blowing.

It was in a nightmare that she ran, her legs heavy, feet dragging in the hard rutted dirt. Her lungs burned as she gasped air, pain stabbed the pit of her stomach, and she clasped her hands over it. A small green grasshopper flew up from the ditch, wings whirring against her cheek, and she hit wildly at it, knocking it away. She half walked, half ran, looked back again and again thinking to see the black car coming after her, looming like death, and when the sun went behind a cloud she thought a shadow moving in the road was the car. She cried out and ran harder, stumbling, nearly falling, the dark woods, the chalky road strange, unfamiliar, and she did not know where she was running to. But then she saw the streak of highway that led to her father's house, and knew she had been here many times, knew all the time where she was heading.

Her ankle twisted in a rut, and she pitched forward and crashed into a ditch, long, sharp spikes of Johnson grass cutting her arms and legs, drooping over her, wrapping about her. Pain shot through her stomach, and she lay staring into the sky where low on the horizon a three-quarter moon was rising. Irritably she shifted against a warm wetness between her legs, thought for a moment that she was at her mother's house and had wet the bed again, that her mother would be sad and shake her head at her. *It just makes extra wash for Hattie, you ought to think about poor Hattie having to wash sheets every day....*

She felt the vibrations before she heard the heavy crunch of tires against the earth, and she watched a big white sidewall tire and dust-spattered fender move slowly past. Only it had nothing to do with her, and she closed her eyes, she was so tired, so sleepy. But minutes later the vibrations came again and she opened her eyes and watched the tire and fender move past in the opposite direction. Not far away a car door slammed and someone walked up and down, now close, now receding, calling in a singsong voice *come out come out wherever you are.* And then footsteps crashing through the woods, great thumping explosions of fury against the ground, and her name shouted over and over.

High above the blurred edge of the moon the North Star rose, from its bright shining she traced downward to the star at the beginning of the curved handle of the Big Dipper. Ursa Major. Funny. She hadn't known she knew that. Out of her high-school science this information had surfaced from her subconscious, and she was pleased that she remembered.

Fireflies swarmed in the pines, and she smelled the warm sweetness of the honeysuckle tangled in the ditch with the Johnson grass. And coming toward her down the road in the falling darkness was a round spot of light moving back and forth and growing larger and larger as it came closer.

8

Late Sunday afternoon, John Lasseter parked his car on the side of the road and decided to walk the last mile through the woods to Zella's house. He followed the river for awhile and then sat on the hump of a tree root near the bank and took off his coat, lay it on the ground beside him. On top of the coat he placed a package wrapped in gold foil and tied with a red ribbon with curled streamers. Inside the box was a pink negligee.

It was smothering hot, and he wished he'd gone ahead and taken the car all the way to the house; even now he could be sitting on the porch looking out to the river, the fan turned on him. After the sun went down they could go inside and make love, and now it was going to be just about dark when he got there. But at the same time he was reluctant to be with her, afraid of what she might tell him, and he watched the minnows darting at the water's edge, conscious of his heart's slow, hard beat. It was uncomfortable but not dangerous, and brought on by not enough sleep from sitting late with patients and drinking too much coffee. He worried, though, because he was at the prime age for a heart attack, with not as much chance for survival as a much older man would have whose body would have formed new arteries—if a clot blocked one passage, why, then, more than likely the blood would be shunted to another one.

He thought again of Zella. No matter where he was or what he was doing she was always in his mind; he longed again for the time when he could concentrate totally on his work. Each morning when he awoke his first thought was that this might be the day she left. When she had been with him a year, she had told him she had never stayed so long in one place. She had lived in Birmingham and Selma and Carden; she had even been to Detroit. Each time she left Asheton she had stayed away longer than the time before, not understanding what pulled her home again. Her daddy was a cropper and she was born a couple of miles down the road from Wesley Turner, but her family was gone now, her mother and father dead, all those sisters and brothers scattered. She said every now and then she'd just had to come back, and this last time when she came home from Detroit she left her grandmother and started living with Henry Jerald. But always she had this restlessness ticking away like an inner clock, telling her when it was time to move on. He felt deeply grateful that she had stayed with him so long, had tried so hard to deny her impulses. She loved him, but only because of gratitude for what he had done for her, and that was all right with him, he wanted her under whatever conditions.

The vial of morphine pressed against his leg deep in his pocket, and he shifted until the pressure was gone, watched the river where it churned into white water as it passed over a root snag near the bank. And he knew he could not bear it if she left, he imagined the house vacant, no more laughter echoing through the rooms when she ran from him after she had, like a child, pounced at him from behind some door, he pursuing, until finally they fell onto the bed together, the scuffling ending in lovemaking. No, he could not imagine her gone, of not having to scold her for forgetting to eat or for swimming on frosty December mornings in the river. Last summer, at dusk, she had coaxed him into the river with her, he naked also: she called forth from his stiff dignity another self he had not known, a frolicking playful self who splashed and cavorted with the dusky woman, her black hair streaming, slick skin caught in her lover's embrace.

He slumped, head sinking upon his chest, longing for the way things used to be. She seldom laughed anymore, she was no longer playful. For weeks she had not talked of leaving and that was more ominous, more terrifying, than when she had talked of it constantly. He did not think she would say good-by when she left, it would simply happen: one day she would be there, the next gone, and with the thought, panic leaped, his heart beat faster. That night when she had come whispering at his door he had not known how lonely he was—it was only in comparison, in looking back, that he understood.

He moved his leg and the sharp edge of the bottle bit into his flesh, and he stood up and took it from his pocket, raised his arm high overhead to throw it into the river. But then the light caught the clear fluid and made a sunburst of color, and he dropped it back into his pocket, sat down again. No need to waste such valuable medicine—waste was never justified. Though he had become a rich man, his mother's training would never allow him to become a wasteful one.

He considered going away for awhile, when he came back Zella would be gone; he knew she would take that chance for freedom. He could always pretend that when he came back she would still be here. Once Lillian Hodge told him he ought to travel, to go and see the great cities of the world, the ruins of great civilizations. Sail the Grecian isles, she said, walk over the Scottish moors in September when the heather blooms, stroll through an English garden in the springtime. Walk down a French country road. Griffith and I have, she said, and when I'm old in my wheelchair I'll have all that to think about. He'd considered thoughtfully what she said; it had merit, he knew that. He told her he just might do that one day, but then he had thought but why in God's name should he? He lived in the most beautiful land in creation, even Canada couldn't compare. And if he needed ruins, well, he had those too, slave cabins and Negro shacks. If Lillian wanted ruins she ought to take a good look at that poor wreck of an alcoholic, Ellard Willoughby.

When the train had pulled into the Asheton station all those years ago when his mother sent him to Canada, before he even went to see her he climbed an oak down by the tracks and gazed at the town, at the single block of buildings, the houses of the neighborhood set neatly in a row and beyond them the farms scattered randomly like cardboard boxes across an attic floor. And his heart had nearly burst with love, he had known that he wanted nothing more from life than never to have to leave again. And yet he'd had to go to Baltimore to learn to be a doctor, and he left now and then to go to conventions; but for all practical purposes he'd never left home again. In the tree that afternoon he planned his life as neatly as those houses laid out in a row: school, an office somewhere on that street, a house farther out in the countryside. A wife.

And he had made it happen like he planned. In those early days of his practice, in the mid-thirties, he'd made his rounds on horseback. He'd been up all night delivering a baby that spring morning he met Jenny. He was on the way back to the Bide-a-Wee where he was living at the time, and nearly asleep in the saddle, the reins slack in his hands. He thought at first he dreamed, she was white and gold, her hair tumbled about her shoulders and glistening with light. When he came even with her he thought she would vanish like a vision conjured from his tired brain, but she continued staring at him, studying him. She was barefoot, and the early breeze whipped the white dress close about her slender form, revealing soft curves, budding young breasts.

"Who are you?" he said. "I've not seen you around here."

"I haven't been home for a long time. My name's Jennifer McKinley."

So, he thought, she is Angus McKinley's daughter. He hadn't seen her since she was eight years old, when her mother died. Mr. McKinley had sent her to live in Glasgow with his sister. He looked over his shoulder to the two-story white board farmhouse he had just passed. It sat far back off the road with a field on one side, an apple grove on the other.

He looked again at her. "You've come back home."

"As you can see."

"I didn't think you were real. I thought I was dreaming. I'm John Lasseter—"

"I know who you are."

"Then you know that I couldn't save your mother and the baby."

She shook her head. "It was chance, or fate. Who knows?"

"Your father hates me." And he saw again that raw December afternoon, mother and baby together in the coffin, the baby boy swaddled and cradled in the crook of the mother's arm. "Your mother was so weak, she just faded away, and the baby was born too early."

"I know all that, you don't have to explain," and the pity in her eyes answered the pain in his face. "If there was fault," she said, "it was my father's; he blamed himself and turned on you. He knew my mother wasn't strong and past the age she ought to be having babies, and you told him so; I heard you, I was listening through the door that afternoon you told him she ought not to be allowed to have it. You told him it could kill her and it did. And I heard him tell you that what you proposed was murder, and that if it came to a choice between one or the other you were to save the baby, for that was what his religion taught."

At that moment he fell in love with her and knew he would marry her. "How old are you?" he said.

"Fifteen."

Well, then, he would have to wait, she was still a child, though she spoke with a woman's maturity and authority. Her gaze was straight and honest, and in three years, when she was eighteen, he would marry her. That would give him more time to get his practice bigger and to save money for the house he would build for her in a spot he had already picked out on a knoll above the river. He was still young, only twenty-four: he could spare the time.

"When will you be sixteen?"

"March thirty-first."

She stood gravely watching him, and they were silent, enclosed in the brilliance of morning; a mockingbird sang in the apple grove, a bob white flew up from the grass that edged her father's field. He loved her, and joy surged that he had found the woman who would share his life.

"When you're eighteen I will marry you," he said.

Her face revealed no trace of what she felt or thought. He slapped the reins softly across the horse's neck, gently dug his boot heels into her flanks, and when he looked back, she still watched him, her dress blowing, her hair shining.

They had no conversation at all during those three years, they only nodded and said "hello" when they met. But he noted the progress of her physical development, pleased that she was lithe and sturdy as a sapling, her cheeks rosy with good health. Her jawline lengthened from its childish roundness, her breasts developed high and full. But her hair was the same, he could find her instantly in a crowd by its gleaming. It was her glory, it lit her face, and he wished she would wear it up, when they were married he would make her twine it into a bun so that only he could see it down. When they met, knowledge was in their eyes that they only waited.

He knew the things she did, it was the curse and the blessing of the town that there were no secrets: he knew that she went to Selma to the movies on Saturday nights with Byron West and that she wore Byron's friendship ring on her right fourth finger. And that was all right, he could allow that, for he would rather she be with the one rather than the many: he wanted Byron West to dance with her, kiss her, give her the ring. He wanted those three years to be gay and frivolous, for after they were married she belonged to him and he did not want her yearning for that which she had missed. As for himself, he had no desire now for anyone else. He'd known women in college, and in the Biblical sense, but never with love; none of them had made him want to spend the rest of his life with them . And he would be faithful to Jenny—empty, loveless passion was not for him. He yearned toward the time he could gently love her, wished for their babies when he delivered others, and though the three years passed in a dream of anticipated joy, at times desire came so strong he thought he could not endure the waiting. Jenny would be for always, they would grow old together, he would but love her more with shared years etched upon her face.

In the late afternoon of the completion of the three years, and a few days before her birthday, he went to the farm and walked across the wide front porch, the sound of his steps hollow on the board floor. The sweet smell of privet hedges filled the air, birds were nesting, flowers blooming in fields and ditches, and his heart beat with wild joy; but his face became cold and stern: he was afraid to reveal the intensity of his feelings until he made sure of hers.

He peered through the screen door into the gloom of the house, and a stairway stretched in front of him to the upstairs, and he pictured her in her bedroom in her white dress, somehow knowing that today was when he would come for her. He gripped the door pull, thinking to carry her away, that they would fade into the twilight into a long dream of love. But then he took his hand away; how foolish he was, he could not go into Angus McKinley's house and spirit his daughter away, he owed him the respect of telling him that he loved Jenny and wanted to marry her.

He knocked on the door and the sound boomed into the silence, though he thought he had only rapped, and she appeared at the top of the steps, her hair shining with light from the window behind her, and he watched, enchanted, for she seemed an angel floating down to him in the white dress, just as he had imagined her.

She came onto the porch and he stepped back, still watching but unable to speak, for he thought, what if he had only imagined that she returned his looks of knowledge these three years? She was still so young, a child, and he a man close to thirty; he was making a fool of himself, and he held his arms rigidly at his sides. He would make up some other reason he had come, but she looked him straight in the eye as she had that first morning and he knew he couldn't lie to her, and he gestured awkwardly.

"I can't marry you," she said. "I have to marry Byron West, Papa says he's getting old and Byron has said he will come here to live and help to run the farm. Papa says he needs a son."

Anger, hot and deep, shot through him. He shook his head, denying what she said. "You'll be no man's wife but mine, you'll be mistress of no man's house but mine. Byron West has no rights at all with you." He wondered how he had tolerated those years of her going with Byron, was shocked at his jealousy. He did not remember being jealous before in his entire life—it was terrible, made him feel sick. "You'll be wife to no man but me," he said again. He took her hand and kissed the palm, gathered her into his arms, and she felt exactly as he had known she would, firm and slender and strong. Already her shape was as familiar to him as if he had held her many times, and lightly he stroked her hair, breathed in the essence of her purity.

"When we're married, Jenny, I want you to pin up your hair, I want no one to see it down but me."

She sighed and relaxed against him, and love flooded so strong that tears stung his eyes. "You belong to me, I will love you forever. I promise I will make you happy."

I promise I will make you happy. How many times had that been said by lovers? In how many languages, at that precise moment, was it being said all over the world? The arrogance of youth, ah, to have it back again. So young, so young they had been, he and Jenny. He shook his head at their innocence, watching an egret skimming over the water, scooping a small fish into its beak, then wheeling skyward, the scales flashing sunlight.

He had tried to keep his promise, he had put his mother's sapphire ring on her finger that afternoon and gone to stand at the fence to wait for Mr. McKinley to make his return trip from plowing a furrow. He had told him of his love for Jenny and of hers for him.

"No," Mr. McKinley said when he finished. His long weathered face had remained impassive as he listened, his hands never loosening the grip of the plow. "No, she canna do it. I need her here to keep my house and I need Byron West to farm my land. You lost me one son and you'll not deprive me of anither." The words formed into a stone wall leaving not one small chink for argument; and they were said slowly, as if he were unused to talking. "And now I'd appreciate it if you'd get off my land and niver come back."

He slapped the reins across the mule's back, turned him around and began breaking ground for a new furrow. And then

Jenny was there, she touched his arm as she slipped through the
barbed wire to run alongside her father, looking up into his face
as she talked, stumbling in the soft dirt as he strode away, stiff,
unyielding back moving ahead of her. She stopped and watched
him, called after him, but he never looked back.

They were married the first week of April at ten o'clock in
the morning in the apple orchard. She wore a long white or-
gandy dress that was to have been for graduation, and her hair
hung loose about her shoulders; a wreath of apple blossoms
crowned her head, and they stood among the trees, his hand
covering hers that held his arm. The spring day spread about
them flower-scented and pale green, fresh and shining as a newly
made promise; and he thought that everything was ahead, their
future a snow-white sheet of paper on which to record their
lives, glorious day following glorious day.

Mr. McKinley stood watching from the front porch, the
breeze lightly blowing his thin gray hair. When they left the
orchard (he and Jenny and the preacher; Griffith and Lillian
Hodge as witnesses), he had wanted to go to him and beg his
forgiveness for taking Jenny away, he looked so lonesome, so
solitary. He half-turned toward him, but the old man abruptly
went into the house and closed the door.

They had had only two days for a honeymoon, and he had
taken Jenny over to the Albert Hotel in Selma. When they came
back to Asheton they lived at the Bide-a-Wee and each week
Jenny went to see her father, and after about three months she
came home one evening and said that Mr. McKinley wanted
them to live at the farm with him. Already he had deeded the
farm and land to her, all he wanted was a home. And he had
gone willingly, grateful that Mr. McKinley could forgive him
to such an extent, after all that he, John Lasseter, had done to
him.

He stood up, brushed the pine needles from the seat of his
pants; his feet tingled from the long sitting and he stamped them
up and down, waved his arms around to get the blood flowing.
He took his watch from his pocket and saw that he had been

sitting there for a full hour and was amazed at the swift passage of time. Strange, the past coming in on him that way and it seeming that all he had remembered had happened yesterday. Still fresh when he had thought he had it all packed away and didn't care anymore. But Byron West's name was still the bitterest gall on his tongue, even after fifteen years.

He stooped and picked up a thin, flat rock, and with a deft flip skimmed it across the water, counting the circles. Three. Used to be he could easily make eight or even ten. He watched until the circles faded and blended into one another, then stood and leaned against a tree and gazed to where the waves lapped the far shore.

When they had gone to live with Mr. McKinley, he had hired a maid and a cook for Jenny, he would not let her wait on them, though her father resented the strange women in his house. He still said "my house," and he and Jenny did still consider it so, and he let one of the women go but would not give in on Mary Betty, who was young and strong and who could both clean and cook. But he suspected when he was gone that Jenny did a great deal of the cooking her father liked— potato soup and fresh-baked bread—and also that she was the one who ironed the stiff-collared shirts he wore on Sundays, though he went no farther than to sit on the front porch.

And so he began taking her on rounds with him, and she was delighted; she'd put on a pair of boots and jodphurs and twist her hair up, and she'd ride behind him on the horse, her arms tight around his waist, and when he had an emergency and had to gallop the horse, she'd hang on and was never afraid. She wasn't afraid because they had no money either, the Depression was on and he couldn't seem to get his hands on more than a few dollars at a time; nobody seemed to have any cash. He wouldn't let her have a baby, though she talked of it constantly; but not only did he want to wait until they were richer, she was too young: he wanted her to have a few more carefree years, and not only that—he wanted her to himself for awhile. If he had thought he loved her before they were married, it was nothing compared to afterwards.

He was surprised at how tough she was. She could have

been a doctor as easily as he, he had no chance to show off for her because she took the awful things that went with his work right in stride. When he had to amputate a boy's leg in a cropper's shack because he didn't have time to get him to the hospital in Selma, Jenny assisted. The boy had hit a tree on his motorcycle, and the full weight had fallen on his left leg, bones, tissue, nerves mangled. She scrubbed and handed him the instruments after he'd chloroformed him, and he'd kept an eye on her, kept the ammonia handy for when she felt faint, only she never flinched—never batted an eye that he could tell. She performed as if she'd seen legs sawed off every day.

Afterwards, the boy went out of his head, when he told him he'd lost a leg he started screaming gimmie my leg, gimmie my leg, and later he told them cajolingly to please give it back, he wanted to mount it over the fireplace. And Jenny had sat beside him, day and night, for three days, holding his hand, talking to him, dozing when he was quiet, waking at once to calm him when he would again become hysterical. He tried to get her to go home, he said he'd be there with the boy, but she just shook her head and kept sitting in a rocker with a pillow behind her head, and he'd made the coffee and comforted the grieving mother and father. They had no other children and the grief was not only for the mutilated son but that in those hard years they'd lost a helper in the field.

He respected Jenny's courage, and he admired her, and he was ashamed that he was jealous when she began doing those things he counted *his* duty. He wanted his wife and home separate from his work, and besides, he did not think that doctoring was for women—at least women such as Jenny, who should not have to look upon horrible things. She needed cherishing and protecting, and it pleased him to have her need him, to depend on him. But they hadn't been married a year before she let him know that she didn't like having to ask for money, she said having nothing to do and sitting around waiting for him to come home, which was sometimes days at a time, was not *her* idea of marriage. *In my next life, John, maybe I'll come back as a clinging vine for you, but not this time.*

A clinging vine. Well, she certainly hadn't been that. He

had begun giving her a set amount of money after that, no longer doling out a five or a ten hoping to see an adoring look on her face. He smiled and shook his head. What a fool he had been, he recognized that now. So young and eager and wanting somebody to look up to him and need him. And he knew if he'd found a girl like that he wouldn't have liked her, Jenny was more like his mother than any woman he'd ever known. Working like a man and thriving on it.

After the first couple of years, she hadn't needed his money. Gradually she began taking over the farm, her father grew skinnier and weaker, his heart began to fail, and she hired tenants to plow and plant the fields. She made money from the first year she took over, and the Negroes called her "Cap'n." She didn't ask to go on rounds with him anymore, and he was surprised at how much he missed her: he had thought he was going to be happy for it to be only him and for his patients to stop asking where she was. He invited her to go with him again, but she was always too busy, and when he'd ride off he'd look back and see her in pants and a shirt and boots and riding off on her own horse, going to round up a stray steer or to see someone sick in one of the tenant shacks. She got so she could deliver a baby about as well as he could.

So he began to long for a son to go with him, and when the war came and people worked in the defense plants in Selma and Carden, when they paid mostly with money instead of corn and pigs and chickens, he let Jenny get pregnant. For the last two months of her pregnancy she'd hired an overseer, and their marriage was, for that short time, as he had dreamed it in the beginning. She needed him, only he could interpret the fetal heartbeats; he put the stethoscope in her ears and she'd listen intently, then ask if the beat should be so fast, and he would explain. They'd lie together on the bed trying to guess if it was a girl or a boy (he'd been sure it was going to be a boy), and she'd clasp his hand and hold it to her cheek; and he'd have to turn his head, ashamed of his tears. He hadn't thought it possible for one human being to love another as he did her.

At dusk, on a soft June evening in 1942, when the crickets

thrummed outside the window, he delivered their son, perfectly formed, golden hair and pale skin like Jenny, but dead. Over and over he plunged the cyanotic body into tubs of hot, then cold, water, over and over he suctioned his bronchial tubes, turned him upside down, slapping him, until Jenny pleaded for him to stop. She raised her arms for the child, and he placed the dead baby in her arms and knelt beside them. Over and over he told her he was sorry, just as he had told Mr. McKinley. "Hush, hush," she said, "it wasn't your fault," and pressed his hand to her cheek that was dry and not wet with tears as was his. They buried their son beneath a hovering marble angel, and the inscription said Infant Son of John Lasseter and Jennifer McKinley Lasseter, *a rose born to bloom in Heaven.* That was for Mr. McKinley; he wanted the angel and the message.

Always summer twilights when the crickets sang brought a somberness of spirit that was not dispelled until he turned on all the lights and drew the curtains against the coming night.

Three months later Jenny was pregnant again, and the next July he delivered her of a girl, dark like him. They named her Sarah Louise after his mother, and a year after Sarah, the birth dates only two days apart, they had twins (just a minute, Jenny, I think there's another one), and they were identical, two peas from the same pod. They named them Marjorie Frances and Elsbeth Jean for Jenny's mother and her twin sister. He told Jenny she'd have to wait awhile before she got pregnant again, she had bled too much, and the horror of Mrs. McKinley had come back. He moved into another room, he didn't trust himself to be sensible when Jenny wanted to make love; after the son she didn't seem happy unless she was pregnant. He made her stay in bed nearly a month, hoping she'd let the overseer run the farm permanently, but within six weeks she was out on the land again, riding, herding, checking cotton.

The color came back in her cheeks, but she stayed thin, and he had to coax her to eat. He stayed in the spare room so she wouldn't be wakened when he was called out at night—he had taken the old storage room that opened onto the porch for his bedroom. When, after several months, he finally went to her room, the door was locked, and he thought it was because she was still weak, or else uneasy with him downstairs. That was the mistake he was doomed always to make, thinking Jenny needed him. The next time he went to her room it was unlocked, and they made love, but she told him she didn't wany any more children, at least not for a long time, and he respected that, she'd been pregnant almost continuously for three years. He believed when she got strong again she'd change her mind. But she didn't. Not until a few weeks after he'd found Bird in the summer of 1947.

She came to his room in a long white gown, her hair about her shoulders. He had loved her with the same tenderness he had always had for her, and nine months later Johnnie was born. When she gave the blonde girl his name, he knew there would be no more visits in the night, never an unlocked door—never a son to bear his name. And he could not forget the child he could not save.

When he came out of the woods into the clearing, horizontal sun cut a molten path across the water, glanced off the windows of the small white house beneath the trees. At first he thought the sun was a lamp set there to welcome him, but as he got closer, saw the house was dark. He began to run, Zella was gone, he would never see her again, and when he reached the front door, flung it open, crashing it against the wall. "*Zella!* he called, his voice harsh with fear.

A dove cooed beneath the eaves, the river hummed, but that was all the answer he had, and he rushed into the gloom, calling to her. He found her in the bedroom lying naked on top of the twisted covers, and he sagged against the doorjamb, relief causing the anger to rise. What a terrible homecoming when all day he had been working for this moment; through all he had done, she was in his mind. He dropped the gold package onto the floor and went to the window and pulled the heavy green draperies, switched on her bedside lamp. He pulled a sheet up to her waist, then sat in a deep-cushioned wing chair by the bed.

He wanted to wake her, he thought she had probably been sleeping all afternoon; people who slept in the daytime depressed him, and he watched the rising and falling of her breathing, amazed that she could sleep through his calling and the noise he had made coming in. He would have to make her promise to start locking the doors, just anybody at all could walk in and she'd never know it until they were harming her. He couldn't believe how deeply she slept, always he was on the surface of sleep, listening even then for the voices who might call to him, telling him to come. But Zella had to struggle with awakening, sometimes she looked at him dazed, as if sleep had been the reality and he the dream. Sometimes she didn't know him, it was eerie to see her look at him with no recognition, no familiarity.

In the electric light her skin took on a reddish glow, the high cheekbones emphasized. There was Indian blood somewhere in her ancestry, and white also. Her long, delicate fingers plucked at the sheet, her eyes moved behind the lids. She was dreaming. But of what? of whom? And he was jealous that her dreams could be secret from him—did not have to include him.

Shortly after he brought her here, she told him Jenny's overseer, Grady Lawson, a white man from Carden, had raped her. He had fired him the next day even though Jenny had been coldly furious. *You had no right to interfere in my business; what if I heard something bad about Gertrude and came down to your office and fired her? The woman's a prostitute, how can you possibly believe anything she says?*

Zella shifted and turned on her side, pushed her hand beneath her cheek, and he thought how like a child she was when she slept. But she was not a child; that first time he made love with her after he had seen her naked in the river he had lain beside her afterwards unable to speak. There had been no reserve, no restraint between them. And he had been glad for her musky angularity that was so different from the airy fragility of Jenny. He tried never to think about Jenny that way again.

Zella wanted him as no woman ever had, she ripped away the barrier that kept a part of himself for himself. Every person, he believed, was entitled to this area, this identity, that no one else could invade. But apparently Zella knew nothing about areas or identities, he had the feeling she would laugh if he said such things concerning lovemaking, and she had plunged into a dark whirlpool of passion and had taken him along with her, though at first he had struggled to hold back. But she would not have it, she arched her back and rubbed the dusky breasts across his face, pushed the nipples into his mouth, took his hand and guided it to the places on herself she wanted him to touch. She pulled him into her and they were hurled into some strange land where he lost all sense of himself and of her too—a land where nothing existed, nothing mattered, except ecstasy.

Afterward he could not speak. She was his youth, the adolescence he had skipped in his determination of attaining his goals. His abandon had astounded him. He would never have believed such ardor lay within his capabilities. They had lain still connected, had made love the second time, and she would have gone the third but he told her no more, no more. And she laughed softly and kissed his ear, mistook his silence, his exhaustion, and said that love was supposed to make you happy, not sad. And he smiled at her and shook his head, not trusting himself to speak, for the thoughts racing through his head were those of a pubescent boy.

She was highly sexed, and she was also moody. She had headaches that kept her in bed sometimes as long as a week, she'd see flashes of light signaling a migraine. He could not bear her pain, and gave her heavy doses of codeine, anxious for her to be well again: like a chameleon, his mood changed with hers.

As he sat watching her now, he thought her breathing had become shallower, faster, and he lay his fingers lightly on her pulse. It was fast, and he saw scattered on the night table the yellow capsules he had given her last Sunday night. Only six of eighteen Nembutal left, and he scooped them up and returned them to the bottle. The aspirin and caffeine tablets were at least half gone from a new bottle of one hundred given to her a week ago. Too many drugs making her heartbeat fast. Making her sleep too much. But what to do? The headaches were coming more often, and he knew it was because of the stress of trying to leave and him holding her there. He should tell her to go and mean it, let her go without guilt. And as he gazed at her imagining her gone, imagining not having her at the end of each day, he thought better never to have known her than to lose her. Than to go back to the way things were.

She sighed and opened her eyes and sat up, the mass of her hair tangled about her shoulders, a dark cloud that framed her face. Her eyes widened when she saw him, but she recognized him, she was awake.

The bedclothes bound her legs and she thrashed about, struggling to free herself, and he reached to help her, unwinding the twisted sheet. He thought how small her breasts had become, her chest almost flat as a boy's. She pulled the sheet up, covering herself, and with despair he knew this: she was no longer free with him as she had been in the beginning, she did not want him to see her naked, because she did not want to make love. She was gone already in spirit, and he wondered what day, what hour, what precise second had she stopped loving him? He wondered what he had been doing, not knowing that such a cataclysmic happening had occurred in his life. Had he been listening to one of Dave Crenshaw's jokes or been on rounds with Bird or simply sleeping? He could not have been sleeping, such a happening would have awakened him.

She lay upon her pillows watching him. Yet she was not really aware of him, her eyes were unfocused, far away, and he wanted to yell at her, shake her, make her see *him*, and the gladness come into her eyes. He wanted to bring back their past.

He picked the package up off the floor and handed it to her. "I've brought you a present," he said, and she took it and laid it aside. "I'll unwrap it for you," and he tore away the foil, spread the pink negligee with the fluffy feathers across her chest, but she flung it away.

"I don't need no more nightgowns, I need dancin' clothes, party clothes—"

He picked the gown up from the floor, laid it again across her chest. The feathers fluttered when she breathed. "See how pretty it is, I got the gown with the feathers because it reminded me of you with your birds, of how you've taken care of the babies and the hurt ones."

She let the gown stay on her this time, but she looked past him, shaking her head. "I'm smotherin', Docta, I feel like I can't breathe. Why'd you close the curtains, I need to see out—"

"It's dark, there's nothing to see."

"There's the moon shinin' on the water, I can see that."

"I'll open them if you want me to."

When she did not answer, he undressed and got into bed with her, switched off the light and pulled her to him, gently kissed her. But she did not respond, she lay perfectly still, and he released her and lay on his back staring at the window where, above the curtains, the dying light reflected on the ceiling.

"Henry's back," she said, and fear like electric shock shot through him.

"Here? In Asheton?"

"He was at the river; I took a baby swift that fell down the chimney into the woods to let it go and Henry come out of the woods and we talked. He says he been to Chicago, he says things is different up there, that black people can eat anywhere they want and go to picture shows and get jobs—"

"Don't tell me anything else that Henry Jerald says. Have you forgotten what he did to you, that he made you sleep with other men and give him the money? I can't believe you'd even speak to him."

She turned to face him, bracing on her elbow. "I got to go, I can't stand it in these woods no longer, if the devil himself come by I'd go with him. I'll go crazy if I see that sun sink in that water one more time."

"I don't understand what it is you want, what more you could ask for. You go places, over to Selma, you go to church—"

"I go to Selma to buy clothes I got nowhere to wear, I go to church to hear that Uncle Tom preacher tellin' all the sisters and brothers to knuckle under to the white man. That's some fun all right. I got to have me a *young* life—"

"You want to go to some Whiskey Alley and prostitute for Henry Jerald," he said bitterly.

"You got to quit worryin' 'bout me, you been so good to me I won't never forget you, I'd of died without you. But I got to go, I got to dance and walk down streets where there's lots of people and lights and music. Tell me to go, tell me you want me to be happy. I want you to be happy, that's why I haven't gone already. I got to make sure you're all right."

Her eyes burned into him, they were bright and piercing as if with a fever. And for a moment he hated her for telling him those things. She was all he needed, why could he not be the same for her? He wanted her to need him again, and the hatred was gone, he felt calm and certain that he knew what was best for her.

"I'm amazed that you don't recognize lies when you hear them, you're still a child—"

"Docta, *I'm thirty-five years old*! I got to be *free*, I got to be young while there's still time."

"We'll go somewhere, I'll take you up to Canada, we might even go to Europe, I understand Europeans are very tolerant of mixed couples, I'll divorce Jenny—" He stopped. He was making a fool of himself, he was deeply embarrassed for his begging.

"Hush, hush," she said. "I know you ain't goin' North, I know you ain't gon' divorce your wife to go with me. And I don't want you to, not anymore. I used to thirk you might do that, but it was a dream. You got to recognize lies too, Docta, the lies you tell yourself. You already gave up too much for me, and I thank you. I couldn't never repay you. But I got to go, I lie out here listenin' to this house creakin' and these walls feel like they're creeping' in on me, like they squeezin' out my breath. I got to have light and music, I feel like I got a jewel in me and I want to walk down the street and let folks see me shinin'."

"Tomorrow I'll find Henry Jerald and make him understand he can't bother you anymore. I'll have him arrested if he comes around here again. Then I'll figure out something that's fun for you, maybe get you a place in Selma where you can stay part of the time and go to the picture show, go shopping."

She left the bed and took her hairbrush from the night table, opened the draperies to the darkness and sat in the chair beside the window; her profile was reflected in the pane and she took a swatch of hair and held it over her shoulder, brushing the dark waves that fell almost to her waist. And he watched her and thought he would go home and pack and take her North, but knew that he would not. Whatever Jenny had done, they were bound together by long years, by their children—by their dead son. And he was bound to this land that was bred into his cells, into his soul. His ancestors had come into this flat, black land before the War and he could not leave it.

But Zella ought to go. She was right, she was still young and she was intelligent and there was nothing for her here. And she did have a zest, a radiance. But she was also gullible, she believed Henry Jerald's lies— he would have her prostituting again.

"You really are going with Henry?"

"Henry ain't the same. Henry's changed, he's gon' get a job and we'll get married. He wants me to go to school to learn to be a nurse or a teacher." She leaned eagerly to him, let the swatch of hair fall over her breast. "You could come to see me, I wouldn't tell Henry, we could go dancin'—"

He went to stand behind her, took the brush and pulled it firmly, regularly, through the tangled strands, and then she dropped her head forward, and he massaged her neck, for the tendons were tight and bunched, sweeping the strokes of his hands down her back, her hips, her buttocks. He pushed her hair up and kissed her neck, cupped her breast in his hand. Her head fell back, and he leaned over and kissed her, picked her up and carried her to the bed and knelt beside her, kissed her stomach and the mound of coarse pubic hair. She pulled up her legs, moaning and writhing, rotating her hips.

He climbed upon her, and their lovemaking was brief and harsh, the climax for him more like pain than ecstasy, and she turned over, her breathing almost at once deep and regular. But he lay staring into the night and watching a nearly full moon rise over the trees across the river. He slept, and when he awoke she was leaning over him, pulling at him.

"My head hurts, Docta, and I'm sick at my stomach."

He got up and picked up his clothes and went into the

bathroom that connected with the bedroom, and when he was dressed took the hypodermic syringe out of the medicine cabinet, opened a fresh needle, took the vial from his pocket. He went back into the bedroom and switched on the lamp, and she was sitting up, holding her head in her hands. He told her to lie down and turn over, he was going to give her a shot for the pain, the pills were upsetting her stomach. "I want my codeine," she said, and he told her the shot was better.

But he hesitated, the syringe poised above her hip. She was so thin, the buttock so childlike, so innocent, and he teetered on the edge of indecision—he almost flung away the needle, and then did not. The morphine was for the pain and nothing more, she deserved some relief, a good night's sleep. Maybe after she slept soundly she would be able to make a wiser decision about Henry. If tomorrow she still wanted to go he would not try to stop her. Quickly he plunged in the needle, released the fluid into her bloodstream, then lay the needle on the table and sat beside her until the worried lines between her eyes had smoothed and she slept.

He went to the window and stared at the light shining from Uncle Josh's cabin across the river, and he pictured the old Negro man lying in his iron bed alone, and thought how terrible to be blessed with long life and have no one at all to share it with. He took care of Josh and let him live free on the land where he was born and his parents and his grandparents. Josh went further back on this land than he himself did—Josh went all the way back to the slaves.

He pulled the draperies against the night and against Josh's lonely light, and he went to lie on top of the cover beside Zella, careful not to wake her, but she stirred and turned to him, lay her arm across his chest. He stroked her forehead and she said, "I feel so good, honey, so good." And he kissed her temple and thought that he could not lose her, he could not go back to being lonely again. After awhile he slid from beneath her arm and tucked the covers about her. He had only just remembered that he was supposed to be home at six o'clock for his birthday celebration, and he still had to walk all the way back to his car.

▼

It was nearly eight o'clock when he got home, and bright rectangles of light shone onto the front lawn. He parked the car in the graveled drive and felt a fleeting joy that the light was for him, that people waited for him. That they are still gathered for holidays and birthdays was Johnnie's doing, and she was the reason he came. She really loved him, and when she was little he had taken her almost everywhere with him; after he had sent Bird away they had turned to each other. He took her on rounds and to the office, and she was like Jenny, none of it bothered her, not the needles or the blood or the cutting. And he thought he loved her especially because Jenny hadn't. She wouldn't nurse her, he'd had to put her on the bottle, and Mary Betty took care of her as she had Bird. It wasn't that Jenny was ever mean to the child, it was that she was disinterested—disconnected.

Johnnie was four when he began to take her with him. She was always good and stood close to him, unflinching when he stitched up cuts and lanced old sores that spurted blood and pus. Sometimes he had to tell her to stand back, not to poke her head in so close. The Negroes laughed and called her "little Miss Doc," and he thought she would have made a great doctor, she had Jenny's nerve. If only she'd been a boy.

About a year after she was born he'd gone one midafternoon in late August to Byron West's hardware store. He had walked into the warm dimness and passed between the kegs of nails and faucet washers and hose nozzles. He had gone there for a screen for the back window of his office to replace the old one that had a hole in it, and he stood at the counter looking around for Byron, had even called to him. But no one was there; he stood in the silence wondering what it was a man lacked that he could spend his life dealing with such cold, bloodless merchandise. He had just turned to leave when he heard voices in the storage room, and he thought Byron had gone there with a customer. He went behind the counter and down the dark hallway, had just raised his hand to knock when he heard gasps and heavily expelled breath. Byron had had a heart attack, he was trying to call for help, and quickly he flung open the door, already planning how he'd get Bryon into his car, thinking who he could get to bring his satchel from the office.

They were lying naked on a stack of croker sacks. Byron covered her, her arms twined about his neck, and they did not move but lay like fallen marble statues of lovers. In the gloom there was no mistaking Jenny even if he hadn't seen her face, for her hair lay strewn like golden threads across the rough brown burlap. She looked up at him, her face shocked and turned dead white, and he backed away, shaking his head, denying what he saw; and then he was on the sidewalk in the white glare of sun; in the heat he was icy cold.

He went to the office and got a piece of cotton and stuffed it in the hole in the screen, and then he went and sat in his car parked in front of his office. He sat behind the wheel staring at the dash, unable to decide what to do, remembered that it was time to go on rounds and turned on the ignition but forgot to put in the clutch, and the car lurched as the motor caught and died. He had to think how to drive it, how to shift the gears.

He called on his patients, through a mist watched himself giving shots, applying bandages, scolding, comforting, prescribing. He went home at dusk, entering the house through the back door into the kitchen, where Jenny waited for him. She had sent the girls to Mary Betty's room, and in the electric light her face was white, her hair pulled into a tight bun. But she said nothing, gave no explanation or apology.

"If you are pregnant," he said, "I'll leave so you can be with Byron. I understand now what our problem has been, that you have always loved him and never me." Coldly, he noted the tears that glittered in her eyes, and also that her gaze never wavered, that her chin was tilted up. "If you go to Byron I'll take the girls, you can visit them but you won't ever live with them again, just as it's been with Bird and me. If you aren't pregnant, you can stay, but only for the children so that they can have the security of a family. But if you ever go near your lover again I'll divorce you." He waited, but she did not speak, the tears did not fall.

Heavily he climbed out of the car, the anguish of fifteen years ago still just beneath the surface. The passage of time ought to count for something, soften his feelings, mitigate the anger, but it had not. As he had sat in the car remembering, he had wanted to strike her down even as he had all those years ago when she would say nothing against his condemnation. If she had only said something, told him why, told him she loved him, he thought he could have forgiven her; but he took her silence for consent that what he had said was true. The subject had never been brought up again.

He walked across the yard and stood at the foot of the steps watching his children through the window of the living room. They sat as if they had been posed, the lamplight illuminating them softly so that their images were diffused, their features indistinct. The scene looked like an impressionistic painting, the twins on one end of the couch in clouds of lavender voile, their heads inclined to each other, smiling, whispering, as they turned the pages of a magazine. Short, yellow rippling hair fanned their round cheeks. Twenty-one years old and graduating from college next year, but still looking fourteen—still dressing alike, one person divided in two.

Johnnie sat on the other end of the couch, her pink eyelet dress billowed about her, her legs drawn up beneath it, but bare feet protruding. A love surged, for the dress was to do him honor on his birthday, she knew he hated slacks on women, and so for this day she had given up her loved jeans and shirt. But even for him she had not been able to manage shoes, and in her pristine loveliness and purity he hated himself for his weakness of Zella. With brutal honesty he knew that Jenny's sin did not excuse him or justify him. But Johnnie did not judge him, she had never mentioned Zella to him. And the town had not punished his family for her, at least not that he knew about: Jenny's Wednesday-afternnon study club met here once a month, the boys came around to see the twins and Johnnie. It was only him they hated, and he was grateful for that. He wondered if he could have given up Zella if they had punished his children as well as him.

He looked at Sarah sitting off to herself beside the fireplace, her hair the black cloud among the sunny fairness of the other three. It fell darkly shining just below the strong slash of her jaw, and in her starkly tailored white shirt and black slacks he thought she seemed like some dark stranger with no connection to any of them in that room. She looked like him, olive-skinned, tall and lean. And that was ironic, because she hated him.

She had been born in the morning, just as the sun rose, and as Jenny labored he thought it was a good sign that this son would be born at a beginning rather than an ending. At the moment the sun flung its rays into their bedroom, he lifted this dark girl from Jenny, she was squawling and waving her fists before her feet were out. God, she was so alive, so strong, he had had to do nothing but wipe her off, swab the mucus from her nose and throat. Her muscles were strong and taut beneath the washcloth, and as he examined the genitals, disappointment struck hard that it was not penis and testicles that adorned her.

He had kept his back to Jenny, knowing she would see at once his sorrow, and when, finally, he lay the baby naked beside her, she was laughing and crying, not letting him cover Sarah with diaper or blanket, but holding her against her, putting her at once to the breast, kissing the downy hair. He turned away, he did not think she had even looked at him, and he was bitter at her joy, it seemed somehow disloyal to that first child. And though he had hoped for a son each time the girls were born (such joy for that second baby when the twins were born, thinking surely, surely, it would be the son), somehow with Sarah it was the worst—it was as if she owed him maleness, she was to have been his redemption and had failed him.

By the time Sarah was thirteen, she was smoking and Jenny was buying the cigarettes for her. He was furious when he found out, he had told Jenny not to, and she'd listened without comment as he stormed about, then calmly told him that she and she alone would decide about Sarah. "She's my child," she said, "and don't you interfere, just as I don't interfere with you about Johnnie. If I don't buy Sarah's cigarettes she has other methods of getting them."

Sarah was rude and cold to him, and at fourteen and fifteen she was going with men ten and fifteen years older than she. And many times when he went for a haircut he heard them snickering about her, the men casting sly, sidewise glances at him to see if he'd react. But he just kept reading his newspaper and then went home and tried again, he told her she couldn't smoke under his roof and that she couldn't go out anymore. And she had looked at him the way she seemed to the morning she was born, as if she knew all about him and could see right through to the heart of him. And Jenny had come into the room and said he must have forgotten that the roof Sarah lived under was her—Jenny's—roof, left to her by her father, and Sarah could smoke and date whom she pleased. After that he marked Sarah off—he never said another word about what she did.

He looked now at the water color Jenny had hung over the mantel. Sarah had painted it, and it was of Mr. McKinley's old cornfield, grown up now in weeds and wildflowers. She had painted it as it was in the spring, bright blue forget-me-nots blooming in the undulating furrows beneath a washed sky, new-green leaves of the hardwoods smeared among the dark green of the pines. It was a happy picture except that a flock of crows was flying in at the horizon, turning the simple picture ominous and darkly portentous. The picture depressed him, and he wished Jenny had not hung it there, but then, of course, it was her house.

When he crossed the porch and entered the living room, the twins hurried to greet him, one on each side standing on tiptoe to lightly kiss his cheeks, and then Johnnie throwing her arms about his neck, squeezing him, kissing him soundly, her hair warm and sweet from out-of-doors. She was the only person who had ever loved him just as he was, accepting the whole of him, faults and virtues, without judgment. Even his mother hadn't loved him like that. And because she was unplanned (at least on his part), unexpected, she came with no burden of conditions or hopes or fulfillments of other people's dreams placed upon her. She was free as his other children were not.

Sarah glanced up from the fashion magazine that lay open on her lap, and when he smiled, she nodded and looked down again, and Johnnie hooked her arm through his and they walked into the dining room to where Jenny waited. She stood at the head of the table, and in the electric light she looked still young, her face smooth, unwrinkled. She was almost into her mid-forties, but she looked not much different than when she was a girl—still slim, her stomach flat beneath the slacks even after all the babies. She wore a shirt the color of cornflowers, and the intense color made her eyes more bright, more blue. Oh, yes, she looked much the same in the soft light. Except for her hair. She had cut it off the summer of Byron West. He had come home several nights later after he had found them to-gether, and it was cut almost to the scalp, a shining cap of golden curls close about her head. It had shocked him to the core, and he had stared at her, too stunned to speak. But he had never mentioned it and neither had she, but it was agony to him. It still was; it was a mutilation he still averted his eyes from—it was as if she had castrated herself.

Johnnie and the twins lit the candles while Sarah stood in the doorway watching, not stepping into the circle. And grimly he saw that Jenny had put all fifty-three candles on the huge white cake, always it had been a fetish with her to tell the truth about age. But he thought it would have been a nice gesture to have simply put on seven for good luck.

When each year of his life had leaped into flame, Johnnie flipped the electric switch, and they sang happy birthday to him while on the buffet gaily wrapped packages sparkled in the blaze of light, and the blue tallow of the candles melted and ran down onto the snow-white icing.

CHAPTER

9

Bird came into the examining room of his father's office at four
o'clock on Monday afternoon, and a fat Negro girl sat on the
black leather table, her head bent back. The doctor's arm was
wrapped around her neck like a vise, and he was probing stain-
less steel pincers down her throat. His sleeves were rolled above
his elbows, the white cotton shirt damp and clinging across his
back.

"Come over here, Bird, and help me," the doctor said. "Get
the flashlight out of my desk drawer and shine it down Sue
Ella's throat. Gertrude had to go down to Mrs. Logan's house
to take her some cough syrup, you know Mrs. Logan can't wait
for me to make rounds."

Bird got the flashlight and shone the round beam of light
down the girl's throat, and he saw a large, peg-shaped bone
sticking out just below her tonsil. Her large eyes rolled fearfully,
her hand fluttered toward her throat.

"Here now, Sue Ella, be still," Dr. Lasseter said. "If you
like fish you've got to learn to be a little slower about eating it,
stop gulping. Fat people always gulp; learn to chew your food
thoroughly before you swallow, gives you a chance to find foreign objects in the mouth like fishbones. And cut out eating so
much fat food, candy and things like that; every time I see you
you've got a Baby Ruth in your hand. Where do you get the
money to buy all those candy bars anyway?" When she grunted
and tried to speak he said, "Hush now, you're moving the muscle in your throat so I can't get hold of the bone, and if it drops
out you might suck it into your windpipe. Be quiet now, hold
still," and the pincers grasped the bone and when he pulled it
out a trickle of blood flowed behind it.

"There you are," he said, and proudly held aloft the bone for them to see. "Catfish."

"Brim," Sue Ella said.

"What?"

"It was a *brim* bone, Docta," and she grinned. "You don't know nothin' 'bout fishin'."

"Well, whatever. I don't eat river fish anyway and you ought not to either. The water's polluted from the paper mill over in Carden, they're pouring chemicals into the water and they've bought up most of the timberlard and cleared out the hardwoods to plant pines. Pretty soon the whole South's going to be one great pine grove."

"Yassuh."

"All I can do is tell you," he said, "the rest is up to you. Keep on eating river fish and you're going to have a whole lot more wrong with you than a fishbone stuck in your throat. You ever heard of mercury?" He glared at Sue Ella.

"Nawsuh."

He shook his head and sighed, handed Sue Ella a pan and told her to spit into it, then went and washed his hands.

Bird sat in his father's swivel chair at his desk, looked at the pictures of his children: Sarah, the twins, Johnnie, all together in a row, his beneath, and centered. And he felt a rush of love that he had been included among his children, and he watched his father as he went to the window and raised the blinds, letting in a burst of late-afternoon light, dust motes swirling like tiny golden suns.

"The river used to sparkle like wine," the doctor said. He was staring out the window. "Something's happening to our fair land. Oh, we don't really feel it yet, but we're going to. We're going to." He looked out into the hot and deserted street, his arms braced on the window sill, and Bird thought how big his father was, and how strong, black curly hairs covering the tight muscles of his arms.

"The storm is raging all about us, sit-ins and freedom rides and civil rights marches—strangers coming through here almost every day on their way to Selma or Birmingham. One of these days they're going to stop here and those of us who love our land had better try to ward off the trouble. We better start looking at each other, listening to each other, the blacks and the whites."

"Yassuh," said Sue Ella.

Bird saw the closed, guarded look come on the Negro girl's face, and he thought he never would have noticed that if he hadn't lived with blacks. He did not think his father saw it. But he, Bird, did not think anyone was going to talk to anyone; Asheton, Alabama, still ran on slave time—its clocks were a hundred years slow. There weren't more than a handful of people in this town who felt as his father did, too few to change anything. He expected that a hundred years from now Asheton would still be essentially the same—that is, as regarded the white man's attitude toward the Negro. Slave yesterday, slave today, slave tomorrow.

Sue Ella slid off the examining table and Dr. Lasseter said, "Go on a diet, Sue Ella, you've got to take off some of that weight," and she smiled and ducked her head, and Bird saw that she was embarrassed. He was amazed sometimes at how blunt his father was with his patients, and he wondered how someone so empathetic could also be so unaware: didn't he see the girl's pride in the straight set of her shoulders and in the haughty tilt of her chin? She wanted to be pretty or else she would not have wound the red ribbons into the braids of her hair that began at her forehead and ended in a thick, turned-under loop on her neck. And Bird thought she *was* pretty, with her round dark eyes and the tendrils of coarse hair curling about her face.

This was the enigma that was his father: he was compassionate and gentle with sick people, he would go for days without leaving a bedside. He would change the bed sheets and empty the bedpan, cook the food if there was no one else. Some people had told him that the doctor had simply refused to let them die, he would not have it. But for those who did not measure up to whatever standard he set for them, he could ignore, discard. It was as if they did not exist for him. He had done that with Sarah. He had done that with the Woman. It was as if he did not understand, or else could not accept, imperfection.

"My mama say she pay you when the welfare check come in," Sue Ella said. "We didn't get no welfare las' month 'cause the worker come and she found out Moleskin been comin' 'round—"

"*Moleskin*, what is he doing here? I thought he was in jail."

"He back. He say he gon' kill Mama if he ketch her wid anybody—"

"Don't tell me, spare me the details of Moleskin. Tell your mama to keep her money, the fishbone is on me. I'll just get me some corn next time I pass by your place."

"Mama kin spare the money the first of the month 'cause she don't buy nothin' from Mr. Miller no mo' 'cause on the first he raise the prices when he know she get the check."

"I understand, Sue Ella. Tell your mama what I said."

When Sue Ella had left, Bird watched his father pack his satchel, putting in ampules of penicillin and extra needles. "I don't see how I ever practiced medicine without penicillin," he said. "Damndest drug I ever saw, a true miracle. You'll see what I'm talking about when you start practicing. Old Man Ned Jones—you know, he lives in that shack out on the turnoff to the Selma road—he was dying one winter, it was in forty-nine or fifty, I forget which, sometime along about there. I was riding by one afternoon and I thought it strange no smoke was coming out of the chimney, and I went in. He was lying on the floor by a cold grate and wrapped in a blanket. He didn't know who I was, he was nearly dead, I could hardly get a pulse and I'd of hated to have seen an x-ray of his lungs. He had pneumonia, and I got him into bed and got the fire going and gave him a whopping shot of penicillin, and damned if the next morning he didn't look up at me from that raggedy old bed and call my name and tell me he was hungry. By God, he ate breakfast, too, ham and eggs and coffee."

He looked directly at Bird then for the first time. "My God," he said, "what happened to your face?" and he strode to where Bird was sitting, turned his face to the light.

"Coy Watson hit me yesterday when I went out there to work."

"He hit you? Why did he hit you?"

"Because I was talking to Faye Watson, I was raking straw and she called me and asked me to drink a glass of tea with her. I was sorry for her, she was lonesome, and after we drank the tea we fell asleep on the grass under the tree—"

"You what?" He straightened, glared down at Bird.

"We fell asleep, is there any law against falling asleep?"

"There is with Faye Watson if you aren't Coy. My God, what were you thinking of, I thought you had more sense than to pull a stunt like that or I never would have sent you out there. Fell *asleep* with Faye Watson?"

"We didn't do anything wrong, we just talked," and he stood up and glared back at his father, pushed away his hand that kept probing at the purple bruise beneath his eye.

"Here now, keep still, Bird, just be thankful the man didn't kill you. Have you forgotten Saturday morning so soon? The man would as soon kill you as look at you, would rather, I expect, knowing how he feels about things. He's been beating Faye ever since they got married; oh, she doesn't think I knew it until she got pregnant. Made up all kinds of stories to explain her broken hand and those bruises on her face and arms. I'd report him to family court if I thought she'd back me up, but she wouldn't. I don't know what makes women stay with men like that."

"I wasn't doing anything wrong." Bird repeated stubbornly.

"Since when did anybody have to do anything wrong for Coy Watson to go after them? He's insane, he ought to be in an institution. Stay away from him; don't ever go there again."

"Are you kidding? I may be lazy, and I may get sleepy, but *I'm* not crazy." They smiled at each other, the doctor shook his head.

He saturated a piece of cotton with witch hazel and swabbed at the bruise, and Bird said, "He kicked her when she crawled out from under the tree and it looked to me as though she was headed for her father's house."

"The lousy bastard, I better get out there as soon as I can and check on her, it's been sort of touch and go with that baby," and he dabbed harder at the bruises, said "here now, hold still," when Bird winced.

"I pushed him away when he kicked her, and he turned on me, that's when he hit me. I told him he better not touch me again or you'd have him arrested. I just turned around and walked off and he didn't try to stop me, but I was scared. I thought he was going to grab me any minute, but he went bellowing toward the restaurant yelling for Mrs. Watson. I felt really bad leaving her, but I didn't see how I could help her, he could chew me up and spit me out, he's so big. There were some trucks pulling in so I thought maybe they'd help her. He called me a white nigger."

The doctor slammed the cotton ball into the trash can. "You did the right thing, leaving, no sense in getting yourself killed. Faye's the only one that can help herself in the long run, but you should have come and told me, I ought to have gone out there to see about the baby."

"I didn't even think of it. I just went home and crawled in the bed and went sound asleep." He looked guiltily at his father. "I just didn't think of it," he said again. "I just wanted to sleep."

"Well, she's probably all right, I haven't heard from her. No news is good news. I ought to have him arrested for assault, I'm your guardian, but if I do he'll take it out on Faye. The man's dangerous." He looked hard at Bird. "I'm sorry you had this humiliation, but you understand that you brought this on yourself? Coy goes insane if any man looks at Faye, but most especially you. I ought to have sent you away like the tutor told me to years ago, she was right, only I wasn't seeing things straight then, and you've had to suffer. I was selfish, I wanted to keep you close to me. I let you believe...certain things too long. It was that *I* wanted them to be true."

He walked to the window, bracing his arm on the window sill again, looked into the street, and Bird wished his father had said he was going to defend him to Coy Watson and tell him his son was not a nigger. He went to stand beside him, needing to be close to him, and their shoulders touched as they stared into the dusty street.

"You ought to have known better," his father said, not looking at him. "You ought to have realized that even if Coy hadn't caught you with Faye, somebody would have told him. In this town people are always watching; believe me, I know what I'm talking about. They would have told him and he might have caught you out alone somewhere and killed you and no one would ever have known he did it. One day you might not have my name as magic words to protect you, I won't live forever, and I *have* to make you accept those things that will keep you alive."

"We didn't do anything, we just talked, we were lonesome."

He sighed and turned to Bird, his voice patient. "Don't be obtuse, son, you know what I'm talking about. You live in a dream world, and I know it's my fault, but my acknowledging fault isn't going to help you unless you accept what I tell you. The truth is that *by law* you are Negro—"

Bird turned away the horror of the words washing over him; his father had never called him that before. It was not true, one obscure black gene did not make him Negro. His father's hand was on his shoulder, turning him back.

"You have to stop pretending," and a bar of light from the Venetian blind fell across his father's eyes that were hard, unrelenting. "I stopped pretending the day I sent you to Emma Bonner, and I explained your situation to you then. I thought you understood. If you do not accept what is real you might destroy innocent people like Faye Watson. But you *are* my child, you are my child of the spirit, I have loved you with all my heart. That is what is real, what is true. And I also know what lonely is."

Bird turned from the window and the stripes of light and dark fell across his father's oak desk and across the pictures of his children in the silver frame, and the familiar room seemed somehow strange now, and fearful.

"I am not a Negro," he said, his voice barely heard in the whispering stillness of the antiseptic room.

There was a long silence, and then the doctor rolled down his sleeves and said it was time go on rounds, and together they walked out into the hot afternoon.

They passed a white, two-story house on the way to the blue Buick that was parked down the street beneath the cool shelter of a water oak tree. In the front yard, behind a low picket fence, a blond-haired child about two years old was playing in a sandbox. A Negro nursemaid sat beneath a tree dozing, her chin drooped onto her chest, her hand loosely clutching a bamboo fan. The doctor stopped and leaned across the fence, roaring, and the nurse screamed and jumped from her chair, flinging the fan into the air. Her hand clutched her chest over her heart. The baby squealed and laughed, clapped his hand.

"You are the beatenes' one man I ever saw, you are for a fac'," the woman said. "A grown man actin' like a chile, scarin' ole women, givin' 'em heart attacks."

She was a big woman and wore a white uniform, her gray hair braided across her head. She glared at the doctor, muttering, and went to pick up the baby who had begun chewing on a red plastic spade, sand caked about his lips. She wiped his mouth with the corner of her white apron, then settled him on her hip. "Some folks is jes plain silly," she said to the baby. "Some folks ain't got the sense God give little green apples."

"You're just mad, Cora," the doctor said, chuckling, "because I caught you napping when you're supposed to be watching the baby. That child could have eaten the whole box of sand and you'd never have known it."

"You ain't gon' tell Miz Garner, is you? I jes been dozin' fo' a minute, I ain't even hardly closed my eyes fo' you come by. I been up mos' all night helpin' Miz Garner wid Howard. He been real sick all week and she lyin' down now sleepin', an' I got to watch de baby. You ain't gon' tell Miz Garner?" She pulled the child's hand away from her braid.

"You know I'm not going to tell, Cora, but you've got to

stay awake and watch that baby, you hear me? He could run out into the street before you know it or choke on a rock—"

"He behind the fence—"

"You know that fence wouldn't keep him in, he can slip between the bars. What's the matter with Howard? It isn't the asthma, is it? He ought to have outgrown that by now."

"Nawsuh, he ain't outgrowed it, he couldn't hardly breathe atall las' night, the docta had to come from Selma and give 'im a shot, an' he say that don't do no good he gon' have to take him over to the horspital."

"But he's better today?"

"Yassuh, he better, the docta say it was Miz Garner puttin' that rug in his room, he say he told her not to put no rugs on that boy's floor to catch dust, but Miz Garner say she like things purty."

The doctor looked toward the house, his face pensive, thoughtful, and Bird thought he was thinking that once he'd been Howard's doctor, that he could straighten out Mrs. Garner's decorating notions. But he wouldn't get the chance because the young doctor from Selma was Howard's doctor now as he was for most of the white people in Asheton. Bird watched his father and wondered how he could give it all up, his reputation, his white practice, for the mulatto prostitute.

They drove to the edge of town, leaving the highway to wind through the narrow, deep-rutted roads into the colored section of cotton millworkers and sharecroppers. Because the doctor had to drive so slowly, dusty barefoot children ran ahead of the car yelling, "Yonder comes creepin' Jesus," and idly he blew the horn for them to keep out of the way. And he cursed the county commissioner.

"The man paves roads all over the place, every little cow trail, he puts in driveways for his cronies, but you think he'd put one drop of cement in the colored section? Hell, no. But you can bet he would if they could vote. One of these days it's going to do me a lot of good to see him have to go and shake black hands and ask for their votes, and believe me, that day's coming and it's not too far away. And he'll lose, the blacks are onto him, and there's lots more blacks in this county than there are whites."

They stopped in front of a two-room shotgun, unpainted board house where dusty zinnias and marigolds grew around the steps; on the ledge inside the front window stood two gilt angels with their wings spread, and they were blowing bugles as if announcing Judgment Day. At the end of the porch a man and a woman sat dozing in a swing, and when Bird and the doctor came up on the porch they roused, the man smiling and rising to shake the doctor's hand.

"Afternoon, Bill, afternoon, Thelma," he said. "I believe it's the hottest summer since nineteen fifty-two, when it didn't rain for two straight months. Remember? Remember the river dropped twelve feet and the slews all dried up?"

"Yassuh, I remembers, Docta," Bill said, and Thelma said, "Sho' did," and Bill said the doctor was certainly correct in his facts. And he offered them some lemonade, which the doctor refused.

"I came to see how your mother is, Bill, since she got out of Bryce."

"She doin' well as could be expected," he said. "She ain't really crazy, she jes old. Bubber the one sent her there and I ain't gon' let him take his turn wid her no mo', me and Thelma kin look after her all right. God as my witness, Docta, I couldn't stand to see my mama in there wid them folksies talkin' to theyselves and messin' in they clothes like they was babies. Bubber say Mama spooked him talkin' about hearin' voices, but she ain't nothin' but old, now that's a fact."

"You did right to bring her back," the doctor said. "It's only right for children to look after the people who raised them and cared for them. Do you know that at one time, back in the early forties, I was looking after nine old people whose own people wouldn't take them in? One old woman I brought back from Bryce after her son left her on the steps with a note pinned to her dress like an orphaned child. Abandoned." They all of them stood considering this, shaking their heads. "Is your mother in bed?" the doctor asked finally.

"Nawsuh," Bill said. "She sittin' by the winda lookin' out.

She sit there mos' all day lessen I bring her out here, but it be too hot right now."

"Hot weather is hard on old people. Keep her inside until after the sun goes down," and the doctor motioned for Bird to follow him, and they went inside.

Near-dark engulfed them, and the smell of beans and old grease hung in the close, heavy air; in a rocking chair by the window sat a small figure outlined in the diffused light that shone through yellowed lace curtains. Outside glowed the hard clay earth neatly swept clean of topsoil, and in the distance was the cornfield and the pines. Over the mantel was a royal blue velvet wall hanging of Martin Luther King and John Kennedy, and on the floor in front of the fireplace lay a small hand-braided rug of many colors. A vase of yellow plastic roses sat on the mantel on a white crocheted doily beneath the pictures. On the opposite wall was a sagging dark-green plastic couch, and on the other rickety wicker chair that faced a small television set. Through the door to the bedroom was a day bed spread with a colorless spread; a square of worn, flowered blue linoleum covered the floor. On the back of the door on a steel hanger were a few dresses and a man's black suit.

Bird shrank back as his father advanced softly toward the old woman, and he thought how he hated coming here. This was like a social worker's model house of defeat and hopelessness, and it would be repeated over and over through the afternoon. His throat closed up and his chest got so tight he thought he couldn't breathe; his father had told him he couldn't give in to feelings like that. He told him he had to concentrate on helping these people, they needed him. "If we don't take care of them, who will?" he said. "You have to learn different things dealing with the poor, they have diseases like pellagra and rickets, and I've even seen scurvy. And you have to treat their minds too; sometimes people get so discouraged they give themselves diseases, they lie down and will themselves to die. It would be more merciful if they put a bullet in their brains. That's why I wanted you to have this year with me before you go to school. You'll understand beforehand you don't learn half of doctoring through books and in hospitals—at least, not the kind we do."

"Jessie," the doctor said, leaning over the old woman and taking her hand. "It's Dr. Lasseter come to see how you are."

She looked up at him, her face shriveled as a coconut, framed with an aureole of white hair. "You come to take me back?" she said.

"No, no, Jessie, I didn't come to take you back. I just want to visit with you. You remember me, don't you? and Bird? I've been taking care of you for a long time, and Bird's going to school in Birmingham and he's going to take care of you too when he gets to be a doctor."

He sat his satchel on the mantel and took out his stethoscope. "I'm going to listen to your heart," he said, and as he lay the silver disc against her chest, she closed her eyes.

Bird watched, and he became the old woman, his skin was dry as an old leaf, the light passed dimly through his milky eyes, he saw people only as dark forms moving across his vision. His thin, clawed hand grasped the chair arms while somebody he only vaguely remembered and couldn't see touched him. He looked at her and thought that she had once been young, she had run and played and climbed the chinaberry tree outside the window and had gotten married and made love to her husband and had Bill and Bubber. But he did not believe it: that frail women had never made love; he thought that any moment she would topple from the chair and lie broken on the floor, delicate, vulnerable, like butterflies sometimes crushed by nothing more than a random breeze.

"Your heart sounds fine, fine, Jessie," the doctor said, and put the stethoscope back in his satchel. "Of course, you're not sixteen anymore, and I'm going to give Bill some tablets for you to take." He picked up his satchel and started for the door, then turned back. "Tell me, Jessie, do you still hear those voices that you heard when Bubber sent you away?"

"Yassuh," she said, "I does. I hears the voices, sometimes in the night they wakes me up, they come 'round my bed and plucks at my hair and they whispers to me that they's come fo' me, but when I tell them I ain't ready they lets me stay. Sometimes they come and tells me things to do, like go down and walk by the river 'cause that's where my mama and daddy be waitin' fo' me. Sometimes they tells me I got to cook supper fo' Abraham Lincoln, and when I was at Bubber's I use to put on some peas and salt po'k and set the table real nice fo' the president."

"I thought the doctors at Bryce had cured you of that," Dr. Lasseter said. "I thought maybe the doctors at the asylum had made the voices go away."

She laughed, shaking her head, covering her face with her hands. Then she looked up at him. "They couldn't do nothin' 'bout the *voices*," she said. "They jes mens, then cain't stop the voices 'cause they *spirits*, they wouldn't pay no attention to little old *doc*tas. Cose it might be they done *some*thin', because I don't do what the voices tell me no mo', I sho' don't," and she turned from them and parted the curtains to gaze toward the sky.

"What do you see, Jessie, what are you looking at?" Dr. Lasseter said.

"My eyes is watchin' fo' the glory-light of the comin'," she said.

They had just driven a short way up the road when a teenage Negro girl came running after the car, shouting and waving her arms. "Miz Wesson's havin' her baby," she said, leaning into the car window, breathing hard. Her eyes were wide with excitement. "I'm the onliest one that knows it, Mr. Wesson's out to the field and she be standin' on the po'ch hollerin' and screamin'. I seen your car passin' by awhile ago and I run to get you—"

"Well, I thank you, Rachel. The day had to come sooner or later, and I'm glad for Maxine to get it over with. You run out to the field now and find Mr. Wesson and tell him to come to the house, and then go tell Gertrude when she gets through at the office to come down here and give me a hand. Tell her to give you a couple of dollars out of the cash box for helping me."

He turned the car around and when they were back to the highway headed for the big stretch of bottomland that Frank Wesson farmed on halves for the county commissioner. Bird pushed the ventilator window out so that the air blew hard on him, and he leaned back and watched the landscape flash past like pictures on a wall: flat green meadowland where cattle cropped red clover in the long-shadowed afternoon; rows of cotton streaked between with black earth; a vacant, falling-down shack with rusted tin roof and covered with honeysuckle and blackberry vines; a Negro cabin where an old black man sat in a straight chair beneath a tree, a naked baby playing at his feet. And over it all, the azure stain of sky, the harsh, crystal glare of summer.

They turned off the highway and went down a long dirt road, parking the car beneath the trees near a whitewashed house. The sun glared off the tin roof, the slam of the car doors flat in the still air; from the open window came a floaty, airy moan as if a singer practiced scales.

They climbed the two wooden steps to the porch, and the sound came again, and the doctor flung open the front door, calling for Maxine. They walked into a room where the shades were pulled, the light leaking around the edges making a pale, eerie glow so that the heavy furniture seemed crouching, ominous. And then the sound came again from the room adjoining, and they went into a bedroom that was also dark except for the light of a small lamp set on a table next to a heavy mahogany bed. It was empty, the patchwork quilt thrown back.

"Maxine," the doctor called, and when she whimpered, they saw her crouching naked in the corner of the room, her stomach ballooning against her drawn-up knees, her breasts thrusting and huge. Her black hair hung limply about her shoulders.

The doctor strode over to her and she hit at him and bared her teeth like a cornered animal. "Don't you touch me, don't you dare touch me. ain't no man never gon' touch me again, I'm gon' kill Frank if I live through this—"

"Here now," Dr. Lasseter said, leaning to take her arm, but she jerked away, shrinking farther back into the corner. "You're acting like a fool, Maxine, you had as much to do with this as Frank did—"

"Did not! All that fucking was his idea, I never once wanted to, he forced me, and I ain't having this baby neither, and you kin git away from me!"

"You can't just decide not to have the baby, you're nine months gone and it's ready to be born—"

"*I* kin, *I* kin decide not to and you cain't make me!" and she crossed her arms over her stomach, but then a pain caught her and her face contorted, became mottled red, and she screamed.

"Come here and help me, Bird," the doctor said, and as Bird walked toward the huge mound of white flesh it seemed to glow in the dim room like a moon.

"Take her other arm, help me raise her," his father said, and when Bird touched her she screamed and tore her hair.

"My God, my God, somebody help me—"

"We *are* helping you, Maxine," the doctor said dryly, "if you will simply stop your hysterics; you're all right, you're just having a baby, it'll be over in a little while."

They raised her and she sagged between them; they half-carried, half-dragged her to the bed, and she turned begging eyes to Bird saying, "*He* won't help me, will you help me? I don't want to have this baby," and she dragged out the last word as a long moan.

When she was on the bed he stared at her stomach that looked as if it would explode, and he did not see how the baby could get out without splitting her in two, and he turned away because his sight was fading, walked toward a rectangle of light. Fresh air hit him as he went out the back door, and a dingy white dog with one liver-colored spot sidled up to him, wagging his tail. And then a scream split the air, and he ran across the yard and hid behind the barn, clasped his hands over his ears, but began to laugh thinking of the naked woman with the bursting stomach. He thought how funny she looked squatting in the corner, he thought he could never stop laughing, but then the tears streamed down his face.

He stayed behind the barn for a long time, then walked slowly toward the house. He was ashamed of his weakness, and he knew he had to go back inside and help his father, though he loathed with all his heart to do so. He had started up the back steps when someone spoke to him.

"Ain't no use goin' in there."

He turned toward the sound of the deep male voice that came from beneath a chinaberry tree. A man with black hair and in bibbed overalls and a faded blue workshirt sat in a cane-bottomed chair with his legs crossed.

"I have to, I'm supposed to be helping the doctor."

"The doctor's nigger nurse come down and they ain't no need of you; besides, warn't yore place nohow, warn't no place for a boy."

"I'm going to be a doctor, I'm the doctor's apprentice."

"Don't make no difference what you're *gonna* be, it's what you are now, and you ain't nothin' but a boy. Just sit down on the steps, the doc says it's liable to be awhile, this bein' her first and all."

Bird was glad to let himself be persuaded, and he sat down on the steps and petted the dog that came up to him tongue hanging out, mouth seeming stretched into a grin; it pressed its head upward against the affection of Bird's hand.

"I don't see why it has to be like that," Bird said. "I don't see why it has to be so terrible."

"Oh, pshaw, it ain't that terrible, most of it's just Maxine; you should've heard her when I busted her cherry, she yelled like a banshee, you'd of thought I killed her. Tell you the truth, it was worse on me than it was on her—I should've been the one hollering, a man's dick is a tender thing."

Bird looked toward the field where the cotton bloomed, and he was acutely embarrassed that the man revealed such intimate matters, he felt himself blushing, but Frank Wesson seemed not to notice, he leaned back in his chair, bracing it on two legs against the tree. He tucked his hands in the bib of his overalls.

"Not only that," he continued, "they have to have *some* pain because of their sin."

"Their sin?"

"Hell, yes, don't you go to church? The Lord requires it of

them, Coy Watson read us that in church yesterday. 'In pain and sorrow shall she bring forth children.' Something like that. That's what the Bible says. It's because Eve tempted Adam with the apple, made him eat it."

"How could she *make* him eat it? What'd she do, push it in his mouth and make him chew?"

"Shit, *I* don't know, that's just what the Bible says. Are you an infidel, son?"

"I guess I am if I have to believe that."

Frank nodded. "Well, I wouldn't argue with what you believe or if you have to believe anything. I'm not sure I believe that myself." He grinned. "A little far-fetched, ain't it."

They were silent, no sounds came from the house, and the shadows lengthened, deepened. And then Frank said, "You hear what happened out to the Kountry Kitchen yesterday afternoon?"

And Bird was suddenly afraid, and puzzled; what did he mean "hear of it", he *was* the "happening."

"Are you talking about what happened while I was cleaning up the yard?"

"You were there?"

"Yes—"

"Then you know about that bunch of niggers come in and sat down expectin' Coy to serve them?"

"No, I didn't know about that. It must have happened after I left."

"Well, it's all over town, I'm surprised you ain't heard it yet. Three niggers from up North somewhere and driving a great big car come in the restaurant and sat down big as you please and expectin' to be served. The way I heard it down to the barbershop was they come in and Coy told them what was what, told them to go around to the back door and place their order. Well, they did, only they didn't wait for their food, and they talked real mean to Coy, said it wouldn't be long before the *Nee*groes would be taking over and running this restaurant. Well, you know Coy, he took out after them with what they'd ordered and made them pay for it. I tell you, I wouldn't never want to tangle with Coy, he's mean as they come. Them niggers sat in at the wrong place that time."

So, Bird thought, that was where Coy was while he and Faye lay beneath the tree. And he thought how people like Frank Wesson forgot that he was supposed to be Negro and talked to him without patronization or using code words or phrases to get points across. Like that they knew it was Northern agitators coming down and stirring up trouble, and the Negro saying that was right, *they* certainly didn't want integration. Stock messages, stock replies. Stock lies.

But when they sat on their porches talking, or Jake and his friends at the table in the kitchen drinking, they talked of going to Birmingham or Montgomery or Selma to join the Movement. They talked of the men and women who gave importance to those places: Rosa Parks who wouldn't give up her seat to a white man on a city bus in Montgomery because her feet hurt; James Forman and Ralph Abernathy organizing, recruiting, leading marches; Martin Luther King, Jr., the preacher from Georgia who led the boycott that integrated the buses in Montgomery to protest Rosa Parks's arrest. Bird saw him on the evening news many times being taken off to jail, he had seen the dogs attack the marchers he had led. He would go to jail for a few days or a week or a month and then he was back in the streets again, leading some other march in some other place. L.L.J. That's what Jake and his friends called King as they sat around the kitchen table drinking white lightning. Little Lord Jesus. Black Moses sent to deliver his people into the promised land.

At dusk, a long piercing scream came from the house, and Frank jumped to his feet, cursing, began to pace beneath the tree, hands jammed into his pockets. "Well, by God, I wish she'd hurry up and git it over with, I got to feed and water the stock." He looked at the sky, measured the remaining daylight. But he looked at Bird with worried eyes, his jaw was clenched.

There came another cry, but this time bleating and angry,

and Frank strode from beneath the tree, grinning. He grabbed Bird's hand and pumped it. "Well, now, lissen to that, will you? That's a man baby's cry, them's some pair of lungs, ain't they? Got me a boy for sure, got somebody to help me git off this rented land."

The doctor came to the door and called to Frank, and Bird followed him inside; they walked hesitantly into the bedroom, and his father was washing his hands in an enamel basin set on a table at the foot of the bed. Gertrude in her white uniform, her head bound in a white cloth, was holding out a towel to him.

The room had a moist and musky scent, and Bird stood just inside the door watching as Frank went to stand beside the bed, not smiling now, looking down at the baby wrapped in a thin white blanket and lying in the crook of Maxine's arm. Her hair was wringing wet and clinging to her head.

"Come on over here, Bird," Frank said, motioning to him.

Bird went to stand beside him, and he kept his face poker stiff so he would not reveal his shock at this ugly creature Frank beamed upon. Its skin was wrinkled and scalded, its dark hair plastered wetly to a misshapen skull that had a soft spot in the middle and where he could see a fluttering pulse. Its mouth was pursed, now and then making sucking noises; it stretched its face as if trying to pull it from its wrinkles.

"It's a boy," Frank said, "I told you so, I could tell."

"A fine boy," the doctor said absently, drying his hands. "A perfect child."

Bird looked at him, his jaw dropping. He thought how awful for him to lie to them, he should tell them straight out that the baby was deformed. But his father's face was bland as he replaced his instruments in his satchel.

"We gon' name him after you, Doc," Frank said. "Ain't that right, Maxine?" and when she said that was right, they all turned to look at her, as if they had forgotten she was there.

Now his father would protest, Bird thought, now the time for evasion was past; he would never consent to having this poor being named for him.

"I'd be proud to have him bear my name," his father said.

"It'll be John Frank Wesson then," Maxine said. And she smiled at her husband, clasped his hand.

Bird looked at her in disbelief. Only a few hours ago she had been screaming her hatred of this man who stood beside her smiling, who had so offhandedly proclaimed her not only hysterical, but deserving of her agony. He did not understand, and it was something he would have to think about—ask his father about.

"I suppose you're mad at me."

"No," the doctor said. "I'm not mad. Why should I be?"

"Because I didn't help you with Mrs. Wesson. I just couldn't stand it."

"Well, that was natural. I've seen interns faint in the delivery room the first time. I gave her a few whiffs of chloroform and she got all right. She was even able to help after she calmed down. Besides, she won't remember the pain. They never do, it's nature's way. You know, nature would have to provide for that or else the human race would have died out long ago. Next year she'll probably be having another one. She'll want a girl to go with that boy. They're good people."

The car sped along the highway, and Bird stared toward the horizon where a sliver of pale moon was rising. "I keep wondering why they do it, if I was a woman I wouldn't ever have a baby."

"They do it because they like to. I've never seen a woman yet, black or white, didn't look like the cat that swallowed the canary after it was all over. Birth is a miracle; think of it, life where there was nothing at all. A human being, with a personality and hopes and dreams and visions, all of that already in that tiny body. You have to remember that just because it happens so many times, that doesn't take away the miracle. You'll see what I mean when you get used to it. Don't run from life, son."

There flashed in Bird's mind that night on the back porch when the sky was nearly solid with stars and fireflies swarmed in the trees, when he had learned of his Negro heritage. Had not his father run from life by accepting the world's—society's—definition of him whom he had taken for his son? Was that not a worse denial than his this afternoon when he was unable to accept Maxine Wesson's pain?

"I think I'll drive you on home now, Bird," his father said. "I'm bone tired, and there's nobody that can't wait until tomorrow. I was up all last night delivering Cattie Andrews' baby down in the flatwoods. I swear, you'd think the moon was full the way these babies have all decided to come at the same time."

But when they went around the curve, Wesley Turner stood in the middle of the road waving his arms, and when they stopped, he ran up to the car and stuck his head in the window.

"I was coming for you, Doc, Faye's at my house. Coy's been beating up on her again. She's pale as a sheet and she went to bed and she won't eat and she looks like she doesn't even know me. I've been on the porch all day with my shotgun across my knees, I was scared to leave because he might come looking for her—"

"Get in the car, Wes," the doctor said. "Let's go see about her, calm down. I've had my doubts about whether she was going to carry that baby to term."

"I don't want anything to happen to her, but I wouldn't care if she lost it, I never wanted to be granddaddy to that son-of-a-bitch's baby," and he climbed in the back seat of the car.

They parked in the dusty road up close to the porch, and Bird felt the hard knotting of his stomach as he had that afternoon at Maxine Wesson's, for as they went up the steps he heard low moans coming through the open window. He had not known when he got up that morning that this day was to be marked with the cries of women because of what men had done to them.

"Stay out here, Wes," the doctor said, "while I see about Faye. You keep that gun handy."

"Don't worry, Doc, if he sets foot on this place I'll blow his head off. If I was the right kind of a daddy I'd of already killed him."

Bird followed his father into the front bedroom and in the light that angled across the bed from the living room he saw a huddled white mound lying on top of the covers.

"Faye," his father said, touching her lightly on the shoulder.

At his touch, her eyes flew open. "Who are you?" she said. "Leave me alone." She pushed back on the bed away from them.

The doctor switched on the bedside lamp. Her uniform was ripped at the waist, her hair wild with bits of grass clinging; she was barefoot.

"My God," the doctor said. "My God."

Her eyes filled with tears. "I don't know who you are," she said. "Are you going to hurt me? Please don't hurt me."

"It's Dr. Lasseter, Faye, I've come to help you. You don't have to be afraid of me. Did Coy do this to you?"

"I don't know, I can't remember. I don't know where I am or what day it is—"

"You're at your father's house, and it's Monday night."

She nodded. "I'm at my father's and it's Monday." She smiled as if expecting approval.

"Yes, that's right. Now, lie back," and the doctor pushed her gently back onto the pillow. "You rest now."

"But I don't know who you are."

"I'm Dr. Lasseter, you'll remember me after awhile, just lie still and let me take care of you."

"I'm at Daddy's?"

"Yes."

"But I thought I was in the ditch, Coy's found me, he's going to hurt me some more."

"No, he's not, you're safe now, we'll look after you."

She rolled her head back and forth on the pillow, moaning as the doctor probed her scalp, his long yet blunt fingers moving over it inch by inch. "She needs her head x-rayed, she's got a lump behind her ear big as a goose egg, she's got a concussion, I'd bet on it. She ought to be in the hospital but I can't risk moving her."

Bird stepped back and looked away, anguished to remember how happy she had been yesterday when they sat talking beneath the willow tree, so laughing like a child having a tea party. Such an innocent thing they did, so without harm to anybody. And he thought if he only hadn't gone beneath the tree with her, this wouldn't have happened, he should have known better; it was as his father had said, he had hurt an innocent person.

She cried out, pulling up her knees, clasping her arms across her stomach, and the doctor took his watch from his pocket, observing the sweep of the second hand. Wesley appeared in the doorway holding the gun, barrel pointing upward, his face white.

"It's all right, Wesley, she had a contraction. There's no way of telling if they're regular yet, we'll just have to wait and see. Go back and make us some coffee, will you, then close and lock the front door."

He looked around for Bird, and when he saw him standing in the shadows he said, "Bring me a straight chair from the kitchen, Bird, and then you go on home. There's nothing you can do here. I expect you've stood about enough for one day. Just go by Gertrude's and tell her what's happened, tell her I probably won't be in until late tomorrow, if at all. If there's an emergency she'll have to send them over to Carden."

Bird brought him his straight chair, and as he left, turned to look back at his father who sat so straight and still beside Faye's bedside, one hand on her stomach, the other holding his watch. And he thought he ought to stay with him, he ought to try to be what his father needed. He wanted to tell him he was sorry for running away, but then turned and walked out into the night.

When he rounded the curve out of sight of the house, he was enclosed in the breathless night, and overhead the bright stars proclaimed an illimitable, terrifying universe of worlds far beyond the boundaries of Asheton. But for him, at this moment, reality was that small house and that room where a new life pounded upon the door of time, demanding to be let in, but too soon; and again he thought he ought to be with his father to keep the vigil. Instead, he went into the woods to lie awake the rest of the night in his magic place.

In the blood-red August twilight that shone through the plate-glass window of the barbershop the story spread from mouth to mouth like a children's game of gossip. It was embellished with repetition and increased in intensity. The window air conditioner that fit in the transom above the door circulated the air and blew back upon them the odors of sweat and hair tonic and soap. *Naked? Johnnie Lasseter? Faye Watson? Forced?*

"It's a lie," Mason Posey said. "The most preposterous bunch of hogwash I ever heard in my life. Bird Lasseter wouldn't do anything like that."

"Well, it's come from two different sources, one of them your own wife, Mason," the barber said, waving the straight razor. "Don't you believe your own wife?"

"Not so's you'd notice it," Mason said, and when the laughter died away the barber said, "Well, Maybelle's the one told my wife. She saw them buck-naked down in the woods." The barber was hollow-chested, pink scalp gleamed through thin gray hair. He was shaving the Garrett-snuff salesman from Marion.

"Maybelle exaggerates," Mason said. "Besides, what was she doing down in the woods to see them? We need to find out what she was doing there."

"Well, by God," the traveler said, "she was probably taking a walk. Ain't no law against a person taking a walk, is there? Have times got so bad a decent white woman can't take a stroll by the river at sunset? I'll take a white person's word against a nigger's any day."

"Bird Lasseter is no nigger, sir."

"Well, it's not only Coy's word we're taking, Mason," the

barber said. "Your wife saw the boy with Johnnie Lasseter. That's enough by itself. Where there's smoke there's fire. I've seen this coming for a long time the way Doc set that boy up making him out to be white. It's more his fault than the boy's, I'd say."

"I think we all know what Coy Watson is," Mason said. "Running that so-called cafe bootlegging place out on the highway, peddling dope and beating his wife in between times. How can any of you—" he leaned forward and swept the air with his arm to include the others who had only been listening— "take the word of a man like Coy Watson? I don't believe Bird attacked Faye and I don't believe Maybelle either when she said he attacked Johnnie Lasseter. Has anybody asked the principals involved?"

"All of y'all know niggers lust after white women," Bro' Abel said, leaning forward. They all turned to look at the heavy-jowled man who chewed on a twist of tobacco. "Bird Lasseter ain't white, though he purely thinks he is the way he struts down the street."

"Bird Lasseter walks down the street like everybody else. What you mean, Bro', is that he doesn't step off the sidewalk when you pass by."

"Well, ain't no use in discussing it with you, Mr. Lawyer, ever'body knows whut a nigger-lover you are, defending them nigger rapists the way you did."

The traveling salesman sat up in the chair, half the foamy beard shaved away. He glared at Mason through narrow, judging eyes. "We don't need your kind here," he said. "Why don't you go back where you come from?"

"I *am* where I came from," Mason said. "I was born in this town, sir, and my parents and my grandparents."

"Well, by God, you're a mighty poor Southerner," and he sank back into the chair.

"I think we ought to find out the facts, go to Johnnie and Faye and ask *them* what happened. Seems to me the parties involved ought to be consulted," Mason said.

"You're some hell of a white man," a teen-age boy with

yellow wavy hair said. He was reading a 1959 Christmas issue of *Life* magazine.

The men turned to look at him, but he didn't say anything else and the shop was quiet except for the rumble of the air conditioner. The street was deserted, for it was nearing the supper hour and the shops had closed. Only the barbershop stayed open late on Saturday nights and the men gathered there to talk. Tonight they had come specifically to discuss Bird Lasseter. The door opened, and in the surge of warm air Coy Watson walked in, his boots clunking against the wood floor. He sat down beside Mason.

"Well," he said, "what we gon' do about our resident white nigger? We gon' let him keep on attacking our white women?" He tilted his chair back against the wall, propped his feet on the rung. "He's pretty near broke up my family, my wife's left and gone to her daddy's, she's scared Bird Lasseter will come looking for her while I'm gone—"

"I wouldn't have believed that even you could lie like that, that you would have the *gall* to put out a story like that. I've talked to Wesley Turner, the whole town knows how you beat your wife, that she's lost the baby."

"By God," Coy said, thumping the chair to the floor and staring back at Mason Posey. "By God, I guess you're bound to take up for the white nigger because he takes you home when you're drunk and crazy—"

"Bird Lasseter is kind to me," Mason said. "And it's true, I do get drunk and that is my weakness, just as yours is that you are always too eager to commit violence."

They were all silent, unmoving. Late sun moved in to cancel the electric light.

"Well, now, Lawyer Posey, if you are referring to Otis Helms, he threw up his gun on me, there are plenty of witnesses to that fact. He got what was coming to him."

"And you're glad Otis pulled his gun. The truth is that you have no remorse whatsoever for having to shoot a fellow human being."

"Listen here," the barber said. "There's no cause to get

personal, either one of you. The way I see it, you're both right, we have to defend our way of life, defend our women. But on the other hand it might be we ought to do what Mason says, talk to Johnnie and Faye." He held the razor poised in the air, and gently the traveler pushed the barber's hand away from his throat.

"Ah, shit," Coy said. "I've already talked to Faye, she's half out of her head she's so scared, but ask the doctor, he admitted that Bird was under that tree with my wife, that they was lying as close together as nobody but a man and his wife ought to be."

"You want somebody to beat up because your wife's not available at the moment—"

"You shut your fucking mouth!"

They glared at each other, Mason and Coy, and the barber made clucking sounds, shook his head. "It's no use talking if you two keep getting personal." Coy turned flat, cold eyes upon him, and he resumed shaving the traveler.

"*As* I was saying," Coy said, "we got to put the niggers in their place before it's too late. Y'all heard what happened out at my place, how those three black bastards come walking in and *told* me it was the law I had to serve them. Well, by God, I guess I showed them." There was a general murmur of approval, Bro' Abel nodded and clasped Coy's shoulder, the teenage boy said "by God, by God." And Mason looked at him beneath half-closed lids and shook his head.

"What I want to know," Coy said, "is are y'all with me? You want us to make an example of the white nigger?"

"Hell, yes, I'm with you—"

"Me too—"

"I guess so," the barber said, but he looked at the floor, his expression frowning, doubtful. And then he quickly shaved off the last of the foam from the traveler's face, wiped it with a damp towel that he threw into the sink.

The saleman sat up, buttoning the collar of his shirt, tightening the knot of his tie. "I don't live here, but I'm with you. I live in Memphis, and let me tell you things have been rough up there, sit-ins and freedom rides. Can't go anyplace a bunch of niggers ain't shoving you around, we got to take a stand."

"Listen, men," Mason said. "Don't do anything until we talk to John Lasseter—all of us together." He looked significantly at Coy. "We ought to hear what he's got to say and we ought to talk to Faye and Johnnie. What can it hurt to wait one day. *One day!*"

"If we wait, Lawyer," Coy said, "you gon' be with us?"

"I will never be with you in anything. I'd rather die first."

"There you go," Coy said. "You heard what he said, he's just trying to give the nigger a chance to get away."

They all of them looked at Mason, considering.

"What is it you plan to do?" Mason said, turning to Coy.

"Hell, I don't have to tell you what I'm gon' do," Coy said, and he stood up and reached into his boot and pulled out a flask of white lightning. He pulled the cork, turned the bottle up and drank deeply, then passed it to the rest, who had also stood up, circling him. Mason still sat and was staring at the floor. The teen-age boy turned up the bottle, his Adam's apple in the thin, adolescent neck convulsing upward as he swallowed the raw-gut whiskey.

He coughed and turned red, and the men laughed and gathered around to slap him on the back. The boy was game, they said; he was one helluva fellow; they were proud to take him along with them to show him how men handled themselves. They strutted before the boy, drinking the whiskey, their faces flushing with excitement and alcohol. They drank until dark and then filed out the door, Mason following behind them down the sidewalk and begging them to come back, to reconsider. But they did not answer or even look at him.

Finally he became quiet, and the only sounds were the squeaking of bats swooping in the yellow circles of the street-lights and the heavy tread of their feet against the concrete. After awhile they crossed over to the dirt road that led into the Negro section, and a full moon, through the hot, thick haze of August, cast a sulphurous light over the tin roofs, the shadows of the houses black and angled. Now and then one of them coughed when dust choked in their throats, and then Coy would stop and take the bottle from his boot and pass it around. They left the road and cut between the houses to the alley where patches of yellow light shone from the windows.

The smell of hickory smoke and burned meat hung in the air, red coals still glowing in the dug pits where pork had been barbecued all that afternoon. The shadows of the men shot before them like dark searching fingers, their feet scuffed against the ground, the dust hanging about their heads, and they huddled close as they drank, their bodies sweating where they touched. When the bottle was empty, Coy tossed it into the parched grass at the edge of a field.

"Let's go—"

"Well, by God, where is it, which one's the house—"

"That last one there, that one with the built-on room sticking out, that's where the white nigger sleeps—"

"I insist on knowing what you plan to do," Mason Posey said. "If you hurt Bird Lasseter I'll go for the sheriff and swear out a warrant—"

"Go ahead, go for the sheriff," Coy said. "Chances are he'll come with us unless he's got a still to raid."

"Let's have less talk and more action," the teen-age boy said.

"If you go ahead with this terrible thing," Mason said, "I'll swear out a warrant against every one of you, your names will be in the newspapers, the whole state will know what cowards you are—"

"Shut the fuck up, you impotent son-of-a-bitch," Coy said. "Maybelle's told everyone down at the beauty shop how you can't get it up, so why don't you go on back home while we take care of men's business?"

They left him standing in the road and, crouching, crept up to the house, and up and down the alley the dogs barked, and then came a sharp yelp as someone kicked one of them that ran up to them. Like shadows they drifted up the steps and into the house, from inside came scuffling and muttered curses and grunts, the thump of flesh against flesh, the hiss of expelled air

from lungs; and then they were outside again and dragging a
dark shape across the porch and across the road, bare feet drawing wide, protesting lines in the dirt, the wildly thrashing
shadow projected by moonlight onto the dusty road.

Mason ran after them into the cornfield, the dark rope of
a snake whipping across the furrow in front of him; and then
they stopped in the clearing just outside the woods, striking
random blows across Bird Lasseter's face and shoulders, and he
struggled and kicked at them silently, but Mason yelling for
them to let the boy go.

"Mr. Posey," Bird cried, "go get my father!"

"Your father, *hell!*" Coy said, and kicked him to the ground,
and Bird lay with his legs drawn up and clutching his stomach.
"Thought you'd get away with trying to fuck my wife, didn't
you?" and he kicked him in the chest, and Bird sprang up,
screaming, and flinging himself on Coy so that they fell together
rolling in the dirt.

"Kill the son," somebody said, and all of them grabbed him
and dragged him to the edge of the woods, shoved him against
a tree and began to hit him and kick him. They held him while
Coy smashed his fist into his face and the blood spurted and fell
in great black drops onto the ground.

"Get your white-trash hands off me," Bird screamed, lung-
ing at him so hard it seemed as if his shoulders would rip from
the sockets.

"Don't have much respect, does he?" Coy said. "Shows how
bad he needs this. Take his shirt off, boys," and the men ripped
it off and turned him toward the tree holding his arms outstretched, winged shoulder blades almost touching in the middle.

Slowly Coy took off his belt, doubled it, slapped it against
his palm.

"Trouble with you, boy, is you don't know your place.
Therefore it is my duty to educate you. Living with white folks
confused you, a nigger's brain just naturally don't understand
that living white don't make you white. So it looks like we got
to teach you."

"Mr. Posey," Bird said. But he did not turn from facing the tree, the words only sighed into the hot, still air.

The belt hissed through the air like spit sizzling on a hot stove, it slashed across Bird's back and lay open the flesh, the blood darkly flowing. Mason Posey dropped to his knees and covered his face with his hands as Bird cried out, "You have no right, you *have no right!*"

"Oh yes, we got every right," Coy said. "You got to learn a nigger's place," and he slashed the belt across Bird's back again. "When you tell me you're sorry for what you done and that from now on you understand your place, you can go back home."

But Bird held his head high, his shoulders stiff and straight, and the only sounds were his harsh expulsions of breath and the *hiss, thunk! hiss, thunk!* of the belt. And of Mason Posey's sobbing.

The blows became more frenzied, more vicious, and finally Bird's head sank against his chest and he sagged onto his knees, and the barber said, "That's enough, Coy," but when the blows continued, he stepped forward and grabbed the arm that held the belt. "No use for that kind of abuse, Coy, we only wanted to scare the boy, not kill him."

The men turned Bird loose and he pitched to the ground.

"He's fainted," someone said.

"He's dead, I didn't come here to kill nobody—"

"Let's go—"

"By God, by God—"

They ran from the clearing, crashing back through the field; but Mason still knelt, hands clasped over his chest; and then he rose and followed them through the broken cornstalks, following the path they had made. And the white moon, straight up in the sky, shone onto the crumpled figure that did not move and made no sound.

Music, hollow and rippling, awakened him. But he did not open his eyes to the ringing of the silver breakfast bell. Mary Betty was calling the family to breakfast, but he was not hungry, and he was so heavy he felt as if he could never rise, as if some enormous weight held him down.

He shifted, squeezing his eyes against the throbbing pain in his head, and when he moved, water flowed over his arm and shoulder. Water was in his bed, and alarmed, his eyes flew open, and in the gray light could not position himself in place or in time: he was sprawled on his stomach with his cheek resting on a patch of packed wet dirt, his legs angled downward into cool water. He looked upward, and in a faintly luminous sky saw a pale star, but whether of the evening or the morning, he could not tell. Birds twittered, and light mist rose from the water, and because of the mist he decided it was morning.

But where was he? He lay in the dark green shelter of huge pines that touched the sky, and felt separated from the earth and drifting, as when he swam through deep water. He needed to see farther, but when he pushed himself up, the earth rocked and pain shot through his head, and he fell back onto the ground, vision fading. He trembled, his teeth chattering, brackish water seeping into his mouth.

He lay until the sun rose, and then, digging his fingers into the ferns that drooped over the bank, hoisted himself up and crawled through the whirling, tilting green world until he reached the sunlight shining down through the circle of the pines converging on the sky. He rolled onto his back, unable to focus his eyes, trees and sky blurring together; his stomach convulsed, and sour, burning bile heaved into his throat, and he turned his head to the side so that it ran out of his mouth and down his cheek. When the heaving stopped, he scooped pine straw over himself trying to get warm, but still he shook so violently he panted, his breath coming in short, hard gasps.

Consciousness faded, and when he came to, the sun was on the westward slope, and through the aperture of treetops a white mass of angels gathered, hovered over him, their robes rosy-tinged with sunset. And as he watched, they shaped themselves into hawks that swooped down on him, and he cried out, flailing his arms, and gradually they flew away, trailing bloody wisps of clouds in their talons.

His throat burned, his tongue was dry and cleaving to the roof of his mouth. Down the slope, water sparkled in the day's last burst of light, and in its flowing against the rocks it called to him to come and drink. But he was too heavy to move again, for some fierce and terrible gravity pinned him to the earth; on the horizon a white moon rose round and flat as a plate.

He slipped in and out of sleep, and once, awakening, thought Johnnie lay naked beside him, her skin pocked with moonlight, and joyfully he reached for her, but she leaped up and dissolved into a man who cavorted about him shaking a club, and he moaned and closed his eyes, wrapped his arms about his head.

As the night advanced he grew hotter, seeming to radiate heat, and he pushed the pine straw away and was cold, then heaped it back again, for the gentlest touch of breeze made him tremble. Yet his mind seemed to grow sharper, his skin acutely sensitive, he felt the blood flowing through his arteries, in his veins, it throbbed in the soles of his feet and in his fingertips.

Shadow monsters crouching beneath the trees leaped at him, grotesque white faces loomed out of the dark, and he cried out, hitting at them; he saw his spirit, shimmering and opaque, on a tree limb watching him while the branches of the trees mourned over him: soul and body had separated, and he closed his eyes, heard again the tramp of feet running across the porch and the men dragging him from his room where he had sat at his desk writing. And he saw Mrs. Bonner in her long gown hitting at them, and them shoving her aside so that she fell across the bed; they flung away his notebooks, ripping out the pages, and dragged him from the house.

They had no right, they had no right, and their voices, thick with hatred, screamed *nigger.* He wept, not wanting to live, and knew only then that he was in his magic place and that he had come there to die; he closed his eyes, accepting death.

He heard angels singing, and thrills of joy skittered up his chest and down his arms and legs. He was in heaven, and he opened his eyes to gaze upon its jeweled halls and saw, instead, walls of leaf and bark. So he was still of earth. But what was the singing and the rippling joy on his skin? He raised his head, and in the gray light saw three deer mice playing on him, their velvet feet soft as pattering rain. He did not believe them, he thought they were from his fever, and suddenly, in the dead-silent dawn, they rose on their hind legs and sang a high, trilling note that trembled and slowly faded. Their tiny bodies vibrated, their white stomachs glowed faintly, and in that half minute he saw the earth as it must have been in its innocence, that time when man and animal lived together, trusted each other. In that half minute evil had been held at bay.

And then they left, all at once and together they skittered across his shoulder and down his arm, disappeared beneath the leaves as if they never had been. Slowly he lowered his head, and wandering tendrils of fog drifted over him. There came then the music of the river. He thought that he had dreamed, that the mice had come from dreams, but knew they had not: they were nature's compensation for his suffering, a balancing of the ledger, an evening of the score.

He had seen deer mice before, when he had lain reading or drowsing for a long time beside the river. Sometimes they came at dusk to play, the mud on the bank patterned with their rosebud prints, and those that had come this morning should have long been back at their nests, for they were nocturnal. He used to climb trees when he was little to look at baby birds, and many times found instead, in the flimsy beds of sticks and straw, hairless pink mice. That they sang he knew, he had read of it, but it was so rare as to be almost unheard of—anyone who knew about such things would never believe it. And he did not care, for he knew it was meant only for him—his agony had demanded a miracle for him to live: the mice had come to prove his innocence.

He listened to the birds twittering themselves awake and to the lizards rustling the grass and in that suspended dimension of time between dawn and full light, when the earth seems to stand still, he thought he also heard the shifting of rocks in the mud on the riverbank, and that it was true what Mrs. Bonner had told him once when she had taken him fishing at daybreak. *Sometimes, when ever'thing's quiet and still, if you listens real hard you kin hear the rocks move jes a little bit. Some folks says in de dawn dey got life.*

He slept, and when he awoke the sun lay across him, but from the western sky, its rays shredded through the pines. With great effort he pushed to his feet, and the world tilted, then steadied; his legs barely held him up, but he could walk, and he went slowly to the pool, knelt and drank. And the fluted voices of the birds called from the deep woods.

He stood in the dark of his father's office, and the sweet familiarity of the squeaking hinges of the door, the floor with the paint worn into a trail from the waiting room to the examining room, the cotton poked in the hole of the window screen, filled him with such joy that tears came to his eyes. He longed for the scolding he was sure to get along with his shot of penicillin—he was a child again, he had hurt himself, and his father would comfort and heal him.

As he stood just inside the door, it seemed for a moment the end of an ordinary day, and that he had merely stopped in to visit for awhile. Enclosed within these walls, he was back to where he was before the beating—he was Bird Lasseter, cherished son of Dr. John Lasseter, and he walked toward the bar of light that fell through the partly opened door that led into the examining room and the office.

His father stood beside his desk counting the day's receipts. On the desk beside the stacked bills lay a gun, and Bird thought how easy for someone to slip up on him and rob him, he was so absorbed in the counting. He delayed going in, savoring the shape of his father, the broad shoulders, the noble shape of his head.

"Father," he said, and the doctor whirled, his hand flying toward the gun, his face draining deadly white into anger.

"By God, I didn't think you'd have the gall to come here," he said, and Bird took a step toward him, terror washing over him.

"Father," he said again, stretching out his hand and advancing, not understanding, and then the doctor struck him across the face, and he fled backward, crashing against the wall.

"They ought to have killed you; by God I would have strangled you with my bare hands if I could have found you."

He stared at his father, whose face was white as the moon
that night outside the cornfield, and he put up his arms to shield
himself, for his father leaned toward him, seeming ready to
spring on him.

"Why are you mad at me! I didn't do anything to you—"

"*Didn't do anything to me!* When you hurt Johnie, you
hurt me—"

"I didn't hurt Johnnie, I didn't do anything to her!"

"You have disgraced an innocent girl, you've ruined her,
and I trusted you. I trusted you."

"Father, Father," he said, anguished, and he stretched out
his arms.

"Get back, get away from me, don't come any closer or I'll
kill you," and his hand clasped the gun, though he did not raise
it from the table. "You are disgusting, you are loathsome—"

"I didn't do anything, I didn't hurt anybody," and he began
to cry, dropping to his knees, covering his face with his hands.
He waited for, hoped for, the bullet that would smash into him
and release him from his shame and from the hatred in his
father's eyes. Through his tears, through the cracks of his fingers, he saw the scuffed brown leather toes of his father's boots.

"How could you hurt someone so pure and so innocent?
I've protected you and now you've betrayed me."

He looked up and his father stared down at him as if he
were someone he had never seen before, and this was more
terrifying than anger or hate. "I don't know what you're talking
about, I have never hurt Johnnie, why do you think I would
hurt Johnnie? I love her—"

"Don't say that to me, don't even speak her name, you're
not fit to be in the same world with her, pulling off her clothes,
seducing her."

"I didn't, I never did, she—" He stopped and slowly rose
to his feet. "Did Johnnie tell you that?"

"No, by God, Maybelle saw both of you naked in the woods,
she said you were chasing Johnnie. I ought to kill you," and his
jaw clenched, his hand still tight about the gun.

"We were playing, nothing happened. It was a game."

"My God, man, how old do you think you are? A brother and sister can't go running around the woods naked like children."

"She's not my sister."

Suddenly the fury drained from the doctor's face, and with the anger gone Bird thought he looked old, the flesh drooping around his mouth.

"No, she's not your sister. I keep forgetting." Slowly his fingers released the gun. "Don't you know I understand that your life's unnatural? I remember being seventeen and how strong the urges are. Until you accept who you are you can't have a normal life; you ought to be with girls. But you *cannot be with Johnnie!*" His face was hard and unyielding as stone.

"You want me to find some nice Negro girl?"

"You're every bit as prejudiced as Coy Watson or those men that took you out and beat you. I'm sorry, but I can't even pity you right now because in your own way you're as bad as they are. And you can't even have the satisfaction of telling me I don't practice what I preach. If I could live my life over I'd marry Zella. You ought to go to Meharis, you'd meet women there you could respect, you'd see Negroes aren't all ignorant, downtrodden sharecroppers."

"I'm not going to Meharis, I'm going to Birmingham. And you believe what Maybelle says without even asking me. How does she know what Johnnie and I do anyway?"

"She walks every evening before bed because she has trouble getting to sleep. She said the other night she decided to walk by the river."

"So far from her house? That's more than two miles."

"That's what she said."

"She was spying because she hates me. When I take Mr. Posey home she tries to get me to do things I don't want to do."

"Like what?"

"She cooks strange food and she tries to get me to go in the ballroom and dance with her. Last time she made me touch her."

"Touch her?"

"She put my hand on her breast." He could not meet his father's eyes, and he looked past him out the window. How terrible to have to confess such a thing. Something he had done had made Maybelle think he wanted to dance with her, touch her.

"She just took your hand and put it on her breast? And you let her? That's hard to believe."

"It just happened before I knew it, I've been trying not to go inside but you told me I had to help her."

"Well, how in hell could I know what was going on? Why didn't you tell me? All this could have been avoided."

"I started to once, but then I didn't, I was ashamed."

"I wish you had told me, I could have talked to her. I wish I had known you and Johnnie were meeting; she says it's been going on for a long time. I ought to have suspected, I blame myself for being so blind. She was so sad after you left and then suddenly she was happy again and I know now it was because of you. I had thought she'd finally adjusted. I've got to send her away now, off to school somewhere. There's nothing else for it."

"Please don't," Bird said. "I'm sorry, it's not her fault, don't punish her because I was so lonesome."

"You don't have to be lonesome. I know there are fine colored people in this town who would like to be your friend if only you'd stop acting like you're better than everybody. All this talking and explaining hasn't made any impression on you at all, has it? How come I'm doing my damndest to accept and you won't make any effort at all?"

"Because I will never accept that I'm supposed to shuffle and grin and confine myself to the Negro race. Maybe I will marry a Negro, but not because you tell me I don't have any choice. It's so easy to tell somebody else what they ought to do because it doesn't affect you. Coy Watson's not going to take you to the woods and beat you if you speak to his wife."

"Well, I've tried and my conscience is clear. But you're going to have to learn the hard way because you're hardheaded. You did more than speak to Coy's wife. I think even you'd have to admit that didn't look right, falling asleep with Faye. Race wouldn't make that much difference to Coy where she's concerned."

"That didn't give him the right to beat me."

"I didn't say it did. But the fact is that in this town a Negro cannot be with a white woman. You have to accept that and go on from there."

"Have you seen me with any white women?"

"Just my daughter and Faye Watson, that's all," the doctor said dryly. "We can't have our plans anymore, you understand that. If I could have foreseen this day that morning in the woods when I found you, I would never have taken you home with me. That act led up to this night, and I'm deeply sorry. But that's water over the dam, and what we have to do now is make a clean break. You have to leave here, go someplace and start over, go to a trade school, find yourself a job. There's no future for you here."

"You won't stand up for me to Coy Watson and to those men who helped him. You're on their side."

"That's not so. I'm trying to save you. You have to understand the realities of your life. You can have a good life if you will learn from what has happened. And I hope you will forgive me for the part I've played in making your life hard. I was selfish."

"Right now all I feel for you is hate. You wanted to kill me just like those men did, why didn't you? What have I done except get born?"

They were strangers now, wary and suspicious. Bird felt his old life breaking away—soon he would leave this room forever, where on the pale oak desk stood the yellowed, eyeless plaster-of-Paris man who so impassively bared his entrails. Next to him was the typewriter where all these years his father had pecked out prescriptions with two fingers, and next to that the pictures of his children; only his own was gone from the silver frame, the cardboard faded around the blank rectangle—if he looked in the wastebasket he knew he would find the shredded remnants of his image. Childhood's death was bitter on his tongue, and yet he did not feel a man, he seemed to dwell in some sort of limbo between the two. He was bereft of all whom he had loved, he was empty, hollowed out, as if his father had taken his curette and scooped out his insides.

He turned to leave, and at the door looked back, and his father was standing with the light behind him, tall, implacable, the gray in his hair reflecting the pale light of the crookneck lamp so that his head seemed haloed, and Bird loved him again, sorrow tearing through him that when he went through the door their lives were forever separate. He wanted to cry, to lay his head on the broad cotton shoulder and feel the heavy comfort of his father's hand on his head.

"For awhile you were my father and you did love me."

Compassion darkened the doctor's eyes, then faded. "My love makes you weak, and if you are weak they will kill you. You have to be strong and be what you are. And that is the plight of us all."

He went back to the woods and lay down beside the river, thinking *he did not even ask to see my wounds*, thinking *twice now he has rejected me*, and as he shot off into gray oblivion, wondered if he could survive alone and without love.

He lived beside the river, lying on the bank in the sun, and the healing, protecting mud caked in the gashes; he drank the muddy water for medicine as he had read the Indians had done. And, also like the Indians, he caught small bass with his hands, trapping them between the bank and the tangled roots of the willows. He found flint, and after much practice was able to light a fire from pine straw and twigs and roast the fish on a stick. After a week, his wounds were healing and covered with thick, tough scabs.

At dusk of the eighth day, Johnnie came; he was wading in the water catching fish, and he saw her shimmering reflection in the green water of the pool. Quickly he looked up, and she was there watching him; his heart began to race with fear and gladness, and then she reached her hand to him.

"Leave," he said, and her hand dropped away. He did not

know if she was real or if he imagined her, but when he closed his eyes and opened them again, she was still there.

"I love you," she said.

"Don't love me. Go home." He freed the small wriggling fish he had held in his hand. "Don't ever come here again."

"I love you and I will always love you." She walked toward him.

"Get back, don't come closer. We can't be together anymore." Those were the words his father had said to him, and like an inheritance, he passed them on to her. And whom would she pass them to, whom would she tell they couldn't be with her anymore? And a great sadness came over him that people who loved each other couldn't be together.

She stood beneath the tree, and in the dying light her face was bleached white, sorrow drew her face into lines of age so that she seemed old, an ancient goddess too wise and too suffering. His heart wrenched with pain and with love for her.

"We have to grow up, Johnnie, we can't play games anymore."

"Loving you was never a game—"

"It *was* a game, that's all it could ever be for us. If I could touch you I would shake you until you understand that we're not children."

"Because we got big we can't love each other? That's stupid." Her mouth drooped at the corners, her chin quivered. "I will always love you."

"And I will always love you. But we can't be together, they won't let us."

"We can go away, we can go somewhere they'll never find us."

"Hide our children in a slave cabin?" He smiled, but with tenderness and with longing.

"Don't make fun of me."

"I would never do that. But you have to forget me."

"How can I live without you? I love you."

"I'll show you my back, maybe that will convince you that next time they will kill me."

"I don't want to see it, and I won't listen to you anymore. It doesn't have to be like this, we don't have to do what they say, we can find ourselves another magic place far away from here."

"Listen to me!"

"I won't!" She clapped her hands over her ears.

"Take your hands down, Johnnie!" Slowly her arms dropped to her sides.

"We cannot go away together, we cannot love each other—"

"I *will* love you—"

"You have to go home and never come here again." His voice was weary with patience, but he wanted still to hold and comfort her, tell her they could be together. But he would not bring her into his torment.

"You don't love me anymore," she said. "I see it in your eyes. If you did, you wouldn't let anybody keep us apart."

He looked over the water toward the horizon where towering dark clouds edged with sunlight were building, and he was not aware of when she left, but only that she faded as the light failed; and he could not look directly at where she had stood, for the spot was agonizingly lonely.

She would not come again, and now all he had left of her were memories, electrical impulses shooting images of her to his brain. He held his hands out before him, looking at the fingers that once had wound in her hair, that had touched her face and never would again; in sorrow he cried out against his chosen solitude.

He left the pool and walked through the brittle straw to lie in the place where she had stood, the crickets quieting, the tree frogs trilling coming rain; late in the night he woke to the rain pounding on him heavy and warm, flooding up from the saturated ground so that he thought he might be swept into the river and washed away on the currents into some dark and velvet forgetfulness.

The dusty days of late summer passed into fall, and he lived between woods and house, and Jake didn't say anything, but just looked at him with pitying contempt. The first night he came back home, Mrs. Bonner had held his hand to her cheek, her tears washing over it, saying, "Po' little baby, po' chile," but he did not want her pity, he wanted only to be alone in his room, but could not hurt her feelings. And so he had stood patiently waiting for her grief to slacken, then pulled gently away from her. She gave him a small package wrapped in tissue paper that his father had left with her to give to him, and he sat at his desk and opened it, sat staring for a long time at the stack of money—fives and tens and twenties, wrinkled and limp and musty, the smell of dirt and sweat caught in them. It was two thousand dollars, he counted it twice, then wrapped it up again in the thin paper, retied it with the string, and put it in the bottom drawer of his desk beneath his journals. The money made it real as his father's words never could have, that their relationship was over; it was conscience money, get-out-of-town money. His father could now truly forget him, put their life together behind.

At first he thought he would rip the wrinkled bills into shreds and fling them into the river, and by that act he would also be free. But then he thought he ought to keep it, it would help him in his plans for medical school—not his father, not Coy Watson, not one thousand Coy Watsons could make him give up his plan that one day he would again live white, that he would be what he was. He was still enrolled in pre-med at the university in Birmingham, he had passed his high-school equivalency, won his partial scholarship. All that was still his no matter who beat him, no matter who disowned him. He would go ahead with his plans as if nothing had happened, and he would take the two thousand dollars and be glad for it. It wasn't nearly enough, even with his scholarship, to cover the first year, but he would earn the rest.

Wesley Turner hired him to help pick the cotton, and he didn't say a thing about what had happened, but Bird knew how he felt, in the deep sympathy of his eyes, the hard line of his mouth. At night they'd sit on the porch before Bird went home, and Wesley told how Coy had come night after night to see Faye, his Bible pushed up under his arm and how he'd cry and read scripture, begging her to come back. He said a woman was supposed to leave mother and father and cleave to her husband.

"By God, I'm glad she lost the baby," Wesley said. "I never wanted my blood mixed with that hypocritical bastard's."

He'd light a cigarette and prop his feet on the banister and say he wished he'd had the guts to shoot the son-of-a-bitch because then Faye couldn't have gone back to him.

Bird worked for Wesley through the long hazy days, and when cold weather came, helped plant the oats and rye. One brilliant, starry night some men came in white robes sometime after midnight and burned a cross down in the woods back of Wesley's place and scrawled in black paint across his barn *nigger lover*. Calmly, Wesley painted over it and said you had to consider the source, and when Bird said he wouldn't work there anymore, Wesley said, "Son, the world's full of fools. Let's just you and me rise above it. Don't mind what they call you, it's what you think of yourself that matters. And that's part of their problem, they realize you don't have any problem with self-esteem." Their eyes caught, and they smiled, and Bird started staying at Wesley's nights too, he was too tired to walk the long way home. Some nights he'd fall asleep at the table waiting for Wesley to put his beans or soup or rutabagas in front of him, and then Wesley would gently shake him awake and he'd go sleep in the front bedroom where Faye had lost the baby.

Bird gave part of the money he earned at Wesley's to Mrs. Bonner because his father wasn't giving her any, but he saved part of it too, adding two hundred more to the two thousand his father had given him. At night he sat on his bed and counted it, stacking the bills as his father had done in his office, and he was amazed at his pleasure in what he had earned himself. And as time passed he got so he didn't mind the work so much, he didn't get nearly so tired, he didn't jerk himself awake as he had in the beginning, when his muscles had ached so bad. The blisters in the palms of his hands turned into calluses, and he became leaner and harder. He took his shirt off and admired himself in the mirror, flexing his biceps, turning sideways and rotating his fists to make the muscles pop up in his shoulders and upper arms and, forgetting, thought how pleased his father would be.

As the weather turned colder and there wasn't anything left to do in the fields, when he knew Wesley was giving him jobs he could as easily have done alone, like chopping wood for the fireplace and shucking corn, Bird knew it was time to go. Besides, a restlessness had come upon him, a longing for something he could not define. He thought at first it was that he missed the woods, that he missed sleeping to the sound of the river, but then one morning when he awoke in Wesley's front bedroom and looked out onto the bleak landscape he knew what it was: he wanted to get on with his life, he was tired of marking time. He wanted to go on to school and get his degree so he could go North. Nothing was left for him here, Johnnie was gone, he'd stood behind a water oak tree and watched the bus pull away from its stop at the drugstore. Her father was the only one there to see her leave, a tall solitary figure in a dark suit, alone on the sidewalk in the heat of mid-September, yet there was an underlying chill in the air, a presage of fall. He had caught a glimpse of her face as the bus turned the corner; she pressed against the window looking back toward her father. He shrank behind the huge tree so she wouldn't see him.

With her gone, the heart went out of him, he'd think of things to tell her, feel glad on his way to his magic place thinking he was going to meet her. And then he would remember, and the day would turn flat and purposeless, without flavor. He became lethargic after there was no more work at Wesley's; he lay on his bed reading and listening to music, and he hurt Mrs. Bonner's feelings because he hardly touched the food she cooked for him; he'd shake her hand away when she felt his forehead. He had taped the torn pages of his journals back in place, and he would take them from the drawer, run his finger down the cellophane that held together the ragged edges, and thought his life was like those pages, torn and flimsy and patched. He wrote about that night when the men came for him, but the terror would come back and he couldn't write more than a few sentences before he had to put the notebooks away—he'd begin to sweat and his heart would pound. Then he'd sit at the window to look at the turning leaves that had begun to fall, reluctantly, one by one.

He watched the clock, and every day at four o'clock thought, "Now is the time we would be going on rounds," and he would wonder about the patients, about the old woman who sat at the window watching for God; and he wondered if Maxine Wesson still loved the ugly little baby they had named John. It was like not finishing a book, he longed to know how the stories came out, and he'd think maybe it would be all right to go just once to see his father, to talk with him like they used to do. But he did not, he knew the finality of the money his father had sent him, and so he did not go into town at all: everybody knew what had happened to him, and he did not want to see their hate or their pity.

As the days passed from fall into winter, the compulsion to leave grew stronger; his time here was over. He would go to Birmingham as he had planned, get a job and find a place to live, then he would go to the school and see if he could start in the spring term of the next year rather than waiting until the fall. He needed to get on with his life, get the schooling behind so he could go North. But even if he couldn't start school, he had to get away from Asheton, and he had to get these last years he must live as a Negro over with. His admission forms had specified his race as black, and when he thought of setting up a practice as white he wondered if there was something that would give him away, something he hadn't noticed. *I kin always tell a nigger,* Bro' Abel would say loudly as Bird passed the barbershop taking Mason home. *I don't keer how white some folks skin is, I kin always tell.*

Once, not even thinking about it, he just suddenly climbed on a city bus in Birmingham and had ridden a few blocks as a white person, and no one had questioned him. But he didn't consider that a true test, the bus was crowded and no one paid much attention to him. He needed some acid test, something bold and daring that would convince him beyond all doubt that he was right in his thinking, that he was truly white. He believed that then he could put this ridiculous fiction behind that this mote, this speck of dust of black gene he carried, had defined him Negro.

And so it was that on a cold, gray December afternoon he stepped from a Greyhound bus onto the hump-backed Edmund Pettus Bridge that spanned the Alabama River into Selma. He had come for his own private sit-in in the dining room of the Albert Hotel, that bastion of white supremacy where the only blacks who entered were maids and waiters and bellhops. He was afraid, but he thought that he was also brave to make his test in this place of luxury and wealth. No tacky diner, no dime-store counter would serve as well.

A north wind blew thin rain mixed with stinging needles of sleet into his face as he walked over the bridge, and he hunched into the fleece-lined overcoat his father had given him last year for Christmas. Beneath it he wore the dark wool suit his father had also bought for him last winter at Steinberg's in Selma. They were white men's clothes, expensive, well-cut. He had no fear about them, he knew that people judged mostly by appearances—by externals. But nevertheless he was afraid, and his palms sweated inside the cowhide gloves as he walked along the sidewalk down Broad Street.

He came to Jeff Davis Avenue, and if he had turned right, he would have entered the Negro section of shanties and rows of government-built houses, the olive-drab paint streaked with diesel soot like dark tears. Beyond the houses were the L & N tracks with the train engines strung out in a row and hooked together, chugging back and forth on the sidings, coupling with the freight cars. But he kept his course straight ahead—he did not come here to feel sorry for those he could not help, and after several blocks came into the business district. The store windows were filled with dancing elves and Santa Clauses and Christmas trees brightly lit and with glittering silver and gold packages piled beneath. Gathered around the trees were laughing children, all of them white, and he thought if the store windows were true, blacks did not celebrate Christmas. On the corner a woman in a black uniform and black hat with a huge red ribbon tied beneath her chin intoned to keep the pot boiling, and from the loudspeaker of a store happy voices sang *have yourself a merry little Christmas*.

He pushed through the crowds, and then he saw the Albert cater-cornered across the street. Before today he had seen it only from the car window when his father took him to see patients with him at St. Francis Hospital. It was not a tall building, only four stories high, but it was imposing nevertheless, its dully glowing white stone quarried from Alabama soil; a six-columned arcade led into the hotel entrance on Broad Street, and above this arcade was another smaller one, extending from the second story. The hotel was a replica of a doge's palace in Venice, and during the War both Yankees and rebels had stabled their horses in the lobby. His father had told him this, and he had also told him that the Albert was Selma's pride and joy. And that was why he must cross its portals—he must prove that he belonged in places such as this; but he allowed the traffic light to change from red to green many times, and twice he counted the fourteen small columns of the second-story arcade of the hotel, then he crossed the street, suddenly swinging into step with the crowds pushing by.

He stood in the splash of light from the arched windows onto the sidewalk and stared into the lobby at the darkly gleaming mahogany tables, the fading, opulently worn magnificence of red velvet Victorian couches and chairs. A broad oak stairway curved gracefully to the left and to the right leading upward to the balcony. Stained-glass windows faced those stairways and muted blue and red light fell across the pale floors. Encircling the balcony was an oaken balustrade entwined with pine boughs decorated with bows of red ribbon. A huge crystal chandelier reflected the colored lights of a tall Christmas tree that stood in the middle of the lobby where a few people sat, their feet resting on a plush, flowered carpet. A gray-haired woman dozed in a deep-cushioned chair, two men sat on the stiff couch talking, gesturing. A third man sat across from them in a straight-backed chair reading a newspaper. A waiter in a red jacket served tall amber drinks on a silver tray to the two men on the couch, and they smiled up at him, the black man nodding, smiling widely. When the waiter left, one of the men looked out the window pointing, and quickly Bird moved away. They had seen him, they knew who he was, and he stepped into the light to look through the window once more, anger rising. There was no law against looking in a hotel window; besides, they probably weren't even talking about him but were noticing the weather, how snowflakes had joined with the sleet.

Before he went inside he studied the arrangement of the lobby so that when he entered he would be assured, confident. He wanted it to seem as if he had been there before, or in places like it, and he noted that the desk was to the far right behind the lounge, and the dining room on the balcony overlooking the lobby—dimly, through the window he saw white-coated waiters moving among the tables lighting candles. Soon he would be sitting at one of those tables and those black faces would be watching him, measuring him. Would they see who he really was, would they spy something he had missed? But even if they did, they couldn't say anything, couldn't be sure.

As he pushed through the door he felt beneath his topcoat and into the inside pocket of his jacket to make certain he still had his billfold. He had also checked when he left home and on the bus. How horrible if, when it came time to pay the bill, he had no money, and he fingered the soft slickness of the leather wallet and knew that inside was a ten and two fives. And he was proud that the money he would spend tonight was earned with the sweat of his brow.

The streetlights flashed on when he entered the building as if stage lights had signaled his entrance, and then warmth smote him and a faint odor of rich mustiness: the opulence, the grandeur, reached out like tentacles and wrapped about him, trapped him, and he was suddenly terrified, for all those faces in the lobby had turned on him: Christmas lights winked on and off on the rimless glasses of the man who had lowered his newspaper to gaze at him; the gray-haired woman had roused also, her tiny, narrow feet crossed on the deep rug.

Heat washed over him. *They know who I am*, he thought,

and visions of a black Maria rose in his head, he saw himself being arrested and shoved into it as had happened to the Negroes in Birmingham. The desk clerk and the men drinking the amber liquor and the woman with the slender feet were going to rise and point their fingers at him and scream *nigger*, and he half turned to leave, then turned back again. He must make this test; even if they killed him he had to know if he could pass in this place where only genteel whites were allowed. As the deer mice of the woods had told him he was special, so would this place reaffirm it, and he raised his chin arrogantly, pulled off his topcoat, and imperiously called to the bellhop lounging against the desk.

"Boy!" he said to the gray-haired man who straightened and hurried to him. "Take my coat."

He handed it to him, and thought his manner precisely that of master toward servant. It was the tone he had heard whites use toward blacks all his life.

The man bowed and smiled, but behind the smile hatred flattened his eyes. "Yassuh," the man said, and Bird put a quarter into his hand. "Yassuh, thank you, suh. Did you need a room?"

"No, I came for dinner."

"Then I'll hang yo' coat over here, suh," and the old man in the organ-grinder monkey hat walked away from him, hung his coat on the rack at the foot of the steps that led up to the dining room.

The people in the lobby still watched him, but lazily. He had imagined the hostility, he was merely a momentary diversion in the monotony of their afternoon, and casually he ascended the red-carpeted steps into the dining room.

Silverware gleamed on the tables, and bouquets of holly in cut-glass vases were set in the centers. Red candles flickered in hurricane lamps. He stopped when he reached the landing, afraid again—he was conspicuous, the only diner. He had come too early. Quality white did not eat so early, it was barely five-thirty according to the clock over the lobby desk. Habit had tricked him into carelessness, supper at Mrs. Bonner's had always been at four o'clock. And he became unsure and hesitated, thought he ought to leave. The enormity of what he was doing swept through him, but then a Negro man walked toward him in a black suit and black bow tie, smiling at him, but the smile remote, superior.

"Good evening, suh," the man said. "Are you meetin' someone? Would you like a table now or would you rather wait in the lobby?"

"I'm alone," Bird said, "I'm meeting no one. It's a party of one," and he relaxed again, he thought the phrase "party of one" had exactly the right touch, the right amount of sophistication.

"Certainly, suh, right this way, suh," the man said, and Bird thought the eyes were keenly appraising. But he did not shrink from the scrutiny: he was properly dressed in his soft, white oxford-cloth shirt with the button-down collar, the red and dark blue striped tie. Let this man with the close-cropped hair who was probably called "Blackie" or "Shine" when he went home to his shanty on the railroad tracks each night look him over all he wanted to—he was not afraid.

The man seated him at a table by the balustrade and overlooking the lobby; he looked down onto the Christmas tree, the star of Bethlehem winked up at him, the desk clerk handed a room key to a man who hurried toward the muffled elevators that rang softly in the dimness of a hallway beyond the lounge. And he breathed the sharp resinous smell of the pine boughs in the warm, rising air, and sadness jabbed, for it was the smell of the woods, and he wished it were summer and innocence and Johnnie, the time when they had played their games and not known they were wicked. And then another man was there, a black man in a snowy-white jacket, and with a long, sad face. And this man smiled too, but like the others, his face revealed nothing. In the hypnotic glow of candlelight, in the obsequious courtesy of those who served him, he relaxed, thinking *I belong here, I am at home here*, and he wanted to talk, he became lighthearted and he smiled up at the waiter who was arranging his silverware.

"Are you responsible for this weather, waiter?" he asked. His voice gently accused.

The man smiled, shook his head. "No suh, this weather must of come down from the north. Maybe, though, we'll have us a white Christmas."

The man left and returned with a huge gold menu, opened it, handed it to Bird, then went to stand in the corner and wait. Bird studied the menu, reading the strange dishes, reading the prices, astounded at the cost, relieved that he had brought extra money. He rejected the braised calf's liver, he liked it but it was too ordinary, he ate that at least once a week at Mrs. Bonner's. He rejected the bass too, he did not think he would ever be able to eat fish again, it reminded him too sharply of those days by the river after the beating. He also passed over the roast beef and the steak in sour cream Hungarian, though it did sound poetic, as did the shrimp en brochette. But ah, last on the menu was what he would have: breasts of chicken Nanette. How could such a dish not be delicious? Who was this Nanette? and visions of some apple-cheeked peasant girl in a gingham dress rose in his mind; and he thought that someone had created the dish for her, had made something special for love of her.

He looked up and the waiter hurried over to him.

"Yassuh, do you wants to order now?"

"Yes. I'd like the chicken." He could not say "breasts," for somehow he thought that disrespectful to Nanette, and wished that whoever had concocted this tribute to her had chosen some other part of the anatomy to honor her. But what, leg? thigh? Those, also, were too familiar.

"What would you like on yo' salad, suh? Blue cheese, Roquefort, Italian—"

"I'll have Roquefort," he said. He had heard of it but he had never tasted it, and for that reason he chose it. He did not think a Negro would order Roquefort dressing.

The waiter wrote, and then he asked what he would like to drink, and Bird told him water. "But with no ice. Strong beverages with food detract from its enjoyment, except, of course, a delicate wine would go well with chicken." He had picked up that bit of information from a gourmet magazine at Maybelle Posey's one afternoon while he waited for her to put Mason to bed.

He looked up into the man's face then, thinking to see admiration, and saw instead a flicker of amusement in his eyes. And he looked quickly down at the menu again, anger flaring, his cheeks warm with embarrassment. Very well, let the man laugh at him, but he dare not show it openly. He, Bird Lasseter, was white, and what did he care what this black man thought? What difference to him?

As he stared at the menu, the words beneath *Desserts* jumped out at him, and he said haughtily, looking again into the waiter's eyes, "I'll have cherries jubilee for dessert," for suddenly he *was* jubilant. No one was paying any extraordinary attention to him, he blended with his surroundings, he was accepted.

The man held his look, told him he could order his dessert after he had finished his meal.

"I'll order it now," Bird said, and knew the man would not have looked so boldly at an older person. He was young, not long past the age when blacks could still have properly called him by his first name. Mrs. Bonner had begun calling him "Mista Bird" when he was thirteen, much to Jake's disgust. "Little yella boy look mo' lak mista shit to me," Jake said. "Gran'mamma ought to be ashamed of herse'f."

"Yassuh," the waiter said, looking away; he smiled and nodded, his manner ingratiating. "Anything else, suh?"

"No, that'll be all, waiter," and he looked away from him, idly scanning the lobby, dismissing the thin-faced man. He decided that after he ate he would also go to the movie, to the one the Negroes had been trying to integrate. He had never been, for he would not humiliate himself by sitting in the balcony. He had stood across the street from the huge theater in Birmingham whose sign announced it was the Showplace of the South; he had looked at the big posters of Clark Gable and Lana Turner and wished he could go in. Tonight he *would* go in a theater, right in the front door, and he would sit downstairs. If he passed the test in the Albert, he could do anything. By God, eating here should surely prove he was white.

A man and a woman came into the dining room, and the waiter seated them at the table in front of Bird, and they nodded and smiled, and Bird nodded and smiled back. A fever of joy tingled through him, everything was going right, and he felt suddenly festive as he watched the woman who wore a sprig of holly in her fur coat drape it so carelessly over the back of her chair. He tried to imitate their ease, forced his shoulders to relax, his face taking on the bland, for-granted look of his right to be here. The knot in his stomach dissolved, he felt a faint stirring of hunger. He belonged here just as much as they did, and he thought how beautiful was the word "belong."

And he looked at the people, the desk clerk and those who sat in the lobby and the man and woman at the table in front of him. He thought how grand for all of them to be in this place together on this festive night; and he thought that never again would they all be gathered again in exactly this same way: this time, this place, these people, arranged as they were on this evening, were unique and would never again be duplicated. It was a pattern, and if no black faces were included in this pattern (he did not count the black servants), why then, he was sorry, he was truly sorry—but there was nothing he could do about it. He believed that if they were in his place they would do the same; he had heard the talk over the years of those who had crossed the color line, of those who had made it into that rarefied world of not having to forever play the child; of being able to believe that if you tried hard you might become president or governor or mayor.

The waiter had placed his salad before him, the shredded dark green lettuce topped with a thick dressing studded with chunks of cheese. He was careful to eat only about half of it, though now he was truly hungry and could have eaten it all; he did not think refined white people cleaned their plates, and the waiter took the dish away and in awhile brought back a gold-rimmed plate on which lay a large chicken breast covered with a creamy sauce and toasted bread crumbs and cheese. The sweetness of spices steamed into his nostrils, and saliva flowed from beneath his tongue.

He cut into the meat and the flavor was so succulent it was almost sensual and he, who was seldom really hungry, who sometimes at the end of the day would realize he had not eaten at all, now wanted to eat greedily. But he ate slowly, and when he was finished nothing remained on the plate, for the chicken was boned. Mary Betty would have fussed at him for eating every morsel. Many times she had scolded Johnnie for eating too fast, for chasing one last pea around on the plate. He lay down his fork and sighed, thinking someone must have loved Nanette dearly to have created such a dish.

He decided not to eat the vegetables in the tiny white bowls, did not want to spoil the taste of the chicken, and besides, black-eyed peas and potatoes were commonplace, though the potatoes were cooked with cheese and, therefore, somewhat special. Au gratin, the menu said. He leaned back in his chair and thought how well he fitted in with his surroundings; he watched the people coming and going in the lobby, caught up in their gaiety of the holiday season, the old man bellboy carrying the suit-cases; a young black boy in a white jacket came and cleared away his dishes. He started to say something pleasant about Christmas or about the rotten weather, but was unsure if white people spoke pleasantries to the servants. And besides, he didn't want to patronize the boy, he was suddenly ashamed at having somebody his own age waiting on him. So he stared into the lobby, angry because he felt sorry for the boy whose arms were too long for his sleeves, the skinny wrists somehow pitifully vulnerable.

The waiter set up a small table next to his, and on it was a bowl of ice cream and black cherries and Bird was deeply disappointed at its ordinariness—he could buy ice cream from the store, and canned black cherries. So where was the jubilee? He did not know what he had expected, but certainly much more than this. But then the waiter poured a golden liquid over the dessert from a long bottle that said on its label Hennessy Brandy. He struck a match and touched it to the liquid, and dancing flames leaped and spread. Speechless, Bird stared at the sputtering blue fire.

"How did you do that?" he asked. His voice was filled with awe, gone were all attempts to impress. Gone were all thoughts of why he had come to this place. He was a child again watching the magic show at the State Fair in Birmingham.

"Why, didn't you know, suh, that brandy burns?" the waiter said. "You jes slides it easy into the dish and sets it afire. Nothin' to it. I'm surprised you never saw that before."

The man was amused, and now patronizing him, and Bird straightened stiffly. "That will be all, waiter," and he waved his hand at him, dismissing him. The Negro's face became impassive, he nodded and left, went to stand against the wall.

Bird ate the melting ice cream and the fibrous cherries that he thought too cloying, too sweet. But he liked the bite of the brandy and its warmth in his stomach. He did not eat it all, he was unused to so much food. And he was tired, his mood had changed and he felt dejected and depressed. What glory, what value in intimidating old black men and young boys? Was that what he really wanted? And the truth was, the food at the Albert was not nearly so good as Mary Betty's or Mrs. Bonner's. But then, that was not what he had come here for. His evening had been successful, he had passed for white. Why then was he not happy?

He was ready to go home now, he wanted to lie in his bed with his back against the chimney and think about this evening, make some judgment about it. The waiter discreetly placed a small silver tray before him, and the check was turned face down, the black man withdrawing while Bird turned it over to look at it. Amazing, he had eaten seven dollars and fifty-seven cents worth of food. Mrs. Bonner could have made dinners for a week with that amount of money, and he had lived for days beside the river without spending any money at all.

He took out his wallet and placed a ten-dollar bill on the tray, pushed back his chair to leave. The change from the ten ought to be enough for a tip. But before he had time to stand up, two Negro men came through the door into the lobby, walked briskly to the desk. One man was dark, the other tan. They wore black overcoats and black felt hats, and when the clerk who had his back to them sorting mail into the pigeonhole boxes did not turn, they rapped insistently upon the marble counter.

"We need a room for the weekend," the paler-skinned Negro said when the clerk turned. "We've been traveling all day and we're very tired, but first we'll want our dinner." He inclined his head toward the dining room. "The bellhop can take our bags to our room."

The clerk stared slack-jawed, and silence fell across the lobby and in the dining room, which was now nearly half filled. It was as if all of them had become suddenly frozen, shocked into rigid stillness that these two black men had invaded their sanctuary. Bird did not believe how boldly they stood, how straight and confident they seemed. They were never going to be mistaken for white, so why were they not terrified?

"I beg your pardon?" the clerk said.

"I said," the man said, bracing his hands against the edge of the counter, "that we require a room for the weekend. I said that we're very tired."

"You want a room *here*?"

"That is correct."

Color rose darkly in the clerk's face and all the way into his scalp where the thin blond hair receded. "You've made a mistake," he said. "We can't accommodate you, we have no room for you here. The Albert is for whites only. You'll find a nigra motel on the outskirts; I'll be glad to give you directions."

"We need no directions. We've made no mistake. I insist that we be given a room just as would be done for any ordinary white citizen. It is the law."

They stood stubbornly waiting, shoulders touching, staring at the clerk without shrinking. And Bird recognized Martin Luther King; he had seen his face many times on the five-o'clock newscasts and from pictures in the newspaper; the dark, heavy-set man was Ralph Abernathy.

A bulky man in a plaid sports coat suddenly stood up from

a chair in the lounge and walked slowly toward the two men, tapped Martin King on the shoulder. And when King turned, the man smiled at him. "I believe I've seen you on television," he said, and lacing his hands together, smashed his arms down upon King's head. As he fell, the man kicked him in the groin, and when Abernathy whirled on him, grabbing his shoulders, they began to struggle, moving slowly across the floor.

People began to scream, jumping from their seats and running into the street, some up the stairs into the dining room. The hats spun across the floor, people ran in from the street, men screaming "kill the mothers," and King and Abernathy dropped limply to the floor, pulling their knees to their chests, wrapping their arms about their heads.

Bird stood at the railing, and it was as if he stood on a hilltop watching a battle, observing and yet knowing that what was happening below was, in some way that he did not yet understand, crucially and intimately involved with him. A woman sobbed close by, "My God, my God, niggers, niggers," and the people milling about him and in the lobby were as in slow motion, as if they drifted through water, yet the movements seeming precise, rehearsed.

White men punched and kicked the Negroes, and like him that night outside the cornfield, they never cried out, and he became them, felt their terror. He understood also that they were afraid when they stood at the desk spewing out the brave words about the law and how they deserved a room simply because they were human beings and tired. The star shining in the Christmas tree was the evening star above the pines the night he was beaten.

Sirens shrieked far away, blended with the women's screaming, and after what seemed a long time policemen rushed in with silver stars gleaming on their chests and waving nightsticks, and slowly he inched away from the railing, moving back and back, the men in white plastic riot helmets yelling *stand aside, stand aside*, dragging the black men to their feet, shoving them toward the door.

Photographers' bulbs flashed and television floods lit the

lobby bright as midday; the police handcuffed King and Abernathy and dragged them from the lobby yelling "disperse, disperse," to the white people, who dropped back, making a path. But the rumble of the white people's wrath was like faraway thunder, their anger building, piling upon itself.

The people who had fled to the balcony were leaving, the policemen waving them toward the front door with their sticks, but Bird knew he dared not pass by them, they would see who he was, those sticks would crash upon his head, and wildly he turned and ran through the swinging doors into the kitchen. Long wooden work tables rushed past him; in sharp detail he saw heads of lettuce and tomatoes and cabbage, silver and copper pots and pans gleamed on the walls, flashed brilliant light.

And then he was in the alley, sharp wind blowing sleet and snow into his face and piling it thinly against the brick walls of the buildings; as he fled, the clanging notes of Christmas bells from the churches crashed in his head, and the colored lights and grinning neon Santa Clauses strung overhead reflected back from the wet and shining streets.

Faye sat in the corner booth next to the window reading the Sunday paper, and already it was dusk, though it was barely four o'clock. Red and green Christmas lights strung across the eaves reflected on the thin film of snow on the parking lot. She had kept her eye on the sky all afternoon, watching it turn ever more heavy and lowering, and she pulled the blue cardigan sweater tighter about her shoulders, took another sip of scalding coffee. She wore dark glasses to cover the greenish-yellow bruises of her eyes that had been purple two weeks ago. It had not been a bad beating as Coy's beatings went—he'd blacked her eyes for talking back to him in front of a driver. She'd told him to get his own coffee when he'd ordered her to, so naturally, later that night, he'd hit her several times in the face. Ever since she lost the baby, she did the opposite of what he told her to do. If he told her to sit down, she stood up; if he told her to stand up, she sat down. The morning after he blacked her eyes, he told her he was sorry but she knew he wasn't, he was only afraid she'd go to her daddy's and tell him what happened. Her daddy had told Coy he was a dead man if he ever touched her again. So he'd gotten her to pack her suitcase and go to Florida; he said they'd never had a honeymoon. But the real reason he wanted to take her away was for the bruises to fade before her daddy saw her.

But she didn't care what the reason was as long as she got to take a trip. She hated taking it with Coy, but then, life wasn't perfect, and besides, she got to go to a state she'd never put in her notebook. No truck from Florida had ever stopped at the restaurant; she'd never been anywhere else except once to Mississippi and once to Georgia to visit her mother's relatives.

When they had come onto the highway that stretched along the ocean, she'd been glad for the beating. It didn't matter what had gotten her there, she thought she surely dreamed when she saw that great heaving mass of water stretching off forever to the horizon, blue water streaked with rose and emerald meeting the blue sky, blending. And when at the end of each day they stopped along the way at some motel in their drive along the coast, while Coy sat in the bar drinking beer with the manager and talking about how he'd never sleep in a bed where niggers had slept, she would walk to the beach and know that home was here too, that the Alabama crashed upon this shore: she had followed the river to its heaven, and she walked in the dawn with boiling rainbow foam dissolving the sand beneath her feet so that she was dizzy, feeling she was being sucked out with the tide, and not caring.

Sometimes when she walked far down the beach past the motels and the stilt houses and the restaurants, all the way down to where there was only sea oats and white sand and hot wind and burning sky, she'd feel the baby moving in her, at least she'd think she felt the baby move, but then knowing it was gas bubbles or hunger gnawings. But nevertheless, for a moment she'd become afraid, even though her brain had told her the baby was gone; she'd stop and lay her hand on her stomach, remembering that Dr. Lasseter had delivered her of a dead boy fetus. She'd asked him what it was, she had to know, and with the streaks of fear now came sadness. What would it have been like to have a son? She would never know, for she no longer slept with Coy, and after the first few times he'd tried to touch her, he'd stopped. He'd known there was something different about her, something hard now, and unyielding. She wasn't afraid of him anymore, she wasn't afraid of dying anymore. The only thing she thought she was really afraid of was bringing children into a world that could be so cruel.

She'd walked along the beach remembering her flight down that hot, dusty road, and later, when she had lain in the ditch after she had fallen, Coy shining the light in the dusk looking for her, back and forth, back and forth; and only luck or fate or God or whatever decided such things had made him miss her; his boot had come even with her head, and she could not close her eyes, she had had to follow the arcing beam that raped the dark, revealing the sharp-edged, green-glowing Johnson grass. He had gotten back in the car and gunned it down the road toward the restaurant, spewing dirt and gravel that clattered into the ditch.

Her daddy was sitting on the porch when she came up into the yard, and all she remembered was him calling to her, that he ran to catch her as she fell up the steps. And the next thing was happiness when Dr. Lasseter took her hand and told her the baby was gone out of her. Days later, Coy had come; through the door of her bedroom she could see her daddy standing at the top of the steps with his shotgun ordering him away, her willing him to pull the trigger so they'd get the money back and the restaurant would belong only to her. But he didn't pull the trigger, Coy had left, and her daddy had come and sat on the side of the bed not saying anything, and her knowing if Coy wasn't dead she had to go back to get the money.

Coy had come almost to the top of the steps before he stopped. Her daddy had leveled the gun at him, but he'd held the Bible high over his head like a magic charm, crying and saying scripture. When she knew her daddy wasn't going to kill him, she'd let him come into the house, and he knelt by her bed and read the verses that said a man and a woman should leave father and mother and cleave to each other. He thought he'd fooled her that he'd changed and had always loved her, but she knew better, he was only afraid he'd lose the restaurant if she divorced him. She lied and told her daddy she still loved Coy, and when the doctor said she was well enough to get up, that all she had to do was take it easy for a few weeks, her daddy went to the field and wouldn't even wave good-by when she climbed into the car with Coy. She nearly went back, her daddy looked so sad, his shoulders slumped, his hair gray and scraggly on his neck—and that was why she had to leave, to make things right, give him back his money. But she didn't sleep with Coy anymore. He'd come up to her smiling, saying how cute she was, and she despised him, knowing hatred showed in her face.

She sighed and folded the paper, laid it on the seat next to her, and watched the highway where a car passed slowly by now and then, sound and shape muted by the snow falling faster, now thinly covering the ground, drifting against the trunks. The scene looked like a Christmas card; all that was needed was a house with peaked roof and a plume of smoke curling out the chimney. That's what she'd wanted when she married Coy, a house with a hooked rug and a fireplace and a cat sleeping on the hearth. She'd always loved the Peter Rabbit stories when she was little, the snug house beneath the ground, yellow firelight, the rabbits cozy in their beds, and Mother Rabbit, fat and smiling, spooning soup to them out of cups. It seemed such a simple thing to want, a snug house and somebody to love and to love you. And so hard to get. The impossible dream. A fairy tale. What was real was a high-ceilinged house, cool and dim in summer, cold and drafty in winter. Massive mahogany furniture and four-poster beds. Her mother's house. Reality was this apartment with plastic furniture and diesel trucks grinding in the night and fumes coming in the windows into smothering rooms in summer, but close, gas-heated in winter.

But in between those two homes was her father's small house with pegged pine floors and raftered ceilings and coffee and biscuit smells coming from the kitchen. Her daddy's house. It was the only place the wolf had never lived.

She sat looking out the window thinking how good it felt to be by herself for awhile. Hardly anybody had come in today because of the snow and also because of the holidays. Coy had gone to pick up the help and was staying the afternoon. He didn't make excuses about staying gone so long anymore, he just left, and thanks to Nellie she knew where. Coy thought Nellie spied for him, but she really spied *on* him, and that was how she knew he was with Roxanne, the seventeen-year-old, big-breasted waitress he'd hired when she had lost the baby.

She took a pack of cigarettes out of her pocket and lit one, let the smoke billow about her head. She didn't hide her smoking anymore, Coy glowered at her but he didn't say anything.

But he was furious, and she enjoyed it, reveled that she was no longer afraid of him, felt glorious with power. Coy looked at her, puzzled, sometimes he'd start to hit her and then stop, as if he understood that her hatred fed on his violence: the pain, the not caring, the despising, were delicious after all the years of terror and trying to please. But she also knew that the story was about done; she felt on knife-edge, as if something was just before happening. She knew her life with Coy would soon end. How, she did not know, only that this was a fact.

She took long drags off the cigarette and thought she'd probably never have found out about Roxanne if Nellie hadn't kept track of Coy for her. She smiled to think of fat old Nellie as a counterspy, of how she kept strict account of when Coy left and when he came back and whether Roxanne was gone at the same time. Nellie said that nearly every night since he'd hired her he'd taken her out in the car and stayed gone at least two hours, sometimes more, and that several times while she was at her daddy's he'd even taken her into the apartment. Nellie said she'd heard Roxanne bragging to the other waitresses that it wouldn't be long before Coy divorced Faye to marry her, and then she'd own the restaurant and be their boss so they'd better watch their step.

Nearly everybody thought only Coy owned the restaurant, and many times when she sat at the register Faye heard him saying to some driver "my restaurant" this or "my restaurant" that. She watched his huge hands picking at the damp label of his beer bottle and thought how she hated him, wondering how it ever could have been that she let those hands touch her. She'd look at them and remember how they had hit her. And her hatred would rise.

A Red Ryder truck pulled into the diesel fuel station, the deep rumble of the big engine muffled through the snow and gradually dying away as the driver geared down, finally stopping. Steam poured out the tailpipes and dissolved in the gusting wind, and Faye walked quickly to the window, peering through the snowy gloom to see what state was on the tag. *California.* She smiled. *Hooray,* she whispered, but pushed down the joy.

She was wicked and a sinner, for she had also been glad of her son's death. *It was a boy, Faye, it was a boy.* Dr. Lasseter's voice was filled with sadness.

He came across the parking lot, hands shoved into his pockets, his breath steaming about his head, but he did not hurry. He never hurried, he walked as if he were ambling along on a spring afternoon. But his deliberate movements were deceptive, for he could be fast as lightning, as he had been that morning he hit Coy.

Faye watched him, unable to push away the love or the gladness. God would just have to punish her, she was glad Hayes was here; she loved the shape of him, he was lean and broad-shouldered, giving the impression of tallness though he was about the same height as she. As he came into the light from the window she saw the snow catching in the coarse darkness of his beard. Part Cherokee, he had told her, explaining his dark skin and jet hair.

She had often wondered how the beard would feel if he kissed her, but pushed those thoughts away too. She had known him only a few months, had never been outside this room with him, and yet she knew him better than anyone in her whole life, even her father. Hayes was honest and open, willing to risk showing his feelings as she believed she never could again. She had loved and trusted Coy, and so much for risk and trust.

But when she went back to the booth, she felt a faint stir of desire as he walked toward the door, and viciously she stubbed out her cigarette, rubbed the red coals into ashes. *It's a trap, I won't be trapped again,* and she thought she had had all she ever wanted of the touchings of men, remembered the boys who had walked her home from church in the dappled moonlight, their fuzzy cheeks hot against hers, their hands pulling at her clothes. In Coy's mindless lovemaking she could have been anybody, he didn't care who she was. Once he told her that women were all the same in the dark. Pussy, he had said. She closed her eyes against the vulgarity of the word, the humiliation. When she opened them, Hayes was smiling across the booth at her, snow melting in his beard and on his cheeks.

"How you been?" he said, and she could not keep from smiling, but when he reached for her hand, she pulled away. She saw the hurt in his eyes and was sorry for it.

"I've been fine," she said. "Where all have you been?"

"Oh, all over, here and there, out to L.A. and Seattle." The hand she had rejected was now curled about the pale blue mug of coffee he had brought with him from the counter. "Why are you wearing the glasses? Sun too bright for you?"

"Very funny. It's the glare, I've had a headache, and the glare hurts my eyes."

"You could sit with your back to the window."

"Yes, but then I couldn't watch the snow."

He nodded, smiled, and again would have touched her, and she settled back in the booth, the insular bubble wrapping around her, and he stared down into the cup. They were quiet for a long time, and then he looked up at her again with such longing and intense love she had to look past him out the window, tears coming to her eyes. He would not love her if he knew how wicked she was, if he knew she had wished her baby dead. Her son.

"What is it?" he said. "What's wrong?"

"Nothing, I'm just tired—"

"No, it's more than that, I can always tell. He's been hitting you again, hasn't he."

"No, it's not that, you don't have to worry—"

"Take off the glasses."

She shook her head, and he reached and pulled them down, his face going hard, anger flaring in his eyes. "I knew it, I'll kill him this time, so help me, I'll kill the bastard—"

"Stop it!" she said, the words a whispered scream. "I don't want you to kill for me, I don't want you to be like him. Please, let's just sit here and talk for awhile before he gets back. Let's forget that he's even in the world." She firmly pushed the glasses back in place.

He sighed, leaning back, and she took out another cigarette and lit it, and he shrugged out of the fleece-lined suede jacket and hung it on the back of the booth.

She smiled at him. "I like your shirt." It was bright-red flannel and she had never seen it before.

"Thank you. But let's not talk about my shirt. Let's talk about your bruised eyes and swollen face. Let's talk about when you're going to leave Coy Watson."

"No."

"No what? No, you won't leave him? No, you don't want to talk about it?"

He was angry, and disappointment made her angry too. She had wanted to be happy with him for awhile, to tell him about Florida. Ever since she had come back she had looked forward to telling him about it, wanted to find out if he had ever been there.

"I'm not going to leave Coy right now. I've told you that."

"Not even him making you lose the baby changes your mind?"

She mashed out the cigarette that had burned almost to the filter tip, began to slide from the booth. "I have to go now," she said. "I have things I have to do."

He caught her hand, and when she tried to pull away, would not turn loose. "Why won't you leave him? I can't keep coming here seeing you all beat up like that—"

"Then you'll have to stop coming—"

"Please don't go, let's talk."

She slumped back into the seat. "I've told you, I can't go yet, I have to get the money back. *I will not go* until I get my daddy's money back."

And then Nellie was there, she had brought Faye a mug of coffee, refilled Hayes's cup from the Pyrex pot she carried with her. "I'se keepin' watch, Miss Faye, you jes' relax an' enjoy yo'sef 'cause I kin see de headlights when he come in de parking lot. You don' have to worry."

"I appreciate it, Nellie, thank you," Faye said, and the Negro woman went back to the kitchen, her hair knotted tightly and covered with a hair net, her uniform starkly white against her dark skin.

"I'll leave if Nellie says he's back, Faye, but what I really want to do is stay here and tell Coy that I love you, that I want to take you with me."

"You never said it before." She felt like crying because he loved her.

"That I want you to leave him? Only about a million times—"

"That you love me."

"I've never said it? I thought I said that about a million times too. You mean I really never have said it?"

"No."

He smiled and shrugged. And because her response was supposed to be *I love you too*, quickly, she said, "I went to Florida."

"You went to Florida?"

"Yes. While you were gone. We drove all the way down the coast to the Keys."

"By 'we' you mean you and Coy?"

"Yes. He wanted to go on vacation so Daddy wouldn't see my face."

His jaw clenched, but he said nothing. She looked past him to where the snow was blowing harder against the darkening square of window, the flakes flashing red and green and gold in the Christmas lights. And she told Hayes about the sand that melted beneath her feet and how she had walked on the beach every morning at sunrise and every afternoon at sunset.

"And do you know what?" she said. "It was the strangest thing, one morning when I was walking on the beach and the sun wasn't up yet, I looked off to the horizon and just as the edge of the sun came over the water there was a green flash of light that lit up the whole sky. It was the purest, clearest green you can imagine, and every morning after that I got up and tried to see it again, but there were always clouds or mist. Maybe I just imagined it."

He took her hand again that he had released when Nellie came to the table, and she did not try to withdraw it this time. "You didn't imagine it," he said. "I've heard of it, it's a phenomenon. I wish I could have seen it with you."

"I needed to see it by myself."

He looked hard at her, then nodded, agreeing.

"It was kind of like a good omen, or a sign. You understand, don't you? It was like it was meant just for me, if I had seen it with someone else it wouldn't have meant that. I didn't hurt your feelings, did I? I wouldn't ever want to hurt your feelings."

"No. I understand. I'm glad you saw it alone. Maybe sometime we *can* see it together and it'll mean good luck for both of us."

After her mother died she had felt so anguished, so guilty, and the morning of the funeral she had walked in the yard and she'd seen a ruby-throated hummingbird darting among the crimson blossoms of the althea bushes. She had stood perfectly still watching it, and it had come so close she had felt the air on her cheeks from the whirring wings. And later she had thought of that after she had gone to live with her father, and had taken it for a good sign.

"I saw a ruby-throated hummingbird once," she said. "They're very rare, you know."

"You're very lucky," he said, his eyes filled with tenderness.

A truck pulled into the parking lot, and when the driver came in and passed the booth, he spoke and she asked him where he was from. When he said "Oregon," she took her notebook from her pocket and wrote it down.

"What are you doing?" Hayes asked. "Writing down my faults? My sister used to do that; when I did something she didn't like she'd write it down and somehow that seemed like the worst thing she could do to me, and I'd beg her not to, I'd promise her anything if only she'd erase it—"

"Will you *hush*,' she said, laughing. "I don't know what you're talking about, I'm only writing down 'Oregon'."

"Why? Why are you writing down Oregon?" He took the notebook to read what she had written, handed it back to her. "You really did write 'Oregon'. Why did you do that?"

"Because nobody from Oregon's ever been in here before.

I write down all the states and then look them up in the World Book. The next time a driver comes in from there I'll know all about it and maybe we'll talk about it and he'll think I'm smart."

"You *are* smart, why do you put yourself down?"

"No, I'm not, I quit high school to marry you know who."

"So what? I said you're smart, school has nothing to do with it."

She smiled, gently touched his hand. "Thanks. You almost make me believe it. You know, I think about all the places I've never seen, and I wonder if they're *really* there or if somebody made them up. Like Florida. Now I know it's really there, and I can think about the ocean and the green flash. But I also think about all the people in the world who don't know me and live in those strange places that are only names as far as I know, and if I died nobody in Arizona or Oregon or Nebraska would care; the world would go on and none of them would know that the world had stopped for me."

She looked down at the table, embarrassed that she had said too much, revealed herself too much. She pushed at a drop of water, smeared it on the dark Formica table.

He took her hand again. " 'She lived unknown, and few could know when Lucy ceased to be; But she is in her grave, and, oh, the difference to me.' "

Tears burned, if she looked up they would fall.

"Wordsworth wrote that about a girl he loved when she died. 'She dwelt among the untrodden ways Beside the springs of Dove, A maid whom there were none to praise and very few to love—' "

"Stop," she said.

"I would miss you if you died," he said. "Even if I had never met you I would have known you exist. All my life I've known you were out here somewhere. Why do you think I'm thirty-two and not married? I was looking for you."

When she looked up, he was watching her.

"I love you," he said.

"There are things about me if you knew you wouldn't love me."

"You are the best person I have ever known. Just don't tell my mama I said that."

Because his kindness was unbearable, she blurted out, "I wished my baby dead. I was glad when I lost him." Now he knew the truth about her, now he would leave the booth and never come back. If she looked into his eyes she would see his contempt. "I killed my baby."

"Faye," he said, pain coarsening his voice, "don't do that to yourself. Nothing about losing the baby was your fault."

"Lots of times I wished I could get him out of my stomach, I wished him dead. The Bible says the thought is the same as the deed."

"Stop it," he said gently, "Stop punishing yourself. The Bible also says that you must grow up and put away childish things. Like believing you can make something happen by wishing it so."

"I thought I was going to die when the baby was born, I was glad when Dr. Lasseter said it was dead. Now you know what a terrible person I really am."

She had whispered the words of horror that hung between them like a barrier, and outside the window was the night and the frantic snow, in a moment he would leave her, despising her, and though she did not blame him, still a terrible dread of coming loneliness swept through her. But he continued holding her hand, and she saw pity and tenderness and love were mingled in his face and far more terrible to bear than his hatred would have been. The hatred would have been deserved.

"Faye, darling Faye."

She would cry now, but not here where the curious waitress and the driver could see her. She would go and walk in the snow and weep for herself and for her dead son who now seemed to have had nothing at all to do with Coy.

"Don't go," he said, catching her arm when she started to leave.

"I have to be by myself."

"You're all right?"

"Yes."

He released her and she slid from the booth and left him there, one hand curled about the coffee mug, the other, palm up, empty where hers had been. She went into the apartment and got her coat and walked out into the night.

She stood out of sight beside the restaurant and watched him fill the glinting aluminum tanks on the side of the truck, and the densely falling snow outlined him darkly, emphasized his solitude. She had to stop him from driving in such dangerous weather; if she let him leave she would never see him again. She knew that when she went to bed she would turn on the all-night radio station that played easy-listening music from midnight until dawn and that on the hour and half-hour gave weather bulletins and newscasts. And sometime during the night some newscaster would tell of a truck skidding off the icy highway and turning over and over and sliding down into a chasm, flames bursting bright through the snow and against the dark sky. In a few minutes, when he pulled out, it would be the last of him—never again would she feel the warm roughness of his hand holding onto her, anchoring her.

She ran toward him, calling to him, but the sound was sucked away in the trough of wind tunneled across the parking lot. When she came up to him, she caught him around the waist from behind, and, turning, he leaned down to her, his cheek cold against hers. He clasped her against him, trying to still her trembling.

"Don't go," she said. "Don't go, don't go. If you go I'll never see you again." She cried, the tears coming from the beginning of her life, from before her life, from some deep and ancient well of grief.

He led her around the truck, helped her up the high step into the cab and into the sleeper behind the seat. They lay together, he murmuring to her, stroking her hair, and after a long time she stopped crying, finally stopped shaking.

"I'm going to California tonight," he said. "It's all right, nothing will happen to me, I promise. You can believe me. I'll never lie to you. I'll be back after Christmas and I'll want your answer about marrying me. I won't argue with whatever you decide, I won't try to change your mind. But if you do marry me, I'll spend the rest of my life helping you forget all the bad things. We'll go see every one of those states you've got written down in that notebook and then some. I'll take you home to California to meet my mama and my daddy and my sisters and brothers and they'll be your family too. I want your daddy to come with us—I love him, he's part of you. But there's one thing, you're never coming back here where the bad memories are. Make up your mind to it, you'll never see Coy Watson or Alabama again."

They lay for a long time, the snow glancing off the windows, and then she sat up and he kissed her gently on the lips, without passion. As she left the truck, she turned back to him. "Hayes," she said, "you're lucky for me too, like the hummingbird and the green flash."

She cut across the parking lot that was strangely lit with the blurred blend of colored lights and fluorescent glare of the lights over the gasoline pumps; and when she looked back he was standing at the side of the truck watching her and barely seen through the swirling snow.

CHAPTER 13

Zella lay sprawled on top of him, her small breasts flattened against his chest, her face contorted into the ecstasy of orgasm. Her breath came in short, hard gasps, and gently he lifted her face and kissed her lips, then rolled her off him, lying in his own fading passion. And he thought how joyless and without purpose their lovemaking had become, and he turned on his side away from her breath that puffed against his cheek and from the smell of stale sweat. He had fussed at her about that, told her she must bathe every day and keep her hair clean, but she had become apathetic, lazy.

She fell now into a heavy sleep, drugged with sex and the grain of morphine he had given her a couple of hours earlier. When he had first begun giving her morphine she had been so happy, so gay and carefree, as she had been in the beginning, in those first days when he had brought her here. She had loved him for giving it to her, for taking away the pain of her headaches, and the result had also been to ease her restlessness, her urge to move on. She talked no more of leaving, but as the dosage increased and she grew tolerant of the drug, she grew sullen and demanding, with wild swings of mood—happy in the afternoon, depressed in the morning, and gradually she had become careless with her grooming and slovenly about the house. When he became alarmed and tried to cut back on the dose, she had cried, and then begged and cursed, and he'd had to go back to the full grain.

Low gray clouds hung like a pall over the trees, and a longing for Bird came over him; but with the longing came also rejection: he and Bird could never be together again, the boy had to accept the realities of his life. He was Negro, and to ignore this fact was disastrous; it was unfair to him if he kept contact with him. It encouraged fantasy. But the pain of losing another son had lessened in his concentration on Zella. One thing he had learned in his life was that people came and touched you briefly, then were gone, leaving you in the confinement of your flesh, solitary, always solitary. Giving Zella the morphine had bought him a few days less of loneliness, nothing more. Inevitably, they would part.

He thought of Jenny. When he had sent Bird away, even though she had been the cause of.it, the old impulse to turn to her for comfort on the loss of a child had come over him, and early one morning he went to her room needing to be close to her. She had not heard him coming, she sat with her back to him at the window, the light shining through her hair, making her seem glorified, holy. Righteous. But when she turned and saw him standing in the doorway, she clutched her nightgown high about her neck, her face turned granite, without expression. He had left without saying a word.

Zella moaned, and he turned and propped on his elbow, watching her. A thin film of sweat glistened on her upper lip and on her forehead, and he pulled the sheet up over her shoulders so she would not be chilled. Her face even in sleep looked worried, and she frowned and shifted, a muscle in her jaw twitched.

In the first euphoric days of the drug, she had told him over and over how much she loved him, and he had told himself that he had done the right thing, that it could not be wrong to make her so happy. To make her feel good. But she had become quickly addicted; in only two weeks he'd had to increase the dose from a quarter grain to a half grain, and in the past two weeks he'd increased it again to a dangerous one grain every six hours.

She moaned and turned her head restlessly on the pillow, and he shook her shoulder gently, and when she did not respond, more roughly. "Zella, wake up!" She opened her eyes and in the dim light the pupils were constricted, barely pinpoints. Slowly the lids drooped shut and she slept again.

He sank back on the pillow, fear dully heavy in his chest.

She slept too much, the drug was poisoning her, and he closed his eyes and behind his lids flowed the words *I will give no deadly medicine to anyone if asked, nor suggest any such counsel.*

He opened his eyes to erase the words. He had broken his oath, he had wronged this innocent woman—he could not continue to excuse himself, to try to justify what he had done. He had to get her off the drug and let her go, let her live her life. But he was afraid, not of the letting go, but of getting her off the morphine. He'd seen people coming off drugs in the psychiatric ward when he interned, seen the pain and the vomiting and the torment, seen those poor souls doubled up with cramps.

He could not stay in the bed; quickly he rose and put on his clothes, wondering how long it would take for Zella to forget him when she was free.

When she left, she'd go straight back to Henry Jerald. But he had to stop believing he could control people's lives; if she started prostituting again what could he do about it? He had tried to help her, but she was with him now not because she loved him or was grateful to him, but because of the morphine. He was no longer her lover but her source. Sometimes, when he had been delayed on a case and was a few minutes late to give her her shot, she'd be pacing the floor and would scream at him as he came in the door, cursing him.

It was nearly dark, and he pulled the draperies, then went to the kitchen and rolled up his sleeves and washed the dirty dishes that smelled sour, as if they had lain in the sink many days. He checked the refrigerator and found that most of the food he brought here a week ago was still there and some of it spoiling. He sniffed the milk carton, gave a snort of disgust, then poured the milk down the drain, emptied the molding cottage cheese into the garbage sack beneath the sink. What did she eat? Two eggs were gone from the carton, a slice or two of the whole-wheat bread, a half-inch of the stick of butter. The potatoes and onions in the vegetable bin were sprouting, one can of soup of the half dozen he had bought more than a week ago was gone. No wonder she was so skinny; he was going to have to start coming out earlier and cooking her supper, *make* her eat. Gradually, gradually, reduce the morphine.

A gust of wind rattled the magnolia tree outside the window, and he pushed the curtains apart and saw the broad leaves sheathed in ice and sparkling in the light from the window; if he knew anything at all about the weather, and he did, it would be a white Christmas. He couldn't remember that happening since he was a boy, and he wished he was that child again, thrilling down the small hill in back of his mother's house on a flattened cardboard box, the wind whipping his cheeks, the undulant fields streaking away on either side of him, brittle with crusted snow. So long ago, so long ago, that innocence. That exhilaration. Exhilaration took a different form now, and snow was only a nuisance, an inconvenience. Deadly, when he couldn't get through to a sharecropper's cabin or a Negro shanty where someone might lie dying.

There came a noise like the scraping of a limb against the house, and he dropped the curtain and went to peer out the pane of glass in the back door into the deep twilight. The sound came again, and he opened the door a crack, calling out, "Who's there?"

A Negro man came around the corner of the house to stand on the flagstone patio, swaying slightly, as if the wind moved him as it did the tree branches. He was in a dark jacket with a cap pulled low over his forehead, his hands shoved into his pockets. Even in the dim light, and with the cap obscuring his face, the doctor recognized the broad-shouldered shape of Henry Jerald.

"What are you doing out here, Henry? Zella said you were gone—"

"Zella lied, I come fo' her." His voice was thick, slurred.

"Why, you're drunk, man—"

"You stole Zella and killed my baby, mine and Zella's." He walked toward the door, wobbling from the whiskey and from the blasts of wind. As he stepped into the light that fell through the kitchen door the doctor saw the hatred carved in the black face, and shocked, he stepped back. He had seen that look on

Negroes' faces many times when they huddled around fireplaces in bitter cold shanties waiting for some child beneath ragged quilts to die of pneumonia, or for some mother or father to simply fade away because they were too tired to fight, or else didn't want to fight, whatever disease they had caught. But the hatred was never directed toward him, but to God or the white man who owned the land.

"Zella was raped," he said, his voice harsh, defending. "Grady Lawson raped her."

The man laughed as he came closer. "Zella's bad to lie, she knows that was my baby."

"Get back, get back, I say," the doctor said, pushing the door almost shut, and Henry stopped, but still laughing, the sound rising, falling, like the wind.

"Zella wasn't raped, Zella and me love each other, but she got mad and say she don't want the baby, she say the baby make her have to be still and she cain't stand that. She told me she was gon' leave here and go up North wid me and have some fun. But now she say she too tired. How come Zella look so bad lak she gon' die, Docta?"

"You stay away from here, do you understand? Have you been coming in this house? How do you know what Zella looks like? If you come in this house I'll have you arrested—"

Henry laughed again. "I know whut you're doin' Docta, I ain't one of your croppers don' know they ass from a hole in de ground. Zella say you givin' her something she got to have—"

"You're trespassing on my property, sir, get out of here," and he clapped his hands at Henry as he would at a stray cur dog that had wandered onto his land. "You know nothing about medicine, what treatment I'm giving for her headaches."

"I knows 'bout yo' treatment, all right."

"Get, sir!"

He slammed and bolted the door and through the pane of glass saw Henry Jerald fade back into the night heading toward the woods, wondering if he was really gone or if he would hide someplace close around and come back to the house after he left.

He went from room to room locking windows, bolting doors, thinking it was probably true what Henry had said, that Zella had not been raped. Zella knew too well how to take care of herself to get raped. But the night she'd come to him, he couldn't have saved the baby, he had to use all his skill to save her. She had really done a job with the coat hanger.

He went into the bedroom and stood looking at her and thought how different things had turned out than he had meant them to, not just this relationship with Zella, but all his careful plans. This tangled, disorderly turn his life had taken was not his way. Sometimes he felt paralyzed, as if he could not move or think how to resolve anything.

He sat down in the chair next to the bed and did not turn on the light, though he hated sitting in the dark. But he could not risk waking Zella, and he leaned his head back, sighed, and closed his eyes. He had intended that he and Jenny would grow old together. The thought had never entered his head that it should be any other way. But over the years people had crowded between: the children, Bryon West, Jenny's father.

The old man had lain upstairs in the hospital bed he had bought for him; it was the same room Mrs. McKinley had died in and where Jenny was born. They had turned him toward the window so he could see his fields, and he had lain with his long, knotted fingers laced across his chest, staring for hours as if he could see himself guiding the mule down the furrows he had plowed so straight. That last year there really wasn't anything wrong with him you could treat, it was just that he was ninety-one and the machinery worn out, only his heart wouldn't quit. How bitter that he should live to see his land that he had loved turn back to weeds and scrub brush. When he saw old people in this condition, memories mostly gone and with no purpose anymore save one and that was waiting for death, he questioned severely, like a man doubting his religion, whether antibiotics were, after all, the blessing he had believed. If not for penicillin, Mr. McKinley would have died at seventy-eight with pneumonia. He thought maybe that would have been best—a man shouldn't be required to live beyond his time.

But even before Mr. McKinley and Byron West, he and Jenny had grown apart. She was busy with the farm and the children, and he worked longer and longer hours as his practice grew. Gradually they lost the urgency of the beginning years to share their lives; some days when he was on a hard case they didn't see each other at all. Maybe not for days. It was like a dream that once they had comforted and drawn strength from each other. That they had been united and of one mind and one flesh. But after the girls were born, it seemed they stood on opposite shores, the river flowing between them and widening as the years passed, the banks wearing away, the mist thickening, obscuring, until at last they were polite acquaintances and he couldn't remember why he had loved her so dearly.

He passed his hand across his mouth and stood up. He did not want to think about these times. What was done, was done. He looked down at Zella, watched her sleep. He thought how small she looked, and vulnerable. He was filled with pity for her, but forced it away. If she needed pity, it was because of him and what he had done to her. What she needed now was not his guilt, but clear, hard, impartial thinking. He must treat her as someone he did not know, as much as he was able to keep emotion out of his decision as to what he must do. He took her hand, and its fragile smallness was like Katie Hunt's tiny hand that he had held that last night, when they had said their silent good-bys.

Katie lived in a small white house across the street from the high school where she'd taught Latin from the first year after she'd graduated college. She'd never married, she seemed to care for nothing except this ancient language that so enthralled her. But she'd found a large lump in her breast and he'd sent her to a doctor in Selma and before she came back to Asheton she'd had her right breast amputated. The cancer had spread into the lymph glands and into her lungs, and they sent her home to die. She taught another year, and when she came to him that last summer her skin and eyes were jaundiced, and he didn't even have to feel her liver to know it had spread there too.

He'd seen her through those last months, watched her waste away, enduring the pain until she'd chewed her lips bloody, and he'd sat with her, held her hand. Gave her as much pain killer as he could, shaking his head when she begged him for more. *Give me something, John, please give me something. You're a kind man, you won't let me suffer.*

Her hair which when she was young had been fiery red, lay faded and strung out on the pillow. Her skin was dry and thin, her arms blotched with dark bruises of spontaneously rupturing capillaries. Her green eyes were bright with pain and pleading.

He'd left her a bottle of Seconal on her bedside table one gentle fall evening when the misted, failing light shone through her window. The leaves were barely turning, only beginning to spot with red and yellow, and he'd held her hand for a long time and already her eyes had turned peaceful, accepting. *Don't be so sad*, she'd said. *I always worried about you, you take things too hard. You need to learn to bend, to absorb. But you're a good man.*

A good man. He wondered what she'd say about him now if she could know what he'd done to Zella. He'd kissed her hand that evening and gone back to the office and called Gertrude and told her not to come to Miss Katie's, and he'd sat the rest of the night in his office at his desk, not sleeping, just sitting. The next day he signed the death certificate, wondering where all that knowledge had gone, where thought had gone. Were those thousands of words she had spoken to her students still out there floating around in the universe? As he signed his name he remembered the joy she'd had teaching about Rome, calling the people she told about *my Romans*. And she'd told them that she believed she once had walked among them, that she had lived before, and the class snickered, but she hadn't seemed to mind that they laughed at her. She'd been dead ten years, and he doubted anybody ever thought of her anymore except maybe when they walked in the cemetery reading tombstones. Someone might say "Remember nutty old Miss Hunt how she thought she'd lived before and was a Roman page boy in Caesar's court?"

Zella sighed and rolled over, facing him, and he leaned to pull a long strand of hair from across her face. He stared intently at her, and it was his detached, medical opinion that he must get her into a hospital. He was fooling himself thinking he could do it alone, she needed twenty-four-hour supervision. And when she was well again he would lose her as he had lost Bird. He would have to go back to loneliness; already he felt the heavy warmth of it wrapping about him like a blanket. In its heat, he shivered, and he lay Zella's hand on the quilt and paced the hall outside her door.

The day after tomorrow was Christmas, it was the day before Christmas Eve, and he had forgotten. All at once he longed deeply, tenderly, for home—not his mother's, but his and Jenny's and those early years when the children were little and there was a Christmas tree and colored lights and tinsel and tissue paper and the smell of Mary Betty's fruitcakes baking in the old wood stove. Oh, to be young again, to be blind to fault and error, to see through the glass darkly—to have not put away the dreams of youth.

He went to Zella's bed and adjusted her electric blanket to medium and turned out the light, turned off the gas space heater. She would sleep the night and not need another shot before ten in the morning. He thought briefly of Henry Jerald and decided he was gone, it was too cold to skulk around the woods, and besides, he'd threatened him with arrest for trespassing. He kissed Zella gently on the forehead, left on all the lights for her should she happen to wake during the night, and he locked the front door behind him as he left.

The house was dark when he pulled into the driveway, except for a light upstairs in Jenny's room. He turned off the headlights and the motor, wondering why no Christmas candles shone from the windows, why no Christmas tree flashed on and off in the living room. Why was there no laughter, no voices coming from the house? Johnnie should be trimming the tree while Sarah bossed the placing of the ornaments—the twins should be at the piano harmonizing.

He got out of the car and went up the walk, the soft, cold touch of the snowflakes on his cheeks, and he felt a glimmer of satisfaction that his weather prediction had been correct. They would have a white Christmas. He unlocked the front door calling *hello* into the darkness, deeply disappointed that no warmth met him, or light or voices, but only silence. Why did the children not sit by the hearth wrapping clumsy packages, the firelight leaping on their faces, their stockings hung from the mantel? But no, no, that was not now, he was confused, that was a long time ago, they were grown now. The light and the laughter was from the time they all loved one another, and he fumbled along the wall until he found the switch, standing in an island of light from an overhead bulb. They were gone, all of them. But where? Why were they not celebrating Christmas?

"Mary Betty!" he called, and he pictured her lying in her bed in the dark back room, deliberately silent, her black face set in disapproval of him. She had hated him since Zella, though she had not hated Jenny for Byron West. Sometimes he felt her strong-boned face, solemn and judging, turned on him.

He climbed the stairs that leaped upward into darkness, flipping switches in the hallway as he went so that the dark sprang backwards in the path of advancing light; faintly, from Johnnie's room, came the hollow, echoing call of her cuckoo clock. Seven o'clock, he counted. Much earlier than he'd thought, with dark coming now before five. *That bird's calling you, Johnnie,* he used to say to her, and she'd giggle and say *no it isn't, Daddy, it's calling you.*

The door to Jenny's room was open, and he proceeded slowly toward it, afraid of the strangeness, of the unfamiliarity of this house that once was so familiar, so loved. He had presided over life beginning and life ending in this house, but his heart beat fast now and he did not understand why he was so afraid. He still came here several times a week, but always in the daytime. He wished now he had stayed at the river house.

Pale light splashed against the floor into the hall from Jenny's room, and when he got to her door saw her on the bed in the green velvet robe he had given her one Christmas years ago. She lay on her side in the mahogany four-poster bed they had once shared, and where the babies had been born. She had not turned back the covers but lay on top of the white, flowered chenille spread. She was asleep, a paperback novel still held loosely in her hand near her cheek. An open box of chocolates was on the bedside table, brown, accordioned paper cups scattered about. The dim glow of the lamp shone on her crumpling face, and on the mutilated hair that she permanented now into a colorless frizz about her head.

He watched her, thinking it was an unkind thing to do to examine her without her knowledge, and despair and sadness caught him for her destruction. What had they done so wrong, at what point could they have made things come right? What incident could they have said, "Now, now, *this* is the place we have to turn back, to go no further." He didn't know. He used to think he did, he thought it was Byron West, but he understood on this day before Christmas Eve that Byron West was a result, not a cause. What had gone before to cause him?

He felt her solitude, it creaked in the boards of the house, in the trapped, sighing air whorling through the chimney. Her feet were not covered by the robe, he remembered that morning a thousand years ago when her toes had curled in the dust of the summer morning. Little-girl feet, dainty, slim. He reached to pull the robe over them because they must be cold. The room was cold. But when he moved the soft green material, she awoke, and she looked up at him, not recognizing. Her eyes were puffy.

"Jenny," he said, "where is everybody, why is the house dark? It's nearly Christmas—"

She sat up, still staring, bewildered. "Christmas? What are you talking about?"

"Tomorrow's Christmas Eve. Where is everybody, where are the children?"

"The children?"

"Stop repeating what I say. Why isn't there a Christmas

tree and everybody celebrating and wrapping packages? Where
is Mary Betty, she's supposed to stay up all night tonight baking
her fruitcakes."

Comprehension crept into her face, and she laughed.
"You've lost your mind, John. What are you doing here?"

"Where is everybody, everybody should be here, the girls
come home; the last I heard, Johnnie was coming home."

"The last you heard has changed. Johnnie called and
wanted to spend Christmas with a new friend she's met, the
twins have gone to the Coast with their friends. Mary Betty has
not baked fruitcakes for the past three years since she misread
the label on the bottle and aged them in vinegar instead of
sherry. She's gone to her son's as she did last year and the year
before that. But I'm here, won't I do?" The words were slurred
with sarcasm. "To think, once upon a time I was all you
needed."

When he said nothing, she said, "Oh, I forgot, you probably want to know about Sarah too, you just didn't think to
ask. She won't be here either, she's gone to New York with her
rich lover. Isn't that nice? And we don't have to worry about
her getting pregnant because her lover is a woman."

Dully, he stared at her. He heard the words but they meant
nothing. Long ago he had learned to live with the constant,
aching guilt that he had never loved her, did not deceive himself
that he'd only hated her those brief moments when she was
born and was not his son.

"I don't want to hear any more," he said. "I told you years
ago I left Sarah to you—"

"Like an inheritance?"

"You wouldn't listen, I'm not surprised at how she's turned
out." He turned away from her and went to the window to look
out to the fields shining white with snow, watched the snowflakes strike the window, illumined briefly in the light before
they passed into darkness.

"You're incredible," she said. "I cannot believe your un-
awareness, your selfishness. You ignore us for years, put us out
of your mind, come here mainly on matters of business and

always in a hurry, then walk in here tonight expecting things to be the way they used to be. My God, we've been *living* all this time, thinking, feeling. Growing old." When he did not answer, she said, "Why haven't you written to Johnnie? answered her letters. Couldn't you have managed even to send her a Christmas card?"

"What do you care, you've never loved her."

"Oh, yes—" She stopped. "What's the use. Why are you here, what made you decide to grace this house with your presence? Why aren't you with your nigger whore?"

He whirled on her, arm upraised, and he heard Mary Betty's voice that night of Byron West. *Don't you hit Miss Jenny, Docta, if you hits her you better hit me too and make it a killin' blow*, and she had taken a stick of stovewood from the box behind the stove. He had only now let himself remember that he wanted to smash Jenny that night.

Slowly his arm dropped to his side as she looked up at him now, unflinching. "Who are you," he whispered, "to condemn me for Zella? Who do you think you are? After Byron West you had no right to require anything at all from me."

"Ah, so pure, John, so blameness. And me so wicked. I'm sorry for all the times I failed you."

"I thought you were an angel standing in the road that morning."

"Such hell to condemn me to. An angel would have had another son for you, wouldn't she? It tore the heart out of me to see your disappointment when the girls were born. I could see it in your face each time that you loved me less. Oh, no, don't say anything. I don't care about chromosomes or genes or who's responsible technically for the sex of a child. In your heart you blamed me."

"It's not true. How can you know what I thought? Do you read minds?"

"I read faces. I read actions."

"I wanted us to share Bird. Don't you know I brought him home to you? Don't you know that the look on your face when I lost our son was the same look on your father's face when I lost his son? I always loved you until—" He stopped, unable to say the hated name again.

"Until Byron?" Jenny said. "Byron was because I needed someone to love me because I was me, not because I had to produce a son. I loved you that morning we met in the road. I'd have married you then if you'd asked me to, gone anywhere you said. I wanted to make you laugh and forget all that sorrow and guilt you had for things you couldn't help. I thought it would be so simple. The ignorance of youth."

"We did, Jenny. We did laugh together."

The wind slammed against the house, the boards creaking and settling, a draft of cold air circulating around the loose windows. "It's cold in here," he said, and took a packet of matches from his pocket and went to the fireplace and knelt and lit the heater. The smell of sulphur and the sweetish fumes of gas were faintly in the air.

He was suddenly exhausted, as if some great weight pushed him into the floor, and he thought he would go to the office and sit in the dark and think about what had been said here tonight. He would remember that which he had forgotten, that his work was his life. It had never failed him, in his work he knew what to do. He walked to the door.

"I'm sorry everyone wasn't here for you tonight, John, that we have disappointed you again. I'm here, but I suppose I wouldn't do. All I can offer you is some chocolates."

He had just started into the hall when he heard a jagged rush of strangled air, and when he turned, Jenny had fallen back, her face and lips deadly pale; her hand clutched her robe over her heart as she gasped. He watched her for what seemed a long time, heard the ticking of the cuckoo clock, the wind whipping against the window. Her eyes were round and frightened, and as he started toward her she jumped up and tried to run.

He caught her before she fell. "Don't be afraid, Jenny, I'm here, you're all right." He picked her up, surprised at how light she was, how fragile her body, and he lay her on the bed and felt her pulse. It was weak and irregular, and he ran into the hall shouting for Mary Betty, remembered, and cursed her for being gone. He ran down the steps, two and three at a time, stumbled and caught the newel post, and then was running up the steps again, not remembering going outside, but cold air blasted through the front door he had left open and he was carrying his satchel.

When he got back to her room, she was standing and holding onto the bedpost, and he set the bag on the table and put his arm about her shoulder, gently eased her to the bed, made her lie back, and she closed her eyes. He took his blood-pressure cuff from the bag, and the stethoscope, listened to her heart that was still irregular, still weak. He wrapped the blood-pressure cuff about her arm, shocked at the flaccidness of the muscle. He remembered her body as strong and hard, the muscles tight with youth and exercise.

Her pressure was low, she was having a coronary; he removed the cuff, quickly put it and the stethoscope back in the bag. He had to get her to the hospital, he could do nothing for her here. Her breathing was labored, and she frowned as if she hurt.

"Jenny," he said, taking her hand, "are you in much pain? I can give you something for the pain."

She rolled her head back and forth on the pillow, and that was the way it had been with the babies, she had never wanted the chloroform—she would never even admit the pain.

"I can give you something," he said. "You don't have to hurt. I have to get you to the hospital, it's your heart." He kept his finger on her pulse, and thought how vulnerable they were in the board house and the pale lamplight that were no defense at all against death. He had tended her many times in this bed, but never alone, never with only the two of them. The house seemed so echoing, so lonely.

"You can leave now, John," she said. "I'm all right, I've had these spells before, it's only indigestion from too much chocolate."

"Why didn't you tell somebody? Why didn't you tell me?"

She smiled, but did not answer.

But when she looked up at him he saw the fear in her eyes, and with a rush of sadness he picked her up, wrapping the spread around her, and carried her down the stairs and into the swirling night, put her into the car.

"You'll be all right, Jenny, I won't let anything happen to you, you'll be all right," but she was silent, and in the light of the dash when he switched on the headlights her face was pale, her eyes closed.

He drove as fast as he could on the ice-slick streets, the rear end of the car fishtailing as he turned the corners heading toward Selma. A crowd of teen-agers walked along the sidewalk laughing, shouting, their faces turned to the sky, arms outflung as they cavorted, scarves and bandannas blowing in the wind. In a spot of light in front of the red-brick Baptist church from which they had just emerged was a manger with plaster statues of Mary and Joseph leaning over the crib that held their new-born son.

He sat on a bench a short way down the hall from her room. It had taken him an hour to get her here. He should have called ahead that he was coming, but had not wanted to waste even that much time. He had admitted her to the emergency room and a young resident doctor had set up a cardiogram. While they were running it he had filled out the admitting papers, and he had not been able for the life of him to remember whether Jenny had ever been baptized, since there was no Catholic church in Asheton. Mr. McKinley had never been devout. So he had left the space blank on the form. What difference anyway? Each person's soul was his own affair, and when he handed the dark-haired nurse the papers she glanced over them quickly.

"I'm sorry, Doctor, you've missed one."

"I didn't miss it. I didn't answer it because I don't know."

"You mean you don't *know* whether your own wife has been baptized?"

"I said that I did not. Besides, it's not your business anyway, I don't see the point of it."

"Well, Doctor, I certainly am not prying, it's the hospital wants to know, I only work here." Her voice quivered with indignant hurt.

He had walked away down the long corridor and the woman called after him, "You'll have to answer the question," her voice rising as the distance widened.

He looked now at the green whorls on the tile floor made by the waxing machine, wondering how many atrocities had been committed in the name of that phrase of someone doing his job. Excutioners springing trapdoors, throwing switches, letting the ax fall. Doctors leaving sleeping pills on bedside tables, scraping away embryos.

Quickly he pushed the thoughts away. The things he had done were done, he could change nothing. The thing at hand was that Jenny was going to die, he had seen it in the resident's face as he listened to Jenny's heart, took her blood pressure in the sterile grimness of the emergency room.

He leaned his head back against the wall, took a deep breath, remembering how she had looked as they wheeled her past a short while before, taking her to her room. Her eyes were closed, the frown gone from between her eyes. They'd given her medication for the pain and a tranquilizer. They were preparing an oxygen tent for her. He supposed the tranquilizer took away the fear and he was glad. He hated thinking of her afraid, she was so strong. He pushed his back against the wall, the cool plaster easing somewhat the ache between his shoulder blades, and he thought how odd that he should have been at the house this night. If he had not gone home, he would have found her dead the next day. And he wondered what time that would have been, for he would have gone to the office first.

Footsteps approached hollowly down the vacant hall, stopped in front of him, and he looked up into the face of the chubby-cheeked resident with the light, silky-blond hair. Rubber tubes dangled from the pockets of his white jacket, a stethoscope hung around his neck. An apple-cheeked doctor garbed in super-hero clothes. Probably the boy had changed in a phone booth.

"Doctor?" the boy said.

He stood up.

"Your wife's had a coronary, you know that."

He nodded curtly.

"She's critical."

He made no acknowledgment of this statement, and the boy looked away at some point just beyond his left ear. "I'd like to show you the cardiogram, explain the medication we have her on."

"It won't be necessary."

"Dr. Garber concurs in my opinion that she's critical. If you'd like to talk to him?"

"No."

"Dr. Garber and I concur that you should call your children home."

The boy's cool blue eyes were suddenly compassionate, the veil of detached professionalism dropped away. "I'm sorry," he said.

The wall clock clicked to seventeen minutes past nine, a page bell rang. A nurse walked briskly past carrying a tray filled with small paper cups. And beyond these cold green corridors that smelled of wax and alcohol, where the muffled door of an elevator clanged and the sad lights of a small Christmas tree on the admitting-room counter glowed, was the other world of last-minute shopping and happy families gathered together. An unreal, cruel world that could laugh and celebrate while Jenny died. He turned and walked quickly to her room, leaving the young doctor standing beneath the electric moon that shone from the ceiling, radiant in his shimmering white clothes.

She lay on the high railed bed, her arms on top of the cover, a blood-pressure cuff around her left arm; a nurse stood beside her counting her pulse. The green robe Jenny had worn from home now hung on the closet door. A small crucifix of Jesus was on the wall in front of the bed, a bright crimson drop of blood swelling from His heart.

"It's all right, nurse, I'll stay with her now."

"They'll be putting her under oxygen any moment—"

"Tell them to wait a few minutes, I want to be alone with her."

"But, Doctor—"

He only looked at her, and she left the room in an energy of starched disapproval, and he adjusted the long, tubed, fluorescent light out of Jenny's eyes, though she seemed unaware it had been shining in her face. He pulled the green plastic lounge chair close to her bed, took up her hand, startled as he had always been at the callused palm. Strange that it should still be so rough. Used to, when he had shaken his head over her scarred, worn hands, she had laughed and said *in my next life, John, I'll come back as a clinging vine.*

But finally he had given up trying to change her. He would have liked to have her depend on him, need him. He had hated it when she put on slacks and had ridden the horse across the fields checking on stray cattle, going to the sharecroppers' cabins to nurse the sick. He was afraid of what she might catch. Those last years before she'd hired a permanent overseer she had carried a doctor's satchel on her saddle that he had given to her. It was a Christmas present, and when she unwrapped it, she had looked up at him with eyes so full of love he had had to turn away. He understood at last that she had to do what she had to do. He'd even been big enough to tell her she would have made a good doctor. He was glad he had told her that.

He rubbed his thumb gently back and forth across the back of her hand, and for the first time noticed that she no longer wore his mother's ring, wondered when she had taken it off. A negation, a rejection of him and their life. An acceptance of the failure of their life together.

"So. You're here."

Startled, he looked up. "I thought you were asleep. I didn't mean to waken you."

"I haven't been asleep. I wouldn't sleep away my last hours." The words were weak, whispered.

"It's not your last hours—"

"Please give me credit, John. Why are you here?"

"I brought you here, where else would I be? Don't you remember me bringing you here?"

"Of course. It's just I expected you to go back home."

Pain stabbed at the hurtful words, but she said them idly, and he thought they really didn't mean anything special or have any hidden significance. They were merely an observation.

"Raise the blind," she said, "so I can watch the snow, will you please? It's so pretty, I always loved riding in the fields when there was snow, it was like sailing through the clouds. There was ice on my minnow pond this morning. It seems so long ago, this morning. Is it still today?"

"Yes, it's still today, Jenny."

"Good, I'm glad, for I won't be here tomorrow."

"Of course you will."

"I won't be going home again."

He went to the window and raised the blind, came and sat again by her bed, took up her hand. "I'll take you home now if you want to go, you can be in your own bed where you can see the snow on the trees from your window."

"I never want to go back there. Promise me when I die you won't take me back there." She struggled to sit up, and he pushed her back.

"You're not going to die, Jenny, you've got lots of fish to catch out of the pond and new babies to see about—"

"Promise me."

"But it's where you were born, where the girls were born—"

"And the boy." Through the drugs came the slurred bitterness.

"Yes. And the boy."

"I hated him. Not at first, but later I hated him. How could a little dead baby destroy us, John?"

He went to the window and thought that most of this night had been spent looking out of windows. Over the white rooftops he saw in the distance a white neon star of Bethlehem, and he thought that he didn't know her at all. All these years she had been his wife, he had known the intimate, physical parts of her, and yet he had never known her soul. So skillfully she had kept herself secret, had hidden herself from him.

When he sat beside her again, when he had had taken up her hand, her eyes were closed, and a terrible grief came over him for their lost years. She went far back with him, and there were too few people left who knew him when he was young—who could remember with him. And he knew he did not want her to die, he wanted them to start over and do things right this time, he thought he had learned how. He would wake her and tell her he loved her; through all that had happened, for all his sins, he had never stopped loving her.

Gently he touched her shoulder, called her name.

"What can I do for you, Jenny? I'll do anything."

She opened her eyes. "I would like for you to tell Byron I'm sorry for how I used him. He'll understand. And the girls, tell Johnnie I always loved her, I don't think she knew. Tell Sarah that's she's always had a special place in my heart, she's the most damaged by what we've done."

He slumped back in the chair, releasing her hand. Nothing for him, nothing at all. It was too late for one kind word for him. But not too late for him to tell her he had never stopped loving her, for he had only just understood that. He leaned close to her ear, took her hand. "Jenny?" he said.

She looked vaguely at him as if she were already cut loose from this world.

"I love you still," he said.

She closed her eyes, and for a long time she didn't say anything. But then she looked at him, and he had to put his ear close to her lips to hear the words she spoke.

"John," she whispered, "I hate you still."

After a few minutes they came and put her under the oxygen tent, and from the doorway her face, through the thick plastic and in the dim light, looked young again. Blindly he walked down the hall and stood at the door at the end of the corridor and stared out into the night, watching the snow build up against the curb and beneath the trees. The lines of an old song he'd heard his mother sing ran through his head: *There's a minor in the carol, and a shadow in the light, and a spray of cypress twining with the holly wreath tonight.*

It was just turning light when he heard the crackle of the long starched skirt, and when he turned, a nun in blinding white robes was hurrying toward him, a large cross of Jesus swinging like a pendulum from her waist.

14

Midafternoon of Christmas day, Coy Watson sat at a table in the Kountry Kitchen drinking Jack Daniels. It was a present from a driver he kept supplied with bennies, and he had broken it open after he finished off a six-pack of beer. He drank the whiskey straight except for one ice cube in the bottom of the glass.

Hot air blew from the big ventilator on the ceiling, and combined with the liquor his face grew red and he was sweating, so he kicked off his shoes and took off his shirt, sitting in his undershirt with his hand curled around the glass, scowling. He blamed his foul mood on Roxanne leaving town and going over to Selma to her grandmother's for Christmas. It wouldn't have been so bad if the restaurant was open, he'd of had something to do, talk to the customers. But Faye had closed it, not even asking him if she could. And that was because she was calling the shots—she'd caught him two weeks ago fucking on the living room couch with Roxanne. Hell, he'd thought Faye was asleep, she'd been up all night in the restaurant, but hell no, she'd come pussyfooting into the living room right before daybreak and caught them humping away.

He was tired of screwing in the back seat of the Continental, it about froze his ass off, so he'd thought it was worth the chance. Ordinarily you could send in a brass band and Faye would sleep right through it, but that night the couch springs creaking must have woken her up. He hadn't hardly got started good when he just happened to glance up and there she stood in a white robe, winking off and on in the neon light that shone through the window. It liked to scared the hell out of him, he'd thought she was a ghost or an angel pulsing there in the dark.

Shit, he'd fallen off Roxanne and hit the floor, felt like he'd broken his back. Faye hadn't said a word, she'd just gone and brought Nellie back there and flipped on the light and both of them had stood watching him and Roxanne trying to get their clothes on, Roxanne crying and saying he'd made her do it. Faye had fired her the next day, had walked up the road to Roxanne's daddy's and told him to tell Roxanne not to come back, she wouldn't be needing her anymore. But she didn't tell him about the fucking, and that was a good thing, the man was a wrestler when he was young and still had legs like fence posts—he would as soon kill you as look at you. Of course, Coy wasn't scared of her old daddy, he had his equalizer, but he'd just as soon not tangle with him if he could help it. And Faye knew it. That probably accounted for the smug look, she'd look at him with a smile that meant she might tell and she might not, and he'd want to smash her.

He took a long swallow of the smooth, mellow whiskey, his mood turned blacker: he only then remembered she had invited her daddy to come for Christmas dinner, and that meant he was going to have to sit while Wesley Turner turned that hard blue stare on him. The man hated him, and he thought that the feeling was certainly mutual. One of these days, some-how, some way, he'd get even for him holding that shotgun on him and keeping him from his own wife. Hell, nobody had the right to keep a man from his wife, that was a sacred condition, a man's relationship with his wife.

Faye was up to something, she was planning something. She looked like the cat that swallowed the canary, and he had to watch his step until he could find out what it was, and then he'd get even with her; and that would be a definite pleasure. It was almost worth letting her play her little game, thinking of the ways he'd get even with her later on. He'd never gotten to complete his plans from that afternoon when he caught her under the tree with Bird Lasseter. Got even with the little white nigger, though. He sure got even with him. Even got some of the good citizens of the town to help him. Easiest thing in the world to do, whip up people's hate. It was always there, just under the surface. Except for those thin thinker types like Mason

Posey. Well, they showed him, the impotent little son-of-a-bitch standing sniveling, begging them to think it over. And the doctor hadn't done a goddam thing either, he'd expected some reaction from him, but not a thing. He was mighty liberal until it came to his daughter, and then he was just like everybody else. Nobody wanted their women corrupted.

A car eased down the highway, chains on the tires thunking against the ice, and he thought they would probably have stopped in at least for some coffee if they'd just been open. Hell, what he ought to do was go ahead and divorce Faye, he could buy her out, she never had been anything but a millstone around his neck. Then he'd fix this place up, turn it into a roadhouse with gambling and prostitution and bootleg whiskey. Hell, that's where the money was, not in blue-plate specials and a few bennies on the side. And the beauty of a roadhouse was that it would be with the sheriff's blessing; shit, he'd be a rich man in a year, he'd bet his right ball on that. That's what he'd wanted all his life, to be rich and wear snappy suits and have a different woman every night. Money might not buy happiness, but he sure wouldn't mind being miserable with a million bucks in the bank. Yessir, a million bucks sure would ease the misery.

He drained off the last of the liquor in the bottom of the glass, sloshed in another couple of ounces, and thought what a shit-eating way to spend Christmas, Faye back in the apartment making a family dinner. She was stuffing a turkey and she'd made two pumpkin pies and a pecan pie last night. Damned if he knew who was going to eat all that pie, but Faye was playing the typical little housewife planning the typical shitty, mother-fucking Christmas feast. Hell, she knew what he'd rather be doing, and she twitched her shiny, nylon-covered butt on purpose, taunting him. She knew he couldn't demand his rights anymore after catching him with Roxanne. He had committed the big "A" and she had a witness. That is, if the court would count a nigger as a witness.

He drank the last of the whiskey in his glass, poured another inch, thought how horny he was and knew he didn't stand a snowball's chance in hell of getting any until after the new year when Roxanne got back. He went into the kitchen and got another ice cube for the whiskey, watched Faye buzzing around setting the table. She had on a ruffled apron over the red slacks, and a white sweater that clung to her small round breasts. He stared at her, and for a flash understood that she was beautiful, that she probably could have married anybody, with that red hair and soft curved figure. He just got used to looking at her in a uniform, and then she turned and saw him watching her, and her look turned to such cold contempt that he went quickly back into the restaurant, anger flushing in his neck and face. Who the hell did she think she was to look at him like that? He was the one got her off that pissant dirt farm and into a place that had a little sophistication.

He looked out into the white day, and the quiet came down on him, and he thought that later on it might cheer him up to go hunting, maybe do a little target practice on some squirrels and rabbits with the new shotgun he'd given himself for Christmas. He'd bought a gift only for himself this year. Faye didn't deserve one. He had a black nightgown he was going to give to Roxanne that a driver who hauled Movie Town lingerie had given him in exchange for some bennies. But then he decided not to waste it on her, he'd never get to see her in it, the only way he ever saw her was on the back seat of the car with her pants down around her ankles. Now and then he saw a flash of white butt when a car went by, but what the hell, that wasn't worth a nightgown. Nah, save it for somebody else.

Thinking of his gun made him want to handle it, and he went into the living room and took it down from the rack over the television, went into the bedroom and sat on the side of the bed, breaking it open, closing it, loving the feel of the slick steel as he ran his fingers down the barrel. The feeling was so sensuous, he almost got a hard on, and he loaded in the shells, aimed it out the window at a redbird perched on the stark limb of a maple tree. "*Tch*" he said, his finger resting lightly on the trigger, and rising, he lay it on the dresser, breaking it, but leaving the shells in.

He continued drinking for almost another hour, though his

stomach was beginning to ache and burn. Goddam ulcer, always something to take the joy out of life. Vaguely, on his trips back and forth to the bathroom to take a piss, he noticed that the floor seemed to jump up when he stood, and that the long cylinders of fluorescent light had become blurred and fused into a solid rectangle. It seemed such a long trip to the bathroom he decided just to pee on the bush outside the front door, shit, the world was vacant, no cars passed, he had become Nanook of the North. He chortled. Nanook of the North. And Faye was Na*nooky*, only she wouldn't give him any. And he scowled, and pulled his bottle closer as he sat down at the table, and when he poured, more liquor sloshed onto the table than in his glass. Wasting his present. Well, hell, what's the difference, he didn't pay for it.

The ice had again melted, and he went to the kitchen and Faye was bent over the oven door basting the turkey, and he stood in the doorway watching the way the slacks pulled tight across her ass. Quietly he walked up to her, reached around and cupped his hand about her breasts, squeezing.

She whirled on him, color leaping into her face. Through clenched teeth, the words hissed, she said, "Don't you ever touch me, Coy Watson, don't you ever put your hands on me again."

"Cunt," he said, stepping back, stumbling, grabbing the door facing. "Switching your ass around, you know what you're doing." His words were slurred, and he reached for her again, and she sidestepped, and he fell against the table she had covered with a white cloth and set with her mother's Rambler Rose china, her King Richard sterling silver. "You think you're some hot shit, don't you? Think I'm just dying to get in your pants, don't you? Hell, I'm tired of sniffing around after your pussy, you're my wife, you got a legal obligation—"

"You *leave me alone*!" she said as he reached for her again, and they faced each other in the blast of heat from the oven. The white tablecloth was twisted, the china on the edge of the round table.

"Saving it for Haysie boy? Izzat why you switch your ass around his table? Haven't seen him in here for awhile; he knows what's good for him he won't never set foot in here again."

When her eyes widened and she stepped back, he looked hard at her. "He's been coming in here behind my back, hasn't he, you been slipping around with him, you can't fool me. You bitch, you whore, I'm gon' beat your ass—"

She braced her hands against the counter. "You're not going to touch me, I've done nothing wrong, I've done nothing to be ashamed of."

"Hell, neither have I. A man don't get service at home, he's justified in going someplace else. You owe me a little service for keeping a roof over your head and clothes on your back. Hell, you even got a big car sitting out in the parking lot."

"This roof and my clothes and that car that you won't let me drive was bought with my daddy's money, with *my* money that Daddy intended for me to have. Your name is on the deed to this restaurant because I *let* it be there, and I was a fool, Daddy warned me—"

His sight blurred, he lost all vision except the round moon of her face and her red lips saying the lying words. Rage roared down on him and he fell upon her, knocking her down, the smug face turning white with fear, and he straddled her, wound his fingers into her hair, beat her head against the floor, as in a dream heard her screams, his own voice saying softly, *die, goddam you, die.* And then pain ripped into his groin, and he fell onto his side drawing up his legs, the bright shining of the tile dimming, and he closed his eyes. A high, thin hum buzzed in his head.

After a long time he opened his eyes and she was gone, but a small puddle of blood was darkening on the floor where she had lain. He sat up, the room darkened, then cleared, and he pulled up by the handle of the refrigerator, and he went to the oven and pulled out the blue, white-dotted enamel coffin that held the turkey. He felt no pain but smelled his own burned flesh as he walked to the back door and flung it out, pan and bird separating, rolling, settling finally into a drift of snow against a pine tree.

He ripped the cloth from the dining table, smashing the china onto the floor; he picked up the silver and broke it slowly, methodically, in two, opened the kitchen drawer and took the rest out of the box and broke those also in two, all the ornate, darkened knives and forks and spoons engraved with an old English "C." He tore open the drawers and emptied them, stomped the contents, dishtowels, potholders, light bulbs, flowers seeds, grinding them into the floor, took a hammer and smashed the plastic tea-kettle clock on the wall over the stove and all of Faye's collection of salt and pepper shakers on the whatnot stand in the corner.

He went into the bedroom and smashed the dresser mirror, the glass splintering and spewing, stinging shards striking him in the face, his image distorted, his cheeks streaked with bloody tears. He went into the restaurant and smashed the electric wall clock, the juke box, the display cases. He drew pictures of naked women on the walls with ketchup and mustard, and then he went back into the apartment looking for her, calling to her, her name whispered, echoing. In his mind he saw her kneel to kiss his injured testicles before he smashed the hammer on her head, obliterating her, silencing her vile and lying voice forever.

He looked in all the rooms, behind the doors, in the closets. He went out the front door, walked to the highway, looking up and down, and then back inside and out the back door; he had taken but one step onto the porch when she said his name.

She stood at the bottom of the steps looking up at him, her face dead white, her hair wild and flaming about her head. "Coy?" she said, and he had barely time to catch the terror in her eyes as he started down the steps before she raised his shotgun and fired straight into his face, and he pitched backward, spangled pain bursting in his head.

She fled down the road with no thought of where she was going but only that she must run, and again and again looked over her shoulder thinking to see the black car bearing down on her. But each time the road stretched white and empty, and the wind pounded her in freezing gusts though the sun had come out bright that morning.

She ran for her life, this time he was going to kill her, and she heard the throbbing rush of blood in her ears, saw her heartbeat as black dots before her eyes. It seemed she had run forever, that the only thing real in all her life was this picking up and setting down of her feet. The terror of illimitable space came over her and of the immense and boundless arc of sky— of her aloneness in the universe; the frozen fields had always been cruelly barren and silent, the bare bones of the tree limbs had forever clattered in the howling wind; and she cried out but had only herself to hear.

When she came around the curve she saw a figure silhou- etted against the rosy sky and she screamed to it to stop, and when it continued, she ran harder and shouted louder, waving her arms. And then the figure stopped and turned around, a man's tall form approached her, growing larger and larger until at last she collasped into John Lasseter's strong arms.

15

John Lasseter sat in the back seat of the first car behind the hearse. A teen-age boy in a black suit drove the limousine furnished by the Valleydale Funeral Chapel. Johnnie sat in the back seat too, and the procession wound through the streets headed for the cemetery on the outskirts of town where the old Baptist church once had been. After it burned, the new church was built in the town, the old cemetery growing gradually larger as the citizens died off.

Through the small window in the back of the hearse, and beneath the blanket of pink roses, he could see the dark wood of the coffin in which Jenny lay. He was bringing her from the funeral home in Selma without taking her by the house because that was what she wanted, and this was the last thing he could do for her, honor her request. Request. Such a mild word, so bland, to describe her vehemence. And he so unaware of it, not knowing she hated the house. Or him. He had known she did not love him, but the hatred had stunned him. He had thought all the grievance on his side. How hard, how unforgiving her face had been, how typical her honesty that as she lay dying she would be uncompromising with truth. And so he was placing her next to her mother in the McKinley plot, for she would not want to lie next to him for eternity.

The cars passed through the neighborhood, a Christmas sun shining from a pale blue sky; it glinted off shiny bicycles and wagons and roller skates of the children who had stopped to watch the cars creep by. The snow had begun to melt in patches, spikes of yellow grass poking up through the smooth circles; a rope of silver garland, twined through the limbs of a fir tree, sparkled and shimmered in the gusts of wind.

He closed his eyes against it all, the horrible, depressing brightness, the rosy-cheeked children whipping along on their various wheels, and when he opened them again they were going through the business district. As they passed his office, he wished desperately that he could leave the car and go into his office to take care of the patients who were gathered about his door, hunched down in their coats and waiting for him. He was mad at Jenny that she had died and so badly disrupted his life; always in the back of his mind was the knowledge that she was there. And as he had not understood that he had never stopped loving her, neither had he understood just how much he had counted on that. How bitterly she must have hated him all these years not to have been able to forgive him as she lay dying. And he had thought himself so righteous that evening after he had found her with Byron to allow her to stay. The truth was, he was terrified she would go.

Mary Betty was leaving. She had told him yesterday morning when he gave them the news of Jenny that she was going permanently to her son. "I only stayed fo' her, God knows I never would of lef' her by herse'f, but now I'se goin' too, I couldn't stand one mo' night in that house." Her face was pulled into the harsh lines of grief, her gray head bound with a black cloth. Her nearly sightless, watery eyes had watched him unblinking, and he could not meet her gaze.

The gleaming black hearse led them around the corner and onto the stretch of asphalt that shot flat and straight between the wide white fields to the cemetery, and he glanced at Johnnie, aching to take her gloved hand, aching to comfort her. To be comforted. But if she saw him looking at her, she gave no sign, for she was still coldly angry with him for sending her away. She kept her face turned, and he thought how like Jenny she was, her hair glowing palely against the dark cloth of the coat. He looked back at the white fields again, thinking she seemed unmoved by her mother's death, but like Jenny, she suffered inwardly, keeping her feelings to herself. When he had given her Jenny's message of love, her only reaction was a brief and fleeting shadow of pain across her face. And he yearned for that time (only a few months ago but seeming like years) when she loved him, when they could have comforted each other.

He had called the girls home on Christmas Eve morning, and they had arrived at dusk, the twins first, then Sarah, then Johnnie. They stood in the living room before the cold fireplace of half-burned logs and ashes and he told them the circumstances of their mother's death. Johnnie asked him why he had not called them the night before so they could have said good-by. "That last night belonged to your mother and me," he said. "She did not ask me to call you. We started out alone, there was a time before any of you. I know it's hard for you all to understand that once we were just two people and we were in love." They only looked at him. "We had things to say that did not concern you." No one spoke, and he thought how innocently selfish children were, how they thought parents existed only in relation to themselves. He thought they could never understand that first they had been Jenny McKinley and John Lasseter, that becoming parents had not changed who they were. Only it had. Was that not what had destroyed them? the children?

The twins had sobbed on each other's shoulders, but Johnnie and Sarah had stood on opposite sides of the fireplace, never crying, but going to Mary Betty who stood darkly solitary in the dining-room door. They had taken her in their arms, had drawn her into their circle and left him out. Except that, as he left, the twins had touched his arm, and he had appreciated their acknowledging him.

From the car window he saw the pines laden with heavy snow, the ground only thinly covered beneath the dense trees. He saw himself a young man riding his horse into the woods where only paths led to the shacks, his wet boots frozen into the stirrups so that he had to shout for someone to come and pull his feet loose so he could climb down. And Jenny was there too, riding behind him, arms tight about his waist, sometimes on a summer morning when they had been up all night, sometimes in the softness of dusk. And she would say, "John, how can people dream of heaven when they have this glorious earth? What could heaven possibly have that we don't have here?" And she'd say, "I don't believe what the Bible says about heaven and hell, John, do you? Do you suppose God would send me to hell for not believing?" And they'd laugh at her inconsistency, he would spur the horse to a gallop, her laughter ringing through the woods.

The car bumped onto the rutted dirt road as they turned off the highway, and they began the last half mile to the cemetery. They passed the shanties teetering on crooked rock pillars, and the gray-board houses seemed like animals crouching, dark window sockets staring. Pots of red and white plastic poinsettias lined the porches, and he wondered why they did not gather pine and holly bough for their decoration that grew so plenteously all through the woods. Pine had filled his mother's house at Christmas; she had banked it on the mantels, twined it over the doors. She had burned pine logs and resined knots that burst into red and gold sparks that showered upward through the chimney, and he would run into the yard to see them streaking against the night sky like rockets.

The Negroes came onto their porches to watch, hugging themselves against the wind, the women's heads wrapped in dark squares of cloth, their skirts whipping about their knees, children hiding in the material, clasping their mothers' legs. The men stood watching, raising their hands in a somber wave as they passed; the women's tears were strung down their faces like tinsel rain.

When he looked away, Jenny stood in the road not far ahead and in the place he had seen her that first morning. The wind blew her white dress, she was barefoot, and he leaned forward, smiling, joy leaping. In the bright day her hair had turned to sunlight, and his tears blurred her sweet young form. He groped for the door handle, but then as the car came even with her, she faded into the blue shadows that fell across the road. He sank back, trembling, and Johnnie had turned to him, her gloved hand clasping his as they turned into the stoned archway of the cemetery.

▼

They sat in a row on folding chairs beside Jenny's coffin. Gathered behind were those who had ridden in the procession, and behind them the Negroes who stood last, and with a separation of ground between them and the whites.

He stared at the plastic grass that covered the raw black dirt, and the preacher stepped from the crowd, his bald head laurel-wreathed with thin gray hair. He raised his Bible and said that they had gathered to say good-by to Jennifer McKinley Lasseter, whose body must forever rest beneath the soil and the clay, but that if she were saved, even now her spirit was in heaven with her loved ones who had gone before. He said she looked upon the face of God.

John Lasseter listened to the words and thought that if the preacher's words were true, perhaps Jenny at last could hold their son. But he didn't believe any of it; whatever survived of Jenny was in his memory and in the flesh of their children. Her heaven and her hell had been upon this earth, and that fact was true for all of them gathered there.

When the scripture was read, the prayer prayed, he stood and touched her coffin. "God bless you, Jenny," he said, and walked away toward the woods toward the farm to pick up his car; he was already late for Zella's shot.

Their palpable, disapproving silence battered him like stones as he had left. Hypocrites, he thought, most of them hypocrites, coming only for curiosity or pretended sanctimonious bull. Well, let them come for whatever reason they had, he had long ago given up caring what they thought of him. He would, as he always had, continue to live his life the best he saw fit. None of those people put bread on his table.

He walked along the frozen path and as he crossed the back fields of the farm he stopped at the fence to look at the bare, twisted boughs of the apple trees in the orchard where he and Jenny had married that April morning. In the freezing afternoon it was hard to believe that those trees had ever been so thick with blossoms they sprang even from the trunk—hard to believe that he and Jenny had loved each other so much that day that neither could speak after the vows had been said. *To love and to cherish, to have and to hold.* So long ago, and yet seeming like yesterday.

It was all over, their story told, his and Jenny's. Now he knew how it all came out, he could close the book. And in the end he had still loved her, finally understood. And though she had said she hated him, he knew she did not: behind the bitterness he had seen the sorrow. She could not have pitied him if she had not loved him. But as for Byron West, he would never get the message Jenny sent to him, and he continued across the field to the road, then not going to his car but suddenly entering the house, needing to be alone there for a few minutes.

He climbed the steps to the front porch, went through the door where so many years ago he had waited for Jenny, watched her come down the stairs to him. The setting sun streamed brightly through the living-room windows onto the worn, threadbare Persian rug, blending the faded red and royal blue, diffusing the colors so that they glowed. He stood in the empty strangeness of the house and couldn't believe it was all over: never again the cries of babies, never the sweet harmony of the twins at the piano singing old songs, their voices blending, floating in the air as he came up the back walk for supper. Never again, never again Bird a little boy throwing his arms around his legs, looking up at him with loving eyes. With accusing, begging eyes that morning he sent him away.

He walked to a small mahogany table beside the fireplace, gently touching the petal of a dried cornflower in a cut-glass vase. It was in a bouquet of asters and chrysanthemums, and Jenny had put them there, saying she couldn't bear it when the flowers were all gone. She'd been doing that for years, gathering the last of the flowers and drying them, trying to keep them longer. But they never did, they crumbled and fell into dust after only a few weeks, just as the cornflower did now, the petal that he scarcely touched falling onto the table, withered, colorless.

Slowly he climbed the stairs to her bedroom. He had to

look once more at the bed where she was born and where the babies were born—the place of beginnings and endings. He stood in the doorway staring at the dark, massive four-poster, and for a moment the windows were thrown open to summer and the perfume of roses and the twilight dotted with bursts of light of the fireflies. And they were young and they had all the time in the world, they laughed and made love beneath the covers on misty winter mornings, their breaths puffing in the cold air before Mary Betty had laid the fire, laughing and scuffling as she crumpled the old newspapers and pushed the kindling beneath the logs. *Don't act lak grown folks atall, act like chee'rn*, but smiling, shaking her head, bringing them coffee and biscuits to eat in bed.

He had not known he showed his terrible disappointment when the girls were born, nor had he known her sorrow and desperation. If only they had talked, had told each other how they felt, but they had not, and the stunning, echoing emptiness of the house bore down on him—the smooth, unwrinkled bed covered now with a blue spread (he did not know what the hospital had done with the white one he had wrapped about her) looked as if nobody had ever slept in it, had ever been joyful or prostrate there—had ever been born or died there. Such an old bed, so strange with its unwrinkled face.

He walked to her dresser, picked up her brush, felt between his fingertips the faded, frizzed strands of corrupted hair caught in the bristles, laid it down again, not wanting to touch it. He picked up a bottle of cologne that sat beside a stern-faced picture of her father, read the label: Windsong. A beautiful word and so like Jenny to choose such a scent for herself. He did not recall that he had ever given her a present of perfume.

He opened the top drawer of the dresser, smiled at the jumbled contents—handkerchiefs, necklaces, a small camera, some pictures, a packet of pins, all jumbled together. Neatness, orderliness, were never Jenny's strong points. And then in the corner of the drawer, as if it had been carelessly dropped there, was his mother's ring, the red and blue stones dusty, the gold setting grown dull.

It lay in the palm of his hand; he thought how the minerals, symbolic of love and hope, far outlasted the human flesh—far outlasted the love and hope. He dropped it into the drawer and turned to leave, at the door looked back, and out the windows saw the blotched fields where the snow was melting; in the corner, beside her closet door, sat Jenny's muddy boots, as if she had only lately returned from a walk there.

He walked down the stairs and into the fading afternoon, and up the road saw the dark specks of cars returning from the cemetery, and hurried toward his car, the rising wind pushing against him. He turned up the collar of his coat, thought he heard someone call, and looked over his shoulder and saw a tiny figure running toward him and waving its arms.

16

Concealed by the trees at the edge of the woods Bird listened as the preacher read scripture over Jenny Lasseter, his gray hair ruffled in the wind.

Like as a father pitieth his children, so the Lord pitieth them that fear him. For he knoweth our frame; he remembereth that we are dust. As for man, his days are as grass: as a flower of the field, so he flourisheth. For the wind passeth over it, and it is gone; and the place thereof shall know it no more.

He saw his father rise and touch the coffin, then walk away toward the woods, and the preacher and the people watched, there was no movement but his father's. No sound but the wind whistling among the tombstones, tossing a withered wreath to the ground.

He cometh forth like a flower, the preacher said, *and is cut down, he fleeth also as a shadow and continueth not.* He closed his Bible and prayed and all the heads were piously bowed, and Bird thought how lonesome Johnnie seemed with the vacant chair beside her, how like a stranger to him in the dark coat. When he thought of her it was always as she had been in summer, green light from the water reflecting onto her pale skin, her hair streaming about her shoulders.

He had seen the condemnation in the hard set of the people's shoulders as they had watched his father leave, and he thought that most of the men who condemned him for Zella had also slept with black women—those same white hands that now so protectively clasped their wives' arms had also fondled black breasts.

He stayed until everyone had left, watched the lowering of

the coffin, the clumps of black dirt thrown in. The Negro gravediggers left, shovels balanced on their shoulders, and the wind fluttered the flowers they had laid on the grave.

And though she was enclosed forever in the confines of her narrow room, she was there, he felt Jenny Lasseter's presence, and a wearying, aching sadness came over him. But not for her, never for her. The sadness was for the little boy who had flung his arms around her legs that morning in the kitchen, not crying or begging but nevertheless pleading, as he looked up into icy-blue eyes. The memory of them, child and woman, came back so strong, and with it the hatred and the pain. He felt again her hands hard as steel gripping his shoulders, ripping him loose from her. He had followed his father to the car, and when he looked back she was watching from the kitchen window, the curtain pulled back, her face pale in the early light. Then some movement made him think she called him back, and happiness thrilled; but then the curtain dropped and his father called to him, and he climbed into the car, his suitcase riding on the seat beside him like death.

Raw dirt seeped from beneath the blanket of pink roses covering her grave, and he was sorry she belonged now to the earth, for he hated her with the same intensity of that morning. But he missed her, he wished her back to continue hating her in the flesh, and he turned into the woods taking the path his father had taken to Zella's house. He was going to say good-by, for tomorrow he was leaving Asheton and would never come back. He was taking the two-o'clock bus to Birmingham, and when he got off and became merged with the crowd in the station he would begin his life as a white man. Odd, that such a momentous journey should begin on the Greyhound—that this journey that would open up the whole world to him was not begun with bells ringing and a marching band.

The cold glaze of twilight was on the river and he walked faster, anxious to see his father, believing his father would be sad to see him go, even though that was what he said he ought to do. He also believed that his father loved him, and he must have the memory of this love he would see in his face to take away with him, for that would be all he would have for a long time. He could love no one until he finished school and went North, he must be far away and invent a new past for himself. It sounded so like a game Johnnie would love, he smiled, and wished he could take her with him. She would go if he asked her. But how long before she would tire of the game and want to come home? And if he refused her, or tried to forbid her, she would hate him. So the road he traveled must be alone, at least for awhile—only he could know his beginnings, perhaps after many years even he might believe the past he made up, this life seeming like a dream.

He walked against the flowing of the river, coming out finally into the twilight of the clearing not far from the cabin, and he thought how strange that no light shone from the windows, that the panes glowed only with the rosy light of setting sun. He stopped, puzzled. Maybe they had gone somewhere, taken a walk in the woods along the river, he knew they sometimes did that. But in the cold growing more bitter as the sun went down he did not think so, and thought they were making love. He would go home and come back later, embarrassed to think of his father that way.

The stars were coming out dimly in the dusky sky, and he stood with his hands shoved deep into his jacket pockets, the gusts of wind freezing cold on his bare head. In the distance the undulant, silver strip of river reflected back a waxing moon. Tomorrow, when he was gone, would the river still be here beneath the celestial sky? So calmly the water flowed between these shallow banks, and when spring should come again, the lilies would bloom, the birds would nest, the willows would trail their tender, new-green branches along its shores. Nature, so cruelly, so implacably, continuing without him.

Something screamed, and he turned his ear to the sound that he at first thought came from the woods, at first thought was a screech owl or some animal caught in a hunter's trap. But then it came again, and it was from the house, a lost, eerie, moan that made the flesh rise on his arms, and he ran for the front door, flinging it open, shouting into the gloom. He heard harsh, rasping breathing and stepped hesitantly inside, saw a

heaped something on the couch, walked slowly toward it, calling Zella's name. He thought someone had broken in and hurt
her, that he might be waiting in the dark for him, and his heart
began so fast a beat he became faint as he crept across the room.

She lay huddled on her side, her legs drawn up, and he
touched her lightly on the shoulder. She opened her eyes and
looked up at him, her eyes dimly glowing, and though she stared
at him she did not really seem to see him. "Are you Doc?" she
asked, and when he said that he was not, she moaned and rolled
her head.

"Oh, God, I thought you was come with my shot, I ain't
had nothin' since las' night—"

"This is Bird," he said, "are you sick? What's wrong with
you, I heard you scream—"

"I got to have my shot, do you know where Doc is? He
promised to come out early." She clasped his hand, and her's
was cold as ice.

"I saw him leave the funeral, he came this way. I thought
he was here. His wife's funeral lasted a long time, they were
late coming to the cemetery from Selma, the roads must have
been icy."

She sat up, still hugging her stomach, and rocking back
and forth. "I'm gon' die too he don't get here with my shot, I
got to have it, I got to have it," and she thrashed her head back
and forth, tore her hair.

"*Stop it!*" he said, pulling her hands away from her head,
and she sprang on him, leaped up and raked her fingernails
down the side of his face. He jumped back, thinking she had
gone mad, that the shot she needed was for rabies, that one of
the wild animals she fed had bitten her. He grasped her arms,
holding her off, pain stinging down his cheek, and she collapsed,
sobbing against him. He picked her up and carried her down
the hall and lay her on the bed.

"Go get Doc, honey, if Doc don't come I'm gon' die—"

"I don't know where he is."

"You can find him, honey, everybody always sayin' what
a smart boy you are, you can find him." Her voice was wheedling, cajoling.

"I don't know where to look." He reached to stroke her forehead, but she knocked his hand away.

"Goddam *man*, take your hands off me, goddam men always hurtin' somebody." She began to tremble, her teeth chattering, and he pulled the jumbled cover up over her.

He switched on the bedside lamp thinking the light might calm her, and he stared, disbelieving, at what he saw: her cheekbones thrust beneath fleshless, jaundiced skin that once had been coppery with undertones of red. Her thick black hair was dull and brittle, her lips dry and pale. The pink satin robe she wore was soiled and smelled of old sweat, a faded stained circle beneath the arm that she had placed across her eyes to shut out the light. He could not match this person with the woman who swung along the street on Saturday afternoons, her tawny skin shining, the coarse hair glossy about her shoulders. He only now thought that it had been a long time since he had seen her downtown.

She lowered her arm and looked at him, her eyes dull and uncomprehending, the pupils dilated almost as big as the golden-brown irises. "Where is he, Bird? Why don't he come, he promised he'd come, how come is he doing this to me? I been good to him, I ain't never refused him, I stayed with him." She cried soundlessly, the tears sliding over the sharp cheekbones, dripping off her chin, spotting the soiled robe.

"Did an animal bite you, Zella?" he asked. "Is my father giving you rabies shots?"

She laughed. "Oh, my yes, honey, a animal bit me," and she rolled up the satin sleeve. "See them bites, see where that animal got hold of me?" And he saw the dusky skin marred with needle punctures, but not understanding; he said nothing, but stroked her hand as her arm fell back onto the bed.

"My guts feels like they's on fire," she said, but began to shiver, sweat forming in a fine mist on her forehead and over her lips.

"I don't understand, Zella, what's he giving you the shots *for*? What's wrong with you? Maybe I can do something until he comes—"

"Can't nobody do nothin' but him, he's got the stuff."

She turned onto her side, drew up her legs. "Have mercy, Jesus, have mercy. Mine eye is consumed with grief, my soul and my belly, my life is spent with grief, my strength faileth." Her voice faded away. For a moment she lay quietly, her eyes closed, and he thought she had gone to sleep, hoped she had gone to sleep.

"My grandmamma used to say that to me, it's from the Bible. She used to say I was bad when I come home from being with Henry; she'd come to my room in her long gown and kneel by me in the dark and make me say the words with her. When I come with the docta, grandmamma say I can't never come back to her house no more. I miss her, I don't never see her." Her mouth turned down at the corners like a child's.

"But she loves you, Zella," Bird said. "People don't just stop loving you." But they did, and he was afraid. Wasn't that why he had come here? to see if his father loved him?

He took up her frail hand and held it tightly, for it was a bond, a strength—she understood what it was like to be him, being more than you were allowed, having the gift or the curse to want more, to maybe be able to get it. To have to struggle, to risk.

She began to tremble violently, he thought she was having convulsions, that she was dying, and he jumped up and backed away from her, and she opened her eyes and looked at him. "Listen, Zella," he said, "I have to go find somebody to help you, to take you to the hospital," and she whimpered and through the chattering of her teeth asked him not to leave her.

And then he was outside, running across the clearing, shadow-wraiths cast across his path from the rising moon, and he ran for the road, but just then headlights swept around the curve, and his father pulled into the clearing in the Buick. He flung open the door, not stopping to shut it, and he ran for the house carrying his satchel. Bird ran after him, and when they got to the bedroom, Zella was sitting on the side of the bed.

"You son-of-a-bitch," she screamed, pushing up her sleeve, shoving the skinny arm to him. "*Where have you been!*"

The doctor did not answer but methodically, efficiently, went about taking a rubber tube from the satchel and tying it about her upper arm, and she balled her hand into a fist, watching him with bright and greedy eyes. From a small bottle he drew a clear fluid into a hypodermic needle, and Bird wondered why there was no discussion between them, no questions asked concerning symptoms. They knew their parts as if they had been rehearsed many times, and Bird closed his eyes and leaned against the doorjamb.

He heard the sighing exhalation of her breath, and when he looked again her back was arched, her head thrown back, a look of purest ecstasy spreading across her face as the crystal fluid flowed into her vein. "Heaven, oh, heaven," she said. "Thank you, Doc, thank you, honey. I love you."

The doctor withdrew the needle, replaced the rubber tube in his satchel, and Zella sank back on the pillow, her pelvic bones sharp against the robe. He counted her pulse, took her blood pressure.

"What's wrong with her?" Bird said. "I thought she was going to die, are you taking her to the hospital?"

The doctor looked sharply at him, surprise and anger flashing in his face. "What are you doing here? You have no business here—"

"I came to say good-by."

"We already said that, last summer—"

"I didn't, I didn't say good-by then. At least not for good. I'm leaving Asheton in the morning, I won't be back."

The doctor's shoulders slumped beneath the black suit coat. "So. You're taking my advice."

"I'm taking my own advice."

"Yes, well." He turned again to the satchel, put back the blood-pressure cuff, the needle. "So many good-bys. Everything's changing—is changed. Where are you going?"

"To Birmingham, to the University—"

"To the University?" the doctor looked at him, his eyebrows raised.

"I still have my scholarship; I've thought about it and I don't see any reason I should change my plans."

"No, I suppose not. I'm just surprised, I thought you'd given up the idea. You could still come back here, the place needs another doctor—"

"No, I'll never come back here."

"I thought not. It's better that you don't, but I could help you some with money, the partial scholarship won't be enough."

"Thank you, but I have to do it by myself. I've made some money working for Wesley Turner."

"I know, I saw you in the field. I was surprised."

"I appreciate your confidence."

"Well, you have to admit you hated it pretty bad."

They smiled, the old understanding, the old comradeship briefly between them. Bird held out his hands, palms up, displaying the calluses like medals. His father took his hands, rubbed his thumb over the tough, raised flesh, and Bird thought that he could not speak or he would cry. He had not hoped for so much, that they would touch, that he could take this away with him too, the warm gentleness of his father's hands. And with the pride in his father's face he felt the child's surge of pleasure for the approval.

"Well," the doctor said, and turned to push a damp strand of hair from Zella's forehead, "you'll have to get over being squeamish."

Bird dropped his hands to his sides. "Have faith," he said.

Their reflections were in the dark window, the circle of lamplight enclosed them, and Zella sighed, and the doctor pulled the cover over her, smoothing, straightening, tucking it about her.

"What's wrong with her?" Bird asked. "She looks so awful—"

The doctor turned to him. "I wish you hadn't come here, I wish you had come to the office." His voice was irritable, scolding.

"I'm leaving before daylight in the morning, you wouldn't have been at the office before I left."

"Yes, I see, I understand. I'm glad you came. I wouldn't have wanted you to leave without any word."

"No. I wouldn't have done that. What kind of medicine

are you giving Zella? I thought maybe she'd gotten rabies, she acted like she'd gone mad, she attacked me, scratched me." He turned his face to the light so his father could see the scratches.

"You'll need to put something on those—"

"Yes, I will, later." He did not want the dread Merthiolate scrubbed into the raw flesh.

His father smiled. "That's not so very much pain, Bird, to disinfect a wound."

"I understand pain, have you forgotten last summer? I made it all right without the Merthiolate."

"I thought you would go to another doctor, maybe over to Carden."

Bird shrugged. "It worked out all right. What's wrong with Zella?"

"Can't you tell?" His voice was deeply patient, deeply weary. "You ought to recognize an addict, you've read the books, you were with me that time Dil Johnson had delirium tremens."

"He was an alcoholic. He was seeing bugs and things. Does Zella drink?"

"She's hooked on morphine."

"On morphine? How did she do that, from Henry Jerald? Has she been going with him again? I've seen him around town. I thought he'd gone up North."

"He came back, he's been hanging around out here. I had to run him off the other night; Zella's been meeting him down at the river, he wants her to leave with him."

"He's been giving her morphine?"

"No. I gave it to her."

"You? I don't understand."

"I gave it to her for the headaches; Henry started coming around bothering her and the headaches got really bad, she couldn't sleep. If she goes with him she'll become a prostitute again."

"Why did you think she would go with him?"

"Because she's been wanting to go for a long time; she stayed with me because she was grateful." He shrugged, spread his hands. "I could have let her go, but not with Henry, not to prostitute."

"But how did she get hooked, you must have seen what was happening, you must have known—" He stopped, their eyes met and held, the doctor went to the window and pulled the draperies, turned to him, but did not come back into the light.

"I thought I could keep her on a low dose, give her just enough to give her some relief, make her feel good until Henry left. It wasn't fair for him to sneak out here and promise her lights and music. The big city. Chicago, Detroit, wherever it was he told her he would take her. I just wanted to make her feel good so she could make the right decision, but a little of anything is never enough for Zella; sex turns her into a prostitute, a couple of shots of morphine into an addict."

"You knew it would happen, you did it on purpose." The horror of the whispered words blended with the hiss of the gas heater that the doctor had lit. "You knew, you knew—"

"No, I did not, I never intended this should happen, I'm not a monster."

"You did it on purpose and you loved her, how could you do this to someone you love? What you have done to her is worse than what Coy Watson and those men did to me. You *are* a monster, I hate you, I hate having loved you."

"You have no right to judge me, who are you to judge me?"

In her sleep Zella moaned, and quickly the doctor walked to her, felt her pulse, pulled the cover around her shoulders. "It's all right," he said, "I'm here," and she opened her eyes, smiled at him, then turned to her side, her back to them.

"Why weren't you here to take care of her? Since you did it to her, you had to know what she needed."

"I was on my way here when Faye Watson caught up to me on the road after I left the cemetery."

"I saw you leave."

"You saw me leave? You were at the funeral? I thought you hated Jenny."

Bird did not answer, but stubbornly waited.

"I went by the house to pick up the car and come here, but Faye Watson stopped me, she'd shot Coy."

"Shot Coy?" He blankly stared, not understanding.

"Coy got drunk and tried to kill her and she shot him with his shotgun. I had to report it, the sheriff's out there now."

"Is he dead?" He felt nothing, only a curious detachment that he should lose two old enemies in one day.

"He's not dead, but it was bad, there was a lot of blood; the gun was loaded with bird shot. Faye shot him when he came down the back steps into the yard after her. I don't know whether he'll make it."

"Why would you even go to help him? You chose him over Zella, she could have died, your medical books say people can die if you take them off drugs too quick."

"Zella wasn't dying, she was a long way from that. I had to go with Faye, she had that deadly calm people get sometimes just before they go completely over the edge. She's not over the miscarriage, psychologically or physically, I went for her, not for Coy. And I don't have to explain myself to you or to anybody. I've always lived my life the way I thought best, and I didn't ask you here. We said all we had to say to each other last summer. Go on to Birmingham and see if they can teach you perfection along with your medical studies."

Silently they waited, unable to cross the infinite division of the narrow physical space that separated them, their divergencies irreconcilable, the doctor's face gone deathly white. "Well," he said, gesturing, the giant shadow of his hand moving on the wall, "you don't have to worry, I'm taking her to a sanitarium over in Atlanta, and when she's well she can go with Henry or do whatever she wants to do. I'm tired, I no longer need close relationships, my work is all I want. It's the most important thing in the world to me. If only I had recognized that years ago."

Bird did not speak; his face was hard and inscrutable as rock. The wind gusted and shook the windows, and loneliness, terrifying and absolute, clutched him; and that the doctor looked suddenly old and desolate, his face sagging into the creases of age, his lips gray, his eyes anguished, was no satisfaction: in grief and despair he ran out into the night, blood and breath pounding in his head, his face turned toward the black woods.

▼

He ran as he had that morning when he fled the dusty horror of Mrs. Bonner's yard. He dodged the trees as they loomed upon him out of the mist, found his way by the sound of the river, falling, scrabbling up to run again, crying without knowing he was crying. Over and over he said, "I hate him, I hate him," and in the patches of moonlight his shadow leaped ahead as if pursued by himself, only he did not know who that self was, and he said his name as he ran but it did not identify him.

When he reached the river it was flat and dark, and in the bitter cold he trembled, and pushed deeper into the fleece-lined jacket. "Father, Father," he whispered, but the words were strange, they seemed spoken from a language he had only just heard and did not understand. The woods seemed unfamiliar, as if he had been conjured onto a strange planet and would never see home again, and he went back to the road that led to Jake's and Mrs. Bonner's to wait for tomorrow, when he could decide what he must do.

And the river flung headlong in its flowing, its urgent waters beating upon its banks and but faintly heard as he walked along the cold and narrow strip of asphalt toward the town.

He walked down the street of the Negro neighborhood, and the houses were dark, the multicolored lights of the Christmas trees in some of the windows shining on the snow that had not yet melted from the front yards. Each spot of light became a milestone when he passed one, another beckoning, leading him to red electric Christmas candles in Mrs. Bonner's living-room window. He walked toward this final glow that pulled him like a magnet.

He had left the house at sunup to walk beside the river, staying close to the road to be able to see the funeral procession when it passed by coming from Selma. He had set his feet carefully in the crusted snow to make his footprints sharp, unsmudged. He thought now that Mrs. Bonner was disappointed that he had not been there for her special Christmas breakfast of sweetmilk gravy and biscuits, scrambled eggs and sausage. She always saved one jar of blackberry jam from the summer for Christmas morning. And he was sorry to have disappointed her, but he had to watch for the cars, had stood behind a tree when the hearse finally came in sight, stared at the long black car that carried her whom he had hated. Still hated.

As he walked, he marveled that once he had been so excited on Christmas Eve he couldn't sleep, and had lain on his cot huddled beneath his quilts looking at this same sky, wanting only for morning to come. After everybody had gone to sleep, Johnnie would slip out and crawl under the covers with him and they'd whisper and laugh and pretend they believed in Santa Claus many years after they didn't. But through the joy was the fear that the Woman would catch Johnnie in bed with him, thought she probably had known it, because that last Christmas before he had been sent away he had not been allowed at the dining-room table with the family. When he had gone to sit in his place beside Johnnie, his father had led him gently into the kitchen, not speaking, not able to meet his eyes, and had pulled out the chair at his new place at the kitchen table.

He sat next to Jefferson, his plate piled with corn-bread dressing and turkey and English peas held in a thick white sauce, but he had sat with his hands in his lap, staring at the fibrous meat, the dots of black pepper in the food. Mary Betty hovered over him, saying, "Eat now, baby," and Jefferson muttering "po' creeter, po' creeter." When they told him he could leave, he pushed back his chair and walked out into the warm drizzly afternoon, and Johnnie followed him, tried to take his hand, but he jerked away, hating her because she felt sorry for him.

His stomach felt the same on this Christmas as on that one long ago, empty and churning, as if he could never eat again.

He came up into the yard and heard voices and laughter coming from the kitchen, walked around the side of the house, and through the window saw Jake and two of his friends sitting with their feet propped up on the table and passing around a Coca-Cola bottle with white liquid. They would take long swallows, and then they dropped their feet, hung their arms about one another's shoulders, and sang, "tuck me to sleep in some moonshiner's arms, cover me with corn and rye and leave me there alone; I ain't had a bit of rest since I left my mama's breast."

He entered the house through the front door, in the glow of the electric candles saw the frail form of Mrs. Bonner asleep on the narrow bed that was a couch by day. "Is that you, baby?" she called querulously into the red light and he went to her and pulled the cover over the thin shoulders, thought how fragile she was.

"I missed you today, baby," she said. "I left you some food on the back of the stove."

"I was with the doctor, I had to see him about something."

"I'm glad, I don't like y'all not seein' each other."

"Good night," he said, and kissed her cool cheek, and she told him she had left a present for him on his desk.

He lay on his bed on top of the covers, pushed his back against the warm chimney, felt dizzy, and pushed hard against the rough stones. The pain made him feel more connected, as if body and spirit were not separating. He listened to the laughter in the kitchen and envied Jake his black skin that imprisoned him, yet at the same time freed him: he knew who he was, he belonged someplace. He was accepted. And he wished he could sit with the Negro men and drink the white lightning until the memory of the doctor holding the crystal fluid, sucking it into the needle, was obliterated. He drew his legs tighter against his chest, wrapped his arms more securely about himself. He closed his eyes and pictured himself an old man with his life over; he pictured himself walking away down some road and never looking back.

When the frosty light was on his windows the men left, the back door opened and closed, Jake came through the house to his bed, the springs creaking as he lay down, the grumble of his snore coming almost at the same time.

He rose and the room tilted, he braced against the doorjamb until the dizziness passed, and he thought he had gone too long without food and went to the kitchen and pulled the dishcloth back from the plate of food Mrs. Bonner had left for him. He stood at the stove and ate a few bites of pork, a few bites of hardened dressing, then left the house and walked through the town, the squat buildings huddled in the cold light. The garland and the neon stars strung across Main Street were depressing and already out-of-date. He thought nothing was ever quite as over as Christmas on the day after. But the decorations would probably stay through spring, the new-green leaves overshadowing them.

When he had reached the woods, dawn was spreading across the sky, the stars fading as it advanced, and he stood on the riverbank in its primal light and thought that the world was as it was in the beginning: the river, the sky, the same as in those African dawns when mankind, hairy, four-legged, scuttled across the savannahs to stand three million years later, black and regal, upon the banks of the Nile. And he had from those black loins descended, he carried those wild genes in his blood— his ancient self had been called forth that last time he had taken Mrs. Bonner to church.

He stood upon the shore of the Alabama, and the river was strange, as if he had never seen it before, and he left and went to stand across the road from the McKinley farm, saw himself a child calling for Johnnie to come with him to the woods. *I can't come now*, she called back, *I've planted myself in the garden, I'm growing into a rose.* And he had found her standing in a hole, the dirt heaped about her feet, her arms spread to the sun, and they had laughed, thrown back their heads and laughed that she should become a rose. The laughter came also from the woods where they had swum that last time in the shimmering green light of the river. But he remembered all this as from great time and distance, as a man returning after many years, looking back on his life.

In the red light he strode across Wesley Turner's field, the frozen cotton stalks crunching beneath his boots, and he saw the slaves chopping the cotton beneath the white-hot sun, dark forms outlined against dark earth; he heard them calling from field to field, chanting *Swing low, sweet chariot, comin' fo' to carry me home.* Harriet Tubman's freedom train was the chariot that would take them North to heaven.

All his life he had heard the Negroes talk, sitting beside hearths and stoves, under trees, on porches, in the doctor's waiting room. Idly he had listened to them, only now remembering the pride in their voices as they told the stories the slaves passed down; it was their black hands that had cleared the land, cut the trees, sawed it into lumber, built the white-columned houses. This town that lay on the banks of the Alabama belonged to the blacks as it never could to the whites who owned it with the flimsy papers of deeds and mortgages. And of tyranny. But the Negro owned it with blood and sweat.

But for all this, he still wanted to be white; he envied the whites their sprawling high-ceilinged houses and wide shaded porches, envied their cool green grass—no grass grew in the swept yards of the Negro section. But even more than the beauty and ease of these physical comforts, he envied them their rights: even the poorest white trash could vote, had hope for escape from their poverty. And they could grow up to be somebody important.

Blanched sunlight struck without warmth on trunks of trees; in the deep shade snow lay in patches on the wet pine straw, and he walked again in the woods and thought he could still be white—he could do many more good things for Negroes as a white man than he could as a black one. But Zella's gaunt face rose before him, and the white hand holding the needle that punctured the bulging vein of her skinny, dusky arm. Gritty dust was in his teeth as he lay in the clearing outside the corn-field, and the pounding vibration of running feet was in his ear as he lay on the ground. He saw again the men's backs as they ran away, through blood-filmed eyes he had seen them running through the corn. When only the trembling fronds told where they had passed, Mason Posey, haloed with dusty moonlight, had knelt watching him, but then he too had risen and run away, taking the path the others had taken.

Oh, no, he could not be white. Too much had happened, he hated too much. Choice had been taken from him. He stopped, shocked into motionlessness that he no longer had this haven, this superiority. And yet last night as he lay on his bed he had greatly desired to have no choice. He had envied Jake's black skin. He sank against a tree, sunlight blurring, his palms sweating inside the leather gloves. Great waves of heat washed over him, and yet he was shivering, and he crossed his arms over his chest, hugging himself against what he knew. But still he denied it. "I am not a Negro," he said aloud. "I am Bird Lasseter." But his name did not identify him by daylight as it had not identified him last night as he fled through the dark. He was not that person any longer. He doubted he had ever been that person. "Then I am a Negro," he said, again aloud.

He gazed through the trees and he thought that to be a Negro meant to live in shacks and sharecrop or to be a janitor or a moonshiner; it meant to go to church and shout yourself into a trance; it meant flashing gold teeth and drinking rotgut whiskey and pimping in Whiskey Alley where the prostitutes stroked children's crotches; it meant shuffling and grinning and moving off the sidewalk to let white people pass; it meant calling yourself "this old nigger." It meant white boys stopping you on the road and grinning and pulling down your pants to see your giant penis. It meant being sent to the kitchen to eat with Mary Betty and Jefferson.

Through a haze of terror he wept, grasping for his old self that was slipping away, his mind screaming with despair at his loss—if that life had been painful, this new life could only be agony, for it was to be without dignity, without hope. "I cannot be Negro," he whispered, but knowing that he was. Even if his skin was fairest of the fair, still he was Negro. He took off a glove and stared at his white hand, wishing God would strike him black so that the world could know at a glance what he was. He despised this white skin, wished he had never known its arrogance, its privileges. He wished that his mother had taken him into the river with her, sparing him this torment. He heard the preacher's voice that Sunday morning telling them of their sins and of the white God who could save them, and he thought that Jesus had accepted His destiny, and that He was born for crucifixion. And Bird knew he now must take up his own cross.

On this thirteenth birthday he had gone on the Greyhound alone to Birmingham on an errand for the doctor. He had sat in the back with the Negroes, and suddenly, walking down the street of the big city, he had become heady with manhood and felt full of himself. Without giving any thought to it at all, he had climbed on a city bus passing by—he was white, he was Bird Lasseter, he didn't have to sit in the back of buses. But the driver had yelled *get on back to the rear door, nigger, what you mean pushin' on here in front of white folks*, and the man's fat face was red and violently angry. He had fallen back, stunned that he had been so quickly identified, but then understanding that it was the slim Negro woman ahead of him who had climbed first up the steep metal steps the driver was yelling at. It was he who was the "white folks" niggers weren't supposed to push in front of, and as he sat down in the front he looked back at her, his heart still pounding wildly. Their eyes caught; for a moment she held him in the flat wrath of her hatred.

Her face came to him now as plain as it was that summer afternoon, he saw the sharp creased sleeves of her white blouse and the stiff dignity of her shoulders as she stood holding to the steel pole, swaying with the motion of the bus, her face set like black marble.

As he stood in the woods he understood that it was also her cross he was taking up, and those of the Negroes marching in Birmingham, fleeing the shepherd dogs set on them by police in battle helmets, and it was of those who were washed like dark leaves down the gutters by floods of water from fire hoses; it was the cross of the mothers and fathers of the four little girls in Birmingham hearing the story in Sunday school of how the white God commanded them to love their enemies, their lives exploding that bright June morning in a klansman's bomb. They came to claim him now, those he had locked behind a door of his brain burst upon him: the unblemished children with the fluffy ribbons tied to their braids, smiling at him from the front page of the newspaper; the marchers; the marble woman; the men and women of the fields. They were not without dignity, they were not without hope.

He closed his eyes. Acceptance would come to him now; he understood, he had thought it through, logically, as the tutor had taught him to do with mathematics and philosophy all those years ago. "I am Negro," he said, again aloud, but without emphasis or passion. The words seemed tangible, like objects hanging about his head that if he wished he could pluck from the air and toss away.

The sun was full risen when he reached Berry's Woods, and faintly, as from distant spring, a redbird whistled, and from farther still, the baying of dogs, the explosions of shotguns. A dove shoot. The men would be joking and laughing, happy to get away from the women through the too-long holidays. Though he did not hunt, the doctor had taken him on one of those shoots; he'd heard the men laughing and cursing, saying all the female-forbidden words. One of the doves had fallen at his feet, and the bird's round eye had seemed to accuse him, then gradually dulled, the grainy lid closing slowly from the bottom. He had run away from the red-stained feathers, sobbing, flinging himself beneath the scuppernong arbor behind the house. He lay on the cold ground hearing again the men laughing and saying it was his mixed blood made him weak. *Mongrelization of the races*, they had said. The doctor had come and sat beside him in the dim shade, sunlight streaking his face, and he told Bird he was sorry. Just that. "I'm sorry," he'd said, and it wasn't until he was banished that he'd known what the men had meant and what his father had been sorry for.

He entered the copse beside the river where his father told him he had found him, and he squatted, touched the ground. His mother had left him here in the basket, wrapped him in soft blankets and tied a tiny gold cross about his neck. When he had gone to the Bonners, the doctor had told him about the cross, intended to give it to him but said it had disappeared from his dresser drawer where he had kept it.

He wandered about the small enclosure, and in the dim stillness thought he saw her running toward the river; he ran after her, calling "Mother, Mother," yet not really excited, but only doing what he ought to do, trying to feel love or concern. He stood at the edge of the bluff looking down at the foaming water; they had found her the next day, the doctor said, her body washed up on the sandy shore two miles downriver and lying beneath a willow, the long branches weeping over her.

In the copse, beneath the vines and briars, he had seen the indented earth of the path that led to the cabin, and he went back and followed it into the woods, thinking of all the feet that had trod it before him—his mother and his grandfather, the slaves who were his ancestors. They too had taken this path to float the logs to the places of the mansions: Montgomery, Selma, Mobile. And had the white man whom they said was his father, had he walked this path going to his mother? He had heard the Woman call her a whore, heard her bitter condemnation that night as he lay on his cot saying to the doctor "that nigger whore whose child you call your son."

He came upon the tilting shanty suddenly. It seemed part of the woods, the rotting boards blending into the trees massed about it, a leafless sycamore thrusting through the collapsed roof. The front porch was fallen, the rock pillars crumbling, and he stared for a long time at this place where he was born, pictured himself a baby cradled in a blurred woman's arms, nursing at a pale breast. "She was white," the doctor had said, "you couldn't have told she was Negro except when she spoke." He was a month old when she left him there with a note pinned to the blanket telling his birthdate: August 17, 1947. And nothing else, no words of regret or sorrow. No name. She had sent him into the world to find his own name.

Slowly he walked to stand on the disintegrating boards that were tunneled with sterile termite nests, and he looked through the window that had no glass or screen, and in the gloom saw the tree trunk palely glowing. Beside it a table lay on its side, cater-cornered was a rusted iron stove, two bottomless straight chairs pulled close as if two people had sat talking there. Maybe it was his mother and his grandfather, and for a moment he saw the stove glowing, firelight flickering through the slatted damper onto their faces. He remembered then a white-haired man in overalls standing at the foot of the back steps at the McKinley farm and clutching a straw sun hat in his hands. Tears ran down his wrinkled, yellow cheeks. *I got to have him, Mista Doc, I got to take him wid me, he's all I got left of her.* But the doctor had ordered him away, and he himself had stood behind the screen door watching, knowing it was him the old man wanted to take. Afterwards, the doctor and the Woman had argued, their voices harsh, angry, and Mary Betty had come and taken him away to her room and rocked him to sleep.

He walked around to the back of the house, and on the wall hung a zinc tub on a nail and straw trailing out a hole in the bottom where the birds had nested. A rotted wooden bucket held together with rusted metal bands sat on a stone well at the end of the porch, and across a wide field of dry sage a cross rose. He ran toward it, excitement rising, his heart beating fast: he was running to his beginning, beside her grave he would find himself, accept himself.

When he had reached the spot, the earth was flat, the grave had become a part of the field, and all that showed she was there was the silvered cedar marker at the foot, the cross at the top. He knelt and ran his fingers over the burned letters in the block of wood. He had always known her name, his father had told him that from the beginning, but he never thought of it, it had no real connection to him then. He traced the letters, softly saying *Phoebe Callins*. A pretty name, but a stranger's name.

He willed himself to identify with this young girl who was his mother, willing her to become real to him, and for some love or kinship to strike. Beneath that sage-covered dirt lay his heritage, inside those bones he had lived. He closed his eyes, waiting, but felt nothing.

As he rounded the house as he left, he stopped and looked back, and the cross seemed suspended, not attached to anything, its shadow huge on the dry grass.

Bird sat across the kitchen table from Jake. Hickory logs burned in the fireplace, slow rain drummed or the tin roof and poured down the windows, blurring the stark limbs of the trees. He had decided the night before to tell Jake he was going to join the Movement, that he rejected his white heritage. He had thought Jake would be pleased, even flattered, to sit down with him, but instead had been sullen and reluctant to accept the cup of coffee Bird poured for him. He scowled and shifted in his chair, speaking only when Bird asked a question that forced a reply.

"I miss Mrs. Bonner sitting in her chair. She's not doing too well, is she?"

"No," Jake said. "She ain't."

"What does my fa—" He stopped. "What does the doctor say is wrong with her?"

"She jes old, ain't nothin' you kin do 'bout that. Ain't no medicine."

"No, I guess not. Maybe we ought to get her out of the bed, it can't be good for her. The doctor used to say you had to keep old people moving around if they were at all able."

"I'll take care of Gran'mamma. You don' have to worry."

"I care about her."

Jake shrugged. "You wants yo' breakfast cooked?"

Bird bit back the angry retort he wanted to hurl at Jake, who watched him with such knowing eyes. He took a deep breath, sipped the scalding coffee he had brewed in the white enamel percolator that sat now on the back burner of the stove, the flickering blue flame turned low. The coffee slowly perked, the smell hanging in the warm air thrown from the half-burned, glowing red logs.

"Maybe she'll feel better when spring is here. This time of year it seems like it won't ever be warm again."

Jake grunted, stared into his cup, tilted it on edge, rotating the coffee. His back was to the window, and Bird thought how this meeting was not going at all the way he had planned, and he searched for some subject that would not make Jake mad or that he could not take the wrong way.

"Corn-shucking weather," Bird said.

"Hah!"

"What do you mean, 'hah'?" He felt a hot flush creeping up his neck.

"I mean you don' know shit 'bout shuckin' cawn."

"It doesn't take a genius to shuck corn."

Jake smiled contemptuously, shaking his head. "Little yella boy thinks you shucks cawn at Chris'mustime? Shit, you're even dumber'n I thought. We shucked cawn back in October when you was lyin' in there on yo' bed listenin' to that crazy music."

Bird had one fleeting thought that he must keep his temper, quickly rejected it, and leaned hotly toward Jake. "Wesley Turner shucks corn at Christmas, he says *any* time it's raining it's corn-shucking weather."

"Warm weather is best fo' shuckin' cawn," Jake said smugly. "Best to git the shuck off so de cawn kin dry befo' wet weather."

"You think you're so smart. Wesley knows as much as you."

"Wesley Turner don' raise no cawn to speak of. He knows a lot 'bout cotton, I give 'im that. But he don't know nothin' 'bout raisin' cawn."

"Well, *I* do—"

"Hah!"

"That's it, when you don't have an answer to something, just say 'hah!' That your best argument?"

"Hah, hah, hah, and *hah!*"

"Well, if that's your best argument there's nothing I can

say. Except that I know a few things too, I chopped cotton last summer, I loaded it, I cut down trees, chopped stovewood—"

"Mule work."

"What?"

"Mule work. It don' take no brains fo' mule work. You didn't plant nothin'." Jake leaned back, balancing his chair on two legs, hooked his thumbs beneath his overall straps. In a patient, singsong voice, as if he spoke to a retarded child, he said, "When's de best time fo' greens? When's de best time fo' oats? How you know when de groun's ready fo' spring plowin'? What quarter is de moon s'posed to be in fo' squash or beans or okra? Huh? You know any of them things? Little yella boy know any of dat?"

Bird slumped back in his chair, the anger gone. He looked toward the withered field and he could not answer any of Jake's questions, he had failed the test; but he would not ask Jake the names of authors of books as he had first thought to do. The expression on Jake's face had been of triumph, but mixed with it fear that somehow Bird might know these things. As he looked at the field, he saw the pride in the straight rows so carefully, evenly distanced, and he remembered now that never a weed had choked Jake's tomatoes or beans that climbed the bamboo poles. Jake tended his vegetable field with as much love as Wesley tended his cotton.

But neither would he be robbed of his triumph last summer. Nobody had made him work except himself, and this time he didn't have Mary Betty to pet him and bring him glasses of iced tea beneath the grape arbor or the doctor to rub yellow ointment into his blistered hands. He had commanded himself to arise each morning, not giving in to the stiff, aching muscles that begged to be sent back to bed; and he had gone to the fields while the moon and stars still shone bright in a sky dark as midnight except that the rosy promise of dawn was streaked across the eastern horizon.

The smell of the turned earth of Wesley's fields came back, and the burning ache between his shoulder blades, sweat running into his eyes, blurring the pale shoots of cotton. Chop the weed, turn the dirt, chop push turn chop push turn, blisters swelling, bursting beneath the gloves. He had quit that first time the doctor had made him work for Wesley, but he had not quit last summer. And nobody could take that away from him.

Bird pushed away his cup of coffee, sad that things had gone so wrong this morning. Last night as he had lain in the dark planning this meeting, Jake had been sleek and regal and noble, but in daylight he was just Jake in faded overalls and flannel shirt. He studied him now, and thought that he was more, too: over the years he had seen Jake at this table late at night poring over the Farmers' Almanac, long black finger tracing the sentences, lips forming the words. When Billy had left, Jake had had to quit school in the fifth grade and take over the farming. He had also worked for Byron West loading people's wagons and pickups, sweeping out the store and dusting the shelves. Just a little boy then, tall but without the years of labor that had grown the muscles. A little boy with close-napped head and solemn face that showed no emotion when, as he grew toward manhood, the white people still called him "boy." And when he, Bird, had been heading for the woods to read because Mrs. Bonner didn't give him any chores, Jake was at the hardware store talking to the farmers about what seed was best and which manure made the corn grow tallest. He'd heard snatches of their talk. He understood now Jake's anger at him for thinking that one summer's work with Wesley made him an expert farmer.

"Whut you starin' at yella boy? How come you all of a sudden come in here an' wants to drink coffee wid me? You too good to eat wid me, ain't you? Gran'mamma wouldn't like it she see us sittin' here together."

"I have decided to acknowledge my African heritage." He saw the bewilderment in Jake's face, heard the stiff pomposity of his words. But he could not say "I am Negro" to Jake, it would be as if he admitted defeat. He had to couch his announcement in more acceptable form. Sugarcoat its hard meaning. He still resisted that he must drink the bitter cup that he was Jake's brother.

"You gon' whut?" Jake said.

"I am going to acknowledge my African ancestry. I am going to join the Movement and help to raise my people up."

"You gon' join the Movement. Now, ain't that some shit. Whut makes you think we wants you? Whut you know 'bout the Movement anyway?"

"I read the newspapers, I hear the television news just about every night. I've seen things you haven't seen when I've gone to Birmingham for the doctor. Don't be so superior."

"Hah! Little yella boy talks 'bout superior." His voice was thick with disdain. "We don' need you, you jes stay to yo'se'f lak you always have."

"I should have known better than to try to talk to you, tell you who I have decided I am—"

"You is who you always was, didn't make no difference you did or didn't admit it. A snot-nose little yella boy struttin' 'round tryin' to be somethin' he wasn't."

"Stop calling me 'yella boy.' " If Jake called him that once more he would lean across the table and smash his fist into his mouth. He saw the flicker of surprise in Jake's face that he understood this, also a flash of what Bird thought might be admiration.

A crow dipped and cawed over the cornfield and he wondered why it chose to live in such a poor neighborhood when it could live on a rich farm with acres of corn. *Blackbirds live with blackbirds.* All the mean words applied to Negroes came into his mind: jigaboos, shines, coons, burrheads. Hambones. Jungle bunnies. On and on, the list went on and on. He was ashamed of the cruel words, he had not meant even to think them. But they were just there in his head as if he had no control, and now they applied to him too.

His mood turned gray as the somber sky, and he wished his rebirth as a Negro had come in spring, with blue skies and flowers and the singing of birds. It would have been so much easier to accept reality when the earth was beautiful with sun and music and flowers. Musingly he said, "Why don't you plant some cotton, Jake?"

"Plant cotton? Whut you talkin' 'bout now?"

"Wesley Turner said he raises cotton as a gesture to beauty. He said hardly anybody raises it anymore except him and Ellard Willoughby. It's because the Negroes are leaving and you can't grow cotton without somebody to pick it. This land is ours, yours and mine. Our ancestors cleared it and chopped the trees to build the houses. By rights, it's ours."

Jake gently lowered his chair, took a long swallow of coffee, and sighed. "I don' know whut it is wid you. How come you doin' this? I thought las' summer when Coy Watson beat the shit outta you and the docta didn't do nothin' 'bout it you'd get some sense, but you didn't. You havin' some kind of a delayed reaction?"

"I don't want to talk about last summer. It's got nothing to do with this morning. I just wanted to be friends; I wanted to tell you first that I'd decided to acknowledge who I am and that I'm going to join the Movement."

"When I was little," Jake said, "when you first come here, I wanted to be friends, but you wasn't nothin' but a little snot-nose, stuck-up—"

In Jake's measuring silence Bird waited, knowing that if Jake said "yella boy" he was going to hit him. He wasn't angry, only certain. From the front room Mrs. Bonner coughed and the bedsprings creaked as she turned over.

"If you'll 'scuse me, I got to go see 'bout Gran'mamma, Docta say it ain't good fo' her to sleep so much."

Bird wished he could go to her and lay his head on her thin chest as he had done when he first came here, knowing she would never tell anybody of his childish need for comfort or a mother's breast. Sadness made his eyes burn hotly that she would not live much longer. Sometimes she became confused, a puzzled frown drawn deep between her gray, wiry brows. "Who is you honey?" she'd say, taking his hand, looking up at him from the rocker. And he would tell her his name, and she'd smile and nod, remembering, or pretending to remember.

He walked down the street of the business district, and habit made him take a step toward Mason Posey, who was shuffling along the opposite sidewalk, heading for the doctor's office. But then Bird remembered Mason in the clearing outside the cornfield last summer doing nothing at all to help him, his hands shoved into his pockets, and he turned away. He had no obligation to help Mason or to protect the doctor against the unloaded gun.

At the Q'n Break Pool Hall he went abruptly inside, walked past the men lounging against the wall, past those bent over the tables where bright triangles of balls exploded across the green felt. He looked straight ahead to the door that led into the back room, conscious of the silence that fell as the men watched him. He walked slowly, his head high, knowing hate and despising were in their faces.

A wall of laughter smashed into him as he opened the back-room door, and he saw a group of men gathered about Dave Crenshaw, who had just finished telling a joke and had at once begun another. No one had seen him come in, and he stood just beyond the edge of light of the bare bulb hanging from a long cord over the pool table. He watched them, and thought he ought to step forward now to declare himself, to become part of them—insert his white face among their varying shades of brown. But he did not want to join them, he wanted still to be separate, he the observer, they the observed.

He edged back to the door, wishing he had not come, wondering why he had, knew it was impulse, a need to affirm his decision to be Negro; but also because Jake had rejected him— Jake did not have the power to tell him he could not be Negro. As he moved back, his arm struck the doorknob, and the silence was instant as they spun on him, the smiles, the laughter, fading. They stared bewildered at his sudden materialization. He was the white intruder in their sanctuary, and they stood as if the freezing air seeping through the concrete blocks congealed their movements.

Their faces became suspicious, hostile. A man stepped into the light, bracing on his pool cue as on a shepherd's staff. He was tall and broad-shouldered, his copper skin made more radiant by the light falling across him from the electric heater in the corner. The sleeves of his red flannel shirt were rolled above swelling, taut biceps. He had never been in Asheton; Bird knew he would have remembered him if he had. Such a man you would not forget.

"Who is he?" the man asked, his eyelids drooping so that he seemed disinterested, idly curious. Bird had seen that look all his life on Negroes' faces, and he saw now beyond the idleness to the wariness.

"Dat's Bird Lasseter," Dave Crenshaw said. "He belong' to de docta—"

"I do not belong to the doctor, I belong to myself."

"Docta found 'im in de woods, raised 'im lak he was white."

"*Like* he was white?"

"He had a white daddy, don't nobody know who he was 'cept Phoebe an' her daddy, an' after she drownded herse'f, her daddy say it was 'cause de white man wouldn't take her an' the baby off someplace—"

"Who my father was and what my mother did have nothing to do with why I'm here. I can speak for myself, Dave."

The copper man stepped forward to look full into Bird's face, and Bird looked straight into the light-brown eyes, thinking how straight was the man's nose, with no flare at all to the nostrils. His mouth was full but not African, and he spoke with no trace of black dialect. The pool cue could as easily have been the feathered lance of a Creek warrior.

"He de boy Coy Watson whipped las' summer," Dave said.

"Ah, yes," the copper man said, "I heard about that." His face softened and Bird felt his anger rise.

The man pitied him. For what? That he had been whipped? That he had a white father who had rejected him and his mother? If that was cause for pity, then half the population of Asheton needed sympathy. Pride rose, and dignity for his deep sense of self, and he raised his chin haughtily. He had come to save, not be saved. He had worked out his own salvation in the woods. Through the door came the twang of of "Your Cheatin' Heart" from the radio, the click of plastic balls snapping against one another, the laughter of the white men. Rain blew softly against the window that was opaque with dust; splintered light shone between the men gathered in a semicircle behind the copper man, who slouched now upon the pool cue.

"Why are you here?" he asked, "I haven't seen you here before."

"Because he ain't never been a *Nee*gro befo' today," Jake said, pushing through the door and joining the men who faced Bird. "He thinks he's white folks, puts white man's oil on his hair, but now he's gon' be one of us, he gon' *admit* he a nigger."

The men shifted and looked darkly at Bird and he thought he ought to tell them they carried the white taint also, not one of them looked like those people in pictures of African tribes he had seen in *National Geographic*. But what use? They still hated him, envied him his white skin. Nothing had happened the way he had imagined, he had thought they would be glad that he wanted to become one of them, to lead them in their struggle. His white blood rose, demanding to be master, his black blood answering *never*; he was split again, he was tormentor and tormented, his black blood had commanded him to Berry's Woods to embrace his heritage, reject his white. He had done that, but these men did not accept him.

"I am Negro," he said to them as he had said to himself in the woods.

"Shit," Jake said. "You ain't black ard you ain't white. You ain't nothin'."

"He is our brother," the copper man said, turning stern eyes upon Jake, the words filled with such compassion that tears stung Bird's eyes. He held his breath, tensed his neck muscles to hold back the tears.

"He ain't *my* brother," Jake said.

Once you would have been my brother, Bird thought. *If I had let you, you would have been my brother*. And he was filled with a great sadness that it was too late: once Jake had wanted to be friends and he had not. He understood how crucial was of timing for love and friendship, but he saw no sorrow in Jake's face.

"When he got the courage to walk through that door," the copper man said, "he became our brother. He has been separated from us, but now he has come home. He is the prodigal son."

Bird took a long, deep breath, held it until he thought his voice would not tremble with tears. "I am a descendant of the slaves of Nathan Ashe. I am also a descendant of white men, but I reject that. You are my people, I choose you. If you won't have me, I'll go find someone who will. I am going to fight to raise my people up, to help them gain their rightful equality. I am going to join the Movement." He listened to his words, and thought how bloodless and without passion they were, as if they had been learned by rote—as if they came from a catechism and not from the heart. He was afraid of the part of himself who seemed to look on, cynically amused, and he was afraid of these dark aliens who stared at him hostilely.

He did not want to be here, wanted to turn his back on that which he must become, to walk out the door he had come in, to deny that which he was seeking. He wanted to be a child again with Johnnie, when on raw winter days like this they had sat at the kitchen table eating the tan gingerbread men Mary Betty handed them hot from the oven.

"The white man will give us nothing," Bird said, the warmth of that long-ago kitchen fadinginto this bleak room, the pale-green walls pocked with mildew. "All my life I've been listening to them, and they consider Negroes as property. You'll have to fight for freedom."

The men gazed at him dreamily, musingly. They shifted, sighed, the light from the window falling across the torn green felt of the pool table handed down to them from the white men.

"He is right," the copper man said. "We're going to have to bleed, some of us are going to have to die to become human beings. Our struggle may be passed down from generation to generation before it is accomplished."

He stepped forward, placed his hand on Bird's shoulder. "Welcome, brother," he said. "My name is Jubal Cato, originally from Carden, Alabama, but for twenty years from Detroit. I do not care what the reasons are that you decided to become one of us. I'm only glad that you did."

And he drew Bird with them into the yellow light.

I say to you today, my friends, that in spite of the difficulties and frustrations of the moment I still have a dream. It is a dream deeply rooted in the American dream. I have a dream that one day this nation will rise up and live out the true meaning of its creed: 'We hold these truths to be self-evident; that all men are created equal.'

The recorded rich, deep tones of the Reverend Dr. Martin Luther King filled the auditorium of the Brown's Chapel AME Church in Selma, and the congregation's cheers blended with those from the speaker. It was a speech he had made after a march to the Washington Monument; two hundred thousand people had followed him to the park.

It was a wet, bleak Friday afternoon in late February, and Bird sat in the church listening to the speech, Jake on one side of him, Jubal on the other. Bird had been to many meetings in this church, he had even been on two voters' registration marches to the courthouse, but each time they had been turned away. After King's speech, they were going to march again.

Twilight shone through the stained-glass windows and across the loudspeaker, the colored light making it seem holy. Bird thought how glad he was that it would be dark when they left, for night hid the ugliness of the drab-green duplex houses with their crumbling concrete steps, blended with the sooty porches and yards where the diesel smoke blew. It muted also the stark red-brick government project houses across the street from the church, and he wondered why housing for the poor had to be ugly, why it was that poverty must be punished. Why could the houses not be painted white instead of olive drab?

Why could they not have shrubbery and flowers and green lawn? But they did have television, and into the rooms of Good Will furniture came the electronic images of the white world of shiny floors and pastel stoves and refrigerators, of green lawns and station wagons. The land of Suburbia, the land of nine-to-five husbands and stay-at-home wives and rosy-cheeked children. The Negroes measured the differences of that paradise where no black could set foot except as maid or yard man, but who had better be out of the neighborhood by sunset or the police would know the reason why. *I get tired watchin' white folks on teevee I feel lak smashin' my fist through the screen.* The old woman at the house where he was staying had switched her chair around, turned her back on the set. Anger, so much anger, so repressed, so controlled it had become apathy.

I have a dream that one day every valley shall be exalted, every hill and mountain shall be made low, the rough places will be made plains and the crooked places will be made straight . . .

Bird looked around him at the people who listened to the recorded voice, who strained toward the invisible presence that united them, bound them, making their purpose holy and noble. Bird glanced at Jubal, whose eyes were closed, his face dreamy but his body taut, as if the rush of King's words pushed against him and he must brace against their tide. He looked at Jake, who was staring at the loudspeaker much as he had stared at him across the kitchen table that December afternoon when he had told him he had decided to become Negro. His expression was skeptical, doubting, the set of his shoulders weary. But Jake's attitude toward him had become grudgingly tolerant and he thought that a great step forward in their relationship.

He saw many white faces dotted among the black—nuns and priests and hippies and plain people. Someone said there was even a movie star there. He wondered if those white people really did want Jake to be their equal, to marry their sisters or their children, for themselves to become aunt or grandparent to some black child. He wondered if they really did accept all that the word "equal" meant. How far would they take it?

When the serpent of sex crawled into their Garden of Eden would their liberal beliefs hold up, or would they castrate a black man for touching their white women or even looking as if they wanted to touch them? Would good and decent men whip a man on the word of a Maybelle Posey or a Coy Watson? Bitterness struck, he let it take him, did not reason it away, did not tell himself he didn't care that those men had thought him inhuman, like an animal that has to be taught obedience. And he thought that the words coming from the loudspeaker were the ravings of a madman: how could blacks love whites, ever forgive, much less forget, what they had done to them? It was too much to ask of them that they should love their enemy.

. . . and if America is to be a great nation this must come true. So let freedom ring from the mighty mountains of New York. Let freedom ring from the heightening Alleghenies of Pennsylvania, let freedom ring from the snowcapped Rockies of Colorado. . . .

The blacks called their "amens" to the voice, tears ran down the faces of the whites; it was as though Jesus had come down from the mountaintop to speak to them, to lead them. But Bird still felt apart and sterile in the midst of all this emotion and love; even Jake and Jubal were clapping and nodding their agreement, they who had been angry and ready for bloodletting. He sat with his hands folded, and knew that he would go on this march tonight and all the other marches, for what else was there to do? And he listened to King's softening voice, the congregation had become quiet and still to hear the words almost whispered through the speaker. And Bird clenched his fists and willed himself to accept, to feel, to care. To love.

Let freedom ring from every hill and molehill of Mississippi. From every mountainside, let freedom ring. When we let freedom ring, when we let it ring from every village and every hamlet, from every state and every city, we will be able to speed up that day when all of God's children, black men and white men, Jews and Gentiles, Protestants and Catholics, will be able to join hands and sing the words of the old Negro spiritual, 'free at last! thank God Almighty, we are free at last!'

His voice had sighed away, his breath exhaled through the speaker magnified into the proportions of a giant. His presence invaded them, claimed them. And for a moment the people sat stunned, unmoving, then they broke into cheers, clapped one another on the back, cried and embraced; Jubal shook Bird's hand, Jake reached also to shake his hand, but the speech had been only words to Bird. Beautiful, poetic, but he could not make them fit the hating faces that surrounded him in the clearing outside the cornfield. He could accept King's words with his mind, but not his heart: the white man did not fit the mold of joined hands and brotherhood. This freedom that King spoke so eloquently of, what did it mean, what would they have when they had gained this freedom? Would they all, black and white, love one another and live together as King said? He did not believe it, for the white man would have to give up his power and he would never do that.

The preacher was in the pulpit, his arms raised to them, accepting the cheers and praise as if he had made the speech. His large, solemn eyes gazed out at them, the sleeves of his black coat fell back over stiffly starched white shirt cuffs. His skin was the color of Mrs. Bonner's old tablecloth.

"We have been tired," he said, "but now we are strengthened. We have thought we could not continue our struggle, but Dr. King has given us new energy, new purpose. We will never give up! We will never rest until our goal is achieved, until we are freed from the bonds of slavery!" Slowly he lowered his arms, and up and down the rows the people began to hum and sway, crossing their arms over each other to reach for their neighbors' hands.

A slight, gray-haired Negro woman reached across Jake to take Bird's hand, and she smiled at him. "You are one of our white brothers," she said.

"No, I am Negro," he said, and she nodded and squeezed his hand with warm and gentle understanding.

We shall overcome, we shall overcome, we shall overcome someday, they sang, arms crisscrossed. *Deep in my heart I do believe we shall overcome someday*. The singing, which had begun slowly, rose to a triumphant intensity that rang into the vaulted ceilings, reverberated against the walls.

Bird looked around him at the dark people whom he had rejected for most of his life, and he looked at those whose skin was white and whom he had envied, and for a moment, but only for a moment, he understood that none of it mattered, not skin color or hair texture or speech patterns. They were all just people. It seemed so simple, this condition of being human; for a moment he understood what Dr. King meant by brotherhood.

When they had finished singing, and dusty night sifted through the windows, the preacher spoke again.

"Do you know why we are here?" he shouted, leaning toward them, hands on hips. "We are here to defy the law! The white man's law," and he stamped his foot. "We are here to march to the courthouse where for the past one hundred years we have been denied the right to register to vote! In the spirit of brotherhood we must challenge the white man's unjust laws, through love we must make him understand that we are thinking, responsible people. We must make him understand that we will not tolerate not being allowed out of our houses after dark like children!"

He braced his arms upon the lectern. "The sheriff has given us a curfew of seven P.M. We will march tonight to protest this curfew. We will march tomorrow night and the next and the next if it is necessary, and I have no doubt it will be. We might have to fill every jail in Selma, every jail in Alabama, but we will overcome! We will shine the light of justice upon this heretofore unknown, unnoticed plot of soil that has become our Armageddon."

And they stood and followed him down the aisle into the raw, wet February night, Bird carried along with them. They strung out along the sidewalk, a hundred-odd people, bumping one another, silent, their feet scraping against the concrete, cold mist beading on their faces. And then a male voice began to sing softly *we shall overcome, we shall overcome*, and hesitantly others joined in, and then more and more until all were singing, their voices strong and floating in the night unlit with stars or moon or streetlights.

The streets were deserted, footsteps echoing through the alleys that ran between the dark buildings, the preacher's flashlight the one spot of light that led them, shining against the curbs to show them where to step so they would not stumble. No crowds had gathered on the corners as they had last Sunday, no one shouted *where's your leader Martin Luther Coon?*; no one carried signs that said *nigger go home* and *Dallas County hates Yankee white niggers*. It would have been too dark to have read them anyway, Bird thought, and he thought too that maybe the pictures flashed around the world of marchers being beaten over the head with billy clubs and white mobs pounding unresisting blacks to the ground were making whites ashamed. Maybe after seeing in newspapers and on television how ugly hate had made them, and that an outraged world was also watching, they would not try to stop them from registering to vote. Unlike the violence of integrating lunch counters and Greyhound buses, it might be that they could get the vote peaceably.

He shivered and turned up his coat collar, shoved his hands deeper into his pockets. And maybe the moon was green cheese. There were too many Coy Watsons in the world eager to break black heads. But he wasn't afraid—he was simply numbly resigned that he was doing what he had to do. He had come to Selma with Jake and Jubal because they said that was where, for the time being, the Movement was concentrated. They also said that Martin Luther King was coming to lead them, and his name was spoken with reverence. Hearing King's voice today at the church had stirred hope in him and a tingle of excitement. But mostly he felt formless, like unmolded clay, like water waiting to take on the shape of the vessel that claimed it.

When they reached the courthouse the people pressed close together on the steps; they stared at the heavy oak doors, willing them to open like portals into heaven so they could write their names in the Book of Life that was the voters' register. The clock on the floodlit wooden tower in the center of the building was stopped at four. Across the front of the long, low frame building were four fluted columns, and he thought what irony that they copied Greek architecture, that land of the beginning of democracy. He thought how enchanted Southerners were with columns, because they symbolized richness and power and genteel living. Most of the big houses of Selma had them—even some of the houses of the poorer sections had skinny, pine-sapling columns as tribute to the past glory of the South.

The preacher climbed the steps to stand in the doorway of the courthouse, raised his arms for order, though the crowd was already orderly.

"I too have a dream," he said. "I have a dream that one day you will climb these steps not symbolically, not in protest, but to indeed write your names alongside those of your white brothers. These steps are our mountaintop no less than was Balboa's mountain when he looked across the Pacific to claim those wide blue waters for Spain. It is no less than the pioneers who at the end of their long journey west on the Oregon Trail looked down from the Cascades in the Willamette Valley at their new home. Our feet carve a path for others to follow as surely as did those of Balboa, as surely as did those of the pioneers. Brothers and sisters, we make history here tonight. Let it be written in the textbooks of our crusade for human rights, for human dignity. Let it be said that though we were afraid— we are not ashamed to admit that we fear pain, that we fear death—though we were afraid, still we were willing to die for what we know is right, and with love in our hearts for our enemies."

They stood, quiet and huddled, the thin rain whispering in the trees; the headlights of a car swept across them as it drifted slowly past and turned the corner, the preacher's face briefly illuminated, making it seem to loom suddenly out of the darkness, making his features overlarge and threatening, like faces in dreams. And then behind him the doors swung open and the helmeted, pot-bellied sheriff stepped out to stand beside the preacher, playing the light of his flashlight upon them. In his right hand he held a billy club; his gun belt was slung low on his hips beneath the huge protrusion of his stomach.

"All right," he said, "you niggers git on off these steps,

you're trespassing on gum'mint property. I am ordering all of you to disperse this illegal night march and git on back down across the railroad tracks where you belong."

"We are where we belong, sir," the preacher said.

And Bird thought how strange, how unreal, this scene played in the darkness, the shadowy people shifting restlessly, merging, the statue of the woman justice in the courtyard holding her balance scales outlined against the scudding sky; the tree limbs clacked against one another like bare black bones.

"We have a right to be here," the preacher said. "It is guaranteed in the Constitution of the United States of America that we have the right to assemble peaceably. We carry no weapons, we have no malice—"

"You got one right," the sheriff said, "and that is to git off these premises or else git your heads knocked in." He brandished the club.

"That is the only law you understand, you are a Southern Adolph Hitler—"

As the blow fell, a sigh ran through the crowd; Bird watched the preacher fall and was aloof, separate; he felt no shock, no horror, only dreamy distance, the scene unfolding like a film in slow motion. And then they caught the clubbed man, the blood ran down his face into his eyes, dripped onto the cement, and they picked him up, struggling back down the steps, dragging him, his head sunk against his chest. The marchers fled down the sidewalk, flowing around Bird like water around a stone, but no one screaming, the only sound the scuffling feet, running. The sheriff and his deputies ran after them, flailing their clubs, the streetlights flashed on and Bird was running too, struggling for the dark beyond the light; from between the buildings of the business district hurtled the dark shapes of men, the blobs of white helmets bobbing in the night like giant moths. The silence was broken now and then by the thud of clubs and random screams.

Bird darted into a dark alley where no glimmer of light shone, and he pressed against a brick wall, saw the deputies run past, their boots thumping against the concrete. A gun fired, across the street he saw the bloom of fire from the barrel and thought they were shooting at him, that they could see his white face in the darkness, and he pushed harder against the wall, edging toward the farther opening of the alley. And then, suddenly, the wall became soft, giving flesh, and he turned and thrashed wildly, thinking he had run into a deputy, thinking to see a white helmet and a club upraised to smash down on him.

"Take your dirty honky hands off me," a woman hissed, wrenching free of the clasp he held on her shoulders. She backed away from him, her eyes round with fear and hatred.

"Wait, wait," he said, whispering, reaching for her, but she struck at him, her fist glancing off his face, and he grabbed her arms, amazed at her strength; he could barely hold onto her. As his eyes adjusted to the dark, he saw that her face was dusky, her hair in long, black corkscrew curls about her shoulders. "I'm sorry," he said, "I thought you were a deputy—"

"Do I look the fuck like a deputy—"

"I couldn't see—"

"How come would you want to hit a deputy, you ought to be helping whitey. Now get your honky hands off me."

"I am a Negro," he said, letting her go, his arms dropping to his sides. "I'm a marcher, I came from the church to the courthouse."

But still she edged away from him, her eyes never blinking, never leaving his face. "Yeah, and I'm Shirley Temple—"

"I'm not white, I'm Negro," he said again, stubbornly.

Warily she watched him, her eyes narrow, judging, but she no longer moved away from him. And then three deputies ran past on the sidewalk, and they shrank against the building, but too late, the men had seen them, had turned back and were running toward them.

He grabbed her, pulled her against him, tearing at her clothes. "*Struggle*," he hissed, "try to get away," and she began to slap at him, claw at him.

The heavy weight of a hand was hard on his shoulder, whirled him around. He pushed the girl behind him as the three men gathered about them.

"This here's mine," he said, "I caught her, go git yore own."

The words were flat with white-trash inflection, and then three beams of light struck his face. He put up his hand to shield his eyes, but they jerked it away. "Come on," he said, "gimme a break, I come here to watch y'all beat niggers and caught me this little ole piece of dark meat." He grinned at them. "I ain't had no good black pussy in a month of Sundays."
pussy in a month of Sundays."

They played the light slowly up and down him and he was happy now for his white man's clothes. "I shore wish I could be a deputy," he said, "I shore wish I had me a uniform and a helmet and could beat up on niggers. I wish I had me a gun." He growled the words, scowled. "All I got me is this little ole nigger gal."

"You ought not to be out," the deputy gripping his shoulder finally said. "You ought to be home with your mama and daddy. How come they let you come out anyhow? You ain't nothin' but a kid." But he dropped his hand and Bird thought there was no suspicion in his voice.

"Well, I'm not so young I couldn't show these niggers what was what marchin' an' stirrin' up trouble. Bunch of goddam Yankees come down here tryin' to tell us what to do."

"You from around here?"

"Naw, I'se born over to the flatwoods outside Asheton. We live close by to the Watsons, we're real good friends."

The deputy nodded, his shoulders relaxing; idly he patted the billy club against the palm of his hand. "The Watsons is good folks, me and Coy been 'coon huntin' together lots of times. And I don't mean just the four-legged kind."

They all laughed, and then the girl wrenched free from Bird's grasp on her arm, slapped him hard across the face. "White trash!" she spat through clenched teeth, and he grabbed her hands, the deputy leaped forward, raising the club. Bird yelled for him to stop, knocked away the club, and the man turned on him then, shook the club at him. "You watch what you're doin' there, boy, you look out who you touch, I'm a officer of the law." The words were soft, ominous, he shone the light into Bird's face again.

Bird willed himself to push down the anger that had leaped

hot and murderous. He thought he could crush the man with no more feeling than stomping a bug. Beneath the bulky leather jacket the man was skinny, he had a long, thin neck, his wrists were bony, and Bird could easily take the club from him. But there were the two other men, who were large and beefy, and he could not take them all. But his anger felt good, like a fresh wind blowing. For the first time in weeks he felt awake, alert and connected.

"I'm sorry, sir," he said to the short deputy. The man was a fool not to catch the contempt. "I shore didn't mean nothin', it's just I got plans for this gal and they don't include her being unconscious, if you get my drift." He grinned, ducked his head. He was enjoying himself, was no longer afraid; he hugged the girl close to him.

All three deputies laughed, and the short one said, "Git her on out of here. I hope you ain't gon' let her git away with hittin' you, I sure hope you know what to do with that smart-mouth bitch." He flicked one of her curls with the tip of his club, and she did not move but glared at him, despising.

Bird eased in front of her, thinking if he didn't get her out of there quick she was going to do something stupid like hit one of the deputies. "Yessir," he said, "I sure know what to do with her, and she shore ain't gon' get away with hittin' me neither, she shore ain't." He shook his head, frowned, as if his plans were already made.

The deputy nodded. "Sure wish I had time for a piece of that. Ain't nothin' I'd rather fuck than a feisty piece of black ass. Ain't nothin' like it on God's green earth."

The three men trotted back toward the sidewalk, and when two black men ran past the alley they began to run, shouting for them to stop in the name of the law.

"*Ofay!*" the girl yelled, "*bastards, sons-of-bitches!*" She flung up her arm, middle finger rigid in an obscene gesture, and Bird grabbed her arm, jerking her around.

"Are you crazy?" he hissed, took her hand as they ran in the opposite direction.

She ran ahead, he following, and he had no idea where

they were going, block after block they ran, and gradually the
buildings changed to houses, they crossed streets, stepped up
curbs, running toward light, toward where the streetlights
burned, where light shone from windows, he pulling back and
trying to turn her toward the darkness, she urging him on
through ragged gasps of breath, telling him it was all right.

They stopped at last beneath a tree, the wind blowing in
his face, making his eyes tear, so that he saw blurred brick
houses on terraced lots, and he thought she had blundered into
a white neighborhood, and took her arm saying they had to get
back to the church, that they would be safer there. "If a patrol
comes here," he said, "they'll take us to jail—"

"We can't go back downtown," she said, "we'll go to my
parents' house."

"We have to get out of here, we have to go someplace else."

"We are someplace else," she said. "Welcome to Honeysuckle Hills, showplace of middle-class black respectability,
showplace of Uncle Toms, of black white people. This is where
good niggers get to live when they play by whitey's rules. This
is where my mama and daddy live."

She pointed to a house one up from where they stood, a
two-story brick and frame with a station wagon parked in the
driveway. Safe, warm light shone from the windows onto the
grassy lawn.

"You live here?" Even the banker's house in Asheton was
not so grand.

"Yes, At least I use to. My daddy owns an insurance agency,
he does a good business—you know, those two-dollar-a-month
premiums that Negroes love to buy. When somebody dies Daddy
usually manages to sell them something extra, like a no-sweat
vault or a coffin that won't leak for a thousand years. They
borrow the extra money from a loan shark or they pay Daddy
out on time. And both my parents pretend he's not exploiting
his own people." Her voice was scornful, contemptuous. "He
puts out a lot of white-shit propaganda to the black community
about how what's good for the honkies is good for the Negroes.
He's on the Downtown Businessmen's Committee. He's their

token black. He goes every Tuesday morning and eats breakfast with whitey, and he doesn't have any trouble at all getting his license renewed every year. And so this is a good place for us to hide, they won't look for agitators in Honeysuckle Hills. We can't go back to the church tonight, we wouldn't stand a chance of making it back there without getting caught. We have a curfew, remember?"

He didn't say it, but he would be able to get back; after all, in the alley he had again passed for white. Just like on the bus in Birmingham. Just like at the Albert.

They went to her room over the garage that her parents let her use. She no longer lived in the main house because she did not want them to know when she was going to march, for it upset them and they tried to talk her out of it. "If you choose to die," she said her father had told her, "we will grieve for you every day of our lives. That is all we can do. We do not want to know what you are doing, we are growing old and we intend to have peace."

The room was bare except for a sleeping bag and a table with two chairs; an electric plate with a jar of instant coffee and a package of plastic cups sat on the table. There was a half bath, and she took a pot and got water from the sink, put it on to boil, plugged in the heater in the corner, and they stood in its warmth until they were no longer shivering.

"This room isn't much," she said, "but its private. For a long time I stayed with other people in the Movement, but it was running me crazy. I have to be alone sometimes."

Bird said he felt the same way and that he supposed he'd slept alone too long. "I hate for strangers to touch me. It's awful the way those people have to live down on the tracks. Worse than the sharecroppers shacks. At least they don't have to breathe diesel smoke."

"That's what we're fighting for, baby, to give those people the chance to get out of there. Just the chance, you understand. That's all they want, they're not dying to marry whitey's sister."

When the water boiled and she had made the coffee, they

me, even my teachers and my parents. If you ever tell I was fat I'll say on the next march you're a spy for the honkies and they'll rip your white flesh to shreds and feed you to the crows."

She set her cup on the floor and stretched out on the sleeping bag, cushioned her head on her arms.

"Daddy sent me away to school," she said. "Mother didn't want me to go, but she listened to him like she always does. He didn't want me to go to segregated schools; back then he was angry too, but he's given up. His favorite word is 'accommodation,' his favorite subject 'facing the realities of life.' There was prejudice in the North too, but not so open as here, but just as cruel. Some of the people were really friendly, they didn't care I was Negro. Do you know a white boy wanted to marry me? He was rich, his daddy owned a mill in Vermont. Daddy said the people who didn't like me I probably made mad with my big mouth. But dammit, I only want what belongs to me, I only want this country to live up to what it claims to be. You know, like what it says on the Statue of Liberty, 'Give me your tired, your poor, Your huddled masses yearning to breathe free.' " She Shrugged. "All that jazz."

He set his cup beside hers, stretched out beside her.

"There ought to be more people with big mouths like you," he said. "I like those words on the Statue too."

"Daddy says I'm going to get killed, and I told him I am more afraid of the death of the spirit than of the body. I never want to become accepting like him."

"Maybe he's not as accepting as you think. Somebody has to sit down and talk with the power structure after we march. Would you really want your mother and father to march? to go through what we did tonight? They're old."

"They're not old!"

"I'm sorry, I know it's scary for someone you love to get old. Mrs. Bonner's old."

"Who is she?"

"The woman who took me in when the doctor sent me away. She's almost blind and she can't remember things and sometimes I feel mad at her."

sat cross-legged on the sleeping bag and drank it black and bitter out of the plastic cups.

"I suppose," she said, "we ought to introduce ourselves. "My name is Deidre Robinson. But more familiarly, 'Luntz'. Who are you?"

"I'm Bird Lasseter from Asheton."

"You're Bird Lasseter?" She peered closely at him, her face shocked. "You're the one Coy Watson beat up."

"Yes. How did you know?"

"My God, who doesn't know? Everybody in the black community knows who Coy Watson is and what happened to you last summer. Then you're not white."

"My mother was mostly white, my father was a white man, though I don't know who he was. Or is. I was raised by Dr. John Lasseter."

"Yes, I've heard of him, I know people from here who go to Asheton to him."

"Well, tell me, why are you called 'Luntz'?" He wanted her to stop looking so intently at him, wanted to tell nothing else about himself. He felt exposed, diminished, as if he had done something wrong and he felt ashamed.

She set her coffee cup on the floor, took off her denim jacket and heavy boots, and he saw she was round hipped and full breasted; her cheekbones were high, her eyes almond-shaped.

"I can't tell you why I'm called that," she said. "It's too embarrassing."

"I won't tell anybody. Didn't I save you tonight? Doesn't that prove my character?"

"Maybe I'd rather have gone to jail."

"Your secret will be safe with me. What can be so terrible about a name like 'Luntz'?"

"All right, I'll tell you, I'll trust you. It's because I was a fat little girl and I used to run home from school to get my lunch, I'd be running along the sidewalk and the people sitting on their porches would call, 'Why're you always running, Deidre?', and I'd say because I was hurrying home to get my luntz. Wasn't that cute? Pretty soon that's what everybody called

She turned on her side, lay her arm across her waist. "Let's stop talking about things. Sometimes I think I know everything, that I've got life all figured out, but then, after tonight, I know I don't know a damned thing." She pushed her hand beneath his jacket, through the buttons of his shirt, and the skin where she touched became warm and tingling; gently she rubbed his stomach in a slow, circular motion, unfastened his belt, unzipped his trousers, stroking his groin. His heart began a slow, hard beat, his chest so tight that he could hardly breathe. She sat up and pulled off her jeans and shirt, and he thought her tawny nakedness beautiful in the red light.

Her hair brushed his face, and the rough unfamiliarity startled him and he became afraid and wished he had not come here, wondering who was this dark woman who now lay astride him, pulling him into her, back arched, buttocks thrusting. He let her take him, and when they were finished thought she must surely know this was his first time, for he had not known what to do; he rubbed his fingers against his palms to see if the revealing fuzz of manhood had begun to grow there.

20

A week later, on a gray Saturday midafternoon, Bird, Jake, Jubal, and Luntz sat together in the back of Brown's Chapel Church, which was filled to overflowing, people standing in the aisles, spilling into the churchyard. The nearly seven hundred people had been waiting more than an hour for what they had come for—another march to the courthouse, only this time led by Martin Luther King.

He and Luntz had come back to the church the night after that last march, and the preacher had faced them from the pulpit, his head wrapped in gauze, for his scalp had been split from the sheriff's clubbing. Only fifty people had been there, and the words the preacher had spoken had had no fire, no intensity. No conviction.

"We have been kicked and clubbed," he had said, "but we will not be turned from our goal. We will register to vote. We will overcome." He swayed, gripped the sides of the lectern, his skinny frame like a withered black stalk. The people listened apathetically as if they did not comprehend the meaning of the words, as if they were too tired to try to understand.

"We had a tragic happening," the preacher had said. "Our brother Jimmie Lee Jackson was shot in the stomach and is in the hospital dying." His voice was without persuasion, and he leaned on the lectern, bracing his hurt head in his hand. They watched him, unresponsive, their hands folded in their laps.

Bird had watched also, thinking that nothing had happened as he had imagined: he had pictured all of them shoulder to shoulder, heads thrown back, proudly marching, deputies and police falling like oats beneath the sickle, awestruck with the majesty and nobility of their purpose. *Right makes might.* That was what he had thought when he had come here, that the simple justice of their cause would make them mighty. But instead he had felt more removed, he had felt helpless; and as he looked around at the people so resigned and apathetic, he thought they were like the Negroes on the streets of Asheton— tired, dogged. But since that night in the alley when he had saved Luntz from the deputies, when the anger had struck, hot and clean and pure, he had felt alive and energetic. He wanted to do something, he was ready to fight, to die—to kill if necessary.

The door had burst open as preacher and congregation had been locked in their mutual silence and apathy, in a blast of cold air a man had run down the aisle to the pulpit. The preacher leaned down to him, the man speaking close to his ear. "Praise the Lord," he said as the man talked, and then he straightened, a smile breaking upon his thin face. "Praise the Lord," he said, "I got wonderful news, brothers and sisters. Dr. Martin Luther King is coming!"

Still they were silent, the words not yet registering. He raised his arms, shouting, "Dr. Martin Luther King is coming to lead us in our fight for the vote!"

"*He* is coming?" someone said, as if the "he" were capitalized, and then someone else said, "yes, *he* is coming," the words gathering force with repetition until finally they crackled back and forth. "Hallelujah," they shouted, and "thank you, Jesus." They began to laugh, tears streaming as they shook hands and clapped one another on the back: they were the dead raised, Lazarus called forth from the tomb; it was resurrection morning.

So I shall see him, Bird had thought. But he could not put the image he had seen on television with the voice that had flowed from the loudspeaker, huge, all-pervading, as if it had come from God. He had wondered why so famous a man was coming to this insignificant place. Such a man went to places like Washington and New York, preached from the pulpit of St. Paul's Cathedral in London, the Southern cadence of his words echoing from the old stone walls of that holy place of kings and queens. Such a man dressed in pinstriped trousers and patent-leather shoes and silk cravat to stand upon the stage of the University of Oslo in Norway to accept the highest honor in the world, the Nobel Peace Prize. What was so important in Selma that he should come there?

And now suddenly he came striding down the aisle in a dark suit and white shirt, the people reaching to touch him as he passed, plucking gently at his sleeves, the hem of his coat. Somberly he shook outstretched hands, patted childrens' heads. And still Bird could not fit the voice to this dusky man with the large eyes and thin mustache. He thought he could more easily have obeyed the voice that had crashed upon them from the speaker, as Abraham had obeyed God when He spoke from the burning bush. Bird looked at Luntz, and she was watching King, but she had not shouted, nor had she cried or clasped hands with the people. Her eyes were narrow, considering.

"We are," King said from the pulpit, raising his hands for order, "going to continue what you have begun. We are going to *finish* what you have begun. You are hurt, you think you are beaten, but I tell you that you must be glad that violence is the white man's response to our petition for the vote, for with our bloody heads we will win the ballot. There are thirteen thousand whites in Selma and fourteen thousand five hundred blacks, and yet we have a minute percentage of the vote. Our battle is to end this outrage. We are a threat to the white power structure, they see us as their ancestors saw General Wilson and his raiders in their muddy, ragged blue uniforms sweeping across the fields one hundred years ago to take this town, to bring freedom to the enslaved black man. It is fitting that we wage our battle here. I tell you, brothers and sisters, that the eyes of the world are upon Selma, Alabama!

"If they refuse to register us for the vote, we will appeal to the governor. If he does not listen, we will appeal to the legislature. If the legislature does not listen we will march by the thousands to the places of registration to arouse the sympathy of the federal government. We must be willing—we must *de-*

sire—to go to jail until the walls bulge—*until they crumble!*"

The people clapped, they called out *amen* and *hallelujah*, but still they were controlled, the words without passion. King leaned forward, his voice becoming louder.

"Our method will be that of persuasion, not coercion. Our actions must be guided by the deepest principles of our Christian faith. Love must be our regulating ideal. Once again, we must hear the words of Jesus echoing across the centuries: 'Love your enemies, bless them that curse you, and pray for them which despitefully use you . . . .'"

"Amen!"

"Say on, preacher!" their voices rising, calling up others to answer him also.

"If we fail to do this, our protest will end up as meaningless drama on the stage of history, and its memory will be shrouded with the ugly garments of shame. In spite of the mistreatment that we have confronted, we must not become bitter and end up by hating our white brothers. As Booker T. Washington said, 'Let no man pull you down so low as to make you hate him.' "

"Dat's right, say on, say on—"

"Hallelujah, amen!"

Their voices blended, joined, became one roar of sound, and King swayed, as if balancing against the current of sound that battered him, as if it had substance, and gradually their shouting diminished, became scattered, receding, as thunder dying away. And when the room was totally silent, the only sound the swish of the tires of the patrol cars that circled round and round the block, he spoke again, softly.

"Brothers and sisters. If you will protest courageously and yet with dignity and Christian love, when the history books are written in future generations the historians will have to pause and say: 'There lived a great people—a black people—who injected new meaning and dignity into the veins of civilization.' This is our challenge and our overwhelming responsibility."

His voice consumed them, and they were silent, not calling back, for only their hearts answered him. But when he came down from the pulpit to walk among them, the diffused light streaming through the windows seemed to halo him in hazy radiance. In that moment Bird knew that this man would become a black Christ. This man was born to die.

King walked down the aisle, he was Jesus come down from the Mount of Olives, and the jostling crowd followed him from the church and down Jeff Davis Avenue, nappy black heads, silken blond heads, black and white, Southerner and Northerner, rich and poor, side by side. And they sang, "I love the sheriff in my heart, I love George Wallace in my heart." And when they passed a car repair shop, two of the mechanics left the bay and came almost to the sidewalk to watch. When Bird came even with them, he heard them talking, knew they meant the marchers to hear.

"Bunch of niggers gon' be killed before this is over," one of them said, wiping his hands on a greasy rag.

"Gon' be killed like flies," the other said. "Them white niggers gon' get it too."

Bird kept his eyes straight ahead, avoiding the hate stares. He knew how it was done, the sliding away of the eyes, face stiff, blank, so that the white man couldn't read anything at all into your expression. He'd watched Negroes do that all his life, but he did hate those men—he could not love them as Dr. King commanded. He did not want to love them.

The doors to the courthouse were locked when King pushed against them; the line of marchers stretched away into the next block, and King turned to them and began to sing *we shall overcome, we shall overcome,* and all seven hundred joined with him, their voices rising into the bleak afternoon, *we shall overcome someday.*

Across the street clots of white people gathered silently, not calling insults, but just watching. And when the song was finished, King led the marchers back to the church, spoke to them from the steps. His face was solemn, his voice tired. He told them he would be back, that they must keep heart, for the courthouse doors would swing open to them, that they would be registered to vote on a day not so far away, and they parted to let him pass as he walked down the steps. He was driven away in a black limousine that waited for him at the curb, and the people began to drift away, aimless, wandering. Some went back into the church.

"Sheriff didn't play little Lord Jesus's game today," Luntz said. She stood just behind him, and he turned around to face her. "Kind of took the steam out of him, didn't it?"

"I don't know what you're talking about," Bird said.

"I said the sheriff's getting smarter. Won't be any pictures of us getting our heads cracked for the newspapers for the five-o'clock news."

"He didn't want us to get our heads cracked, he wants peace."

"Shit. We don't get our heads cracked, marching won't do any good. LLJ's gone home to pray that the sheriff loses his temper next time we march so we can show our bloody heads on teevee."

"I don't believe that, I don't go along with all that loving the white man. I've tried it and it doesn't work. But I don't believe he wants us to get hurt."

"You're so full of it. You been a Negro what, two months? You don't know anything."

"And you know it all?"

"More than you, whitey."

He turned away, hurt and anger welling up; he walked down the sidewalk toward where a smoldering sunset glowed behind thinning clouds over the railroad tracks. He would go back to the shotgun house where he had stayed before he met Luntz, but then he felt her hand on his arm.

"I'm sorry," she said, but he shook her away, and she clutched his arm again, tighter. "You didn't deserve that, you've been really brave. Don't be mad, you know me and my mouth, I just open it and something comes out."

He wanted to stay angry, to punish her for awhile for being so mean. So right. On these marches he had tried so hard to be Negro, to feel Negro, but he did not. He had not felt anything until the anger in the alley with the deputies, and he wanted to hang on to that. When he was angry, he felt real. But he couldn't stay mad at Luntz, he knew how much the apology cost her who seldom apologized. He shrugged, smiled. "All right," and turned and walked back with her into the church.

The preacher was speaking, but without emotion, as he told them they must prevail. And Bird was not listening, but thinking how long the days had become—he checked the time of the rising and the setting of the sun in the paper each morning and already there were about fifteen minutes more of daylight each day. The latitude of the sun was swinging north, the shadows growing longer, and Wesley used to say when spring caught hold like that, there was no stopping it, no holding it back.

For a moment he considered going home for a few days to his magic place, the crocuses were up, maybe even a few early daffodils. He wanted to walk in the woods, he did not think he could bear concrete for another minute. Or ugliness. So much ugliness, mud and soot and rotting houses. But was there really a magic place of singing waters and warm breezes and flowers? He had dreamed it; that place where he had laughed and played tag with Johnnie in starlit darkness was never real. He forced his attention to the flat, languid words of the preacher.

But the preacher stopped talking as the door opened and in a blast of cold air a gaunt man in a black suit walked up the aisle. He stopped at the steps that led to the podium.

"I wish to be introduced," he said, looking up at the preacher.

"You have not been invited here, sir," the preacher said.

"Nevertheless, I wish to be heard. I will be heard," and he turned to the few people scattered up and down the pews.

Bird knew who the man was, had heard the rumors that he was in town, that he had come to defy King's teachings and to try and rouse his followers to violence.

His arms hung loosely at his sides, but his face was taut, his cavernous eyes burned into them, enthralling, mesmerizing. "I am Malcolm X," he said. "White man talks about bloodletting. Well, I say if the black man fears this he is wrong, for that is what we must want also. We will not have our rights until blood flows, until the white man's blood flows in the gutters of every town and city where there is discrimination!" He raised his clenched fist. "The black man must rise from his prayerful knees; we do not have to convince God, we have to convince the sheriff and the governor and that white trash standing across the street who have followed us into our neighborhoods to harass and torment us. We must trade *blow for blow* with them!"

The preacher left the pulpit through the side door, and Malcolm X watched him go, slowly lowered his fist. The people stirred, their murmurs rising like bubbles in water, and someone whispered, "Dat's right, we got to fight fire wid fire." A hum ran among them, buzzing from person to person as if they had been touched with electricity that brought them to life, their faces brightening, becoming alive. And Malcolm X stood straighter, a faint smile on his face, and he stretched out his long arms, his huge, bony hands to them.

"Either we are as good as the white man or we ought to drop this campaign and go home and accept what we are. But the trouble with the black man is that he does not know how tall and strong he is. Prayer and church are fine, I'm not putting them down, but the white man is not God, and I say that God helps those who help themselves!"

"Dat's right, dat's right," they called. "We got to he'p ourselves," and gradually the church filled, word had spread to the street that Malcolm X had come to them.

They began to chant and stamp their feet, and Bird was caught in the rhythm of the chanting and in the hypnosis of the dark, burning eyes of the hollow-faced man who gave expression to their anger; he told them it was all right to hate—he was their repressed fury, at last their hostility was directed not at each other but at the white man. And though Bird sat with his hands tightly clasped, he felt his anger rise, thought how good it felt to think of smashing white faces. Maybe even to kill. That was what Malcolm X meant, though he had not said the words. And Bird knew he had repressed these feelings in himself, knew he had wanted to kill Coy Watson and those good and decent men of the town who had humiliated him, who had helped Coy. It felt good to finally let the feelings flow, to not have to tell himself it didn't matter what they had done—that he could not hate the race he was to have become. But now he could revel, he could luxuriate in his hatred and his anger, thereby escaping that gray void where he was nobody, where he was a ghost lost in a vast and terrifying world of nothingness. Malcolm X had been sent to him.

The preacher and a light-skinned woman with dark hair that curled about her shoulders came in the side door and walked to the edge of the pulpit.

"This is Mrs. Martin Luther King," the preacher said. "She is here to represent her husband while he is away. She has a few words to say to you." He stepped back, and Malcolm X turned from the congregation to stare up at her; and though the people's chanting and stamping died away as the preacher spoke, their faces were still angry. But Mrs. King gazed serenely out at them; she had about her an aura of composure like a garment worn loosely and comfortably. She wore a gray wool coat with black tam and black gloves. Her dark hair framed her face, her hands were clasped lightly in front of her.

"We are not violent," she said. "The white man is violent. He sets deputies upon little children who march for right, he chases them into the countryside and pokes them with clubs, making them run until they are hysterical and exhausted. The white man blows up little children with a klansman's bomb as they sit in church learning how to forgive their enemies. The teacher was reading these words from Matthew when they were killed: 'Ye have heard that it hath been said, Thou shalt love thy neighbour, and hate thine enemy. But I say to you, Love your enemies: do good to them that hate you, and pray for them that persecute and calumniate you that you may be the children of your Father who is in heaven, who maketh—' " She was crying. "It was at this point in the reading of the verse on that Sunday morning that the bomb burst through the window of the church and killed four little girls and injured many others. I ask you. Do you want to be like the white man?"

They were silent as they considered the fierce black man from New York who had intruded upon them.

"We are not violent," Coretta King said. "The Movement has been lifted by my husband from lifeless cause to one that has caught the sympathy of the entire world. The black man in pleading peacefully for what is rightfully his is a nonviolent hero. Nonviolence is the gospel of the Movement and of my husband."

Their love flowed up to her as it had to her husband, and she smiled at them, answering silence with silence. Malcolm X stood for a moment, then bowed slightly to her, turned and walked slowly down the aisle, disappearing into the night and the wind.

The preacher stepped forward and stood beside her. "We thank you for coming," he said. "I know you are tired, but as you can see, we needed you," and he took her arm and they went back out the side door.

Bird leaned heavily back against the pew, his palms sweating, his heart beating hard. He had been willing the people not to listen to the woman with the siren smile, who would entice and beguile them to smash themselves upon the shore. How could they be so easily swayed? first this way and then that. As for himself, his course was set, Malcolm X had shown him the way; as that morning in church with Mrs. Bonner, his black genes had again been called forth—he was ready to act. He was tired of thinking, thinking, always trying to puzzle things out. Hadn't the doctor told him a long time ago he was too cerebral? All that mattered now was to feel.

They lay naked on top of the sleeping bag in the red glow of the electric heater. They had made love nearly every night since he had come to stay with her. He had not slept at the house at the railroad track since that night he found her.

She made love to him those first nights with such fury that he began to feel drowned in her lust. He saw himself as from a distance, as if they were struggling in some dark pool, the lights from her parents' house, from the moon, pouring in upon them.

After the climax the world would rush back, the walls, the ceiling, ordinary sounds—bare branches scraping the window, somewhere a door slamming—seeming unfamiliar. He became afraid, thinking *what if there is a baby* (they never talked about it or tried to prevent it); and he thought *if there is a baby we can marry, her father will give me a job, I'll know who I am.* But what would the children look like? which gene would be stronger, most powerful? He would not want them to be white, for them to have to go into the world tainted, undefined.

She took him twice, sometimes three times every night, placing him upon his back and riding him, pounding down upon him, placing him in whatever position she desired, as if she were the man, he the woman; he became an addict, living for night when in agonized bliss he could forget the day. And he thought this was true for her as well and their desire built and built, flinging them finally upon some strange shore of blank solitude, where they lay, hands clasped yet still alone, still strangers. Her wild passion was a denial of this, yet both knew they would always turn their anger and frustration against the other. And so their parting was inevitable: chill, implacable shadows of winter crept upon the false green of late autumn.

He turned to her now, flung his arm across her, pulling her close; tonight he would take her, tonight, this last time (he only that moment knew it was the last time) he would be the man, she the woman, passive, yielding. He rolled on top of her, not lightening his weight, not kissing or stroking or caressing her, but immediately entering her, not caring whether she was ready; she fought him, and he was glad she did, it would make victory sweeter, and she sensed his feeling and lay as if dead, her muscles flaccid, without tension. He moved her legs, shifted her, riding the power of his manhood like some god poised atop a huge wave that swelled and lifted him: he would ride the crest forever toward an ever-receding shore, but then he spurted into her like a burst of dying coal and fell onto his back beside her.

When his breathing and his heart had slowed, he got up and put on his clothes. She lay pitifully naked and alone, and the sorrow of their parting shot through him. He took a step toward her, turned away, knowing if he touched her now he could never leave her, that his life would be forged.

He closed the door gently behind him.

He sat in a booth in the corner of the New Moon Cafe watching the Negro couples, the mixed couples, writhing slowly to the beat of the Isley Brothers singing "Shout"; thin blue smoke rose from the grill where ground meat patties fried, and the air was rancid with old grease of the French-fry machine. He pushed away the beer that burned his stomach and went back into the cold air. As he walked, he thought of how she looked, arms outflung, hair sprung in wild coils; he was ashamed, he would not think of her, and he turned into the street that led into the black section, his feet crunching on the gravel as he crossed over the tracks, the shotgun shanties row on row on either side of him.

When he came to the house where he had stayed before, people were standing in the yard, talking and passing around a bottle. Yellow light shone in a rectangular patch onto the porch, and dimmer light scattered into the muddy yard. A dark form rose from the metal glider, coming to meet him as he climbed the steps.

"Well, well, I thought you was gone from our midst fo'ever," Jake said.

He started around him, not answering, not caring what he said. He wanted only to sleep, to crawl into some corner and be consumed by darkness.

"How come you ain't out wid Miss Oreo, Miss black on de outside, white on de inside?"

"She's not like that, you don't know anything at all about her. You just shut up!"

"My, my, gettin' feisty, ain't you?"

"What's the matter with you? I thought we'd got beyond this—"

"And I thought you'd gone to where yo' soul really belongs, to the other side of de tracks."

"I've been on all the marches. I was there today. Come to think of it, I didn't see *you*."

"I was there. So was Jubal. Jubal done fall fo' all this love-the-white-man shit. Now, Malcolm X was talkin' my language tonight—"

And Bird thought he and Jake had come full circle, thought how ironical that at last they felt the same, at last agreed. But he did not want to talk about it tonight, he was too tired. "Lots of people believe that Dr. King is right, it's Jubal's right to believe what he wants. Leave him alone." He started around Jake to climb the steps, needing to sleep, to become unconscious.

"Wait a minute," Jake said. "I got somethin' to say. You got mo' guts than I give you credit fo'." He shrugged. "I jes' thought I ought to tell you."

"Thanks." He could not say more, though he had not realized until then how much Jake's approval meant to him.

They walked up the steps together. "I got to tell you somethin'," Jake said. "Jubal went over to Asheton yesterday to de pool hall and he heard some news concerns you."

They stood on the top step, facing.

"Nothing in Asheton concerns me anymore—"

"Oh, yes it does, de docta's been shot but he ain't hurt bad, jes hit in de shoulder."

The pang Bird felt, the shock, was for someone he'd once known a long time ago, someone loved, and quickly he called up his hatred, his unconcern.

"I don't need to know that, I don't care what happens to him."

"They say you done it."

"Me? Why do they think that? Who is 'they'?"

"The sheriff, he say you stole a thousand dollas from de docta. He be countin' his money in his office and somebody shot him through the window. The sheriff come down to Gran'mamma's and search yo' room and found a thousand dollas stuck behind the chimney."

"He gave it to me, I forgot I had it. He gave it to me right after Coy Watson."

"How kin somebody fo'git a thousand dollas? Jubal say de

docta say whut you say, but the sheriff believes he jes' coverin' up fo' you. The sheriff took the money into custody." Jake smiled. "I don' expect you ever gon' see that money agin. I expect it's gon' serve a life sentence wid de sheriff."

"I don't want the money, I don't care what he does with it."

"Man, I don' understand dat."

They moved to the end of the porch where dead morning-glory vines twined around rotting cotton strings attached to floor and ceiling. A train shrieked by, and they stood waiting until its clattering, one-note passing had ceased. People drifted in from the yard, stood in groups talking, their breath billowing about their heads.

"Well," Bird said, "I'm going inside, I have to sleep—"

"Wait, they's somethin' else I got to tell you. Mason Posey's dead."

The words hung flat and stark in the cold, diesel-fumed air. Across the street someone laughed, the sound crashing like a plate thrown against a wall.

"Maybelle found him on de flo' wid his th'oat cut. Used a straight razor. Jubal say Gertrude say Maybelle call up de docta hollerin' an' cryin', he say de docta say he was lyin' on de bathroom flo' in mo' blood than he ever see in his whole life. They had the funeral yestiddy."

Bird edged toward the shining light of the front door, wishing that when he passed through it, he would be consumed as by fire, extinguished forever. "All right," he said. "All right, all right, all right."

He lay on a quilt in the corner, the dark shapes of other sleepers bunched about him, and through the uncurtained window he looked toward the sky where no stars shone and no moon rose. And he wished he had taken Mason home that one last time when he had watched him shuffling along toward the doctor's office. Grief and regret flared, but then quickly faded like fireflies against a summer sky.

Ten days later, Bird sat between Jake and Jubal near the front of Zion's Methodist Chapel Church in Marion. It was a gray Sunday afternoon, and he rolled and unrolled the bulletin they had given him at the entrance, over which hung a hand-lettered banner that said RACISM KILLED OUR BROTHER. Outside the tiny weathered, white-board church two thousand people who could not get inside milled around the graveled churchyard in a steady drizzle of rain. They had come from all over the state to see buried that day the seventeen-year-old boy who had been shot the night Bird had found Luntz. People from other parts of the country had come too, had come to join the Movement in cars with tags that said Michigan and Ohio and New York and Maine.

The shiny black coffin was open and lay below a huge bank of flowers that bloomed along the pulpit: daffodils, roses, carnations, lily-of-the-valley, some with streamers that said OUR BROTHER. Bird could see the brown dome of the boy's head that was crowned with splintered light; now and then his mother, who sat in the front pew, would reach to touch the coffin, then press a handkerchief against her mouth as she leaned back again.

Bird unrolled the bulletin, flattening it against his knee, reading that Dr. Martin Luther King would deliver the eulogy, after which Jimmie Lee would go to his eternal rest in the Sunset Lane Cemetery. He then let the bulletin snap back into a cylinder and drop onto the floor.

Slowly the people walked past the coffin, their solemn faces etched against the gray window. *Dark despairing features where, Crowned with dark rebellious hair, Patience wavers just so much as Mortal grief compels, while touches Quick and hot, of anger, rise To smitten cheek and weary eyes.* But these people weren't angry yet, Bird thought. They were trying still to love, to be patient. If this boy's death did not enrage them, then what would? More blood and more dying, that's what it would take. And if that were the case, they might as well get on with it, stop listening to the preacher from Georgia who commanded them to turn the other cheek.

They drifted past the coffin, their shadows on walls following them in their measured tread, brooding over them like dark ghosts of Africa. The women reached to touch the mother, female in their grief and understanding, some leaning to kiss her, to whisper to her, their hands fluttering about her draped head, her white hair dimly glowing through the gossamer black cloth. A nun enclosed in her cave of black garments knelt and crossed herself, a gold cross with a crucified Jesus clutched in her hand, her lips moving as she prayed; and then she rose and turned, the edge of her habit glowing with the gray light as if the boy's death had made her holy.

The boy did not know and did not care, Bird thought, that they stared at him, that in this greening season he should be walking in fresh-turned fields, or fishing from some sandy bank, the smell of live blossoms in his nostrils. Anger surged for him who could not be angry for himself that he had had to die for such a simple right as being able to vote. So basic, so fair. But then, when had the white man ever been fair? Like a trophy, this right must be won again, and it must be won with fists and bullets. For a moment he wanted to jump to his feet and shout this truth to them in this place of muted crying and thin organ music; he wanted to wake them from their dream. From Martin King's dream. *I have a dream*, he had said from the loudspeaker, *that little black boys and black girls will be able to join hands with little white boys and white girls and walk together as sisters and brothers.* And what if, when that little black boy grew up he wanted to marry that little white girl, what then?

All of a sudden, in the mass of people and in the perfumed air of the forced blossoms of the flowers that bloomed along the pulpit, he felt suffocated and panic clutched his stomach, radiating into his chest so that his heart began to pound; he looked over his shoulder thinking to escape through the open door into space and fresh air, but people jammed the opening, pushing to get inside, and he faced forward again, hands clenched.

Beyond the drizzled windows glowed green and tender spring, and he saw Johnnie standing beside the silver river, laughing, beckoning to him; he longed with all his heart to go to her, to take her hand and never leave their woods again.

Martin Luther King came down the aisle as he had that first time Bird saw him, walking slowly to allow the people to touch him, and they parted to let him pass, patted him, murmured to him. And Bird thought they worshiped him like a Christ, that they were like children to put so much trust in him. When he came even with the row where he sat King looked directly at him, and Bird for that moment saw him clearly and without prejudice: his black suit was rumpled because he had sat up all night on an airplane in order to be here today, his sad, dark eyes were bloodshot, his face weary; he was tired, discouraged, and with a burning ache between his slumped shoulders—he was flesh and not spirit, a man in need of sleep, in need of direction. Understanding of Bird's pity came in King's eyes, and he nodded, but then he saw also the rejection and the hatred that came close behind the pity, and he turned quickly away, pushing through the people who caught at him, climbed into the pulpit and faced them.

"We stand here today," he said, "to give praise and honor to this young boy who is the first casualty of the Black Belt demonstrations. He was murdered . . ."—he paused, leaning heavily on the lectern—"he was murdered by the irresponsibility of every politician from governors on down who has fed his constituents the stale bread of hatred and the spoiled meat of racism. He was murdered . . ."

Jake shifted, and Bird glanced at him: broad shoulders straining the seams of the Good Will suit; strong, big-knuckled hands folded upon his lap. A big man, big hands, to fight the white man. Those hands need not remain impotent, they could clench into the raised fists of defiance that Malcolm X had preached to them that night. Maybe he and Jake could go together and fight, maybe they could even be friends. *Compadres.* A good word, he liked the feel of it on his tongue, its poetry rang in his head, and he wished that Jubal could go with them too; they could be like the Three Musketeers, all for one, one for all. But what a strange threesome they would be: white, black, reddish-gold. But Jubal wouldn't go, he had already joined King's Selma organization. Jubal was nonviolent. What a shame, all that power wasted.

He looked toward the pulpit, the rich tones of King's voice in his ears, and yet not hearing the words, and he thought what a long way he and Jake had come since that morning the doctor had left him in Jake's front yard and driven away in the whorling dust. It might be they would die on some strange street, in some unloved place. Maybe the next eulogy would be for one of them. Would some preacher say that he, Bird, was brave, and that he had died nobly? To live by the sword might be to die by the sword. But he did not really believe in his own death—to simply not be was unimaginable.

". . . unrelentingly to make the American dream a reality. His death must prove that unmerited suffering does not go unredeemed. We must not be bitter and we must not harbor ideas of retaliating with violence. We must not lose faith in our white brothers."

But I already have, preacher, and I will not love those who beat me and enslaved Zella, I will not love those who murdered Jimmy Lee, from now on I will fight back.

The coffin was closed and six teen-age boys bore Jimmy Lee down the aisle, and Dr. King left the pulpit following behind them. Bird and Jake and Jubal merged with the crush of people and emerged finally into the cold, moist air. A crowd of whites stood watching silently from across the street as the hearse drove slowly from the churchyard and onto the road that wound into the cemetery, and the people thronged behind, the soft splat of rain against umbrellas and the tires crunching against the gravel.

They gathered about the grave, two thousand people overflowing the cemetery as they had overflowed the church, and
Bird stood deep in the crowd and yet could see the raw earth—
they had not spread the artificial grass about as they had at the
Woman's funeral. He remembered how the blacks that Christmas day had mourned her whom they had served and cared
for. And he thought, *they have plowed the white man's fields
and built his houses, worked in their kitchens and nursed their
children. They have sung songs and told stories. And they have
been repaid with being murdered and having their children
murdered. They are still slaves, and yet they accept King's com-
mand to love and forgive the white man.*

Dr. King closed his Bible, the rain-misted flowers were removed from the coffin, and beneath the green awning the
mother sank to her knees in the red dirt and wept, the women
in their black clothes hovering about her like death angels. And
Bird thought, *maybe I am next*, and the reality of his own
mortality swept over him: inevitably, dawn and his own exe-
cution must come. And that was the only, the total, meaning
of existence.

They marched the next day in brilliant spring sunshine in
the name of Jimmie Lee, black and white together, priests and
nuns, Southerners and Northerners. Like gentle waves they
lapped upon the courthouse door, and the sheriff—gun, handcuffs, walkie-talkie sagging from the holster slung around his
fat belly—came onto the steps as he had before, flanked by his
deputies. The sheriff told them they must go back down the
steps, the deputies shoved them with their nightsticks, and as
the people retreated Dr. King stepped forward.

"Are you a Christian?" he asked the sheriff.

"A Christian? Yes, I'm a Methodist, but what's being a
Christian got to do with you niggers voting? Now get." He
poked King in the stomach with his club, grabbed his shoulders
and whirled him around.

King turned back to him. "I have a constitutional right—"

"You ain't got no rights except what I say you got." He
jabbed the club into King's stomach again.

The crowd surged forward shouting, and Bird was caught in the motion, elated that now they would fight, but King shouted, "Let us pray for the sheriff," throwing his arms against them, urging them back.

But someone shouted, "Black power!" and someone else, "When do you want your freedom?" the crowd answering "*Now!*"

King dropped to his knees, and at first Bird thought the sheriff had clubbed him, though he had seen no blow struck, and then beside him a nun sank to the concrete, one by one the others dropping until only he was left standing. The people bowed their heads, and King's face was lifted heavenward, his eyes closed, his hands clasped upon his chest. The sun shone full upon him as he prayed, and Bird thought he looked like a black Jesus praying in the Garden of Gethsemane with the holy light upon his face.

Bird stood alone, the pistil in the center of the drooping petals, and he thought how noisy were the twittering birds in the deadly quiet.

"Well, white nigger, ain't you gon' pray too? Ain't you got religion? You one of them Northern agitators come down here stirrin' up our niggers?"

With great clarity Bird saw the dark ring of sweat around the band of the sheriff's Stetson, the white-knuckled grip of his hands about the billy club. The sheriff flicked away a drop of sweat that ran down his temple; a pulse throbbed in the protruding vein of his forehead. "Now I'll smash him," Bird thought, and he thought also, "But I don't know him," and could not remember why he wanted to hit someone he didn't know and who had not hit him first. His mind became paralyzed, he could not think what he ought to do.

"What's the matter, boy, cat got your tongue?" and Bird's anger drained away. He felt sorry for the fat man who looked like a ridiculous little boy come out to play cowboy with all his equipment strapped around his waist: walkie-talkie, handcuffs, flashlight. Gun.

"All right now, all you niggers and white niggers," the sheriff said, his eyes looking past Bird to scan the crowd, "prayer meetin's over, on your feet." He brandished the club. "Ain't gon' be no segregatin' together on my courthouse steps, I don't care what y'all do down on the tracks, sleep together, eat together, I don't care. Registration day's every Monday between nine and three, anybody wants to come back with somebody that can vouch for 'em can take the test and you'll be notified in due course if you can vote. But don't nobody hold their breaths."

The deputies laughed, and King rose and the marchers rose with him. "We will leave for now," he told them, "but we will be back. We will return again and again until every qualified voter's name has been added to the register."

Silently they followed him down the steps and along the sidewalk toward the church, and a redbird whistled and shot from a tree, a red streak against the sapphire sky. The ground was warm enough now for plowing, Bird thought. Wesley said when the redbirds called, you could count on spring. But Wesley would be late with his planting this year, for Jubal said Wesley had let the marchers coming through Asheton on their way to Selma take over the field, had let them pitch their tents there. He also let them use his kitchen and his bathroom.

On Friday night Dr. King spoke again in Brown's Chapel Church. He begged the people to trust him, to follow him. His broad face was solemn, his eyes pleading.

"Only this morning I have flown here from Washington where I was conferring with President Johnson. I told him we want—that it is our *right*—to have a voting rights bill that means something, that does not take away more than it gives."

Scattered, subdued "amens" came from the congregation, and Bird thought that all this talking and praying and marches that accomplished nothing were driving him crazy. He had to leave, to do something, he had to find out where he could join up with Malcolm X's crusade.

"We must expand the action," King was saying, "make it bigger, broader, more horrendous. The President has said that

Southerners dominate the committees in Congress through which another voting rights bill must come, and that they are not in the *mood* to betray white Alabama. Well, I tell you we are not in the *mood* to wait for our rights any longer. I tell you we are ready to do what is necessary to secure those rights—we must beard the lion in his den, we must march on the capitol city of Montgomery, Alabama, and confront the governor face to face!"

The people stirred, their backs straightened, their faces becoming alert, and they nodded, saying, "Amen, we got to go see the gov'nor." But not understanding yet exactly what he meant, responding to the passion of his words and of his hypnotic gaze that held them.

"When do you want your freedom?" King shouted.

"Now!"

They joined hands and sang *we shall overcome, we shall overcome someday, deep in my heart I do believe we shall overcome someday.* The sound bounced back upon them from the walls, from the ceiling, and thrills shot through Bird, the goose flesh rose on his arms. Even King was ready to fight back, and so he would march again, and joined hands with them, sang with them in brotherhood.

"We have waited more than one hundred years for our freedom," King said when the singing was finished. "And I tell you we are tired of waiting! God helps those who help themselves, is that right?"

"Amen, say on—"

"The sheriff's got a mean temper, so we're going to use that temper to win, is that right?"

"Dat's right, amen—"

"Every time the sheriff cracks our heads we get prime time on television and people all over the world see our bloody heads and they sympathize with us. Is that right?"

"Yes!" they called. "Dat's right!"

"We will win if we keep control." His voice was calm, conversational. "The energy of our repressed anger will propel us right into the voting booth, where we will pull the lever for human rights, and we can thank all those who do violence to us. Is that right?"

"Yes!" they shouted, and the tension vibrated, crackled in the air, and King's outstretched arms embraced them, joined them in their common goal.

Bird sank back against the pew, his elation gone, his arms, his legs weighted with disappointment. King was still talking about turning the other cheek, about begging and bowing their heads, asking to be clubbed. He was talking about not fighting back, and it was King who was making him paralyzed, making him forget his anger. He had tried desperately to call it back that morning he had faced the sheriff.

"On Sunday," King said, "we are going to march again. On Sunday, March seventh, we will march on Montgomery, Alabama. We will march on the capitol of the Confederacy, stand on that gold star on the Capitol steps where Jefferson Davis stood and face the governor and demand our rights. We will begin this march on the Pettus Bridge that spans the Alabama here in Selma."

"All right, all right!" they called.

"I can't promise you you won't get lumps on your heads, I can't promise you that you won't get your houses bombed. But the time has come when we must face those who illegally withhold our rights!"

They cheered and sang and embraced, but Bird did not join in, though he knew he would march this last time. Alone, he walked out into the slow spring rain, and turned toward the railroad tracks. He was going to cross that bridge over the Alabama, but not as a coward as he had been on the courthouse steps, and not as a victim, but as a warrior.

The white neighborhoods of Selma were in a holiday mood the Sunday afternoon of the Selma-to-Montgomery march. Confederate flags and firecrackers were for sale on street corners, and one of the women who was a maid said her white lady wasn't cooking that day, but was going to early church and packing picnic lunches to eat at the bridge. A janitor who worked at the courthouse said he had heard that the sheriff was giving his deputies tear gas and cattle prods, and that he had also heard that the chief of police of Selma had had one last meeting with the sheriff to try and talk him out of interfering with the march.

By one o'clock more than six hundred people had gathered at Brown's Chapel AME Church, the pews were filled, the aisles jammed and overflowing the doors. People sat in the choir seats and along the window ledges, they milled in the churchyard and they stood on boxes outside the windows, craning to see inside. The church was as cold inside as out, and the people's breath steamed in the air. Selma had had another cold snap, and the windy sunlight of the week before had turned to low gray clouds. If not for the daffodils and blossoming trees, it could as easily have been midwinter.

In the lefthand corner behind the altar and stacked halfway up the wall were blanket rolls and faded patchwork quilts tied with belts and neckties and twine. Bird stood against the wall in the back with Jake and thought what poor protection the flimsy cloth would be against the raw March weather; but he had brought nothing for himself, for he believed he would not be long on the march—he would either be dead or in jail, in which case on the one hand he would have no need of warmth, and on the other, it would be provided. This time he would not contemplate his rage, thereby destroying it; he would hit first.

From the corner of his eye he saw Jake watching him, and he thought how sad it was that now he had Jake's friendship they must part. He had asked Jake to go with him to join Malcolm X, but Jake had said he was staying in Alabama with Jubal. And Bird thought maybe it was better that way, he would become stronger alone.

"You really gon' come, ain't you?" Jake was looking at him. "Yes."

"Maybe you ought to go home and look after de house now that Gran'mamma's gone. I told you the docta give it to me, an' the land too."

"Yes."

"You ought to go on back and start de spring plowin', you so good at farmin'. " He grinned.

"I can't go back there. I'd be arrested."

"Naw, you wouldn't, Docta wouldn't let 'em, he said he give you the money."

"The doctor wouldn't protect me. And I wouldn't want him to. And I *could* do the plowing."

"I guess you could." This time he didn't smile. Then, "Bad stuff gon' happen today."

"You're worried about me. That's touching."

"Shit, I ain't worried 'bout you. You're full of it."

"*Sounds* like you're worried about me."

"You ain't tough—"

"I'm as tough as you, you're so smug, so superior—"

"All right, all right, don't git mad, I'm sorry. You're tough!"

And Bird wasn't mad anymore but he was annoyed with himself that it took only one "I'm sorry" and his anger dissolved. Why was he so easy? Just once, he wanted to hold a grudge for at least five minutes. "I've been on all the other marches, and I'm going on this one. Have I run yet?"

Jake shrugged, smiled, and turned forward as a tall, light-skinned man pushed through the crowd and climbed into the pulpit.

"You don't know how tough little yella boys can be," Bird said, not looking at Jake.

"What?" Jake said.

"Nothing."

"My name," the tall man shouted over the roar of voices, "is Hosea Williams, and I will lead the march today. Dr. King sent me to take his place, for he could not come. He will join us later."

They turned to one another, their faces at first puzzled, then angry. "He ain't comin'? Is that whut he say, that *he* ain't comin'?"

"Let us have order, *please*," Williams shouted, and they fell silent, turning again to him.

"Dr. King had commitments in Atlanta he could not break. He sends his prayers for the success of the beginning of this historic march upon the Capitol, and he is closely in touch with us by telephone."

Their faces were heavy with disappointment, they muttered and shook their heads, and Jake whispered against Bird's ear that he had heard the rumor the night before that King wouldn't be there but hadn't believed it. "Somebody talked him out of it, they told him he was gon' git shot if he come."

Williams was speaking again, and Bird was glad King wasn't coming, maybe now the people would stand and fight if it was necessary. Maybe, as he was going to do, they would trade blow for blow with the enemy.

". . . I believe in the resurrection, but if you read your Bible carefully, you will notice that resurrection comes *after* crucifixion. If it is necessary to bring out the Southern white man's hatred by letting him beat us, then that is what we must do, because this is the only way to communicate with them; injustice must become the thud of club upon flesh, and this will echo around the world; we must be willing to die for hate-filled white children." He paused, the March wind blew against the windows, there came the faint nesting call of a mockingbird. "If love can work in Dallas County, then it can work anywhere.

We will have shown the way for those who fight tyranny everywhere."

The people shifted and nodded desultorily; they were calm,
accepting.

"We have a medical doctor here from New York City," he
said. "He's going to give you some advice for the march, and I
want you to listen carefully, it could save your lives."

The white doctor came to stand beside Williams; quietly
they waited for the short, plump man with wispy gray hair to
speak.

"I understand," he said, "that every effort will be made by
the sheriff and the state troopers to stop this march today.
Therefore you must know how to conduct yourselves in case of
tear gas. You must keep low because the fumes will rise; you
must also walk into the fumes—your instinct will be to run from
them, but you must not! And do not rub your eyes, breathe
through your handkerchiefs. Everybody got a handkerchief?"
He dangled a square of white cotton. "There are extras here in
the front with the blankets, so be sure and get one if you don't
already have one. You might be glad for it later."

The doctor sat down in a chair at the back of the pulpit,
and Hosea Williams spoke again into the gloomy silence. "If
they attack you, drop to the ground, go limp and cover your
heads with your arms. We must pray that we are attacked, for
if the sheriff does nothing to stop us, if the state troopers help
us accomplish our long walk, if the governor meets us on the
steps of the Capitol and agrees to expedite registration for di-
senfranchised blacks, then we have lost, for his words will be
lies. We will have less even than we have now, for people will
believe him and become weary of our cause. We must pray, in
God's name, for the white man to commit violence, and *we
must not fight back*!"

They walked down the front steps of the church into the
gray afternoon, milling, disorganized, clutching their blankets
and their white handkerchiefs that fluttered like small flags of
surrender. Bird did not take one, and he scorned blanket or

sleeping bag: sleeping on the ground in cold night air was nothing to him, he planned to go off by himself into the woods off the highway and sleep near the river, bedded in ferns and pine straw. He wore a thick woolen sweater and a denim jacket taken off the pile of clothes provided for the marchers; he had thrown away his fleece-lined white man's coat the doctor had given him. But he had kept his soft calfskin gloves, he had not been able to part with them—they were lined with fur and his hands never got cold. The gloves made him feel secure.

Williams and his helpers cajoled the marchers into two uneven columns, and one of them kept yelling, "We got to get organized, we got to straighten up these lines!" They marched slowly, unevenly, down the sidewalk, and in the street news vans with CBS, NBC, ABC lettered on the sides followed them, newsmen with cameras perched on their shoulders walked along the curb. Four ambulances followed behind the vans. In the front yards of the olive-drab houses across the street ruffled daffodils ard tulips bloomed, nodding in the cold breeze. Now and then the leaders turned to walk backward to face them, calling orders, breath blowing.

In a sweet soprano voice a woman began to sing, the notes rising tenuously, ethereally. "Be not dismayed whate'er betide, God will take care of you." Gradually others joined in until finally all were singing. "Beneath His wings of love abide, God will take care of you."

The sound rippled down the columns until finally everyone was singing; except that Bird did not sing, for he had begun to tremble, and he told himself it was that the denim jacket did not protect him as well as had the fleece-lined coat. And he wished Jake was beside him, but they had become separated shortly after they left the church in the milling and jostling of the crowd.

They walked down Sylvan Street and Bird raised higher the tiny American flag he clutched in his left hand; a white man had passed the flags out to the marchers as they left the church, and he held it now as a symbol for freedom and courage—the stars and stripes of his country led him into battle, and he felt a wave of pride: this was *his* land, he was a citizen, an American: *Although she feeds me bread of bitterness, And sinks into my throat her tiger's tooth, Stealing my breath of life, I will confess I love this cultured hell that tests my youth! Her vigor flows like tides into my blood, Giving me strength erect against her hate. . . .*

He looked over his shoulder at the six hundred faces stretching behind him, black and white together, their feet thumping toward the bridge as primal man's had thumped across the savannahs toward civilization. And the black man had been first in that long journey, the force of three milllion years had catapulted them to this day.

They turned onto Water Avenue, marching toward Broad Street, and when their steps flagged, Hosea Williams walked backward to face them, talking to them, urging them on. "We are going, we are going," he began to chant, marking the rhythm with his hand, and they joined in, one or two at a time, until gradually the sound seemed to swell from all six hundred, their voices growing stronger and stronger.

Police cars with flashing red lights blocked traffic at the intersections, and white-helmeted policemen stood along the curbs gripping billy clubs. Whites thronged the sidewalks shouting, "Where's Martin Luther Coon?" and they held crudely lettered signs that said *I hate niggers* and *Yankee white trash go home* and *rent your priest and nun suits here.* A firecracker exploded at Hosea Williams's feet, and when he jumped away the crowd hooted and laughed.

In the distance rose the misted hump of the Edmund Pettus Bridge, and the crowds grew more dense, teen-age boys walked among them in white jackets and white caps selling hot dogs and cold drinks. From the corner of his eye Bird saw the smear of white faces, saw a small boy waddle into the gutter, a man's plaid-flannel arm reach to scoop him up and set him upon his shoulder. He thought it was like a parade, that the marchers were merely entertainment, a diversion for what might have been a boring Sunday afternoon. Well, they would soon see how wrong they were, for without King leading them they would fight, they would not humiliate themselves by bowing their heads and begging to be clubbed. His legs felt strong now, his heartbeat steady—only the breeze caused his flag to tremble.

Finally, the great bridge loomed before them a block away; he saw the maze of the steel arch, heard the muted, rough spring flowing of the river. And he thought that like Wilson's raiders who had crossed the Alabama in 1865 and conquered Selma, so did he cross today to declare who he was. His heart pounded, but from excitement, not fear, and he sang, "Ain't *nobody* gon' turn us 'round," with the rest of them.

When they had come to the base of the bridge on Broad Street, Bird waited impatiently for Williams, who stood uncertainly before the sheriff, to motion them on. The sheriff, in his big hat, stood with his deputies barring the way; whites surged from the sidewalks to cluster at the balustrades. The sheriff ordered them to move back, and some of them climbed on top of their cars, others retreated sullenly to the curbs.

Weak sunlight filtered through the thinning clouds, and Bird longed to push on, to take that road that led toward freedom and manhood. He looked about him, shocked to see fear on the people's faces, and that they shivered, their eyes watering in the cold air. Why, they weren't brave yet, and sorrow rose for them, and he thought he ought to take Williams's place, that he should raise his tiny flag like a banner and lead them forward to crush the tyrants underfoot.

Cameramen walked up and down filming marchers and watchers, and a man standing on top of a car yelled, "Let's see you got the guts to cross that bridge, niggers," and took a long pull on his R.C. Cola.

Bird stared at the wide, vacant expanse of concrete bridge that looked virginal in its emptiness, as if foot had never been set upon it, as if it were unexplored territory that must be conquered.

"We ask you to step aside and let us pass," Hosea Williams said, and without a word sheriff and deputies parted, leaving the way clear.

Williams gestured, shook his head, staring at the gap in the line of the brown-uniformed men, and then he raised his arm, waving them forward, and an old woman with stringy white hair rushed from the crowd at the curb and pinned a large button on the sheriff's black jacket that said NEVER.

As they walked onto the bridge the white crowds screamed and taunted, some ran toward the marchers, but the deputies locked arms and made a fence against them, ordering them to halt in the name of the law.

In the smothering mass of people and smells of wet wool and perfume and musty fear, Bird became claustrophobic and began to gulp air, his heart racing, and he struggled toward the edge of the crowd but was pushed inexorably toward the sum-mit where, suddenly, those ahead had stopped, thronged across the bridge like a dark wall.

He pushed to the front to free himself from the crush of people, to where he could feel air on his face, and saw at the exit on the downside a row of horsemen in black uniforms and black helmets and monster faces: goggled, glass eyes, tin-can snouts. Another man on horseback was out front of them, but he did not have snout or goggles but wore mirror sunglasses.

He raised a bullhorn to his lips, shouting, "Turn about!" and the words were hollow, surrealistic. "You have two minutes to disperse!"

"May I have a word with you, Major?" Williams shouted.

"There is no word to be had, you will not be allowed to proceed with this illegal march. This is an unlawful assembly!"

Williams stepped back, and the sun came out full, the wind gusted, cloud shadows sweeping across them; light glanced off the black helmets, flashed from the glass eyes.

"May I have a word with you?" Williams shouted again, and again the major said there was no word to be had.

Silence fell, heavy, immutable; the sun went out, a church bell rang, but the notes at once flattened, becoming discordant, like strings of an instrument snapping; and Bird saw each gray pore of concrete, stark and individual and somehow of great portent; he saw beyond the buildings to the diminishing of the river into the horizon, and a vast loneliness brooded over it all, land and people. And this he knew: all of them were locked forever within themselves, were forever alone.

"Troopers forward!" the major shouted, raised black-gloved hand signaling the charge, and the troopers spurred their horses, galloping them up the hill with furious rebel yells.

Hosea Williams spun into the crowd, yelling them back, and the people turned and fled down the hill, dark rage of horses and riders galloping into the fleeing mass, scattering them, knocking them to the ground, bullwhips flailing right and left. Shrieks echoed down the muddy river, and many marchers sank to their knees to pray, and the troopers leaned from their saddles and clubbed them, splitting their scalps; bright blood spattered the concrete, and in abandoned joy the crowds at the curbs jumped up and down, screaming *kill the black mothers, kill the white niggers!*

The horses, great chest muscles bulging against the creaking harness, closed off the descent, the sheriff and his deputies blocked the ascent, trapping the marchers in the midddle, and Bird ran unheeding with the rest, icy prickles between his shoulder blades, dreading far more what might strike him from behind than that which he could see ahead.

A whip curled across his shoulders, the biting pain that of Coy Watson's belt that night outslde the cornfield, and he whirled and tore away the whip, jerking the trooper from his horse; together they crashed to the ground, the monster's black helmet spinning across the ground.

With a cry of rage Bird fell upon the creature, ready to beat the head with the spiked, straw-colored hair to a bloody pulp against the curbstone of the walkway. Pale eyes, magnified through the goggles, smoldered with hate, and it writhed beneath him struggling to get loose; *it is afraid*, Bird thought, *it does not want to die;* thought, *behind the mask is a man.* In the round glass eyes he saw his own cloudy image. "Why do I have to kill this man, why do I hate him? *Why am I here?*" he asked his self of the glass, but the tormented face only looked back at him.

He loosed the straw hair, sagged back on his heels.

"Goddam Yankee white trash," the man hissed, the words muffled behind the mask.

"I am a Negro," Bird said. His voice seemed far away, the clamor of battle grayly muted like distant thunder.

"Goddam albino coon," the man said, springing up, and pain shot through Bird's shoulder as he dodged the smashing club.

He fell back onto the cold pavement; through the crimson haze of pain he saw the silver star that shone on the man's pocket like that first star of the twilight sky outside the cornfield.

The trooper remounted, and the horse reared over him, gleaming metal hoofs clawing the twilit air, flared nostrils spewing foam. Cinch buckles glinted on its underbelly, smooth foreskin sheathed the giant penis, mammoth testicles swayed; horse and rider were hugely magnified and etched heroically against the failing sky.

Slowly the hoofs came down, and he thought *now I will die*, and that was what he not been able to tell himself, that he had come here to die: *And dreams I'll send you and horses shod with gold. . . .*

He flung himself against the railing, the shattering clang of hoofs striking beside his head and vibrating through his brain until he thought his skull would burst with the sound. "I'm not Negro!" he shouted, locked his arm about the iron post and looked down into the swollen waters of the river breaking against the concrete buttresses of the bridge. "I'm just me," he said.

He jumped up to tell this to the monster, but horse and rider had been swept away in the thrashing tide of battle, and he too was sucked into the fleeing mass, vignettes of horrors flashing past: a nun in white habit kneeling to pray, her rosary clutched to her breast, kicked in the side by a deputy, and her falling gently like a snowflake to the ground; a trooper, from horseback, flailing the head of an old Negro man with kinky gray hair who collapsed against the rail; a white marcher running, sobbing, a trooper prancing his horse beside her, flicking her with his whip.

There came a horrendous boom, and a gray cloud of smoke bloomed over them, cries of "tear gas, tear gas!" shouted up and down the bridge, and the people panicked and ran from the acrid fumes, and Bird ran with them, caught in their terror, his eyes streaming, his chest feeling as if it were ripped by the smoke. He could not breathe, and he fell onto his stomach, stretching out flat and sucking at the trickle of clean air that lay close to the ground. A black woman thumped down next to him, and through the heavy fog he saw a monster lean from his horse to drop a cannister next to her face.

She tried to rise and could not, and Bird crawled to her and knocked the can away, half raised her up and she vomited and he managed to pull her a few feet away from the pooled, sour mass. "Get up!" he yelled in her ear, the horses galloping past them. He leaned over her to protect her, wrapped his arms about his head, the smells of sweat and fear mixed in the gray mist.

He could not lift her, for she was limp and fainting, and he took a square of folded raincoat from his jacket pocket and spread the thin, clear plastic over her head to keep the fumes out of her face. Clinging to the rail, he made his way slowly, moving into the fumes as the doctor had told them to do, but not knowing whether he had turned back to the descent or whether he went toward the entrance. The vague forms of people staggered past, running blindly like ungraceful animals, the troopers rising from their saddles, snouted centaurs with singing whips, the wail of ambulances mingling with the screams—but the ambulances were blocked from the bridge by a barricade of police cars with flashing red lights.

People leaped over the rail and ran down the muddy banks to plunge into the icy river, trying to wash the fumes from their eyes and skin, and the white crowds laughed and taunted. Someone called, "How you like our brand of baptizing, niggers?"

Other marchers tried to escape around the police cars, the

deputies clubbing those trapped in the narrow passages, and when they went limp, dragged them to the black Marias waiting at the curb.

Bird watched with terrible fascination these people possessed by wild terror, their torn bodies, grimy with the oil and dirt of the street, expressing the awful machinery of the law; in the air was the mournful swell of their moans and cries and petitions directed toward an unyielding heaven.

Again he became part of the stampeding mass, the horror that had fastened his hand to the rail unleashed in his running, and in his flight he saw the whirling lights of ambulances and police cars smeared in red nightmare paint across the dusky canvas of falling night—the sheriff's face flashing by and the cyclops eyes of the cameras aimed at them. He had passed through the barricade between the police cars and the balustrade, and when they had entered the business district a posse of deputies on horseback plunged from between the buildings twirling lassos of rubber tubing wrapped with barbed wire. They circled the marchers, rounding them up like cattle and shouting *ya-hoo;* flesh snapping and tearing.

The screams of this new horror crescendoed in his head, and as he ran he thought he barely moved, as if his feet had turned to stone, and yet the low buildings seemed to streak by.

A whip hissed past his ear, wrapped around his neck, the barbs scraping the tender flesh, but he felt no pain. The split man on the doctor's desk flashed in his mind, how the big jugulars ran down the sides of the neck—if the wire cut them he would die, and he looked up into the grinning face of a posseman who in his excitement kicked and reared his horse, making it cavort as if they performed for a carnival, as if Bird were an animal on a leash.

He grabbed the whip to make it slack between horseman and himself, the barbs slashing the leather gloves as he worked it loose from his neck as he ran, the rider cursing him, spurring the horse down on him, but then he was free and running. The posseman shouted, "Get that white nigger, round 'im up!"

A car roared away from the curb and slammed to a stop

crossways in the street, blocking most of the posse, and the marchers cheered and called, "thank you, brother, God bless you, brother," to the Negro man who had been hiding there. They swarmed over the car, Bird clambered over the rear bumper, then was running again, and when he looked back the possemen were pounding the roof, smashing the windows, yelling for the man to come out. The hollow, metal clanging rang through the streets like a funeral bell, and the man gunned the motor, careening around the corner, and the panicked horses reared and screamed, flinging riders to the ground who, in their fury, pursued the car on foot; and when the sound of screeching tires had died away, they ran up and down the street smashing windows and windshields of parked cars.

When they got to the colored section, some of the marchers ran into the first houses they came to, others headed for the church, but Bird did not go in house or church, for he believed that was where the posse would look for them first, and he fled into an alley behind a sprawling furniture warehouse, hid in the recessed enclosure of a doorway. His heart beat wildly, he wanted still to run, wanted never to stop running, but some cool, rational part of his brain made him stay—through his panic he understood he was safer here than in the vulnerable streets.

His breath came in harsh, ragged gasps, now and then someone hurtled past his hiding place, and he would close his eyes, pressing harder into the narrow space, knowing if they found him they would have to take him—he had run as far as he was able.

When his heart began to slow, the beats came harder, and he became aware of his wounds: his shoulder ached cruelly, the deep cuts of his neck burned, and his eyes stung from the tear gas. And yet through the pain and the memory of the hell that was Selma that Sunday afternoon, he felt a dull sort of gladness. He had learned something today, had come to some conclusion on the bridge that he could not now remember; he needed time to think, to sort things out. He needed the sanctuary of woods and river.

Footsteps throbbed out of the gloom, and he shrank deeper into his corner, and then more footsteps came as if from several runners, and then all of them stopped and there came the sound of feet scraping on concrete and scuffling and cursing, the dense thud of flesh on flesh and grunts of expelled breath. The deputies had caught someone and were killing him, next they would find him, and he plunged from his doorway, running again —but toward the sounds, not away, as he had meant to. He had to help the marcher, though his mind cried for him to save himself.

He raised his fist as he ran, and then he stopped and looked around him, for he saw no one, there were only the sounds that seemed to rise from the earth. Slowly he walked toward a flight of stairs that went down into a basement, and he looked over an iron railing and saw on the landing three men kneeling around a man who lay on his back; he could not see the face, but the legs savagely thrashed, rising and crashing to the ground, and the man screaming, "Let me go, let me go," the words pitched high with terror. His arms waved impotently about their heads, then tugged violently at their shoulders, and he drew his legs up in tormented struggle, cowboy boots thumping feebly on the ground. Rhythmically, methodically, they pounded him, and they were not deputies, but men in dark overcoats and with napped heads.

The man's struggles ceased, his legs twitched and settled, his body arching, convulsing, then settling heavily onto the ground. Slowly Bird's fist came down as he stared at the tableau set upon the concrete stage. All the energy drained from his muscles, and he sank to his knees, his head resting on the cold rail, and the men knelt around the dead man as if they had come to mourn him. When at last they rose, Bird raised his head to meet their fierce gaze: two men were dark, one high yellow and bald. In the far air someone shouted, there came the faint *tlot-tlot* of hoofbeats. The men watched him, judging, speculative, then leaped the stairs, fled down the alley, were blotted up in the night.

He went down the steps, stumbling, lurching, as if he were

blind or drunk, and he looked down into the bulging, fixed eyes of Coy Watson, his skin turned dark, the mouth stretched in a horrible grin over his teeth. Bird stared transfixed, he would stand there forever, the living and the dead exchanging eternal looks, sharing some last macabre joke.

Air gurgled from the crushed throat, and beyond horror, beyond any feeling at all, Bird backed away, turned and walked up the steps, on the sidewalk turned toward the business district. He had come too far, he could not get back home, and fear licked the pit of his stomach; if he ran, he would panic, and he swore never to run from men or death again: he walked openly, his hands pushed lightly into his pockets.

Random cars passed, a hymn came from a small wooden church across the street; he passed two deputies who looked sharply at him, but when he did not look away they resumed laughing and talking. Small groups of people gathered beneath the streetlights, glanced idly at him as he passed. He walked toward the bridge thinking he should feel happy that Coy Watson was dead, that he and Faye need never fear him again. But there was nothing, not joy or triumph or satisfaction for justice done. He felt only relief and a strange sort of lightness, to be finished with hate.

For the second time that day he climbed the steep incline of the Pettus Bridge, and it was deserted—not one person or police car or trooper was left; broken drink bottles and mustard-spotted napkins and tiny, trampled flags lay in the gutter.

The bridge was brightly lit, and with nightfall a breeze had risen blowing the napkins about; a piece of paper blew into his path, fastening onto his leg. He leaned to pull it off, and when he saw it was written on, stood beneath a streetlight reading it: *they went without him. I wonder would it have been different had 'de lawd' been there? but a man is allowed his weaknesses and other christs always seem to rise up to take his place.*

He folded the paper, put it in his pocket. From how far away had the wind blown it? And he wondered too if things would have been different if Martin King had been there. Would they have let him lead the people to the Capitol as they had not let Hosea Williams? If King had been afraid, Bird understood that—he was a man and human, he was not "de lawd."

He climbed to the crest and looked back toward the streets he had fled, and then he turned his back and descended to the highway that led to Asheton and his magic place.

23

He lay in the ferns beside the river. It was the morning of the second day since he had come home from Selma. It had taken him three days to walk the distance, and he had kept mostly to the river, following it to his magic place. He had slept all day and all night, the midmorning sun on his face awakening him.

At first he did not remember where he was, and then the images came: the gargoyle faces of the troopers, the ugly, hate-twisted faces of the screaming whites; Coy Watson on the concrete landing. Himself lying on the walkway of the bridge denying he was Negro. And he thought he had rejected all of himself, his whiteness, his blackness. If he was not Negro and if he was not white, then what was he? Who was he? *I am nobody, I belong nowhere. In all the world there is no place for me.* That was what he had learned, paralyzed with silence, standing on the crest of the bridge.

But he had known something else too when he had looked into the muddy waters of the river and denied his black heritage, he had understood something, but could not catch the thought—when it floated into his mind and he looked at it directly, it vanished like a ghost.

He pushed deeper into the ferns, imagining himself dissolving and sinking into the ground, the struggle and the torment over. His purpose in coming to this place had failed. He had come for a second miracle but had found only a bleak world of dying winter with no beauty, no hope. This place of his youth no longer had anything to do with him.

In his despair he thought of Luntz; he had not let her come full-blown into his mind since that last night when he had so cruelly used her, and the guilt and shame came to him now. They could not love, but could only do battle, unable to let each other past the barrier they had raised against the world. Where was she now? He had not seen her on those last marches. Maybe she was staying home to be her parents' good child, or maybe she had gone North as she had often said she would. But he knew he would never see her again, and he would never forget her lying upon the floor in the red light, alone, her frenzied hair springing from her head.

He stood upon the high bluff of jagged outcropping rock in Berry's Woods, the water far below frothing where the currents crossed. This must have been the place where his mother had flung herself from this life, for it was the highest point near the clearing where she had left him those seventeen years ago. Tall plumes of spray shot up, dissolving in the air like smoke, the roar swirling through his head as if he were already a part of the river.

His mother called him, he saw himself lying broken on the rocks and flicked away in the thrashing water. The sun edging above the trees sparkled in the spray, making the place where he would die suddenly light and happy, and he thought how strange that death should be bright: it should come creeping in the dark, stealing upon you unawares to coil about you, squeezing out your breath. But it was also right and poetic for life's end to blend into the sunlight of beginning day; he closed his eyes, and just as he would have jumped, fell back instead, crashing onto his back, his breath knocked out; darkness spun in his head, it was hard to breathe, and he lay for a long time aware only of the numb throb of his hurt shoulder. When he opened his eyes a tangle of lacy pine boughs drooped over him, a redbird balancing on a thin branch. Overhead, the sun was impaled on the spire of a tall tree, and beyond that the blue sky.

Why was he in this thicket of saplings, why was he not lying on the rocks, or drowned in the river, his spirit loosed into the great void? The filtered sun shone warm on him, an ant crawled across his hand, a bird swooped low, wings whirring, raucously scolding, and he remembered that a mockingbird had flown in front of him so close the wings brushed his face, and he had lost his balance and fallen backwards.

So, he had his miracle. Only this time not in his magic place but in this place of his beginning. The bird had saved him, the birds still looked after him. He lay his arm across his eyes and cried. "I'm still me," he thought. It came to him then, his revelation of the bridge: *I'm just me,* he had said to the river, knowing he was not black or white but only himself.

The faces came again, troopers with their snouted faces, possemen twirling barbed lassos; Coy Watson in the cornfield, the shadow of his arm rising and falling against the dusty moonlit ground; Coy Watson dead on the cold square of concrete. He saw the agony of the doctor's face that night at the river house, and Zella's, gaunt and tormented. He moved the faces along in his mind like beads on a rosary, hatred and sorrow mingled; he whispered their names, and gradually he stopped crying and fell asleep.

When he awoke the sun shone on him obliquely from the western sky, and he was cold and sat up, brushing at the pine straw that clung in his hair, to his clothes. He looked across the river to the blurred new green willows whose tenuous roots had such a fragile hold on the crumbling bank, and he thought how dogged was their coming back, the saplings springing from the mature trees that had fallen.

Gentleness stirred in him: he loved the willows and all the trees, pines and oaks and pale-trunked sycamores; and he loved all the seasons of the woods, when it was stripped and bare in winter and he could see so far, and in summer the dense explosion of foliage, smothering, enclosing, protecting; he loved the red and gold death of fall, the new-green hope of spring. Joy surged that he had fallen backwards into life, and the truth was, the bird had not saved him but her nest, for he had come too close. He had seen the straw and sticks, only partially hidden by the young leaves of the water oak.

▼

He went in through the back door of the house, pausing in the dim mustiness of the kitchen. The rocking chair beside the fireplace was empty, and yet it seemed a frail form watched him, a thin, clawed hand gestured to him. *Where you been, baby, I been worried 'bout you. You didn't come home las' night—"*

She was gone, she would never worry about him again for she had died of a stroke. Jake had left Selma and come home to bury her in the cemetery of the Sanctified Church, then went back for the Montgomery march. He had thought to go to her grave, but did not—he would keep the memory of that last morning when she told him good-by and watched him from the front door as he walked away down the street. But he had loved her, and he missed her.

He went to his old room and packed his suitcase, took nothing but a few clothes and the journals. On his desk was the red tissue package of the Christmas present Mrs. Bonner had given him, and he picked it up, and it was limp and soft, as if it contained some sort of material, and he started to open it but did not, put it back on the desk. Let the contents remain forever unknown, a clumsily wrapped yet poignant memory of her love.

He went back to his magic place and took off the clothes that stank of sweat and tear gas and lowered himself into the baptismal pool where he had swum with Johnnie, and he thrashed about, diving and surfacing, washing himself; the cold water numbed the raw wounds of his neck and hands, eased the pain of his shoulder. He stood on the bank waving his arms, shaking his hair, drying himself, and then he put on clean jeans and a flannel shirt and left the woods, walked down the road in the dusk to Wesley Turner's house. As he went up the walk a deep sense of peace of the rightness of things came over him, for Wesley was sitting on the porch smoking a cigarette, his feet propped on the banister. It was a sure sign that spring was really here, a certainty that winter was gone, just as significant in the cycle of nature as the reappearance of the redbirds and the daffodils.

"Well, well, look who's here," Wesley said, and stood up as Bird climbed the steps. "Come on up and have a seat," and Bird shook the rough outstretched hand and sat on the top step. Wesley sat down again in the rocker, and for a moment it was like last summer when they had sat together in the late afternoon, grass and trees humming softly of twilight. But his field was not yet plowed, charred stalks of last year's cotton covering the ground like a shroud.

"What happened?" Bird said, indicating the field.

"Oh, my son-in-law and his hooded friends did that," Wesley said. "Tried to burn me out, but it was too wet, it don't amount to much. I'll just plow it under when it gets dry enough, it puts nitrogen in the soil. It's good for it, ought to have done it myself, but I'm getting lazy in my old days. Need you here to help me."

They smiled at each other, and Bird said, "I appreciate your letting me work, not only for the money, but I think I finally satisfied the doctor's need for my character development."

"He's a good man," Wesley said.

"Yes."

"Faye got word Coy was killed over in Selma on that march."

"I heard that too."

"Did you go?"

"Yes."

"Rough?"

"Yes."

Wesley nodded, tossed away the cigarette, an arcing red streak in the near dark. "Coy and his buddies come over here and burned my field, tried to set fire to the house too. Ran the marchers off, didn't hurt anybody, though, thank God for that. I held them off all by myself with the shotgun, and they satisfied themselves with burning a cross. Ever notice how the most wicked people love to burn the cross?"

They were silent as Wesley lit another cigarette, a Camel. "Stopped rolling my own," he said. "It got to be too much trouble. But these are so perfect they don't seem like real cig- arettes. I might just go back to rolling my own again."

"I came because I wanted to say good-by," Bird said. "I'm leaving Asheton." He needed to hear the words, to try them out and see if he really meant them, or if he had packed his bag like a child threatening to run away from home. "I'm going North." And though the brave words were scary, he knew he meant them. He really was going. "I needed to say good-by to you and the doctor before I left. I'm catching the Greyhound in the morning."

"Well, I'm sorry, but I'm not suprised. I hate to see you go, but there's nothing for you here. You're too good for this town."

Bird looked off across the field; if he spoke, he would cry. Wesley sighed and took a deep drag off the cigarette.

"We had a good time last summer," Wesley said. "I got to thinking of you as my boy."

"If it hadn't been for you I don't know what I'd have done. Nobody else would have hired me. You took me in."

"Angel unawares," he said.

"What?"

"Just that this town one day will have to meet the Judg- ment. I wouldn't like to be Coy Watson or any of those other men for that matter when they have to stand before the Judg- ment and give account for what they did to you. That's why I stay out here by myself, just me and the cotton. I don't like to be with humans too much, makes you ashamed to be one. Now the doctor, he did wrong, but only because he thought he was protecting Johnnie. I wouldn't hold anything against him too much, try to understand him. Don't let bitterness direct your life."

"I hated him for a long time, but not anymore. Selma taught me about hate."

In the dimness they talked easily, an intimacy built that would not have been possible in daylight, for the twilight hid the revealing deep feelings in their eyes, drawn on their faces— obscured the loneliness, the beginning love.

"Faye got married, I guess you heard."

"No, I didn't know." He was surprised that she should risk giving herself again after Coy Watson. How could she trust so easily?

"She'd filed for a divorce when Coy got killed and saved her the trouble. She had him under a peace bond so he couldn't come back to the restaurant. I heard he'd gone over to Selma. You ever see him?"

"No."

"Doc didn't put on the report that Faye shot Coy. He put 'assailant unknown.' When Coy didn't die Doc went to the hospital and warned Coy if he told it was Faye he'd swear out a warrant for him beating you and that Faye would swear out a warrant for him trying to kill her. Hell, the law wouldn't have done anything, she was protecting her own life. He said a hippie tried to rob him and grabbed the shotgun when he tried to run him off. I'm glad that mess is over, that was an awful thing, being involved with a man like that."

His beating had saved Faye, Bird thought. From evil comes good. It was an amends of sorts.

"She sold the restaurant," Wesley said. "I wouldn't take the money so she put it in the bank in my name, but it'll be hers again someday. Hell, what do I need money for? I've got this." His arm swept the cotton field. "She married Hayes Paulson, he was the driver beat up Coy, you recall?"

Bird nodded that he did.

"They got married in Georgia and went to Florida on their honeymoon. They're gon' stay down there a month on the beach, and then she'll ride on the truck back with him to California. He lives in Santa Barbara. Ever hear of it?"

"Yes, I've seen pictures of it in the encyclopedia, lots of palm trees ard blue water and blue sky."

"It's on the ocean, isn't it?"

"Yes."

"They want me to come live with them."

"You ought to go, it must be beautiful and it's warm all the time."

"Hell, this *here's* beautiful, my granddaddy's house and my cotton field. This here's got memories; I can sit out here the whole evening and think about who's been in this house, all the children jumping up and down those steps where you're sitting right now. My mama died in that back bedroom, it was April and the crab apples were in bloom, the wind was blowing the scent all the way down to the field where I was plowing when they come and told me to come to the house. This here's home and that's the most beautiful place—the most beautiful word—in the world. When I die I'll be buried right out back there with my mama and daddy and my grandmamma and my granddaddy."

They looked out over the darkening land where the woods were on fire with sunset, and Bird sat quietly, hoping Wesley would talk some more. It was the most he'd ever heard him say at one time, and it was this memory of his homeland that he wanted to take North with him, the good people like Wesley and Jubal and, finally, Jake, who had also learned to stop hating.

"Maybe I will take a notion one of these days to get on the train and go out and visit Faye. I've never seen the ocean. Got a lot of salt in it, hasn't it?"

"So I've heard. I've never seen it either."

"Can't grow cotton with saltwater."

"Rain's not salty."

They grinned at each other, and Wesley shifted his chair, recrossed his legs on the banister. "When Faye left with Hayes I believe it was the first time I'd ever seen pure joy on her face."

When it was full dark and the stars shining softly over the burned field, Bird rose and they shook hands.

"I'm going to miss you," Wesley said, standing up and walking down the steps with him. "All the young people and most of the Negroes are leaving; there's not much of Asheton left, just about enough to outlast me. In a few years there won't be anything here but some overgrown fields and maybe the columns on the old Ashe mansion because Maybelle's gon' burn it down. Folks say they see candlelight most nights going from room to room. She's gone crazy, people say she never comes out anymore."

He entered the dark waiting room where all those years the whites and the blacks had sat in their appointed places, acting out their prescribed roles. Through the partly opened door of the office he saw the doctor standing beside his desk, counting the money he had made that day. His gun lay beside the stacked bills.

"Doctor," Bird said.

The doctor spun around, his hand flying to the gun, and then his face shocked with recognition. "Bird, my God—"

"Don't shoot, I don't want your money."

"I got shot, a thing like that makes you cautious—"

For a long moment they did not speak, and then the doctor said, "Well. How are you? I heard you were mixed up in that mess over in Selma." His voice was harsh, condemning.

"Yes, though I'd say it was a little more important than just a 'mess.' " He extended his hands, palms upward to show the crucifixion where the barbs had pierced his gloves.

The doctor stepped forward and grasped them, shaking his head. "What could you expect, you're hardheaded, always have been. You're going to get yourself killed, you won't listen."

Bird said nothing, treasuring the scolding. It was what he had come here for, it was the last one he was ever going to get from him. For a few minutes, for a last few minutes, he could be a child again, pretend that things were like they were before he was sent away.

"Those are puncture wounds, the worst kind, you know that?"

"If I didn't, I'd be pretty stupid, I've heard it all my life."

"Don't be flip, this is serious, what I'm trying to tell you is for your own good. You're going to have to have a tetanus shot, come on over to the examining table," and Bird followed, sat down on the end of it.

The doctor flicked on the overhead fluorescent lights, and

in the brightness gleamed the rows of jars and colored bottles behind the glass door of the cabinet; stainless-steel knives and scissors glowed upon a snowy-white towel beside the sterilizer. If they should turn on the lights in the waiting room, Dave Crenshaw would spring to life and begin to tell a joke.

He rolled up his sleeve, and in his nostrils was the familiar biting smell of alcohol as the doctor swabbed his arm, and the cold sting of the antitoxin flowing into the muscle. "My arm's really going to be sore," he said.

"If you dance you have to pay the fiddler," the doctor said.

"So I've been told. Lots of times."

They exchanged wry smiles, and with a swab bright pink with Merthiolate the doctor probed his wounds, digging deep, twisting; Bird pulled against him, and the doctor said, "Here, now, hold still, I've got to clean them out so they won't get infected. You're going to have to have a shot of penicillin too."

"No."

"What?"

"I said 'no.' I'll take my chances with the germs, I can stand my arm being sore but I've got to be able to sit down."

Bird waited while the doctor studied his face, gauging the strength of his conviction.

"All right," the doctor said. "Have it your way, but you ought to have the penicillin."

"I'll take my chances."

The doctor went to the sink and began to lather up his hands, pushing the long handle of the faucet with his elbow. Bird sat in the swivel chair at the desk, resting his arms on the ink-stained blotter. He looked at the pictures of his father's children, and his space next to Johnnie's was still vacant, but it didn't hurt anymore. And he thought how long ago, how like a dream it was, that once he had been one of them.

"Did you know," he said, "that I used to sit in this chair and pretend I was you? I wanted to be just like you."

"And now you don't." He stopped the motion of the drying of his hands.

"Oh, yes, I do. But mostly I want to be whoever I am."

The doctor continued drying his hands, wadded the paper and threw it in the wastebasket. "I'm glad to hear you've finally accepted your heritage."

"That's not what I meant. You don't know who I am, I don't know who I am. I mean to find out."

Sadly the doctor shook his head, walked to the window and parted the slatted shades to look into the dark street, and Bird thought how old he looked, his hair as much white as black. And had he only imagined that he was big? He heard again the sharp knock on the back door when he was a child and sleeping on the cot on the back porch, waking to scared, whispered words, *kin you come, Docta, he bleedin' bad, I think he dyin', kin you come, Docta,* and him running into the yard to see his father gallop away down the road looking as if he grew from his horse, his shadow giant in the moonlight like a god.

He stood beside him at the window, their shoulders touching. They watched Mrs. Henderson in her dinette across the street hurrying back and forth carrying seconds to the travelers free of charge. The town predicted her generosity would ruin her, but instead she had prospered; she had even expanded into the vacant lot behind her.

"Looks like Mrs. Henderson wasn't such a fool after all. Generosity must indeed be rewarded," the doctor said dryly.

"She knew what she was doing apparently."

"I never will understand the workings of a woman's mind. It is the most amazing thing how sometimes they just know things against all logic. I eat down there a lot now that I'm by myself. The girls don't come home much anymore, they haven't been here since Christmas. Sometimes I wish things could be like they used to be, back before the bad things happened. Back when all of you were little, the twins singing and playing the piano, you and Johnnie playing out in the yard. I wish Jenny—" He stopped. "I guess you knew Mary Betty died?"

"No." Sadness stabbed for another loss.

"She had uterine cancer. She was sick a long time. One by one they go and we're left with ourselves. I'm beginning to think the lucky ones are those who go first."

They stood silently contemplating the enigma of Mrs. Henderson, who had cast her bread upon the water and gotten back a thousandfold.

"I'm leaving too," Bird said.

"What do you mean, you're leaving?" the doctor said, and they faced again.

"I mean I'm leaving Asheton. I'm going North."

Angrily the doctor said, "You won't like it, it's full of Yankees."

"It stands to reason."

Their jaws were set, shoulders squared. "You'll be eighteen in August, you'll have to register for the draft. You'd be deferred if you were in pre-med, you wouldn't have to worry about that stupid war in Viet Nam."

"We have to worry about that war because we're in it. I don't know whether it's right or not, I'll have to decide what I'm going to do. Jake said he's probably going ahead and join the army now that his grandmother's dead. But I'm not going to college, that's not what I want right now."

"Well, then, I see there's nothing for me to say. I just hope you don't go off to get yourself killed in a war we had nothing to say about."

A car passed in the silent street, the headlights sweeping across the slatted shades as it turned the corner. A man laughed and called to someone as he came out the door of the dinette, his footsteps fading away up the sidewalk. The Big Ben clock on the desk ticked the minutes loudly.

"Where up North are you going?"

"I don't know."

"You really plan things well."

"Don't worry about it."

The doctor left the window and went back to the desk, absently fingered the money. His back was to Bird. "I never really wanted you to go, I was sorry later for telling you that."

"You gave a good imitation, you even sent me money that I hear the sheriff is now enjoying."

"What does it matter about the money? I was angry, I felt you'd betrayed my trust."

"We've plowed that ground, let's don't talk about that."

"If we can forget the past, we could still practice medicine together, go on rounds like we used to, consult—"

"If I accept my heritage, you mean. If I pull my forelock in front of the white folks and say 'yassuh' and 'nawsuh.' "

The doctor's gesture was heavy, defeated, briefly he closed his eyes. "You've made your point, you win. Go North and may God bless you."

"I need to know about Zella. What happened to her?"

"She's living over in Selma in Honeysuckle Hills. I bought her a house. I took her over to a hospital in Atlanta and she's off morphine. They think she'll stay off. She's living with Henry and I give her an allowance each month and set up a trust for her when I die. I would have done that even if she hadn't told me she'd take me to court and sue me for misuse of a drug. She still threatens me with that, and if she really does it I'll lose my license to practice. That is the one thing I don't think I could survive."

"She won't do that. If you can't work, how can you pay her?"

"Sometimes people will destroy themselves to bring some-one else down. I'll just take it a day at a time."

"Well," Bird said.

"You're really going."

"Yes. I'll say good-by."

"Wait. Before you go there's something you ought to know." He went to open the safe, turning the dial to the numbers of the combination. "I've worried for years whether I should give this to you. Since we don't know whether we'll ever meet again, it's your right to have it."

He took out a folded sheet of lined school paper, and handed it to Bird. "That letter was delivered to me when you were four years old by the man who sharecropped with your grandfather. I don't know whether it's true or not, but since you say you are going to find out who you are, maybe this will help."

Bird unfolded the paper, leaning to the spot of light of the crooknecked lamp. He could barely make out the trembling, wavery words; some he could only guess at what they said.

"dear mista doc since I will die soon with high blood and

water on my lungs I have to tell you what is on my heart and conscience. you have taken my phoebe's boy I mus tell you that she say mr mason posey was his daddy and that mr mason love her an she love him she tol me this many time an he did come to the cabin an lay wit her. she beg him to run away wit her an to claim the boy an when he would not she drownded hersef an lef the boy in the path of where she know you walk each day."

The words continued down the page, but he stopped reading, and he straightened, his arm dropping to his side. "What does it mean?" he asked.

"I don't know," the doctor said. "Was it an old man's hallucinations or a dying man's confession? Mason started drinking at about the same time Phoebe drowned herself. He came here one night and said I stole you and that was why your mother killed herself, that she was grieving for her baby. I told him I found you afterwards, but he didn't believe me and just starting clicking that empty gun at me. Several times I saw him taking a shortcut through the woods across the back of the farm going to your mother's cabin, but other white men went there too."

Then the Woman was right, his mother was a prostitute. But he felt no anger or shame, for she was a stranger and he could not connect her to himself.

"The white women hated her, they wouldn't hire her for cook or nurse, they were scared for her to be around their husbands. Mary Betty said some of the maids would hear them talking, sitting on the porches knowing where their husbands had gone. Some of the names would astound you. Phoebe was beautiful, with thick, wavy black hair and skin whiter than yours and roses in her cheeks. Sometimes I'd see her running across the field jumping the furrows, she'd skip through our orchard as if she was so happy, so glad to be alive. Sometimes she'd sing, she had a piping kind of voice, clear and airy. I wonder what it is puts each of us into our particular condition in life. In other circumstances she could have been whatever she wanted, a movie star, a princess—"

Bird closed his eyes against the pain of his mother's reality.

"I'm sorry," the doctor said. "I didn't mean to hurt you, I thought you'd like to hear about her, I never told you much. I tried to forget you had a mother, I wanted you to be just mine, as if you'd sprung from my forehead like the child of Zeus. That's a doctor's dream, I suppose, to give life."

Bird walked again to the window. Mrs. Henderson was closing up, putting the chairs on the tables. A Negro man was sweeping. For the first time his mother had been real to him, he could see her, hear her song. He wished he could have known her.

"I'm sorry," the doctor said, coming up behind him, touching his shoulder. "I shouldn't have told you about her or about Mason. Some things are better left alone."

"He killed himself because of me, didn't he?"

"Who can say? He was always a tortured man; he could never forgive himself if he thought he did wrong."

Bird handed the letter back to the doctor. "You were my father, I have no reason to try and find out anything else about that."

Slowly the doctor walked to the safe, stood again in the pooled light. Bird came to stand before him. Fumbling, awkward, the doctor picked up some bills off the stack of money and held them out like an offering, like a blessing, his face stricken.

Bird almost refused, almost said he didn't want it, but then he took it, pushed it into his jeans pocket and went out into the night.

CHAPTER
24

The ruffled, new-green leaves of the willows glowed in the thin light of dawn. He had sat on the bank of the river in his magic place all night after he had left his father, for he could not bear to sleep away the last hours he would ever spend here. From the marsh grass the spring peepers sang, the trill sounding as if their throats gurgled with water; the musty scent of the warming earth was mixed with yellow jessamine and wild honeysuckle. A waxing moon rose on the horizon, sister to the spirit orb that dwelled in the depths of the green pool. Sounds, smells, images, were absorbed into his blood and cells.

He leaned back against the rough trunk of a pine tree, and when the sky had faded from deep rose to streaks of pink and lavender, knew it was time to go: he did not want to leave in full light, to have to see or speak to anyone; this last time he must possess the sky, the earth, the streets of the town with his solitude. He should be gone already, for it was a long way to the highway, but as the sun rose, shrank deeper into the safety of his woods. "There's no hurry, I have the rest of my life," he thought. "I could even wait until tomorrrow, what would it matter? I could have one more night." He teased himself with the idea that he would not leave at all, that he could live from the river and the woods as he had after the beating.

Yesterday, leaving had seemed far in the future; yesterday, he had not really believed he was going, and now the time had come and he was afraid. He had thought he had put fear behind as well as childhood. Time had passed too fast, not only his last days in Asheton, but his whole life. Where did it all go? and why did he have to leave? He could not remember.

A pale image came on the surface of the water super-
imposed upon the reflections of the trees, and when he jumped
to his feet and turned around, Johnnie was standing in the filtered, downfalling light, barefoot and wearing a white dress.
She was not real, he only imagined her, but then she smiled
and his heart rushed to meet her; the force of his love drew her
to him, he held out his arms and she walked into them, he
folded her to him.

He lay his cheek against the coolness of her hair, and she
pressed her slender warmth against him, her arms encircling
him, and he could not speak. They stood thus for a long time,
the ache of his leaving gradually draining away. He had required love as a starving man requires food, a perishing man,
water. But how much greater than this was his need to love
someone, to touch someone. He tilted her face to his and kissed
her.

"I love you," he said. "I will always love you."

"And I love you." Love shone from her eyes.

The sun came above the horizon and struck a ray across
her head, lighting each strand of her hair so that she became
dazzling, like an angel; he pushed her away from him, he did
not have the right to touch her. She was pure and good and
still innocent. She was from another life.

But she clung to him, her hands grasping his, and she felt
his wounds and turned up his palms. "Oh, *oh*," she cried, "what
happened?" and she kissed the injured hands, fell against him,
sobbing.

He held her close again, stroked her hair, ashamed that he
was happy that she cared so much—the icy, frozen parts of him
melted, her tears were summer rains washing through him.

"It's all right," he said, and when she cried harder, said,
"I've had my tetanus shot."

She looked up at him, her chin quivering, her eyes angry.
"Don't joke, it's not funny. I stayed awake all night waiting for
morning so I could come here. I've missed you so much, I've
missed home, I hate that school."

"It was my fault they sent you away, I should never have

let you keep coming here. Your father was right, I should have known better."

"He *wasn't* right, we love each other. We've loved each other all our lives. Before Daddy even told me you were here, I knew it, I felt your presence."

"And I yours. I didn't think it consciously, but when I sat watching the river last night, you were here. I will always love you."

"I'm going away with you."

"No. Too much has happened, I'm different. The world's done something to me now that would never fit with you."

"We can still be together."

He smiled because she looked so like a little girl, with tear streaks on her face, her hair tumbled and wild. She was the last fragment of a dream before he woke and had to go and do real things. "We have to grow up."

"If we grow up, Bird, we can't have our games anymore, you'll go away and forget me." Her eyes brimmed with tears, her head drooped against his shoulder.

"How could I ever forget all of my life?" he said, but then, all at once, he was tired of games, he was ready to leave. She was childhood and innocence, the things he could never possess again. Already it seemed he had left her; already, their time together had passed into the realms of dreams and memories. Gently he pushed her from him.

"I can't live without you," she said. "I don't want to live without you."

She stood in a spot of sunlight, and for a moment was the only reality, the mournful shape of her contained in the cocoon of light.

"Yes, you can. People will always love you, Johnnie. How could anybody not love you? We will always be part of each other." A rush of tenderness came so strong that he pulled her to him and kissed her again and for the last time.

He moved away from her, and she ran to him and fiercely threw her arms about him, then pulled a tiny cross from around her neck.

"It's yours," she said, pressing it into his hand. "I stole it from Daddy's dresser when he sent you away. It was your mother's, you ought to have it."

He looked at it for a long time. "You keep it," he said finally. "Think of me when you look at it." He put it into her hand, curled her fingers over it. Just as he had not needed his grandfather's dying message, neither did he need this parting gift his mother had put around his neck. What he would take with him was that instant of awareness of her he had felt as the doctor talked of her. That was all he had wanted.

She ran away, darting among the trees like a pale shadow, and for a long time he stared into the dappled woods, then picked up his suitcase and headed for the road that would lead him north.

Just before he turned to go down the hill and leave the town behind, he stopped and looked back, but no longer yearning toward this place where he had known such great happiness and such great pain. His love had been deeper than he had known, and the steeple of the Sanctified Church flashed its jeweled scars; in the vacant lot beyond the Standard station blue forget-me-nots bloomed so dense they seemed a reflection of the morning sky. And his heart lifted, he was eager now to be on his way, glad to be going somewhere on this spring-green day. He walked down the hill and crossed the railroad tracks choked with weeds and buttercups.

When he came to the highway he walked briskly for about a half hour, and when he looked back, saw in the distance the blue dot of a Greyhound rolling toward him like a ball of light. He stopped and set down his suitcase, waiting for it to catch up to him, and then, faintly, over the far roar of the river, heard his name. He looked up and saw Johnnie standing on the high ridge at the edge of the woods, waving to him. "Good-by, good-by," she called.

He laughed and waved both arms to her, and then the bus pulled up onto the shoulder of the road just short of where he stood, air brakes squealing, wheels churning up dust.

He picked up his suitcase and swung on board, not looking to see where the sign on the front said they were going, for it did not matter.

"Good-by, good-by," she called over and over, and when he looked again, she was running to keep up as the bus pulled away. "I'll find you, someday I'll find you," her voice but faintly heard on the inconstant breeze.

The doors closed, his last sight of her standing in the blowing sunlight graven forever golden in his mind.